"Abundant details turn this Amish romantic thriller...
into a work of art."

—*Publishers Weekly* on *Where Secrets Sleep*
(starred review)

"Crisp writing and distinctive characters make up
Perry's latest novel. *Where Secrets Sleep* is a truly
entertaining read."

—*RT Book Reviews*

"Perry skillfully continues her chilling, deceptively
charming romantic suspense series with a dark,
puzzling mystery that features a sweet romance and a
nice sprinkling of Amish culture."

—*Library Journal* on *Vanish in Plain Sight*

Praise for *USA TODAY* bestselling author Debby Giusti

"*Amish Refuge* by Debby Giusti certainly lives up to the
'suspense' genre, as it kept me up a good part of the
night reading! I could not and did not want to put it
down! I highly recommend *Amish Refuge*."

—*Harlequin Junkie*

"One of the most original romantic suspense plots
I've encountered in a long time... A promising start to
a new series."

—*Dear Author* on *Countdown to Death*

MARTA
PERRY

HIDE IN
PLAIN SIGHT

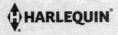

ISBN-13: 978-1-335-40993-5

Recycling programs
for this product may
not exist in your area.

Hide in Plain Sight
First published in 2007.
This edition published in 2021.
Copyright © 2007 by Martha Johnson

Amish Rescue
First published in 2018. This edition published in 2021.
Copyright © 2018 by Deborah W. Giusti

This edition published by arrangement with Harlequin Books S.A.

For questions and comments about the quality of this book,
please contact us at CustomerService@Harlequin.com.

Harlequin Enterprises ULC
22 Adelaide St. West, 40th Floor
Toronto, Ontario M5H 4E3, Canada
www.Harlequin.com

Printed in U.S.A.

CONTENTS

A lifetime spent in rural Pennsylvania and her Pennsylvania Dutch heritage led **Marta Perry** to write about the Plain People, who add so much richness to her home state. Marta has seen nearly sixty of her books published, with over six million books in print. She and her husband live in a centuries-old farmhouse in a central Pennsylvania valley. When she's not writing, she's reading, traveling, baking or enjoying her six beautiful grandchildren.

Visit the Author Profile page
at Harlequin.com for more titles.

HIDE IN PLAIN SIGHT

Marta Perry

For everything there is a season, and a time to every purpose under heaven: a time to be born and a time to die; a time to plant and a time to uproot; a time to kill and a time to heal.
—*Ecclesiastes* 3:1–3

This story is dedicated to my gifted editor on this book, Krista Stroever. And, as always, to Brian.

Chapter 1

She had to get to the hospital. Andrea Hampton's fingers tightened on the steering wheel as that call from the Pennsylvania State Police replayed in her mind in an endless loop. Her sister had been struck by a hit-and-run driver while walking along a dark country road—like this one. They didn't know how badly she was injured. Repeated calls to the hospital had netted her only a bland voice saying that Rachel Hampton was undergoing treatment.

Please. Please. She wasn't even sure she believed any longer, but the prayer seemed to come automatically. *Please, if You're there, if You're listening, keep Rachel safe.*

Darkness pressed against the windows, unrelieved except for the reflection of her headlights on the dark macadam and the blur of white pasture fence posts.

Amish country, and, once you were off the main routes, there were no lights at night except for the occasional faded yellow of oil lamps from a distant farmhouse.

If she let herself picture Rachel's slight figure, turning, seeing a car barreling toward her... A cold hand closed around her heart.

After all those years she had protected her two younger sisters, Rachel and Caroline were independent now. That was only right. Still, some irrational part of her mind seemed to be saying: *You should have been here.*

A black-and-yellow sign announced a crossroads, and she tapped the brakes lightly as she approached a curve. She glanced at the dashboard clock. Nearly midnight.

She looked up, and a cry tore from her throat. A dark shape ahead of her on the road, an orange reflective triangle gleaming on the back of it... Her mind recognizing an Amish buggy, she slammed on the brakes, wrenching the wheel with all her strength. *Please, please, don't let me hit it—*

The car skidded, fishtailing, and she fought for control. Too late—the rear wheels left the road and plunged down into a ditch, tipping crazily, headlight beams spearing toward the heavens. The air bag deployed, slamming into her. For an instant she couldn't breathe, couldn't think.

As her head began to clear she fought the muffling fabric of the air bag, the seat belt harness digging into her flesh. Panic seared along her nerves, and she struggled to contain it. She wasn't a child, she wasn't trapped—

A door slammed. Voices, running feet, and someone yanked at the passenger door.

"Are you hurt? Can you talk?"

"Yes." She managed to get her face free of the entangling folds. "I think I'm all right, but I can't reach the seat belt."

"Hold on. We'll get you out." A murmured consultation—more than one person, then. The scrape of metal on metal, and the door shrieked in protest as it was lifted.

"The buggy." Her voice came out in a hoarse whisper. "I didn't hit it, did I?"

"No," came a curt male voice, and then a flashlight's beam struck her face, making her blink. "You didn't."

Hands fumbled for the seat belt, tugging. The belt tightened across her chest, she couldn't breathe—and then it released and air flowed into her protesting lungs.

"Take a moment before we try to move you." He was just a dark shadow behind the light. In control. "Be sure nothing's broken."

She wanted to shout at him to pull her free, to get her out of the trap her car had become, but he made sense. She wiggled fingers, toes, ran her hands along her body as much as she could.

"Just tender. Please, get me out." She would not let panic show in her voice, even though the sense of confinement in a small, dark space scraped her nerves raw with the claustrophobia she always hoped she'd overcome. "Please."

Hands gripped her arms, and she clung instinctively to the soft cotton of the man's shirt. Muscles bunched under the fabric. He pulled, she wiggled, pushing her body upward, and in a moment she was free, leaning against the tip-tilted car.

"Easy." Strong hands supported her.

"Are you sure she is all right, Calvin Burke?" This voice sounded young, a little frightened. "Should we take her to the hospital?"

"The hospital." She grasped the words. "I'm all right, but I have to get to the hospital. My sister is there. I have to go there."

She was repeating herself, she thought, her mind still a little fuzzy. She couldn't seem to help it. She focused on the three people who stood around her. An Amish couple, their young faces white and strained in the glow of the flashlight.

And the man, the one with the gruff, impatient voice and the strong, gentle hands. He held the light, so she couldn't see him well—just an impression of height, breadth, the pale cloth of his shirt.

"Your sister." His voice had sharpened. "Would you be Rachel Hampton's sister?"

"Yes." She grabbed his hand. "You know her? Do you know how she is? I keep calling, but they won't tell me anything."

"I know her. Was on my way, in fact, to see if your grandmother needed any help."

"Grams is all right, isn't she?" Her fear edged up a notch.

"Just upset over Rachel." He turned toward the young couple. "I'll take her to the hospital. You two better get along home."

"*Ja,* we will," the boy said. "We pray that your sister will be well." They both nodded and then moved quickly toward the waiting buggy, their clothing melting into the darkness.

Her Good Samaritan gestured toward the pickup truck that sat behind her car. "Anything you don't want to leave here, we can take now."

She shoved her hand through the disheveled layers of her hair, trying to think. "Overnight bag. My briefcase and computer. They're in the trunk." Concern jagged through her. "If the computer is damaged…" The project she was working on was backed up, of course, but it would still be a hassle if she couldn't work while she was here.

"I don't hear any ominous clanking noises." He pulled the cases from the trunk, whose lid gaped open. "Let's get going."

She bent over the car to retrieve her handbag and cell phone, a wave of dizziness hitting her at the movement. Gritting her teeth, she followed him to the truck.

He yanked open the passenger side door and shoved the bags onto the floor. Obviously she was meant to rest her feet on them. There was no place else to put them if she didn't want them rattling around in the back.

She climbed gingerly into the passenger seat. The dome light gave her a brief look at her rescuer as he slid behind the wheel. Thirtyish, she'd guess, with a shock of sun-streaked brown hair, longer than was fashionable, and a lean face. His shoulders were broad under the faded plaid shirt he wore, and when he gave her an impatient glance, she had the sense that he carried a chip on them.

He slammed the door, the dome light going out, and once again he was little more than an angular shape.

"I take it you know my grandmother." Small surprise, that. Katherine Unger's roots went deep in Lancaster County, back to the German immigrants who'd swarmed to Penn's Woods in the 1700s.

He nodded, and then seemed to feel something more was called for. "Cal Burke. And you're Rachel's older sister, Andrea. I've heard about you." His clipped tone suggested he hadn't been particularly impressed by whatever that was.

Still, she couldn't imagine that her sister had said anything bad about her. She and Rachel had always been close, even if they hadn't seen each other often enough in the past few years, especially since their mother's death. Even if she completely disapproved of this latest scheme Rachel and Grams had hatched.

She glanced at him. As her eyes adjusted to the dim light, she was able to see a little more, noticing his worn jeans, scuffed leather boots and a stubble of beard. She'd thought, in that first hazy glimpse as he pulled her out of the car, that he might be Amish—something about the hair, the pale shirt and dark pants. But obviously he wasn't.

"I should try the hospital again." She flipped the cell phone open.

Please. The unaccustomed prayer formed in her mind again. *Please let Rachel be all right.*

"I doubt they'll tell you any more than they already have." He frowned at the road ahead. "Have you tried your grandmother's number?"

"She never remembers to turn her cell phone on." She punched in the number anyway, only to be sent straight to voice mail. "Grams, if you get this before I see you, call me on my cell." Her throat tightened. "I hope Rachel is all right."

"Ironic," he said as she clicked off. "You have an accident while rushing to your sister's bedside. Ever occur to you that these roads aren't meant for racing?"

She stiffened at the criticism. "I was not racing. And if you were behind me, you must have seen me brake as I approached the curve. If I hadn't…" She stopped, not wanting to imagine that.

His hands moved restlessly on the wheel, as if he wanted to push the rattletrap truck along faster but knew he couldn't. "We're coming up on Route 30. We'll make better time there."

He didn't sound conciliatory, but at least he hadn't pushed his criticism of her driving. Somehow she still wanted to defend herself.

"I'm well aware that I have to watch for buggies on this road. I just didn't expect to see anyone out this late."

And she was distracted with fear for Rachel, but she wouldn't say that to him. It would sound like a plea for sympathy.

"It's spring," he said, as if that was an explanation. "*Rumspringa,* to those kids. That means—"

"I know what *rumspringa* means," she snapped. "The time when Amish teenagers get to experience freedom and figure out what kind of life they want. You don't need to give me the Pennsylvania Dutch tour. I lived in my grandparents' house until I was ten."

"Well, I guess that makes you an expert, then."

No doubt about it, the man was annoying, but she hadn't exactly been all sweetness and light in the past half hour, either. And he was taking her to the hospital.

"Sorry. I didn't mean to snap. I guess I'm a little shaken."

He glanced at her. "Maybe you should have them check you out at the hospital. You had a rough landing."

She shook her head. "I'll probably be black-and-blue tomorrow, but that's it." She touched her neck gingerly. Either the air bag or the seat belt had left what felt like brush burns there. The bruises on her confidence from the fear she'd felt wouldn't show, but they might take longer to go away.

Apparently taking her word for it, he merged onto Route 30. The lights and activity were reassuring, and in a few minutes they pulled up at the emergency entrance to the hospital.

"Thank you." She slid out, reaching for her things. "I really appreciate this."

He spoke when she would have pulled her bag out. "I'm going in, too. May as well leave your things here until you know what you're doing."

She hesitated, and then she shrugged and let go of the case. "Fine. Thank you," she added.

He came around the truck and set off toward the entrance, his long strides making her hurry to keep up. Inside, the bright lights had her blinking. Burke caught her arm and navigated her past the check-in desk and on into the emergency room, not stopping until he reached the nurses' station.

"Evening, Ruth. This is Rachel Hampton's sister. Tell her how Rachel is without the hospital jargon, all right?"

She half expected the woman—middle-aged, gray-haired and looking as if her feet hurt—to call security. Instead she gave him a slightly flirtatious smile.

"Calvin Burke, just because you've been in here three or four times to get stitched up, don't think you own the place." She consulted a clipboard, lips pursing.

Andrea stole a look at him. It wasn't her taste, but she supposed some women went for the rugged, disreputable-looking type.

Ruth Schmidt, according to her name badge—another good old Pennsylvania Dutch name, like Unger—picked up the telephone and had a cryptic, low-voiced conversation with someone. She hung up and gave Andrea a professional smile.

"Your sister has come through surgery fine, and she's been taken to a private room."

"What were her injuries?" She hated digging for information, as if her sister's condition were a matter of national security. "Where is my grandmother? Isn't she here?"

The woman stiffened. "I really don't know anything further about the patient's condition. I understand Mrs. Unger was persuaded to go home, as there was nothing she could do here. I'd suggest you do the same, and—"

"No." She cut the woman off. "I'm not going anywhere until I've seen my sister. And if you don't know anything about her injuries, I'll talk to someone who does."

She prepared for an argument. It didn't matter what they said to her, she wasn't leaving until she'd seen Rachel, if she had to stay here all night.

Maybe the woman recognized that. She pointed to a bank of elevators. "Third floor. Room 301. But she'll be asleep—"

She didn't wait to hear any more. She made it to the elevator in seconds and pressed the button, the fear that had driven her since she left Philadelphia a sharp blade against her heart. Rachel would be all right. Grams wouldn't have gone home unless she was convinced of that. Still, she had to see for herself.

A quick ride in the elevator, a short walk across the hall, and she was in the room. Rachel lay motionless in the high, white hospital bed. Both legs were in casts, and hospital paraphernalia surrounded her.

Light brown hair spread out over a white pillow, dark lashes forming crescents against her cheek. Rachel looked about sixteen, instead of nearly thirty. Her little sister, whom she loved, fought with, bossed, protected. Her throat choked, and the tears she'd been holding back spilled over.

Cal picked up a five-month-old newsmagazine and slumped into a molded plastic chair. The dragons guarding the third floor wouldn't have let him in, obviously, so he'd just wait until the sister came back down again. Maybe tonight wasn't the time, but he had a few things he'd like to say to Andrea.

He frowned, uninterested, at the magazine, seeing instead the face of the woman who'd just gone upstairs. On the surface, she'd been much like he'd expected from the things her sister and grandmother had said and from the photo on Katherine's mantel.

Glossy, urban, well dressed in a rising young executive way, with silky blond hair falling to her collarbones in one of those sleek, tapered cuts that every television newswoman wore now. Eyes like green glass, sharp enough to cut a man if he weren't careful.

Well, he was a very careful man, and he knew enough not to be impressed by Ms. Andrea Hampton.

Not that her sister or grandmother had ever bad-mouthed her, but the picture had formed clearly enough in his mind from the things they said, and from her absence. Her elderly grandmother and her sister were struggling to get their bed-and-breakfast off the ground, and Ms. Successful Young Executive couldn't be bothered to leave her high-powered life long enough to help them.

Not his business, he supposed, but despite his intent to live in isolation, he'd grown fond of Katherine and her granddaughter in the time he'd been renting the barn on the Unger estate. He'd thought, when his wanderings brought him to Lancaster County, that he just wanted to be alone with his anger and his guilt. But Katherine, with her understated kindness, and Rachel, with her sweet nature, had worked their way into his heart. He felt a responsibility toward them, combined with irritation that the oldest granddaughter wasn't doing more to help.

Still, he'd been unjust to accuse her of careless driving. She'd been going the speed limit, no more, and he had seen the flash of her brake lights just before she'd rounded the curve.

Her taillights had disappeared from view, and then he'd heard the shriek of brakes, the crunch of metal, and his heart had nearly stopped. He'd rounded the curve, fearing he'd see a buggy smashed into smithereens, its passengers tossed onto the road like rag dolls.

Thank the good Lord it hadn't come to that. It had been the car, half on its side in the ditch, which had been the casualty.

Come to think of it, somebody might want to have a talk with young Jonah's father. The boy had said he'd just pulled out onto the main road from the Mueller farm. He had to have done that without paying much attention—the approaching glow of the car's lights should have been visible if he'd looked. All his attention had probably been on the pretty girl next to him.

He didn't think he'd mention that to Andrea Hampton. She might get the bright idea of suing. But he'd drop a word in Abram Yoder's ear. Not wanting to get the boy into trouble—just wanting to keep him alive.

Giving up the magazine as a lost cause, he tossed it aside and stared into space until he saw the elevator doors swish open again. Andrea came through, shoulders sagging a bit. She straightened when she saw him.

"You didn't need to wait for me."

He rose, going to her. "Yes, I did. I have your things in my truck, remember?"

Her face was pale in the fluorescent lights, mouth drooping, and those green eyes looked pink around the edges. He touched her arm.

"You want me to get you some coffee?"

She shook her head, and he had the feeling she didn't focus on his face when she looked at him. His nerves tightened.

"What is it? Rachel's going to be all right, isn't she?"

"They say so." Her voice was almost a whisper, and then she shook her head, clearing her throat. "I'm sure they're right, but it was a shock to see her that way. Both of her legs are broken." A shiver went through her, generating a wave of sympathy that startled him. "And she has a concussion. The doctor I spoke with wouldn't even guess how long it would be until she's back to normal."

"I'm sorry to hear that." His voice roughened. Rachel didn't deserve this. No one did. He could only hope they caught the poor excuse for a human being who'd left her lying by the side of the road. If he were still an attorney, he'd take pleasure in prosecuting a case like that.

Andrea walked steadily toward the exit. Outside, she took a deep breath, pulling the tailored jacket close around her as if for warmth, even though the May night didn't have much of a bite to it.

"I'll just get my things and then you can be on your way." She managed a polite smile in his direction.

"How do you plan to get to your grandmother's? I called to have your car towed to the Churchville Garage, but I don't imagine it'll be drivable very soon."

She shoved her hair back in what seemed to be a habitual gesture. It fell silkily into place again. "Thank you. I didn't think about the car. But I'm sure I can get a taxi."

"Not so easy at this hour. I'll drive you." He yanked the door open.

"I don't want to take you out of your way. You've done enough for me already, Mr. Burke." Her tone was cool. Dismissing.

He smiled. "Cal. And you won't be taking me out of my way. Didn't you know? I'm your grandmother's tenant."

He rather enjoyed the surprised look on her face. Petty of him, but if she kept in better contact with her grandmother, she'd know about him. Still, he suspected that if he were as good a Christian as he hoped to be, he'd cut her a bit more slack.

"I see. Well, fine then." She climbed into the truck, the skirt she wore giving him a glimpse of slim leg.

He wasn't interested in any woman right now, least of all a woman like Andrea Hampton, but that didn't mean he was dead. He could still appreciate beautiful, and that's what Andrea was, with that pale oval face, soft mouth and strong jawline. Come to think of it, she'd gotten the stubborn chin from her grandmother, who was as feisty a seventy-some-year-old as he'd met in a long time.

She didn't speak as he drove out of the hospital lot. He didn't mind. God had been teaching him patience in the past year or so, something he'd never thought of before as a virtue. He suspected she'd find it necessary to break the silence sooner than he would.

Sure enough, they'd barely hit the highway when she stirred. "You said you were my grandmother's tenant. Does that mean you're living in the house?" Her hands moved restlessly. "Or inn, I guess I should say, given Grams and Rachel's project."

She didn't approve, then. He could hear it in her voice.

"I rent the barn from your grandmother. The newer one, behind the house. I've been there for six months now, and in the area for nearly a year."

Healing. Atoning for his mistakes and trying to get right with God, but that was something he didn't say to anyone.

"The barn?" Her voice rose in question. "What do you want with the barn? Do you mean you live there?"

He shrugged. "I fixed up the tack room for a small apartment. Comfortable enough for one. I run my business in the rest of it."

"What business?" She sounded suspicious.

He was tempted to make something up, but he guessed she'd had enough shocks tonight. "I design and make wood furniture, using Amish techniques. If you pick up any wood shavings on your clothes, that's why."

"I see." The tone reserved judgment. "Grams never mentioned it to me."

"Well, you haven't been around much, have you?"

He caught the flash of anger in her face, even keeping his eyes on the road.

"I speak with my grandmother and my sister every week, and they came to stay with me at Easter, not that it's any of your concern."

They were coming into the village now, and he slowed. There wasn't much traffic in Churchville, or even many lights on, at this hour. The antique shops and quilt stores that catered to tourists were long since closed.

He pulled into the drive of the gracious, Federal-style Unger mansion, its Pennsylvania sandstone glowing a soft gold in the light from the twin lampposts he'd erected for Katherine. He stopped at the door.

He wouldn't be seeing much of Andrea, he'd guess. She'd scurry back to her busy career as soon as she was convinced her sister would recover, the anxiety she'd felt tonight fading under the frenzied rush of activity that passed for a life.

"Thank you." She snapped off the words as she opened the door, grabbing her bags, obviously still annoyed at his presumption.

"No problem."

She slammed the door, and he pulled away, leaving her standing under the hand-carved sign that now hung next to the entrance to the Unger mansion. The Three Sisters Inn.

Chapter 2

Andrea had barely reached the recessed front door when it was flung open, light spilling out onto the flagstones. In an instant she was in Grams's arms, and the tears she didn't want to shed flowed. They stood half in and half out of the house, and she was ten again, weeping over the mess her parents were making of their lives, holding on to Grams and thinking that here was one rock she could always cling to.

Grams drew her inside, blotting her tears with an unsteady hand, while her own trickled down her cheeks. "I'm so glad you're here, Dree. So glad."

The childhood nickname, given when two-years-younger Rachel couldn't say her name, increased the sensation that she'd stepped into the past. She stood in the center hall that had seemed enormous to her once, with its high ceiling and wide plank floor. Barney,

Grams's sheltie, danced around them, welcoming her with little yips.

She bent to pet the dog, knowing Barney wouldn't stop until she did. "I went to the hospital to see Rachel. They told me you'd already gone home. I should have called you...."

Grams shook her head, stopping her. "It's fine. Cal phoned me while you were with Rachel."

"He didn't say." Her tone was dry. Nice of him, but he might have mentioned he'd talked to Grams.

"He told me about the accident." Grams's arm, still strong and wiry despite her age, encircled Andrea's waist. Piercing blue eyes, bone structure that kept her beautiful despite her wrinkles, a pair of dangling aqua earrings that matched the blouse she wore—Grams looked great for any age, let alone nearly seventy-five. "Two accidents in one night is two too many."

That was a typical Grams comment, the tartness of her tone hiding the fear she must have felt.

"Well, fortunately the only damage was to the car." She'd better change the subject, before Grams started to dwell on might-have-beens. She looked through the archway to the right, seeing paint cloths draped over everything in the front parlor. "I see you're in the midst of redecorating."

Grams's blue eyes darkened with worry. "The open-ing is Memorial Day weekend, and now Rachel is laid up. I don't know..." She stopped and shook her head. "Well, we'll get through it somehow. Right now, let's get you settled, so that both of us can catch a few hours sleep. Tomorrow will be here before you know it."

"Where are you putting me?" She glanced up the

graceful open staircase that led from the main hall to the second floor. "Is that all guest rooms now?"

Grams nodded. "The west side of the house is the inn. The east side is still ours." She opened the door on the left of the hall. "Come along in. We have the back stairway and the rooms on this side, so that'll give us our privacy. You'll be surprised at how well this is working out."

She doubted it, but she was too tired to pursue the subject now. Or to think straight, for that matter. And Grams must be exhausted, physically and emotionally. Still, she couldn't help one question.

"What was she doing out there? Rachel, I mean. Why was she walking along Crossings Road alone after dark?"

"She was taking Barney for a run." Grams's voice choked a little. "She's been doing that for me since she got here, especially now that things have been so upset. Usually there's not much traffic."

That made sense. Rachel could cut onto Crossings Road, perpendicular to the main route, without going into the village.

She trailed her grandmother through the large room that had been her grandfather's library, now apparently being converted into an office-living room, and up the small, enclosed stairway. This was the oldest part of the house, built in 1725. The ceilings were lower here, accounting for lots of odd little jogs in how the two parts of the Unger mansion fit together.

Grams held on to the railing, as if she needed some help getting up the stairs, but her back was as straight as ever. The dog, who always slept on the rug beside her bed, padded along.

Her mind flickered back to Grams's comment. "What do you mean, things have been upset? Has something gone wrong with your plans?"

She could have told them, had told them, that they were getting in over their heads with this idea of turning the place into an inn. Neither of them knew anything about running a bed-and-breakfast, and Grams was too old for this kind of stress.

"Just—just the usual things. Nothing for you to worry about."

That sounded evasive. She'd push, but they were both too tired.

Her grandmother opened a door at the top of the stairs. "Here we are. I thought you'd want your old room."

The ceiling sloped, and the rosebud wallpaper hadn't changed in twenty years. Even her old rag doll, left behind when her mother had stormed out of the house with them, still sat in the rocking chair, and her white Bible lay on the bedside table. This had been her room until she was ten, until the cataclysm that split the family and sent them flying off in all directions, like water droplets from a tornado. She tossed her bags onto the white iron bed and felt like crying once more.

"Thanks, Grams." Her voice was choked.

"It's all right." Grams gave her another quick hug. "Let's just have a quick prayer." She clasped Andrea's hands, and Andrea tried not to think about how long it had been since she'd prayed before tonight.

"Hold our Rachel in Your hands, Father." Grams's voice was husky. "We know You love her even more than we do. Please, touch her with Your healing hand. Amen."

"Amen," Andrea whispered. She was sure there were questions she should ask, but her mind didn't seem to be working clearly.

"Night, Grams. Try and sleep."

"Good night, Dree. I'm so glad you're here." Grams left the door ajar, her footsteps muffled on the hall carpet as she went to the room across the hall.

Andrea looked at her things piled on the bed, and it seemed a gargantuan effort to move them. She undressed slowly, settling in.

She took her shirt off and winced at the movement, turning to the wavy old mirror to see what damage she'd done. Bruises on her chest and shoulder were dark and ugly where the seat belt had cut in, and she had brush burns from the air bag. She was lucky that was the worst of it, but she shook a little at the reminder.

After pulling a sleep shirt over her head, she cleaned off the bed and turned back the covers. She'd see about her car in the morning. Call the office, explain that she wouldn't be in for a few days. Her boss wouldn't like that, not with the Waterburn project nearing completion. Well, she couldn't make any decisions until she saw how Rachel was.

Frustration edged along her nerves as she crossed to the window to pull down the shade, not wanting to wake with the sun. This crazy scheme to turn the mansion into a bed-and-breakfast had been Rachel's idea, no doubt. She hadn't really settled to anything since culinary school, always moving from job to job.

Grams should have talked some sense into her, instead of going along with the idea. At this time in her life, Grams deserved a quiet, peaceful retirement. And

Rachel should be finding a job that had some security to it.

Andrea didn't like risky gambles. Maybe that was what made her such a good financial manager. Financial security came first, and then other things could line up behind it. If she'd learned anything from those chaotic years when her mother had dragged them around the country, constantly looking for something to make her happy, it was that.

She stood for a moment, peering out. From this window she looked over the roof of the sunroom, added on to the back of the house overlooking the gardens when Grams had come to the Unger mansion as a bride. There was the pond, a little gleam of light striking the water, and the gazebo. Other shadowy shapes were various outbuildings. Behind them loomed the massive bulk of the old barn that had predated even the house. Off to the right, toward the neighboring farm, was the "new" barn, dating to the 1920s.

It was dark now, with Cal presumably asleep in the tack room apartment. Well, he was another thing to worry about tomorrow. She lowered the shade with a decisive snap and went to crawl into bed.

Her eyes closed. She was tired, so tired. She'd sleep, and deal with all of it in the morning.

Something creaked overhead—once, then again. She stiffened, imagining a stealthy footstep in the connecting attics that stretched over the wings of the house. She strained to listen, clutching the sheet against her, but the sound wasn't repeated.

Old houses make noises, she reminded herself. Particularly her grandmother's, if her childhood memories were any indicator. She was overreacting. That faint, scratching sound was probably a mouse, safely distant from her. Tired muscles relaxed into the soft bed, and exhaustion swept over her.

She plummeted into sleep, as if she dived into a deep, deep pool.

Andrea stepped out onto the patio from the breakfast room, Barney nosing out behind her and then running off toward the pond, intent on his own pursuits. A positive call from the hospital had lifted a weight from her shoulders and she felt able to deal with other things. She paused to look around and take a deep breath of country air.

Not such pleasant country air, she quickly discovered. Eli Zook must be spreading manure on his acreage, which met the Unger property on two sides. How were the city tourists Rachel expected to have as guests going to like that? Maybe they'd be pleased at the smell of a genuine Amish farm.

They'd have to admire the view from the breakfast room. The flagstone patio had stood the years well, and now it was brightened by pots overflowing with pansies and ageratum. The wide flower bed dazzled with peonies and daylilies. She had knelt there next to Grams, learning to tell a weed from a flower.

Moving a little stiffly, thanks to her bruises, she stepped over the low patio wall and followed the flagstone path that led back through the farther reaches of the garden, weaving around the pond and past the gazebo with its white Victorian gingerbread. When she glanced back at the house, morning sunlight turned the sandstone to mellow gold, making the whole building glow.

Rounding the small potting shed, she came face-to-face with the new barn. An apt expression, because she'd always thought the barn had more character than a lot of people. Lofty, white, a traditional bank barn with entries on two levels, it had the stone foundation and hip roof that characterized Pennsylvania Dutch barns. More properly Pennsylvania Swiss or German, her grandfather had always said, but the name stuck.

It hadn't seen much use since her grandfather had stopped farming and leased the fields to the Zook family, but the stone foundation showed no sign of deterioration, and the wooden planks looked as if they had a fresh coat of white paint.

A small sign on the upper level door was the only indication that Cal Burke did business here. And how much business could he do, really? The only way into his shop was via the rutted lane that ran along a hedge of overgrown lilacs that bordered the house. She glanced toward the road. Yes, there was a tiny sign there, too, one that could hardly be read from a passing car. The man needed a few lessons in marketing.

She walked up the bank to the door and tapped lightly. Stepping inside, she inhaled the scent of wood shavings and hay. Music poured from a CD player that sat on a wooden bench. Cal apparently liked Mozart to work by. He bent over a pie safe, totally absorbed as he fitted a pierced tin insert to a door.

He obviously hadn't heard her, so she glanced around, wanting to see any changes before she spoke to him. There weren't many. In the center threshing floor he'd installed a workbench and tools, and the rest of the space was taken up with pieces of furniture in various stages of construction. The mows and lofts on either side already held hay and straw, probably stored there by Eli Zook.

She took a step forward, impressed in spite of herself by his work. They were simple oak pieces, for the most part, done in the classic style of Pennsylvania Dutch furniture. There was a three-drawer chest with graceful carving incised on the drawer fronts, a chest stenciled with typical tulips and hearts, a rocking chair with a curved back.

Cal did have a gift for this work, and he was certainly focused. Sun-bleached hair swung forward in his eyes, and he pushed it back with a sweep of one hand, all of his movements smooth and unhurried. He wore faded jeans and a blue plaid shirt, also faded, the sleeves rolled up to the elbows. A shaft of sunlight, beaming down from the open loft door, seemed to put him in a spotlight, picking out gold in his brown hair and glinting off tanned forearms.

She moved slightly just as the music stopped. The sole of her loafer rustled stray wood shavings, and he looked up. The pierced tin clattered to the floor, the sound loud in the sudden stillness.

"I'm sorry. I didn't mean to disturb you."

"It's all right." He straightened, leaning against the pie safe, and watched her approach.

She hadn't noticed his eyes last night. The light had been too dim, for the most part, and she'd been too upset. Now she saw that they were a light, warm brown, flecked with gold like his hair.

He waited until she stopped, a few feet from him, before he spoke again. "Any news from the hospital?"

"We called first thing. Rachel had a good night, and

she's awake and asking for us." She couldn't stop the smile that blossomed on the words.

"Thank God." He smiled in return, strong lips curving, lines crinkling around his eyes, his whole face lighting. For an instant she couldn't look away, and something seemed to shimmer between them, as light and insubstantial as the dust motes in the shaft of sunshine.

She turned to look at the furniture, feeling a need to evade his glance for a moment. She wouldn't want him to think he had any effect on her.

"So this is your work." She touched a drop leaf table. "Cherry, isn't it?"

He nodded, moving next to her and stroking the wood as if it were a living thing. "I've been working mostly in oak and pine, but Emma Zook wanted a cherry table, and Eli had some good lengths of cherry that I could use."

"It's beautiful. Emma will be delighted, although if I remember Amish customs correctly, she won't say so."

A faint smile flickered in his eyes. "'For use, not for pretty,' she'll say. Anything else might sound like pride."

"That's Emma, all right." Nostalgia swept through her. Emma Zook had helped Grams in the house for years, and her sturdy figure, always clad in a long dress and apron, was present in Andrea's earliest memories.

As children, they'd played with the Zook youngsters, so used to them that they never saw the Amish clothing or dialect as odd. She'd caught up a bit with Emma over breakfast. As she'd expected, all the children except Levi were married and parents by now. Levi—well, Levi would always be a child, no matter how old he was.

"The Amish have the right idea," Cal said. "No reason why something can't be both useful and beautiful."

She traced the scalloped edge of the drop leaf. "This certainly qualifies."

"Two compliments in as many minutes." He drew back in mock surprise.

"I believe in giving credit where credit is due. You make lovely furniture. I just can't help but wonder why you're doing it in my grandmother's barn."

Where did you come from, and why are you here? That's what she was really asking. How could this man have made such inroads into her family when she hadn't even known about him?

He shrugged. "I came to this area to learn Amish furniture techniques. When I needed a place to set up shop, she had an empty barn. We came to an agreement."

She'd like to ask what that agreement was, but he could answer that it wasn't her business. Which it wasn't, but anything that affected her grandmother and sister mattered to her, whether she'd been back recently or not.

"You're not from around here," she tried.

"No. I'm not."

Most people liked talking about themselves. Cal Burke seemed to be the exception.

"You're a little hard to find. How do you market your work?"

He shrugged again. "There are plenty of machine-made copies out there, but if people are asking around for good, handmade furniture done in the old Amish style, they'll find me or one of the others who do it."

"That's no way to do business." His marketing strategy, if that's what it was, exasperated her so much that she couldn't stop the words. "You have something people want, so make it easy to find you. You could probably double or triple your business if you did a little advertising."

"I don't want to double my business. There are only so many pieces I can make by hand in a month, and they sell okay. What am I going to do with more customers than I can satisfy?"

She blinked, looking at him. As far as she could tell, he was serious. "If you hired a few people to help you—"

"Then it wouldn't be my furniture people were buying."

"But you could make more money—"

He shook his head with an impatient movement that made the hair flop in his eyes again. "I make enough to get by, and I enjoy my work. Your corporate approach wouldn't work for me."

She stiffened. "If you mean I'm practical, I don't consider that an insult. Although I suspect you meant it that way."

"Just recognizing a difference in how we see things, that's all." His voice was mild, but his eyes had turned frosty. "If you came out here to tell me how to run my business, I thank you for your interest."

"No." She bit off the word. The world needed practical people like her. They kept the dreamers afloat. But she didn't suppose it would do any good to tell him so. "My grandmother wants you to know that we'll be going to the hospital shortly. She asks if you'll keep an eye out for the painters and let them in." Somehow it seemed important that he know the favor was for Grams, not her.

"I'd be glad to."

"I thought she could call you, but she said you never answer your phone."

"Really bugs you, doesn't it?" His expression suggested internal laughter. "I don't like to jump when the phone rings. If anybody wants me, they leave a message."

She bit back another comment about his business methods. Or lack of them. Why should she care if the man frittered away his prospects for want of a few sensible steps?

"I see." She kept her tone perfectly polite. "Thank you for taking care of the painters. My grandmother will appreciate it."

She turned and walked away quickly, suspecting that if she looked back, she'd find an amused smile on his face.

"But I can't. I really can't." Andrea looked from her grandmother to her sister. Both faces were turned toward hers, both expectant, waiting for an answer she couldn't possibly give. "I'm extremely busy at work right now."

"Surely your employer will give you the time off." Grams was serenely confident. "Your family needs you."

Rachel didn't say anything. She just leaned back against the raised head of the hospital bed, her face almost as white as the pillow.

She'd tell herself they were ganging up on her, but that wasn't true. They were depending on her, just as Rachel and baby sister Caroline had depended on her during those years when Mom had relocated the family from place to place, nursing her grudge against Grams and Grandfather and depriving her children of the only stable home they'd ever known.

Andrea was the oldest. She was the responsible one. She'd take care of it.

The trouble was, she was responsible to her job, as well, and there couldn't possibly be a worse time for her to take off. Gordon Walker would not understand his right-hand woman requesting a leave to help her family. He hadn't even taken time away from work when his wife was in labor with their twins.

Of course, he and his wife were now divorced, and he saw his daughters once a month if he was lucky.

She tried again. "I'm in the middle of a very important project, and I'm on a deadline. I couldn't take time off now. It wouldn't be fair to the company."

It wasn't fair to her, either. Maybe that thought was unworthy, but she couldn't help it. The promotion her boss had been dangling in front of her for the past year would be hers when this project was completed. Her position with the company, her stable, secure life, would be assured.

"Can't someone else take over for you?" Grams's brow furrowed. "We've already accepted reservations for our opening weekend. All the rooms are booked. We can't turn those people away now."

Grams's sense of hospitality was obviously offended at the thought, even though these would be paying guests. Andrea could see it in her eyes. An Unger didn't let people down.

I'm a Hampton, too. She thought bleakly of her father. *They're pretty good at letting people down.*

Rachel tried to push herself up on the bed a little, wincing, and Andrea hurried to help her.

"Take it easy. I don't think you should try to do that on your own. Those casts must weigh a ton."

"If they don't, they feel like it." Rachel moved her head restlessly on the pillow.

Looking into Rachel's eyes was like looking in a mirror. Green eyes, cat's eyes. All three Hampton girls had them, even though otherwise they didn't look at all alike.

She was the cool, conservative blonde. That was how people saw her, and she didn't find anything wrong with that. It fit with who she wanted to be.

Rachel, two years younger, was the warm one, with her heart-shaped face and her sunny-brown hair. She had the gift of making friends and collecting strays everywhere she went. Sweet, generous, she was the family peacemaker, always the buffer.

And they'd needed a buffer, she and Caroline. Her youngest sister had been born an exotic orchid in a family of daisies. She certainly looked the part. In her, the green eyes sparkled and shot fire. Her hair, a rich, deep red, had been worn in a mass of curls to below her shoulders the last time Andrea had seen her. Currently, as far as she knew, Caroline was making pottery in Taos. Or maybe it was turquoise jewelry in Santa Fe. Andrea couldn't keep up.

"I could come home in a wheelchair. We could get some extra help and I could supervise." But the tears that shone in Rachel's eyes belied the brave words, and she thumped one hand against the side rail of the bed, making the IV clatter.

"Honey, don't." Andrea caught the restless hand, her heart twisting. "It'll be all right."

But how would it be all right? How could she be true to herself and yet not let them down?

Rachel clung to her, much as she had when Mom had taken them away from Grams and Grandfather so many years ago. "You mean you'll do it?"

"We'll find some way of handling the situation. I promise."

Rachel gave a little sigh, relaxing a bit, though worry still puckered her brows.

"Good," Grams said. "I knew we could count on you."

She'd told her boss she couldn't be back until Monday, though she'd continue working while she was here. She was only a phone call or an email away, after all. By then, she'd somehow convince Grams and Rachel that with Rachel laid up for who knows how long, starting a bed-and-breakfast didn't make sense.

A glance at Rachel's face assured her that now was not the time to mention that. Rachel was far too fragile.

She'd discuss it with Grams later. Giving up the inn was the best thing for everyone, especially Rachel. Once she was healed, she could get another restaurant job in a minute with her skills, and if she needed help to get through until then, Andrea or Grams would certainly provide that.

Right now she had to do something to wipe that strained expression from Rachel's eyes. "Did you hear about my adventure getting here last night? Rescued from a ditch by your handsome tenant. Hope you don't mind my using your car while mine's in the body shop."

"Grams told me Cal brought you to the hospital. He

is a hunk, isn't he?" Some of the tension eased out of the pale face. "So, you interested, big sis?"

"I wouldn't want to tread on your territory." She smiled. "We made a deal a long time ago, remember? No boyfriend poaching."

"Sad to say, Cal doesn't see me as anything but little-sister material." She wrinkled her nose. "I have to admit, when I first met him, I thought there might be something, but the chemistry just isn't there."

Andrea didn't bother to analyze why she was relieved. "I understand he's been around for about a year?" She made it a question for both of them.

"Just about," Grams agreed. "He stayed over at the Zimmerman farm for a while, I think, when he first came to the area."

"You never mentioned renting the barn to him when we talked." Grams and Rachel had come into the city for dinner just a month ago, but in all their talk about the inn, they hadn't brought up their resident tenant.

"Didn't we? I thought you knew about him."

The vagueness of it got under her skin. "Where did he come from? What did he do before? What does Uncle Nick think of him?" Her grandfather's business partner had a solid, no-nonsense attitude that Grams lacked.

"I don't know. Does it matter?" Grams frowned a little, as if Andrea had said something impolite. "And it's not James Bendick's business."

Rachel moved slightly. "He's a nice guy. That's all we need to know."

It wasn't all *she* needed to know. Perhaps the truth was that Grams hadn't mentioned him because she'd known exactly the questions Andrea would ask and didn't want to answer them. Grams did things her own way, and she'd never appreciated unsolicited advice.

"I believe I'll get some coffee." Grams stood, picking up her handbag.

"I'll get it for you, Grams," she offered.

Her grandmother shook her head. "You stay here and talk to Rachel. I want to stretch my legs a bit."

Andrea watched her leave, her heart clutching a little. Grams wouldn't admit it, but she was slowing down. Grams had always been so strong, so unchanging, that age had sat lightly upon her. It had seemed she would never let it get the better of her. But that had been an illusion.

A weight settled on Andrea's shoulders. She had to make the right decisions now. Rachel, Grams—she was responsible for both of them.

"Are you okay, Dree?"

She shook off the apprehension before she turned to look at her sister. "Sure. Just worried about you. Did the police talk to you about the accident?"

Rachel nodded. "The township chief was in before you got here. It doesn't sound as if they have much evidence. He wanted to know if I remembered anything."

"Do you?"

Rachel moved restlessly. "I don't remember anything that happened after about noon yesterday."

Chapter 3

Cal let himself in the side door of the Unger mansion, toolbox in hand. He'd told Katherine that he'd fix the loose post on the main staircase, but that wasn't his only reason for being there.

He'd been mulling it over, praying about it, most of the day. Prayer was still new enough to him that he wondered sometimes whether he ought to be asking for guidance about simple everyday things. Still, it was comforting to feel that Someone cared.

And this wasn't a selfish thing. He wanted a sense of whether he should speak to Andrea about her grandmother. Seemed to him the answer was yes, although that might just be his need to do something.

Two years ago, he'd have found it laughable to think he'd be so concerned about an elderly woman who wasn't even a relative, but he hadn't been much of a human being, either, back then. Now—well, he cared about Katherine Unger.

Katherine was kind, proud and too stubborn to ask for help even when she needed it. She'd be appalled, probably, if she realized how much he'd learned about her concerns just by listening. If she knew he intended to talk to Andrea, she'd be outraged.

But someone had to. Emma Zook could, but she might be too much in awe of Katherine to do it. So he would. He reached the stairs and pulled out a hammer. He'd been watching for an opportunity to speak to Andrea alone since she'd returned from the hospital, but she'd been holed up in the second-floor family quarters. Maybe a little noise would draw her out.

Sure enough, it didn't take more than a few hearty blows with the hammer before Andrea appeared at the top of the stairs, looking annoyed. She marched down to him.

"What are you doing?" She'd exchanged the pants and jacket she'd been wearing this morning for a pair of dark jeans and a green top that matched her eyes. "I'm trying to do some work upstairs."

"Sorry. You brought work with you?"

"Of course. I couldn't just walk out in the middle of the week."

Even when rushing to her sister's side, she hadn't left the job that seemed so important to her. She reminded him of himself, the way he used to be. That probably went a long way toward explaining why she annoyed him so much. He wasn't too fond of that guy.

He rested his elbow on the banister. "Wouldn't your boss give you a break under the circumstances?"

For a moment she hesitated, and he could almost

read her thoughts. She had the kind of superior who wouldn't, as a matter of fact, and she didn't want to admit it.

"I didn't ask," she said finally. "I have responsibilities, and I meet them." She frowned. "What are you doing here, anyway?"

"Katherine asked me to take care of this loose place in the banister." He wiggled the carved wood gently, mindful of its delicate reeding. "I had time to get to it this afternoon."

"I didn't realize you work for my grandmother."

"I don't. I'm just being neighborly." He still hadn't figured out the best approach. "Look, I know this is none of my business—"

"But it's not going to stop you," she finished for him. "All right. You won't be content until you have your say, so get it over with." She planted one hand on the railing, standing up a step so that their faces were level.

"You don't beat around the bush, do you?"

"I try not to." A slight frown appeared between her brows. "Does that bother you?"

"On the contrary, it makes it easier." If she wanted it straight from the hip, she'd get it. "Your grandmother and sister have been running themselves ragged, trying to get the inn ready. They needed help even before Rachel was hurt, but now it's worse. With Rachel in the hospital, your grandmother shouldn't be in the house alone. Did she tell you she's spotted a prowler out in the grounds recently?"

She sent him a startled glance, hand tightening on the railing. "No. Did she call the police?"

"By the time they got here, the person was long gone." He shrugged. "They didn't take it too seriously, figuring it was just someone curious about the inn. Still, there have been some minor incidents of vandalism in the area lately and a few break-ins. I've been trying to keep an eye on things. But she shouldn't be staying here at night by herself."

"You're right about that." She sounded faintly bewildered that she was agreeing with him. "As for the rest, I'm not sure how best to help her."

He was surprised that she was taking it so well, but perhaps she'd been giving some thought to the problem. She just hadn't come to the right conclusion yet.

"Move in, take over for Rachel, get the inn up and running," he said promptly. "Your grandmother can't do it by herself."

"My job—"

"—can get along without you for a while."

"You don't know that." If her glare had been a blow, it would have knocked him over. "I'd be risking a lot to stay here now."

"I get it. I had bosses like that once." He had a feeling he'd *been* that kind of a boss.

"Then you should understand. Maybe I can hire someone to help out."

He shook his head. "I'm not saying more workers wouldn't make things go faster, but what's needed is someone to oversee the whole project. Your grandmother isn't up to that anymore."

"You think I don't know that?" She fired up instantly. "She shouldn't be attempting something so ambitious at her age. She ought to just relax and enjoy life."

"How is she supposed to do that? What's she going to live on, air?" He clamped his mouth shut. He'd gone too far, even though his intentions were good.

"What are you implying?" She grabbed his arm to keep him from stepping away. "My grandmother doesn't need to worry about money."

Was she putting on a front?

"Maybe you ought to have a serious conversation with your grandmother."

Her grip tightened. "Tell me what you meant. What do you know, or think you know?"

Fine, then. "I know I offered to lend her the money for the renovations, but she took out a loan on the house instead. I know Emma works for free half the time. I know the signs of financial trouble. If someone doesn't step in, namely you, your grandmother could lose this place that means the world to her."

He yanked his arm free and grabbed the toolbox.

"I'll come back later and fix this."

Andrea was actually shaking. She watched Cal's broad back as he retreated down the hall. She should talk to Grams—no, she should find out first from someone she trusted if there was any truth to Cal's allegations. Emma. Emma knew everything that went on here.

But even as she thought it, there was a tap on the front door, followed by a quick, "Anyone here?"

"Uncle Nick." She hurried to the door, to be swept into a hug. Soft whiskers and a scent of peppermint—that was Uncle Nick.

He held her at arm's length. "Well, if you're not a sight for sore eyes, Andrea. You're looking beautiful, as always."

"And you're the biggest flatterer in town, as always. You haven't aged a bit."

She made the expected response automatically, but it

was true. Maybe the beard and hair were a little whiter, his figure in the neat blue suit just a bit stouter, but his cheeks were still rosy and firm as apples. He had an aura of permanence and stability that was very welcome.

"Ah, don't tell me that. I know better." He shook his head. "This is a sad business about Rachel."

She linked her arm with his. "She's going to make a complete recovery—the doctors have promised. Come into the library. We have to talk."

He lifted bushy white eyebrows. "Where's your grandmother?"

"Taking a nap, thank goodness. She needs one, after yesterday's upsets."

He nodded, glancing around the room and taking in the computer setup and file cabinets. "It's sad to see this fine old room turned into an office. What your grandfather would have said, I don't know."

There didn't seem to be an answer to that. She gestured him to a chair, sitting down opposite him.

He was surveying her with shrewd, kind blue eyes. "You're worried, aren't you? Tell Uncle Nick about it."

She had to smile. He wasn't really their uncle, nor was his name Nick. Caroline had called him that when she was three because to her eyes, James Bendick, Grandfather's junior partner, looked like St. Nicholas.

"That's what you always said. And you solved our problems with chocolate and peppermints."

"It's a good solution."

"Not for this problem." The worry, dissipated for a moment in the pleasure of seeing him, weighed on her again. "Tell me the truth, Uncle Nick. Is Grams in financial trouble?"

"Who told you that? Not your grandmother." His voice had sharpened.

"No. Cal Burke told me. He seems to think she could lose the house."

"I'd call that an exaggeration." He frowned. "And I'm not sure what business it is of his, in any event."

"Never mind him. Tell me what's going on. I thought Grandfather left her well-off. I've never questioned that."

"Your grandmother never questioned it, either. Sad to say, maybe she should have."

"But the properties, his investments…" She couldn't believe it. "Explain it to me."

Uncle Nick's lips puckered. "I'm not sure I should. Your grandmother—"

"Grams is depending on me." Normally she'd appreciate his discretion, but not now. "I have to know what's wrong in order to help her."

He hesitated, looking distressed. Finally he nodded. "Your grandfather decided, a few years before his death, to sell most of his properties. He didn't want to take care of them."

"I thought he enjoyed that." One of her earliest memories was of riding along with Grandpa when he went out the first day of every month to collect the rents from his tenants. That had been her first taste of business, and she'd wanted to be just like him.

Uncle Nick shrugged. "People change. He wanted to invest the money himself." His gaze dropped. "He wasn't very good. If only he'd held on to the property until the real estate market went up, your grandmother would be sitting pretty."

"As it is…" She could hardly take it in. Still, she'd

certainly known how determined Grandpa was to do as he chose. Something chilled inside her. She, of all people, knew just how stubborn he could be.

"She has this place left, but not enough to maintain it." His voice was brisk, as if he didn't want to dwell on what had been. "I'm not sure how you feel about this idea of theirs to turn the place into an inn."

"I think it's a bad move," she said promptly. "Rachel is a great cook, but she doesn't know anything about running an inn. And Grams doesn't need the stress at her age."

Nick beamed at her as if they were the only two sensible people left on earth. "The practical course is for your grandmother to sell. She could pay off the home equity loan she took for the renovations and have enough to live very comfortably for the rest of her life."

"I wish she agreed."

He nodded. "She has her own stubborn streak, that's for sure. I was worried about her living here alone since your grandfather died, but she'd never listen to me. It was a little better after Rachel moved back, but even so…"

"Cal Burke is out at the barn." With the phone he never answered. What good did that do?

"Burke." He repeated the name. "I suppose he's better than nothing, but what do we know about him?"

Not much. She shared his concern.

"And there have been a rash of thefts. People breaking into isolated farmhouses. You know what this area is like—folks have lived here for generations, never giving a thought that Great-aunt Eva's dough box might be worth a small fortune to a crooked dealer."

She almost wished she hadn't asked, but it was better to face the facts, no matter how unpleasant.

"What are we going to do?" It was good to feel that she had an ally. "Rachel and Grams want me to stay and open the inn. They don't seem to understand that I have a position I can't walk away from."

He patted her hand. "If you make it clear you can't, they'd have to face facts."

"I've tried. Without success."

"You'll have to keep trying." He rose. "Give my best to your grandmother, and tell Rachel that I'll see her later." He gave her a quick hug. "I know you'll do the right thing. You always do."

"Can I carry that for you, Andrea?"

Andrea stopped reluctantly. She'd noticed Cal down the block when she'd left Snyder's General Store to walk back to the house, but she hadn't been eager to talk to him. Just because he was right about her grandmother's finances didn't mean she had to like it.

He caught up with her, and she handed over the shopping bag, taking in the dress shirt and neat gray slacks he wore. She blinked, exaggerating her surprise.

"You didn't know I'd clean up this well, did you?" He smiled, apparently ready to forgive and forget.

"Have a hot date?"

"No, just out for supper at the Dutch Inn. It's chicken and dumpling night. What about you?"

She gestured toward the bag he now carried. "Grams needed a few things from the store, and I didn't want to drive to New Holland to the supermarket."

"So you went to Snyder's, where you get a hot serving of gossip with every bag of groceries."

She couldn't stop a smile. "Some things never change."

"Did you get the latest popular opinion on who I am and why I'm here?"

She was surprised that he spoke so easily about it. "Opinion is divided. You're either a famous author hiding from a deranged fan or a bank robber sitting on his loot until it cools off. That one came from Etta Snyder's ten-year-old son. Her teenage daughter considers you a tragic figure recovering from a terrible loss."

She felt a sudden qualm. What if any of them proved true?

But he didn't seem affected. "I'll let you guess which it is." They walked past the Village Soda Shop and Longstreet's Antiques, their steps matching. "Did you get the whole scoop from Bendick? I saw him come in."

She stiffened. Her family troubles weren't his affair. Didn't he understand that?

His eyebrows lifted. "Okay. Right. I'm interfering."

She fought with herself for a moment. Interfering. Aggravating. But he already knew, so who was she kidding by refusing to answer him?

"Uncle Nick confirmed what you said." She bit off the words, resenting the fact that he'd known what she should have.

"Sorry. I wish I'd been wrong." His voice had just the right degree of sympathy.

Some of her resentment ebbed away. This wasn't his fault. "I can't grasp it. When I was small, I thought my grandfather was the wisest, kindest man in the world."

Her opinion about the kindness had changed when Grandfather let them go without a word, writing them out of his life except for the college funds he'd provided. Surely he could have mended the quarrel with Mom if he'd really cared about them. But even so, she'd never doubted his business acumen.

"You can still have good memories of him." His tone warmed.

She could only nod, her throat choking up. She would like to remember Grandfather as she'd once seen him, without thinking about how he'd let her and her sisters down. Or how he'd apparently failed Grams.

"Why didn't my grandmother tell me? I would have helped."

She could feel his gaze on her face. "Maybe it doesn't matter why. Now that you know, you'll do the right thing."

He sounded like an echo of Uncle Nick, except that they didn't agree about what that right thing was.

"Uncle Nick told me he's been worried about Grams. He said there have been problems with antique thieves. That prowler you mentioned—" She came to a stop, frowning at him.

He stopped, too, leaning an elbow on top of the stone wall that surrounded the church across the street from Grams's house. "Could be connected, I suppose."

"Nick said they hit isolated farmhouses. Grams's place is right on the edge of the village."

"It's also big, concealed by plenty of trees and out-buildings, and for the most part has had only one elderly woman in residence. There aren't any houses to the east, and in the back, the farms are too far away for troublemakers to be spotted." His frown deepened as he looked across the road toward the house.

She shivered a little at the thought. He was right—the mansion was isolated in spite of the fact that it fronted on the main road. Crossings Road, where Rachel had been injured, snaked along one side, leading toward distant farms and making it easy for someone to approach from the back. "Surely no one would try to break into the house."

"They wouldn't have to. The outbuildings are crammed to the roof with stuff. Furniture, mostly. And that's not including the attics of the house itself. No one knows what's there."

"You mean there's no inventory?"

His lips twisted in a wry smile. "I'm sure you'd have a tidy inventory, with the approximate value listed for every item."

"Of course I would." Her voice was tart. He didn't need to act as if efficiency were a sin. "For insurance purposes, if nothing else."

"That's how your mind works, but not your grandmother's."

"I suppose not." Her grandmother was an odd mixture—clever about people, but naive about business, which had been her husband's prerogative. "You're trying to give me nightmares, aren't you?"

He gave a rueful smile and shoved away from the wall. "Sorry about that." He touched her hand in a brief gesture of sympathy. Warmth shimmered across her skin and was gone. "I figured I shouldn't be the only one."

Andrea was still wrestling with the difficulties when she went up to her room that evening, hoping to concentrate on some work. A half-dozen times she'd nearly confronted Grams about the financial situation, but each time a look at her grandmother stopped her. Grams looked so tired. So old.

She'd never thought of her grandmother as needing

someone to take care of her. Now she'd have to, even though she suspected Grams wouldn't take kindly to any suggestion that she couldn't manage her own affairs.

Well, she'd let the topic ride until tomorrow, at least. Maybe by then she'd have come up with some tactful way of approaching the subject and Grams would, she hoped, have had a decent night's sleep.

She opened her laptop. In an instant she was completely engrossed in work.

Finally the numbers began to blur on the screen. She got up, stretching, and walked to the window. Full dark had settled in, and her attention had been so focused on the computer screen that she hadn't even noticed. Maybe she'd been trying to shut out the human problems that she found so much more difficult to deal with than figures.

Her eyes gradually grew accustomed to the darkness. She could make out the pond now, the forsythia bushes along it, and the pale line that was the flagstone path.

She stiffened. There—by the toolshed. That wasn't a bush—it was a person. She froze, watching the faint gleam of a shielded light cross the door of the shed.

He was breaking in. She whirled, racing out of the room and across the hall to burst in on her grandmother, who sat up in bed with a Bible on her lap. Barney jumped up, ears pricking.

"Andrea, what—"

"There's someone prowling around by the toolshed. Call the police and alert Cal. I'm going to turn the outside lights on."

She could hear Grams protesting as she bolted down the stairs, the dog at her heels.

Chapter 4

Andrea reached the back door and slapped the switch that controlled the outside lights. They sprang up instantly, bathing the area with soft illumination. The yellow glow was probably intentional on Rachel's part. It fit well with the style of the two-and-a-half-century-old building, but at the moment, Andrea would rather have harsh fluorescents that lit up every shadowy corner.

She peered through the glass pane in the door, shivering a little. The dog, pressing against her leg, trembled, too, probably eager to get outside and chase whatever lay in the shadows.

The flowers were mere shapes that moved restlessly in the breeze, as if they sensed something wrong. She strained to see beyond the patio. There was the pale outline of the pond, and beyond it nothing but angular shadows.

She heard a step at the top of the stairs behind her.

"I tried Cal, but there was no answer. Perhaps it's him you saw outside."

If so, she was going to feel like an idiot for overreacting. "Does he usually look around the grounds at night?" He'd mentioned looking for the prowler, and after their conversation, that seemed likely. The tension eased.

"Sometimes. But I called the police anyway. Now, don't start worrying about it." Grams seemed to be reading her mind. "I'd rather be safe than sorry."

But she couldn't help the chagrin she felt. City-dweller, jumping to conclusions at the slightest thing.

Well, if so, Cal was the one who'd spooked her, with his talk of prowlers and thieves. He and Uncle Nick had done the job between them.

A heavy flashlight hung on the hook next to the back door, just where Grandfather had always kept one. Clutching the collar of the excited dog, she opened the door, then reached up and took the flashlight.

"Andrea, don't go out," Grams said. "I'm sure it's fine, but wait for the police. Or Cal. He'll come to the house when he sees all the lights on."

Obviously Grams wasn't worried. A little embarrassing, to have her elderly grandmother reassuring her.

"I'll just step outside and flash the light around. See if I can spot Cal. Or anyone."

The dog surged forward, tail waving, apparently welcoming this change in his usual routine. Did the waving tail indicate he sensed a friend?

She edged down the two steps to the patio, lifting the flashlight to probe the shadows beyond the pond. Even as she did, the wail of sirens pierced the night.

She must have relaxed her grip at the sound, because Barney pulled free and darted off toward the lane, letting out an excited bark. Turning, she caught a glimpse of what might be a dark figure. Her heart jolted. She swung the light toward it, but the beam didn't reach far enough to show her anything suspicious.

The dog barked again, a high, excited yip.

If it had been an intruder, he'd be thoroughly scared away by the dog, the lights and the sirens. The lane led to the road—if he went that way, he might run straight into the arms of the police, although he'd hardly be so foolish.

She swung the light back toward the shed where she'd first glimpsed the figure. Everything was still. Reassured by the wail of the police car as it turned in the drive, she crossed the patio, flashing the light around. Nothing seemed to be disturbed.

Cal had said the outbuildings were stuffed to the rafters with furniture. She focused the flashlight on the toolshed. Nothing moved now. The shed was a dark rectangle, with a darker rectangle for the door.

She frowned, trying to pick out details in the shaft of light. Memory provided her with an image of the door as she'd seen it earlier, and tension trailed along her nerves. There had been a padlock on the door. If it was open, someone had been breaking in.

She glanced toward the house. Grams stood in the lighted doorway, peering out.

"Grams, I'm going to check the toolshed. Please don't come out."

"Be careful." Grams sounded a little shaky.

"I will. But if anyone was here, he's long gone by now." She called the words back over her shoulder, mov-

ing toward the shed. If something had been stolen on
her second night here, she was going to feel responsible.

A mental list began to take shape. Get better outdoor
lighting, whether it enhanced the ambience or not. Ask
the police to make a regular swing by the property. New
locks on any building that held something of value. If
what Cal had said was right, that could be any of the
half-dozen or more outbuildings.

Every building should be properly inventoried. If it
hadn't been done when her grandfather died, it should
be done as soon as possible.

Grams and Rachel hadn't thought of that—their
minds didn't work that way, as Cal had pointed out.
Hers did. He hadn't intended a compliment, but she considered her organizational skills an asset. If her mother
had been a bit more meticulous, maybe they wouldn't
have spent so much time evading the bill collectors.

She shook that thought off, because remembering
those days gave her a queasy feeling in her stomach
and an inclination to check her bank balance, just to
be sure she was all right.

Hardly surprising. Other children's bogeymen had
been monsters and snakes. Hers had been collection
agencies.

"Barney! Come, Barney." Her grandmother's voice
fluted over the dark garden.

She glanced back the way she'd come to see the
dog's pale coat as he bounded toward Grams. Apparently Barney hadn't been in time to take a piece out of
their intruder.

Ahead of her, the entrance to the toolshed yawned
open, sending a faint shiver of fear across her skin. She
hadn't been imagining things. Someone had been here.

A few steps took her to the shed door. With a vague thought of fingerprints, she didn't touch it. She'd shine the light inside, that's all. There was no way of knowing if anything was missing, but at least she could see if it looked disturbed. And get an idea of what she had to deal with.

She leaned forward, light piercing the darkness, giving her a jumbled view of wooden pieces—straight chairs, tables, shelves, even an old icebox, jammed on top of each other...

A quick impression of movement, a dark figure. She couldn't react, couldn't even scream as a hand shot out, shoving her into the toolshed.

She barreled into the edge of a table, cracking her head on something above it. Stars showered through the darkness. She stumbled, hitting the floor just as the door banged shut.

For an instant dizziness engulfed her, followed by a wave of sheer, uncontrollable panic. She was shut in, she was alone in the dark—

She bolted to her feet, grabbed at the door, fumbling for a handle, a latch. "Let me out!"

Shout, don't cry, don't let yourself cry or the panic will take over.

"Help! Help me!"

The door jerked open, and she hurtled out. She caught back a sob, her hands closing on the soft fabric of a shirt and solid muscle. She knew him by instinct before she could see him.

"Cal—there was someone here. Did you see him?"

He pulled her clear of the door and slammed it shut. "Are you okay?"

"Yes." They'd had this exchange before, hadn't they? "I'm fine. Did you see him?"

"I saw him." He sounded grim. "Not enough to describe him, unfortunately. You?"

She shook her head. "Just a blur of movement when he pushed me into the shed. I'm sorry."

He grunted, a frustrated sound. "I was following him. If you hadn't sounded the alarm, I might have caught him."

Cal shook his head in response to Katherine's repeated offer of another cup of chamomile tea. "No, thanks, I've had plenty." One cup of the pale brew was surely enough to satisfy the demands of politeness.

"I think that's everything we need." The young township cop sat awkwardly at the kitchen table, looking half-afraid to touch the delicate Haviland cup and saucer that sat in front of him.

"Do you think you'll catch the thief?" Katherine was as much at ease in her kitchen, wearing a fuzzy red bathrobe, as if she sat in the parlor.

"That might be too much to expect, Grams." Andrea spoke before the cop could come up with an answer. "None of us actually saw the man, and he didn't take anything, as far as we know."

While the cop's attitude toward Katherine was one of respect bordering on awe, the glance he turned on Andrea was simply admiration.

Cal understood. Even casual and disheveled, wearing jeans and a loose blue shirt, Andrea was cool and elegant.

And frosty, when she looked at him. Apparently his

comment about her interfering with his pursuit of the intruder still rankled.

"I'd best be on my way, ma'am." The cop rose, settling his uniform cap over a thatch of straw-colored hair as he headed for the back door. "We'll do the best we can to keep an eye on the place."

"Thank you, Officer." Katherine was graciousness itself. "We appreciate that."

Once the door closed behind him, Cal shook his head. "That won't be often enough. The township cops have too much territory to cover and too few men. What you need out there is better lighting."

"That's just what I was thinking." Once again Andrea looked faintly surprised to find herself agreeing with him. "I'll call about it in the morning."

"I don't think that's necessary. If we leave on the lights we have, that should suffice." Katherine set a cup and saucer in the sink, the china chattering against itself, betraying her emotion.

"I can install them," he said, knowing she was probably worrying about the cost, "if Andrea gets the fixtures."

Andrea nodded. "Of course." Her gaze crossed his, and he knew they were thinking the same thing. "It'll be my contribution to the renovations."

"I don't want you to spend your money on this." Katherine's eyes darkened with distress. "After all, you didn't think the inn was a good idea."

She probably still didn't, but she managed a smile. "I have to take part. The sign does say The Three Sisters Inn, after all." She put her arm around her grandmother's waist and urged her toward the stairs. "You go up to bed, Grams. I'll just talk to Cal about the lights, and then I'll see him out."

"Thank you, dear." Katherine patted her cheek, and then came over to touch him lightly on the shoulder. "And you, Cal. I don't know what we'd have done without you tonight."

"No problem," he said easily. "Have a good night's sleep."

She nodded. "Come, Barney." The dog padded obediently after her. "That's my good, brave dog," she crooned, starting up the stairs. "You were so clever to chase the bad man away."

He waited until he heard her door close to shake his head. "I've never been overly impressed with Barney's intelligence, and tonight confirmed that. He ran to me, recognizing a friend, instead of chasing the prowler."

Andrea frowned. "Even if he's not the brightest dog in the world, you'd think he'd go after a stranger."

That thought had occurred to him, too, but he didn't see anything to be gained by pursuing it now. If this was the same person who'd broken into several farmhouses, he could be someone local, even someone who'd been to the house before.

She sat down across from him, apparently willing to forget her annoyance in the need to talk with someone. "Do you think he was planning to steal something tonight, or just checking things out for a future visit?"

"I'm not sure." He balanced the silver teaspoon on his finger. Silver, good china, antiques—there was plenty here to tempt a thief. "He may have wanted to see where the best stuff was. I would expect him to come with a truck of some sort if he planned to haul away any antiques. Pennsylvania German pieces tend to be pretty hefty, to say the least."

"I suppose you're right. He did break the lock, though."

"Meaning he wouldn't have done that unless he planned to take something? I'm not sure you're right. He couldn't know what was there unless he got in to have a look around."

"I guess." She ran her hands through the silky strands of blond hair in a gesture of frustration. "I don't even know what's in the shed. How could they get away without a proper inventory when my grandfather died?" She sounded slightly outraged, as if lack of the right paperwork was a moral failing.

"Maybe that's a good job for you." It would keep her busy, anyway.

"I can't imagine how long that would take. More time than I have, at any rate. But I'll call a locksmith and have decent locks put on all those buildings."

A slight feeling of sympathy surprised him. Andrea was trying to do the right thing for her grandmother, even if she didn't agree with her decisions.

"I can put new locks on. We'll get them when we go for the light fixtures tomorrow."

"We?" Her eyebrows lifted.

"We. Unless you're well-informed as to the best type of light fixtures and locks to use."

Her eyes narrowed, and he could almost see her trying to pigeonhole him. "I thought you were a carpenter, not a handyman."

"I know a little about a lot of useful things."

"In that case, I'm surprised you didn't offer to do the

lights and the locks before," she said tartly. "Since you were so quick to warn me about the danger."

"I did. Numerous times." He rose, carrying his cup and saucer to the sink. "Katherine always turned me down. She held tightly to the illusion that this place was still safe. After tonight, I don't think that's an issue, sadly. She'll let us do it."

"You really don't need to help." Andrea's chair scraped as she shoved it in, the only sound in the room other than the ticktock of the ornate Black Forest mantel clock. "I'm sure my grandmother appreciates your offer, but I can hire someone. I'll pay—"

He swung around, annoyed that she thought this was about money. "I said I'd do it."

"It's my responsibility." That stubborn jaw was very much in evidence. "Why should you be involved?"

"Because I live here, too. Because your grandmother and your sister have both been kind to me."

Because they can accept me as I am, without needing a dossier on my past.

Her hands moved, palms up, in a gesture of surrender. "All right, then. If you feel that way about it, I guess we'd better head out to the hardware store tomorrow."

"Fine." He strode toward the door and pulled it open. "Be sure you lock this behind me."

"You don't need to remind me of that." The ghost of a smile touched her lips as she came to the door and reached for the dead bolt. "I'm a city-dweller, remember? Locking up is second nature to me."

She stood close in the dim light, with the half-opened door between them like a wedge. Her face looked softer in the shadows, more vulnerable.

The way it had looked when she'd catapulted out of

the shed practically into his arms. He'd felt her heart racing in the instant she'd pressed against him. She'd been panic-stricken, although she was hardly likely to admit that to him.

"Katherine could use a few street smarts. But I can't see her changing at this time of her life, so we'll have to take care of it for her."

She nodded, but he thought there was still a question in her eyes. About him. She wasn't like Katherine and Rachel in that regard. She didn't accept anyone at face value.

No, if Andrea stuck around for long, she'd be trying to find out more about him. She'd have to know, just so she could fit him into her neat classification system. And if she did, it would only raise more questions in her mind. Why would a rising young attorney in a prestigious firm throw it all over after winning the case of his career? She'd want to know the answer.

She wouldn't. No one here knew but him. His conscience would never let him forget the mistake he'd made in his rush to get ahead, or the child his stupidity had returned to an abusive father. It had cost his career to right that wrong, and he didn't figure he was finished paying yet. But that wasn't Andrea's business.

"Good night." His fingers brushed hers lightly as he grasped the door to pull it shut behind him. "Pleasant dreams."

"So basically it was much ado about nothing." Andrea gave Rachel her most reassuring smile the next morning. "Really. Stop looking so worried."

Of course Rachel couldn't help it, tethered as she was to a wheelchair by the two heavy casts. The chair was parked by the window, but she didn't look as if she'd been enjoying the view of the hospital's helipad.

"I knew we should have taken more security measures, especially after thieves broke into the Bauman farmhouse and vandals knocked over some of the gravestones in the church cemetery." She brushed a soft brown curl behind her ear with a quick gesture, brow crinkled. "But Grams still thinks this place is as safe as it was fifty years ago, and anyway, she said—" She stopped abruptly, guilt plainly written on her face.

"Relax, Rachel. I talked to Uncle Nick. I know about Grams's finances."

Rachel blinked. "He told you?"

"Yes. What I want to know is, why didn't you tell me?" She forced the hurt out of her voice.

Discomfort made her sister move restlessly in the wheelchair. "You know Grams. She's proud. The only reason I found out was because I happened to be visiting when she hit a low point."

"So you came up with the idea of starting the bed-and-breakfast to help her." How disapproving did she sound? Apparently some, because Rachel's gaze slid away from hers.

"It seems like a good use for the house. Nobody needs a huge place like that just to live in."

"Exactly." She sat down in the vinyl padded chair that was all the room offered for a visitor, turning it to face Rachel. "So wouldn't Grams be better off to sell? The place is way too big for her, and I don't think she should have the worry of starting a business at this time of life."

"You don't understand." Rachel straightened, eyes flashing. "Grams loves that place. Unger House has been her home for fifty years. How can you act as if it would be easy for her to give it up?"

That was as much anger as she'd seen from Rachel since Caroline stole her boyfriend in tenth grade. She leaned forward, resting her hand on her sister's.

"I know it wouldn't be easy, but doesn't that point come to everyone? When people get older, they usually have to move into a place that's more manageable. I'm sure Grams understands that."

Rachel's expression was unusually stubborn. "She's not ready for that. Besides, she always assumed there'd be family to take over Unger House one day. Us."

That was like a blow to the stomach. "She—why would she think that? It's been years since we left."

"Not that long, as Grams sees it." Rachel tilted her head, surveying Andrea with an expression that suggested she just didn't get it. "You're the one who had the most time here. I'd think you'd have lots of good memories."

"Good memories?" Something hardened in her. "What I remember is being dragged out of the house with half our belongings, Caro screaming, Grams crying, and Grandfather standing there like a statue. As if he didn't care."

"Oh, honey." Rachel patted her hand as if she was the one who needed comfort. "I know how bad that was, but can't you think about all the good times, instead? We were happy here once."

She jerked her feelings back under control, shoving the images from that day behind a closed door. In her ordinary life, she never let them out. Here, she'd been tripping over them every other minute, it seemed.

"You've always been the peacemaker, Rachel, trying

to make everyone else feel good." Lucky Rachel had the gift of being able to separate out the bad stuff and remember only the happy times. She didn't, it seemed.

"There were lots of good things," Rachel insisted. "Remember the time the power went off in the big snowstorm, and Eli and Levi Zook brought the horse and sleigh and took us for a ride over the fields to their place? Having the power go off wasn't a problem for them, since they don't depend on it anyway."

"I remember." She couldn't help a smile. "Caroline tried to teach Eli and Emma's kids how to do the hokey-pokey. I don't think they appreciated it."

"The point is that if Grams wants to stay at Unger House, I'm ready to help her do it. The bed-and-break-fast seemed like the logical answer." She rubbed the wrinkle that formed between her brows. "My getting hurt wasn't part of the plan, but I still think if they'd let me go home, we could work it out. Emma's a good cook, and if I'm there to supervise—"

"Absolutely not." That was one thing she was sure of in this situation. "I've talked to the doctors. You need rest, healing and therapy, in that order. No coming home until they give the okay."

Rachel looked at her steadily. "If I do that, how is Grams going to get the inn ready to open? She can't do it herself. Just making all the decisions, let alone the work—"

"She won't be doing it by herself." She'd reached the point she'd probably known all along she would. This wasn't her dream, but she couldn't let her family down. "I'll stay and do my best to get the inn off the ground."

She could only hope that she wouldn't have to sacrifice her job in order to do it.

Chapter 5

Andrea hurried through the center hallway toward the rear of the house, pausing in the small room that had been first a summer kitchen, then later a playroom for her and her sisters. They'd loved the huge fireplace, big enough to roast a whole side of beef. They'd pretended they were Cinderella, sweeping the hearth. Come to think of it, Caroline had always gotten to play Cinderella. She'd been the wicked stepmother.

That was how Rachel had made her feel at her suggestion of selling Unger House—like the wicked stepmother. That stung, with its implication that Rachel cared more, understood more, than she did. She still thought selling was the logical solution, but she was smart enough to know when a plan, logical or not, didn't stand a chance of success.

So she was heading to the hardware store with Cal,

putting off the two things she was least eager to do today. Confronting her grandmother about the financial situation, for one. And then telling her boss she needed a leave of absence. Knowing him, she'd be lucky if he didn't simply give her a choice—her family or her job.

Something winced inside her at that. She deserved that promotion. She'd worked hard for it, sacrificing everything else in her drive to succeed. It wasn't fair that she might lose it now.

She pushed through the swinging door to the kitchen. "Emma, do you need anything—"

She stopped, nerves jumping. Emma was not in sight, but a man stood with his back to her—tall, broad, black pants and a black jacket, his hand in a drawer of the hutch that held the everyday china.

"What are you doing?" The edge to her voice was put there by fear, but she wouldn't give in to the feeling. Wouldn't let herself think about the dark figure that had shoved her into the toolshed. It was broad daylight now, and she wasn't afraid.

The man froze, then turned slowly toward her. It was like watching a mountain move. His face became visible, and something jolted inside her. The face was oddly unformed, as if a sculptor had started working on it and then walked away, uninterested in finishing. Blue eyes, rounded cheeks like a child's...

Emma hurried in from the pantry, her white apron fluttering, eyes worried behind wire-rimmed glasses. "What are you doing, Levi? You remember Andrea, don't you?"

"I remember him." Andrea tried to soften her embarrassment with a smile. Of course. She should have recognized him at once. Emma's oldest son was two years older than she was chronologically. Mentally, he was still the child he'd been long ago. "How are you, Levi?"

"Say good day," Emma prompted, but he just shook his head, taking a step back until he bumped the hutch.

"That's all right," Andrea said, trying to smooth over the uncomfortable moment. "Maybe later Levi will want to talk to me."

Levi's round blue eyes filled with tears. With an incoherent sound, he turned and ran from the kitchen, the screen door slamming behind him.

She could kick herself. "I'm so sorry." She turned to Emma. "I didn't mean to upset him that way."

"He will be fine." Emma didn't seem upset. "He just needs time to get used to new people."

"Doesn't he remember me?" Her own childhood memories were flooding back faster and faster, no matter how much she tried to block them out.

Emma shook her head. "He knows you, for sure. He just doesn't understand about how people change. I'll tell him a couple of times about how you're Andrea all grown-up. He'll be fine."

Certainly Emma didn't seem worried about the incident. Her oval face, innocent of makeup, was as serene as always. Whatever grief she'd endured over Levi's condition had long ago been accepted as God's will, the way she'd accept a lightning strike that hit the barn or a bumper crop of tomatoes to take to market as God's will.

Andrea went to press her cheek against Emma's, affection surging within her. Maybe she'd be a better person if she had a little of that kind of acceptance.

"Well, you tell Levi I was happy to see him, anyway." She dismissed that flare of apprehension that had gripped her when she'd seen him at the hutch. "Rachel was just reminding me of the big snowstorm, when we came to your house in the sleigh. Levi helped his father drive the horses, I remember."

"Ach, I will tell him." Emma beamed at the reminiscence, rubbing her hands on the full skirt of her plain, wine-colored dress. "He will remember that, he will."

They'd all played together then—Amish and English—it hadn't mattered to the children. Emma's oldest daughter, Sarah, had been her exact age. She'd longed go to school with Sarah in the simple white schoolhouse down the road, instead of getting on the yellow school bus for the trip to the consolidated elementary.

"How is Sarah? Married, I know from my grandmother."

"Married with six young ones of her own, and training to be a midwife, besides." Emma's pride was manifest, though she'd never admit it.

"Please greet her for me, too." They'd all grown and gone their separate ways. Only Levi had remained, a child still, but in a man's body. "I'm going to the hardware store with Cal to get some new lights and locks. I wondered if you needed anything."

Emma's plump face paled. "Locks? Why? Has something happened?"

She'd assumed Grams would have mentioned it, but possibly they hadn't had a chance to talk before Grams set off for the hospital.

"We had a prowler last night." She didn't want to alarm Emma, but surely it was better that she know. "He tried to get into the old toolshed."

"Did you—did you get a look at this person?" Emma's hands twisted together under her apron.

She shook her head, sorry now that she'd mentioned it. She didn't want to distress Emma. Probably she, like Grams, still thought of this area as perfectly safe.

"He ran away when he heard the dog and the sirens." Maybe it was just as well not to mention her closer encounter with the man. "We're going to put up brighter lighting in the grounds. Hopefully that will keep any troublemakers away."

"Ja." Emma pulled open the door under the sink, peering inside. *"Ja,* maybe it will. I can't think of anything that I need from the store."

Andrea hesitated a moment, studying the tense lines of Emma's shoulders under the dark dress, the averted face. The thought of a prowler had upset her more than expected, but Andrea didn't know what to do to ease her mind.

"Don't worry about it, please, Emma. I'm sure the lights will solve the problem. And if you're concerned about walking back and forth to the farm, I'd be happy to drive you."

"No, no." Emma whisked that offer away with a sweeping gesture. "I am fine. No one will bother me."

There didn't seem to be anything else to say, but Andrea frowned as she walked to the door. They couldn't afford to have Emma upset. Grams needed her more than she ever had.

They both did, if they were really going to open the inn on time, and though she could hardly believe it of herself, it seemed she was committed to this crazy venture.

From his perch on the stone wall that wound along the patio, Cal watched the black-clad figure vanish from sight around the barn. He and Levi had reached the point that Levi would sometimes speak to him, but today he'd rushed past without a word. Something had upset him, obviously.

Cal latched his hands around his knee. Andrea had said she'd meet him, and he'd guess she was the type to be on time. So he'd come a bit early, not wanting to give her a reason to say he'd kept her waiting.

Sure enough, she hurried out the back door, checking her watch as she did. She looked up, saw him and came toward him at a more deliberate pace.

"Sorry. Have you been waiting?"

"Only for a couple of minutes." He got up leisurely. "I saw Levi come running out."

"I suppose you think I frightened him."

He held both hands up in a gesture of surrender. "Peace. That wasn't aimed at you. I know how shy he is. It's taken months to get him to the point of nodding at me."

A faint flush touched her cheeks. "I guess that did sound pretty defensive, didn't it? I was startled that Levi didn't seem to remember me."

He fell into step beside her as they walked toward the stone garage that had started life as a stable. "I take it you knew him when you were children."

What had she been like as a child? Flax hair in braids, he supposed, probably bossing the others around because she was the oldest.

She nodded, those green eyes seeming fixed on something far away. "They were our neighbors. Emma's daughter Sarah was my closest friend." She shook her head. "It seems odd now, when I think of it. As if it happened in a different world."

That, he thought, was the most unguarded thing she'd said to him yet. "I suppose it was, in a way. Childhood, I mean."

"The differences didn't seem so great to a child. We drove my grandfather crazy by talking in the low German dialect the Zook children used at home."

"He didn't like that?" He gestured her toward the truck. When she hesitated, he opened the passenger door for her. "We may as well take this. Rachel's compact doesn't have much trunk room."

She nodded, climbing in. When he slid behind the wheel, she went on as if the interruption hadn't happened.

"I'm not really sure why he objected. His family was what the Amish call 'fancy' German, just as they call themselves the 'plain folk.'" She shrugged. "He didn't insist—maybe he knew that would just make us more determined. Or maybe he saw that Emma's family was good for us." Some faint shadow crossed her face at that.

"Sounds as if you and your sisters had a good childhood here," he said lightly. "I was an urban kid, myself. Never saw a real cow until I was twelve."

"Good?" Again that shadow. "Yes, I guess. Until it ended."

He glanced toward her. "Ended sounds rather final."

She blinked, and he could almost see her realizing that she'd said more to him than she'd intended. She shrugged, seeming to try for a casual movement.

"Everyone outgrows being a kid. Can we get what we need at Clymer's Hardware, or do we have to go farther?"

Obviously the subject was closed. Maybe only the encounter with Levi had opened her that much. Something had happened to put a period to that innocent time, maybe the same thing that had kept her away from here for so long. Whatever it was, she wasn't going to tell him.

So be it. He wouldn't pry, any more than he wanted someone prying into his life. "Clymer's. I know your grandmother likes to use local businesses if she can."

"Fine."

He pulled into the lot next to the frame building with old-fashioned gilt lettering on the glass windows. He loved going into the village hardware store. It was nice to be in a place where people knew your name, as the song said.

Clymer's was as much a center for male gossip as the grocery store was for female gossip, in the way of small towns. Here they'd be talking about who needed new fencing and how the alfalfa was coming along.

Andrea slid out quickly, and he followed her to the door. She stepped inside, pausing as if getting her bearings.

"Lighting fixtures are in the back." He nodded toward the aisle.

Detouring around kegs of nails and the coil of rope that hung handy to be measured off, they headed back to where sample fixtures hung, gleaming palely in the daylight. Ted Clymer looked up from the counter where he was working a crossword puzzle and raised a hand in greeting. Ted seemed to figure if his customers needed any help, they'd ask for it. Otherwise, he left them alone.

Andrea came to a halt in the midst of racks of light fixtures. She turned toward him. "I'm not too proud to admit when I'm out of my depth. What do you think we need?"

Since he'd already decided, he was relieved that they weren't going to argue about it. He chose two brands and set the boxes in front of her. "Either one of these would do the job."

"Which do you recommend?"

He put his hand on the more expensive brand. "This will cost more to begin with, but it's higher rated. Still, the other one will serve."

She shook her head decisively. "I don't want to worry that they'll have to be replaced in a couple of years. How many do you think we need to cover the area?"

"I'd say six would do it." He glanced at the racks. "Ted doesn't have that many out, but he probably has more in the back."

She picked up the box. "I'll ask him to get them while you're picking out the locks." Her smile flickered. "You don't need to ask my opinion. Just get what you think will work best."

So apparently Andrea trusted him in that, at least, and she wasn't grudging the money spent on something her grandmother needed. He watched her walk toward the counter. Even in khaki pants and a fitted denim jacket, she had just enough of an urban flair to let you know she didn't belong here.

Too bad. Because Katherine would like having her around, not because it mattered to him.

It took a few minutes to find locks that satisfied him. Nothing would keep out a really determined thief, but these would discourage anyone who was looking for a lock that could be popped quickly and quietly.

He headed back to the counter, his hands full, but checked when he saw the person who stood next to Andrea, talking away as if they were old friends. Margaret

Allen. He'd be willing to bet that no legitimate errand had brought her into the hardware store. It was far more likely that she'd spotted them from across the street and decided to check up on the competition.

He approached and dropped the locks on the counter, their clatter interrupting the conversation. "That's it for us, Ted. Ring us up."

He turned, forcing a smile. "Hello, Margaret. How's business?"

She returned the smile with one that had syrup oozing off it. Margaret looked, he always thought, like a well-fed, self-satisfied cat, and never so much as when she was asserting her position as the owner of the finest inn in the county. Just how far would she go to maintain that status? The question had begun pricking at the back of his mind lately.

"How nice to see you, Cal. I was just telling Andrea how wonderful it is of her to come and help her grandmother at such a sad time. Poor Rachel. I'm afraid all their visions of starting a bed-and-breakfast will be lost. Still, I always say that every cloud has a silver lining, and I'm sure in the end, this disappointment will be for the best. Don't you agree, Andrea?"

Andrea looked a little dazed at the flood of saccharine. "Yes, I mean—"

"We have to go." He handed Andrea the credit card Ted had been patiently holding out. "Lots to do. Nice seeing you, Margaret." He scooped up boxes, handing the bag containing the locks to Andrea, and nudged her toward the door.

She shot him an annoyed look. "I'm glad to have met you, Ms. Allen. I'll tell my sister you asked about her."

They reached the pickup, and he started loading fixtures quickly, not having any desire to hang around for another interrogation from Margaret.

Andrea dropped the bag with the locks into the pickup bed. "You didn't have to be rude to that poor woman. She was just expressing her concern."

"Right." He shook his head. "That was Margaret Allen." He pointed to the Georgian mansion across the street with its twin weeping willows overhanging the wrought iron fence. "That Margaret Allen, owner of The Willows bed-and-breakfast."

"She said she was a friend of my grandmother's." Andrea climbed in, frowning at him as he got behind the wheel. "Maybe she did gush a bit, but I'm sure she meant well."

"A bit?" He lifted an eyebrow. "You looked as if you were drowning in it."

Her lips twitched. "Just because she runs another B and B, that doesn't make her the enemy."

"In her mind, it does. Believe me. She takes pride in having the only inn in Churchville, and she doesn't like to share the limelight, or the tourist dollars, with anyone." He pulled out onto Main Street for the short drive home.

"Surely there's enough tourist trade to go around."

He shrugged. "Ask Rachel, if you don't believe me. She's the one who's had to deal with her. The other B and B operators in the county have been supportive, by and large, but Margaret created one problem after another."

"What could she do? Surely you don't think she was our prowler."

That was a thought that hadn't occurred to him, and he filed it for future consideration. "I don't see her wandering around in the dark, no, but she has played dirty. Complaints to the township zoning board, complaints to the tourist bureau, complaints to the bed-and-breakfast owners association. All couched in such sickeningly sweet language you'd think she was doing them a favor by putting up roadblocks."

"Maybe she was." It was said so softly he almost missed it.

"Is that what you'll tell your grandmother when you bail and leave them on their own?" The edge in his voice startled him. He hadn't meant to say that.

He felt Andrea's gaze on him and half expected an explosion. He didn't get it.

"Think what you like." Her tone dismissed him, as if he were no more important in the scheme of things than the barn cat. "But as a matter of fact, I'm not leaving. I'm staying until I can be sure that my grandmother and sister are all right."

It silenced him for a moment. "What about your job?"

Her fingers clenched in her lap. "I don't know. Talking to my boss is a pleasure I haven't had yet."

"I'm sorry. I hope he understands."

"So do I." Her fingers tightened until her knuckles were white.

"It means that much to you?"

"Yes. It does." She clipped off the words, as if he didn't have the right to know why.

She was willing to sacrifice something that was important to her for the sake of someone else. The few people who knew the truth about him might say he'd done the same, but he'd done it as much for himself as for anyone else, because he'd known he couldn't live with himself if he hadn't.

It had brought him unexpected benefits in the long run—helped him to know what he wanted from life, brought him to faith. Still, he couldn't assume that would be the result for Andrea's sacrifice.

"I hope it works out for you, Andrea. Really."

He glanced across the confines of the front seat at her. There was something startled, a little wary, in her eyes. As if she wasn't sure whether she believed him. Or maybe as if it mattered what he thought.

Chapter 6

Andrea sat in the room she still thought of as her grandfather's library that afternoon, frowning over the rather sketchy records Rachel seemed to be keeping on the inn's start-up. Sketchy didn't cover it. Surely Rachel had better records than this. If not, they were in more trouble than she'd imagined.

She flipped through the file folder, her frustration growing. Hadn't Rachel been saving receipts, at least? Grams might know if she had records elsewhere. Maybe, like Grandfather, she preferred to do it all by hand, although he had been far more organized than this.

Grandfather's tall green ledgers had been a fixture of their childhood. Presumably the insurance and real estate business he'd shared with Uncle Nick had long since been computerized, but she'd always associate her grandfather with those meticulously handwritten ledgers. She glanced at the shelf where they'd once stood in a neat row, but it was now occupied by a welter of tourist brochures and bed-and-breakfast books. Rachel must have moved them.

The front door closed, and Barney gave the excited yelp that meant the center of his existence had returned. The scrabble of his nails on the plank floor was followed by the crooning voice Grams reserved for him. Andrea had to smile. She couldn't imagine her dignified grandmother talking baby talk to any other creature but Barney.

"Andrea?" Her grandmother came in, followed by the excited dog. "Good, you're here. I'd like to speak with you."

The determined set to Grams's jaw told her that any questions about Rachel's record-keeping would have to wait. Grams clearly had an agenda of her own.

Andrea swung the leather swivel chair around so that she faced the wingback tapestry chair that was Grams's favorite. The desk chair had been Grandfather's. It was too big for Andrea, and she felt slightly uncomfortable in it, as if she sat in the boss's chair without permission.

"How's Rachel? Did you tell her I'll come to see her this evening?"

Grams sat down, her expression lightening a little. "I thought she seemed a bit stronger today. She didn't look quite so pale. Nick had been in with a lovely arrangement of roses, and Pastor Hartman came just as I was leaving."

"That's good." Good that Rachel seemed better, and good that she was having other company. Perhaps that would keep Grams from feeling guilty if she couldn't be there every minute.

"Yes." Grams fondled the dog's ears for a moment, frowning a little. "I understand from Rachel that you know about my financial situation. That James Bendick told you."

That must really rankle, or Grams would be using the nickname that she'd adopted along with the children. "Please don't blame Uncle Nick, Grams. I'd already guessed some of it, and I made him tell me what was going on."

That didn't seem to have the desired effect. Grams still looked severe. "Nevertheless, he doesn't have the right to discuss my affairs without my permission. I'll have to speak to him about it."

The threat to be spoken to by Grams had been such a part of her childhood that it almost made her smile. *Andrea Katherine, do I have to speak to you?* The words echoed from the past.

Grams was taking this too seriously for smiling, however, and they had to discuss the situation, whether Grams wanted to confide in her or not.

"Uncle Nick probably thought I'd heard it already, from you. Which I should have. Why on earth didn't you tell me about the financial problems? You must know I'd help any way I can."

Grams turned her face away, and for a moment Andrea thought she wasn't going to answer. Then she realized that her grandmother was looking at the portrait of Grandfather that hung over the mantelpiece on the other side of the room.

"I didn't want you to think ill of your grandfather. Or any more than you already do."

The words were spoken so softly that it took a moment for them to register. And when they did, Andrea felt a flush rise on her cheeks. "I don't know what you mean."

Grams looked at her then, her blue eyes chiding. "Yes, you do, Andrea. You've never forgiven him for the quarrel with your mother."

It was like being slapped. She'd never dreamed that Grams guessed her feelings. Obviously she hadn't been as good at hiding them as she'd thought. She took a breath, trying to compose herself. She couldn't let whatever lingering resentment she had affect what she did now.

"It was a long time ago, Grams. What's important is what's going on now."

Her grandmother shook her head slowly, delicate silver earrings echoing the movement. "The past is always important, Andrea. Your grandfather was a good man. He gave me a comfortable life, and I won't hear a word against him just because he made a few wrong business decisions."

It must have been more than a few, some practical part of her mind commented, but she shooed away the thought. She had to help Grams, but she'd hoped to steer clear of Grandfather's mistakes, knowing that would hurt her.

"He loved you very much, Grams."

For the first time since her return, Andrea stared directly at the portrait. Her grandfather's image stared back—blue eyes as piercing as she remembered, the planes of his face still strong even when the painting was done, to commemorate Grandfather's retirement from the state legislature at sixty-five. He looked like a man you could count on.

But he also looked stubborn. In the case of his daughter, the stiff-necked stubbornness had won out over any other consideration, including his grandchildren.

"He loved you, too, dear. I know you find that hard to believe, but he did."

"He let her take us away." The voice of her childhood popped out before she could censor it.

Grams reached out to grasp her hand. "He couldn't stop her. She was your mother." She shook her head. "I know you think he could have mended things with her, but you must be old enough now to see how it was. He was proud, and your mother—well, she was willful. They could never stop the quarrel long enough to admit they loved each other."

Willful, reckless, lavish with both affection and temper—yes, she knew what her mother had been like. How had two such solid citizens as her grandparents have produced Lily Unger Hampton? That had to be one of the mysteries of genetics.

"I'm sorry, Grams." To her horror, she felt tears well in her eyes. "I know it hurt you, too." But her grandmother would never know just how bad it had been for her precious grandchildren, at least not if Andrea could help it.

"He grieved when you were taken away." Grams's voice was soft. "You have to believe that, my dear."

Not as much as we did. You were the grown-ups, you and Grandfather, and our mother and father. Why didn't you take better care of us? She wouldn't say that, but she couldn't help feeling it.

Shaking her head, Grams got up. She dipped her

hand into a Blue Willow Wedgwood bowl that sat on top of the desk, retrieving the small key. She handed it to Andrea.

"It fits the bottom drawer on the right." She nodded to the massive mahogany desk that had been Grandfather's. "I want you to look inside."

Something in her wanted to rebel, but she couldn't ignore the command in her grandmother's eyes. She bent and unlocked the drawer, pulling it open. Inside were long rectangular boxes, three of them—the sort of archival boxes that preserved documents. The top box had a name, written in black ink in Grandpa's precise lettering. *Andrea.*

She lifted that one, setting it on the desk blotter to remove the lid. Her throat tightened. A picture, drawn by a child's hand, showed two figures—a white-haired man in a navy suit, a child with yellow braids. Before she could dwell on it, she flipped through the rest of the contents.

Report cards, more drawings, dating back to the earliest attempts that were no more than ovals on sticks for figures. Always two of them—grandfather and granddaughter. A handmade valentine, with a lopsided heart pasted onto a white doily, signed with a red crayon. *To Grandfather from your helper.*

She remembered making that one, sitting at the kitchen table, asking Emma to aid with the spelling. Emma, always more adept in German than English, had called Grams in to advise.

Tears stung her eyes, and she fought to keep them from falling. Grams meant well. She was trying to prove that Grandfather had loved her. But if he'd loved her enough to save all these things, why hadn't he loved her enough to do whatever it took to stay a part of her life?

A hot tear splashed on the valentine, and she blotted it away. Yes, Grams meant well. But looking at these reminders didn't make the situation better. Seeing them just made it worse.

Cal rounded the shed on his way to the kitchen. His stride checked abruptly.

Andrea sat on the low stone wall where he'd sat earlier, but she didn't seem to be waiting for anyone. Her cell phone was pressed to her ear, and judging by the expression on her face, the conversation wasn't going well.

He detoured to the walk that circled around, taking him toward the door at a safe distance from her. She'd probably come out to the garden to ensure her privacy, and he wouldn't intrude. But he couldn't prevent a certain amount of curiosity. Was it her boss who put that expression on her face?

Or was it a boyfriend, unhappy at her prolonged absence from the city? That thought generated a surprisingly quick denial. No one had mentioned a boyfriend in Andrea's life, but then again, why would they, to him?

He went on into the kitchen, where he consulted Emma about the exact finish on the piece he was making for her, enjoying prolonging the conversation with a smattering of the low German he'd been attempting to learn. It must still be plenty fractured, judging by her laughter.

That had been one of the things that had surprised him about the Amish when he'd come here. He'd expected, from outward appearances, a dour people, living an uncomfortable life as if it were a duty.

Instead he'd found people who laughed readily and who took as much enjoyment in plowing all day in the sun as they did from sitting on the porch on a summer's evening. Work was not something that was separate from play—all things held their own intrinsic satisfaction, because they were done in obedience to God's will.

It was a lesson he'd been trying to learn, but he suspected that even the trying was self-defeating. He couldn't will himself into finding peace and joy in the everyday things of life. That only happened when he forgot the effort and simply lost himself in what he was doing.

When he went out the back door again, Andrea still sat on the wall. Afternoon sunlight, filtering through the leaves of the giant oak that shaded the patio, turned her silky blond hair to gold. The cell phone lay next to her.

"Hi." He nodded toward the phone. "I didn't want to interrupt you."

"An interruption might have improved the conversation." She grimaced. "No, I take that back. It would just have prolonged it."

"Your boss?" That instinctive sympathy came again.

"He did *not* take the news well. Not even when I assured him I'd keep working on the project from here."

"Did you point out that telecommuting is fast becoming the norm in some businesses?"

"He doesn't think telecommuting will do the trick at this point." She shrugged. "I can't really argue with that. He's probably right."

He propped one foot on the wall and leaned an elbow on his knee. "I assume he finally accepted the inevitable."

"Well, he's not firing me outright, so I suppose that's

a good sign. But I suspect my promotion has just moved off into the distant future." Her eyes clouded at that. "I'll do everything I can from here, and my assistant will do what she can, but he'll still be inconvenienced."

"A little inconvenience never hurt anyone. Maybe he'll learn to appreciate you more." He'd like to remove the dismay from her face, but that wasn't within his power.

"Somehow I doubt that."

He sat down next to her. No use pretending he didn't care about her troubles. He couldn't help doing so. "This promotion—it means a lot to you."

A fine line formed between her brows. "It means... security."

Whatever he'd expected her to say—recognition, success, the corner office—it hadn't been that. "Security? That sounds like something I'd expect from a fifty-year-old who's thinking about retirement."

She stiffened. "Security is generally considered a good thing, believe it or not. You don't have to be fifty to think about it. In fact, if you wait until you're fifty, you've put it off too long."

"You're young, smart and, I suspect, talented at what you do." He smiled. "And those are good things, too. They'd be appreciated in plenty of places. Your grandmother says—"

"My grandmother doesn't know anything about business. But you do, don't you?" She swung the full impact of those green eyes on him.

"What makes you say that?" He backtracked, wondering where he'd made a mistake. "I'm just a craftsman."

"You do a pretty good imitation of the country hick from time to time, but that's not who you are, is it?"

He shrugged, almost enjoying parrying with her. She'd never hit on the truth, so what difference did it make?

"I told you I grew up in the city. Any little vestiges of urban sophistication should wear away, in time."

"I'm not talking about growing up in the city." She brushed that away with a wave of her hand. "I'm talking about the corporate mind-set. You understand it too well to be a bystander."

He rose, the enjoyment leaving. He didn't like the turn the conversation was taking. "Hey, I was just trying to be sympathetic."

She studied him for a long moment, her brow furrowed with uncertainty. And he suspected she didn't like being uncertain about anything.

"If that's true, I appreciate it," she said finally. "But I still don't believe you're just a simple craftsman."

His tension eased. She wasn't going to make an issue of it, and even if she did—well, he hadn't committed any crime. At least, not any that the law would call him to book for. Whatever guilt he still carried was between him and God.

"And you're not just a simple financial expert, are you? You're also a granddaughter, a sister, and now an innkeeper."

"Don't remind me." She rubbed at the line between her brows, as if she could rub it away. "I know you won't appreciate how this pains me, but my sister's idea of keeping track of start-up costs consists of throwing receipts in a file."

"She uses a file? I thought my cigar box was pretty sophisticated."

That got a smile, and the line vanished. "You're not going to make me believe that, you know."

"Maybe not." He sobered. "But I hope you'll believe that if anything happens that worries you, you can call me. Any time. I promise I'll answer my phone."

She looked startled. "You mean—but surely with the new lights and the locks, no one would try to break in."

"Sounds a little melodramatic with the sun shining, but I'm still not comfortable about the situation." An ambitious thief might want to see what he could get before the inn opened, filling the place with visitors. And an ambitious rival might think one more incident would be enough to scuttle the inn plans for good. "Just—call me."

Her gaze seemed to weigh him, determining whether and how much to trust him. Finally she nodded.

"All right. If I see or hear anything that concerns me, I'll call you. I promise."

She'd made a promise she didn't expect she'd have to keep, Andrea thought as she drove home from the hospital that evening. She appreciated Cal's concern, but surely the measures they'd taken would discourage any prospective thief.

Now all she had to worry about was hanging on to her future at work, ensuring Rachel's healing, and getting the inn off and running. Those concerns had actually begun to seem manageable.

The layer of dark clouds that massed on the horizon didn't dampen her optimistic mood. Rachel had looked almost normal tonight, joking about the casts and finally rid of the headache that had dogged her since the accident. Andrea hadn't realized how worried she was about her sister until the weight had lifted with the assurance that Rachel was her buoyant self again.

They had spent nearly two hours going over all of Rachel's plans for the inn, and in spite of her sister's undoubted lack of financial expertise, they probably had a reasonable chance of success. They had a beautiful, historic building in an unmatched setting, and Grams was a natural hostess. With Emma's housekeeping ability and Rachel's inspired cooking, they should be in good shape.

The cooking was the immediate problem, but surely they could find a way around that until Rachel was well. If Andrea could just get them set up on a sound financial system, the whole thing could work. She might still have doubts about the wisdom of Grams taking on such a project at her age, but at least she was no longer convinced they were headed for disaster.

She pulled up to the garage, giving an approving nod to the lights Cal had installed. It would take a brazen thief to attempt to break in now, even though darkness took over beyond the buildings with only the pale yellow glow from a distant farmhouse to break it.

She parked and walked quickly to the side door that led directly into the family quarters. From upstairs, Barney gave an experimental woof and then quieted, apparently recognizing her step. Grams must have already gone to bed.

Andrea made the rounds of the ground floor, checking the doors that Grams had already no doubt checked. Everything was locked up and secure. She hurried through the library, not looking toward the portrait. Thinking about her grandfather was not conducive to a good night's sleep.

Upstairs, she opened the door to Grams's bedroom. Her grandmother was already asleep, her Bible open on her lap. Barney looked up, tail slapping the floor. Andrea removed the Bible, open to the twenty-third Psalm. Had that comforted Grams enough to send her to sleep? Faint longing moved through her. She wanted...

She wasn't sure what. Faith, like Grams had? Like Cal apparently had? But faith wasn't to be manufactured just because she felt responsibility weighing on her. She turned off the bedside lamp, tiptoed out and shut the door.

A cool breeze wafted into the hall from the open window. She glanced at it, deciding to leave it open, and went on into her bedroom.

The new lights cast reflections on her ceiling. Comforting reflections. They could all sleep well tonight, including Cal. She wouldn't be calling him.

Andrea jolted awake. Shoving the sheet aside, she reached for the bedside lamp, heart pounding. Then the noise came again, and she subsided, relaxing. Thunder, that was all. The threatening storm had arrived. Even as she thought that, rain slashed against the house.

Jumping out of bed, she hurried to the windows, but no sprinkles dampened the wide sills. The rain wasn't coming in this direction, but it might well be raining in the hall window.

She hurried out into the hallway. The sheer white curtains on the window billowed inward, and she rushed to pull down the sash, bare toes curling into a slight dampness on the floor beneath her feet. She could imagine Grams's reaction if she woke to soaked curtains.

There were no lights on this side of the house. Darkness pressed against the panes, mitigated only by reflections of the dim night-light Grams always left on in the hall. She stood there for a moment, looking into the dark, until it was split by a vivid flash of lightning.

She jerked back, gasping. In the brief instant of light—had that been a figure, standing just by the shelter of the lilac hedge?

She pressed her hand against her chest, feeling the thud of her heart. Imagination, that was all. She was spooking herself, seeing menace where there was nothing... But there had been something that night by the toolshed. Was their prowler making another visit?

Lightning snapped again, closer now, one sharp crack illuminating the grounds below as sharply as a spotlight. Showing her the dark figure of a man.

She drew back, clutching the curtain instinctively in front of her, as if he could see her standing there in the flimsy cotton nightshirt. She slid to the side of the window. Stared out, focusing her eyes on the spot, trying to still the rasp of her breath. If the lightning flashed again, she'd be ready.

A volley of lightning, thunder following it so fast that the storm must be right over the house. It showed her, as if in a series of jagged still pictures, the figure turning, the brim of a hat, tilting up toward the window where she stood, frozen. The face was a pale blur, but the clothing—even in dark outline, the clothing looked Amish.

Impossible. But she had to believe the evidence of her own eyes, didn't she? Even as she watched, the figure moved, raising one arm as if he shook his fist at her.

She stumbled backward, heart thudding, breath catching, and then bolted for the bedroom and her cell phone. The doors were locked, he couldn't get in, call Cal, call the police....

Cal answered on the first ring, sounding as if he fought his way awake. "Yes, what?"

"There's someone, a man, out on the east side of the house."

"Andrea?" His voice sharpened. "Are you sure?"

"The lightning makes it as bright as day. He's there, watching the house. We didn't put lights—"

They hadn't thought they needed to where there were no outbuildings to be broken into. Maybe the intruder's goal wasn't the outbuildings. Maybe it was the house itself.

"I'll be right there. Don't go out, you hear me?"

"I won't. I'll go down to the side door and meet you there." She glanced across the hall. "My grandmother's exhausted. I don't want to wake her again unless I have to."

"Right. Don't call the police until I see what's up. And don't open the door." He clicked off without a goodbye.

It wasn't until she stood there shivering in the dark that she realized that at least one part of her relief at hearing his voice on the phone was the conviction that it couldn't be Cal out there in the dark, playing tricks.

Quickly she pulled sweatpants and a sweatshirt on, stuffing her feet into slippers. She hadn't realized she'd been considering that possibility, even subconsciously. But what, as Uncle Nick had said, did they really know about Cal?

Well, she knew now that he wasn't their prowler. And she knew that comfort had flooded through her at the sound of his voice.

Maybe it was better not to dwell on that. She grabbed a flashlight and went softly down the stairs. Should she have called the police? Maybe, but if she did, Grams would waken, would be subjected to that upset yet again.

Wait, as Cal had said. See what he found.

She huddled against the side door, gripping the flashlight, wishing for even the dubious comfort of Barney at this point. If Cal didn't appear soon, she'd have to do something.

A dripping face appeared outside the glass, and her heart threatened to leap from her chest before she recognized Cal. She unlocked the door, trying to ignore the shaking of her fingers, and pulled him in out of the rain.

She switched on the hall light. Like her, Cal wore sweatpants and sweatshirt, but his were wet through.

"I'm sorry. You're soaked." Well, that wasn't very coherent. "Should I call the police?"

"No use." He shook his head, water spraying from his drenched hair. "He's not there now."

"If he ever was?" She knew her quick anger was just reaction to strain. "I saw him. He was there."

"Relax, I believe you. The lilac bushes were broken, the grass tamped down, as if he'd stood there for some time." His fingers closed over hers. They were wet and cold, but somehow they warmed her. "Tell me what you saw."

"A man. I can't say how tall he was—I was looking down from the upstairs window." She kept her voice low, not wanting to stir up the dog. "I didn't make out the face, but Cal—he was wearing Amish clothing."

He frowned. "Are you sure?"

"I know it doesn't make any sense, but I'm sure. Dark

pants and jacket, white shirt, the hat—if it wasn't an Amishman, it was someone doing a good imitation."

"I'd almost rather believe that." His voice was troubled. "The Amish aren't exactly noted for producing prowlers. You never met a more law-abiding bunch."

She shivered. "That's not all. It—he—the figure seemed to be looking up at the window where I was standing. He raised his arm, as if he were shaking his fist at me. And if you tell me I was dreaming—"

"I don't doubt you." Without seeming to know he was doing it, Cal pulled her closer. "But we've got to think this through before we do anything. Can you imagine the repercussions if something like this hit the newspapers?"

"I hadn't thought of that, but I see what you mean." Like it or not, and they didn't, the Amish were newsworthy. A story like that could get out of control in hours. She glanced up the stairs. "I don't want Grams upset, and that would devastate her."

"Well, whoever he was, he's gone now." Cal brushed damp hair back from his brow. "Are you okay if we hold off making a decision until we can talk this over in the morning?"

She was insensibly comforted by the way he said *we*. Whatever came, she wasn't alone in this. "Yes, all right. After all, he didn't really do anything except lurk. The house is locked up securely."

"Good." He squeezed her hand. "I'll take another look around before I go back to the barn. We'll talk in the morning. Meantime, try to get some sleep, or your grandmother will want to know why your eyes are so heavy." He turned to go back out into the rain.

"Wait. Do you want an umbrella?"

"Why?" Cal paused on the threshold, his smile flashing. "I can't get any wetter than I already am. Good night. Lock the door."

"No chance I'll forget that."

He vanished almost at once into the darkness beyond the reach of the light. She locked the door, realizing that she was smiling.

Amazing. If anyone had told her fifteen minutes ago that she'd find anything to smile about tonight, she'd have said they were crazy.

Chapter 7

Cal frowned at the mug of coffee in his hand and then set it out of the way on the barn floor. He needed something to get his brain moving after the previous night's alarms, but caffeine wasn't doing the job.

He picked up a sanding block and knelt next to a reproduction of an old-fashioned dry sink, running the fine sandpaper along its grain. This was better than coffee for what ailed him.

What he really needed was to talk with Andrea, but he'd known better than to go to the inn first thing this morning. Katherine would be up and Emma already busy in the kitchen, making it impossible to have a private conversation. He'd have to wait until after their breakfast was over, at least.

He ran his hand along the curved edge of the dry sink's top. Smooth as silk—that was what he wanted.

Taking shortcuts at this stage would show up eventually in the finished product, ruining the piece for him.

Even the work didn't chase away his troubled thoughts, unfortunately. He couldn't stop chewing on the implications of what Andrea had seen. Or thought she'd seen.

A few days earlier, he might have been tempted to believe she was making up her tale of a prowler, just to convince her grandmother to sell. Now, he knew her better. Andrea wouldn't do that.

No, he didn't doubt that she'd seen someone, but was it beyond belief that the man, whoever he was, wasn't Amish? She'd seen a figure in dark clothes, but peering out into the storm from an upstairs window, she couldn't have seen all that much. Maybe her imagination had taken the prowler's dark clothing and filled in the rest.

Somehow he didn't relish the idea of bringing that up with her.

"Cal?"

He straightened at the sound of Andrea's voice, dismayed at the flood of pleasure he felt at the sight of her. She stood for a moment in a stripe of sunlight at the barn door.

"Come in. How are you? Nothing else happened, did it?"

She came toward him, the sneakers she wore making little sound on the wide planks of the barn floor. In jeans and a loose denim shirt worn over a white tee, she almost looked as if she belonged here.

"It was quiet enough," she said. "I didn't sleep much, though. I woke at every creak, and believe me, a house that old creaks a lot."

"How about some coffee?" He gestured toward the

pot that sat on a rough shelf against the wall. "It won't be as good as Emma's, but at least it's hot."

"None for me, thanks. Grams insisted on giving me three cups of herbal tea this morning, because I looked tired. I don't have room for coffee."

"She didn't ask any difficult questions, I hope." If she'd told her grandmother about what had happened...

Andrea shook her head. "No. And I didn't mention anything about last night." She ran her hand along the top of the dry sink, much as he had done, a wing of silky hair falling across her cheek as she looked down. "But I can't just ignore what happened."

"I know." He frowned, wondering if it were wise, or even possible, to keep her from voicing her suspicions. "Do you want to go to the police?"

"Depends upon what moment you ask me." Her smile flickered. "I spent my wakeful night going over and over it and changing my mind every thirty seconds or so."

He bent, picked up a couple of sanding blocks, and tossed one to her.

She caught it automatically. "What's this for?"

"Try it." He knelt, running his block along the side of the piece. "It's very soothing."

"Just what I need—to be soothed while intruders trample through Grams's yard and try to break in." But she sat down on the floor in front of the dry sink and began sanding lightly.

"Trample?" He raised an eyebrow.

"You know what I mean." She sanded for a moment longer, frowning. "He was there. He was watching the house."

"I know." He silenced the urge to tell her what he thought she should do. It was her decision, not his.

"You're right. This is soothing. How did you learn to do this? The furniture, I mean, not just sanding."

"My dad's father." His voice softened, as it always did at the thought of his grandfather. Whatever he knew about being a good man, as well as a good carpenter, came from him. "He figured everyone should know how to do something useful, just in case."

"He sounds like a wise man."

She glanced up at him, smiling. For an instant their faces were close—so close he could see the flecks of gold in those green eyes, mirroring the gold of her hair. So close he could feel the movement of her breath across his cheek.

Her eyes widened, and he heard the catch of her breath. He put the sanding block down with a hand that wasn't entirely steady and sat back, away from her. That was—well, unexpected. Not surprising that he found her attractive, but shocking in the strength of that pull toward her. And disturbing that she felt it, too.

Andrea looked down at the sandpaper in her hand. She cleared her throat. "Well, I have to make a decision about calling the police."

So they were going to ignore what had just happened. Maybe that was best.

"If you tell the police the person you saw was Amish—"

"I know. It will cause problems, problems for the community, problems for Grams. I don't want that. But I have to do something. I can't help wondering…" She looked at him again, eyes guarded. "What if it was Levi?"

"Levi." He had to adjust his perspective. "That didn't occur to me. Do you have some reason for thinking that?"

She shook her head. "Only that I've seen him around the house. At one time, I'd have said I knew him, but not any longer. Does he ever come over here at night?"

"I've never seen him." Everything in him wanted to reject the idea. "Look, you know he's like a child—a gentle child. If it were Levi last night, he certainly didn't intend any harm. From what I've seen, his parents keep close tabs on him, so it's hard to believe he could have been wandering around after dark."

"Somebody was." She moved restlessly. "You mentioned there'd been some vandalism in the area. Could it have something to do with that?"

"I don't know. The incidents have been pretty harmless, as far as I've heard. Mailboxes knocked down. Somebody threw a bucket of purple paint at an Amish house. The police seem to think it's caused by teenagers looking for a little excitement. Nothing here was damaged, but maybe they're branching out into intimidation." He'd rather imagine it was random mischief, not deliberate malice toward the inn.

She nodded, frowning. "What do you think we should do?"

We. The simple pronoun stopped him for a moment. Andrea considered him an ally. She didn't want to make this decision alone, and she didn't want to worry her elderly grandmother, or Rachel, stuck in a wheelchair. So she'd turned to him.

All the resolutions he'd made about living a detached life here were on the line. Panic flickered. He couldn't make himself responsible for them.

But he'd put himself in this position. He'd interfered, and he couldn't back away and say it was none of his concern just because his emotions were getting involved.

"It seems to me that the police are already doing about all they can do, under the circumstances. The fact that you saw a prowler again probably wouldn't change anything."

He was being drawn in. He was starting to think like a lawyer again. He didn't want to, but he couldn't help it.

"I suppose not, but doing nothing doesn't resolve the situation."

"Look, why don't you give it a day or two? Let me talk to some of my Amish friends, sound them out about it. See if there's any animosity toward the inn among the Amish community." Doing so might harm the delicate balance of his relationship with them, but the alternative was worse.

She studied him for a moment, as if weighing his sincerity. "All right." She got to her feet too quickly for him to reach out a helping hand. "If you'll do that, I'll talk to Uncle Nick. He may have some ideas, and I'm sure he'd keep anything I tell him in confidence. He wouldn't want to upset Grams."

Obviously Andrea wasn't one to leave everything in someone else's hands, but maybe she was right. Bendick did seem to have his finger in a lot of pies in the township.

"What about Levi? Do you want me to talk to Emma?"

"No. I'll see if I can bring it up without upsetting her." She shook her head. "I'm not looking forward to it."

"Better to talk to her than let the suspicion affect your attitude toward him."

"True enough. If I didn't say it before, thank you, Cal. For last night, and for being willing to help. I appreciate it. And Grams would, if she knew."

"Any time."

He meant it, but he had to be careful. Andrea had broken through barriers he'd thought were completely secure, and trying to deny the attraction he felt was pointless.

But that attraction couldn't go anywhere. The life Andrea prized was the kind of life that had nearly destroyed his soul.

The gold lettering on the plate glass window jolted the cool facade Andrea had meant to maintain for this visit. Unger and Bendick, Real Estate and Insurance. She hadn't imagined that Grandfather's name would still be on the business.

It was a name that stood for something in this quiet country village. Uncle Nick probably hadn't been eager to give that up, and she couldn't blame him.

Grams had assured her that Uncle Nick would be in the office on a Saturday morning. Fortunately she hadn't asked why Andrea wanted to see him.

A bell tinkled when she opened the door. Clever of Uncle Nick to retain the old-fashioned flavor, even when he was dealing with visiting urbanites looking for a little piece of country to call their own. Or maybe especially then.

The woman behind the mission oak desk looked up inquiringly, and in an instant Andrea went from being the appreciative observer to being that ten-year-old trailing her grandfather around town. There was Betty Albertson, her grandfather's faithful secretary, peering at her over the half-glasses she wore at her desk.

Those half-glasses had fascinated Andrea. Betty wore them so far down her pointed nose that they seemed in constant danger of sliding right off, like a sled down Miller's Hill.

"Betty, how nice to see you. It's been a long time." Conventional words, giving her the moment she needed to remind herself that she was no longer ten, no longer interested in the stash of chocolate bars in Betty's top right desk drawer.

Sharp gray eyes now matched gray hair, pulled smoothly back into the same sort of French twist Betty had worn when her hair had been a mousy brown. For a moment she thought the secretary didn't recognize her, but then she smiled.

"Andrea Hampton. Land, it has been a while. You look as if life agrees with you."

Did she? With everything she valued turned upside down in the past few days, it hardly seemed likely.

"I see you're still running Unger and Bendick single-handedly."

The joke had always been that Betty knew more about the business than both partners combined. She'd been so fiercely loyal to Grandfather that it occasionally seemed she resented even the distraction of his family.

Betty's smile tightened. "Mr. Bendick offered to hire more help, but I prefer to handle things on my own."

She'd given offense, even though it hadn't been intended. "I'm sure no one could do it better. My grandfather often said you were worth more than a dozen assistants."

"Did he?" A faint flush warmed Betty's thin cheeks. "That was kind of him. He was always so thoughtful."

Betty had her own memories of Grandfather. "Is Uncle Nick—Mr. Bendick—in? I'd like to see him for a moment."

Betty's gaze flicked toward the closed office door that bore his name, again in faded gold. "This isn't a good time. We get swamped on Saturdays. Why don't I ask him to stop by the house later?"

Andrea glanced around, half amused, half annoyed. "It doesn't look that busy right now. Surely he can spare me a few minutes."

Betty's lips pressed together, nostrils flaring, but then she mustered an unconvincing smile. "He's on the phone. If you want to wait, I'll try to slip you in when he finishes."

Plainly Betty had transferred the devotion she'd once had for Fredrick Unger to his junior partner. "I'll wait." She crossed the faded Oriental carpet to the row of wooden chairs against the far wall and sat.

Betty blinked, perhaps wondering if she'd gone too far. "Well, that's fine. I didn't mean anything, I'm sure."

"I won't take long, I promise."

She couldn't get into an argument with the woman, just because she was hyperprotective of her employer. If anything, she ought to feel sorry for Betty, leading such a narrow life. She probably didn't get out of Churchville from one year to the next. Andrea vaguely remembered an elderly mother that Betty looked after.

The schoolhouse clock on the wall above the desk ticked audibly. As a child, sitting on this same chair, legs swinging, she'd been mesmerized by the jerky movement of the hands. Photos surrounded the clock, recording events from the early days of Churchville. Grandfather at the groundbreaking for the school, at the dedication of the bank, at some long-ago Fourth of July celebration.

The door to the inner office opened. Uncle Nick blinked and then hurried toward her, hands outstretched.

"Andrea, this is a surprise. Betty, why didn't you tell me Andrea was waiting?"

Betty slid the half-glasses down to look over them. "You were on the phone. And now you have an appointment to show the Barker place."

"I certainly have a few minutes to talk with Andrea."

"You know how interested those people are. You don't want to be late."

"Why not? They've kept me waiting at every appointment." He took Andrea's arm, winking at her once his back was turned to Betty. "We have time for a little chat."

He led her into his office and closed the door, then gave her a quick hug. "I'm sorry about that. The woman thinks I can't do a thing unless she reminds me."

"I don't want to mess up a sale."

He shook his head. "Pair of uptight yuppies who think they want a country place but don't like anything that's in their price range." He beamed at her. "I'm glad you stopped in for a visit before you head back to the city."

"As a matter of fact, I'm not going back for a while."

"Now, Andrea, don't tell me you let them talk you into doing something rash. Your job—"

"My job will wait. Right now my family needs me."

His dismayed expression was almost comical. "My

dear, I'm sorry. Is your boss all right with your taking time off?"

She shrugged. "He's not happy, but I'm afraid it can't be helped." Her mind flickered to Cal, saying that maybe he'd learn to appreciate her more. "I have to stay, at least until the inn is up and running."

The elderly swivel chair creaked when he sank down in it. His eyes were troubled, and he ran his hand along his jaw.

"I wish we could find some other way of dealing with this."

"I appreciate your concern, Uncle Nick, but it's all right. Really." She took a breath. How to word this without alarming him or sending him running to Grams? "That's actually not what I came to talk to you about."

He blinked. "Is something wrong? Something else, I mean?"

"Not exactly. Well, you know about the prowler. We haven't had any damage, but it made me wonder if there's anyone who might have a grudge against the family."

"Against Katherine?" He sat upright, outrage in his voice. "Your grandmother is universally respected. You know that."

It was said with such vehemence that she couldn't doubt it was true of him. "Has there been anything—someone who thought Grandfather had treated him unfairly, or some dispute about property lines?"

He was already shaking his head. "Nothing at all. I'm sure the prowler was simply an isolated incident. Those security lights you put up should do the trick."

So he knew about the lights already. She'd forgotten how quickly the township grapevine worked.

"What about turning the house into a bed-and-breakfast? Have there been any ill feelings about that?"

"Mostly from Margaret Allen, maybe a few other old-timers who hate change, don't want to see any more tourists brought in." He shook his head. "They're fighting a losing battle on that one. But I'd say they're not the type to prowl around in the dark, especially Margaret."

He had a point. "She's more likely to bury a person under a pile of platitudes."

"That's our Margaret." He chuckled, then sobered again. "But I'm concerned about you. Your grandmother, dear woman that she is, doesn't understand the sacrifice she's asking you to make. Maybe I could hire someone to help out—"

"Thanks, Uncle Nick." She was touched by his kindness. "I appreciate that, but no."

"Really, my dear." He rose, coming back around the desk. "I want to help. It's the least I can do—"

The door opened and Betty marched in, holding out a briefcase. "Mr. Bendick, you must leave or you'll keep those people waiting." She sounded scandalized at the thought.

"Yes, yes, I'm going." He snatched the case and sent Andrea an apologetic look. "Think about what I said. I'll talk to you later."

She nodded. "I will. Thank you, Uncle Nick."

He hurried out, letting the front door slam behind him.

"He worries about your grandmother," Betty said, her voice almost accusing.

Several annoyed retorts occurred to her, but she sup-

pressed them. "There's no need. I'm there with her, and
Cal Burke has been very helpful."

"Well, he would be, wouldn't he?"

Andrea blinked. "What do you mean?"

"It's none of my business, of course." Betty patted
the smooth twist of gray hair. "But I'm the one who
typed the lease, so I can't help knowing, can I?"

She resisted the impulse to shake the woman. "Knowing what?"

"Why, about his lease on the barn. Mr. Bendick
warned your grandmother, but she wouldn't listen."

She took a step toward Betty. "What?" she snapped.

"She's renting that barn to him at a ridiculously low
price. Almost nothing. It worried Mr. Bendick something awful. Cal Burke is bound to help out. He doesn't
want your grandmother to sell, because then he'd lose
the nice deal he talked her into."

The lease clutched in one hand, Andrea charged toward the barn, anger fueling her rush. When she found
Cal, he wasn't going to know what hit him. She held on
to the anger, knowing at some level that if she let it slip,
even more hurtful feelings would surface.

Betrayal. She'd already experienced enough betrayal
in her life.

She hurried up the slope and shoved the heavy door
aside. Her rush carried her several feet into the barn
before she realized she was alone.

She stood for a moment, looking at the scattered
pieces of furniture as if Cal might be hiding behind one
of them. Nothing split the silence except her own
labored breathing.

Instinct sent her outside again, where she looked

around, frowning. The inn grounds and the surrounding farmland dozed in the Saturday-afternoon sunshine.

And already the anger was seeping away, leaving space for pain and regret. How could she have been so foolish as to trust the man? She knew better than to let herself be taken in by a plausible stranger, the way Grams undoubtedly had.

Maybe he was in the apartment he'd created for himself in the tack room. She followed the path around the corner of the barn. She'd find him and make him admit that he was taking advantage of her grandmother. If there was an explanation for this...

But there couldn't be. She stifled that notion. There could be no logical reason for Cal to have talked Grams into renting him the barn at what anyone would consider a token amount. No wonder Uncle Nick had been upset.

Upset didn't begin to cover it for her.

She rounded the corner and stopped. She'd been prepared to find the story-and-a-half tack room annex changed, but she hadn't expected this.

The rough-hewn door had been replaced by a paneled one with nine-pane beveled glass. A bow window curved out at the front of the building, with a flagstone path leading to the entry.

Irritation prickled along her skin. He'd probably talked Grams into paying for all this, creating a cozy nest for himself at someone else's expense.

Her feet flew over the stones, and she gave a peremptory rap on the door.

The door swung open before she had a chance to raise her hand for another knock.

Cal stood there, smiling. Welcoming.

"Good, you're here. How did you make out with Bendick?"

For a moment she could only stare at him. They'd become partners. She'd agreed to investigate with him.

Before she'd known he was a cheat.

She stalked inside. The old tack room had certainly been transformed. Wooden built-ins lined the walls on either side of a fieldstone fireplace. The wide plank floors were dotted with colorful Navajo rugs that contrasted with the solid Pennsylvania Dutch furniture. The open space was living room, dining room, and kitchen combined, with an eating bar separating the kitchen section. An open stairway led up to a loft that must be the bedroom.

Cal closed the door. "Do you like it?"

Anger danced along her nerves. "Yes. Did my grandmother pay for this?"

He blinked. Then his face tightened, brown eyes turning cold. "Maybe you should ask your grandmother that."

"I'm asking you." Small wonder Grams hadn't confided in her about this dubious rental. She'd have known how Andrea would react. If Grams planned to run the inn on these lines, she'd be bankrupt in a month.

Cal looked at her steadily. "You'd better tell me what this is about, Andrea. I'm not good at guessing games."

He leaned against the bar between kitchen and living room, elbows propped on it. The pose might have looked casual, if not for the muscle that twitched in his jaw, belying his outward calm.

"This." She thrust the lease at him, appalled to see that her hand was shaking. "How did you talk my grandmother into this? She might be naive about business, but surely she realized how ridiculous the rent is. And for both your home and your business—you really got a great deal, didn't you?"

He made no move to take the paper, but his hands curled into fists. "Did you talk to your grandmother?"

"I'm talking to you. The person who's cheating her." *The person who lied to me and made me let my guard down. The person I thought I could trust.*

Cal thrust himself away from the counter, taking a step toward her. "You don't believe that." He stopped, shaking his head. "My mistake. I guess you do."

"I was the one who made the mistake. I trusted you." She would not let her voice break. "How could you do this to an old woman?"

His face might have been carved from a block of wood. "That lease is between your grandmother and me. You don't come into it at all."

"My grandmother asked me to help her with her business."

He raised an eyebrow. "As far as I know, Katherine didn't sign a power of attorney, turning her affairs over to you. If she wants to talk to you about my rental, she will. Are you worried that she's squandering away your inheritance?"

Fury boiled over, threatening to scald anyone in its path. "I'm trying to protect my grandmother from people who would take advantage of her."

Like you, Cal. It wouldn't have been hard to get her to trust you. I did, and I'm a much tougher case than Grams. Something twisted and hurt under the anger.

"I see." Nothing changed in his expression, but he seemed suddenly more distant. "I can't help you, Andrea. The details of my lease are between me and Katherine."

"Anyone who knows the rent you're paying would know you're cheating her."

"That's for Katherine to decide. You're not the owner. And even if you were, you can't throw me out." He nodded toward the paper in her hand. "I have a lease, remember?"

She stared at him, baffled and furious. Then she turned and slammed her way out.

Chapter 8

"I don't know what you thought you were doing." The glare Grams directed at Andrea left no doubt about what Grams considered her actions. Interfering.

"I'm trying to help you. That's all." Andrea sat up a bit straighter. Being called onto the library carpet made her feel about eight.

"Going to my tenant behind my back is not helpful, Andrea Katherine."

When Grams resorted to using both names, the situation was serious. "I'm sorry, but I'm worried about you. If you'd let me know how bad the financial situation is—"

"You'd have told me I should sell the place." Grams finished the thought for her. Her face tightened, and she suddenly looked her age. "That's why I didn't tell you. I didn't want to argue about it."

That was more or less what Rachel had said, but how

could Andrea keep silent when the people she loved best in the world seemed bent on the wrong course?

"Are you so sure selling wouldn't have been for the best?" She kept her tone soft.

Grams shook her head. "You're more like your grandfather than you want to admit. That's what he would have said, too, even though this place has been in his family for close to two hundred years."

Grams was right about one thing. She didn't care to be told she was like her grandfather.

If saving Unger House meant enough to Grams that she'd go against what she believed Grandfather would have wanted, then no argument of Andrea's would sway her.

"I've already agreed that I'll do all I can to help you. But if you want to involve me in the business, I have to understand what's going on. When Betty told me—"

"Betty!" Grams's nostrils flared. "What right does she have to talk about my concerns, I'd like to know."

"I'm sure she was just reflecting Uncle Nick's feelings." She shouldn't have mentioned Betty. Relations had always been strained between Grandfather's wife and his secretary.

"Nick is a good friend." Grams's face softened. "He worries too much, but he means well."

"I mean well, too, even if you think I'm going about it the wrong way."

"I know that." Grams's voice gentled a little. Maybe the storm was over, even if the problem wasn't resolved. "Rachel and I appreciate the fact that you're willing to stay here and help us."

"I want to get you on a good business basis, so that you have a chance to succeed. As far as the rental is concerned…" She couldn't let it go without trying once more to show Grams that Cal was taking advantage of her. "The barn is yours to do as you like with, but I have to tell you that the rent you're charging is extremely low by current standards."

Grams was already shaking her head. "You don't understand."

"How can I, when you won't tell me about it?"

For a moment the situation hung in the balance. If her grandmother continued to treat her like a child who had to be protected from the facts, this would never work.

Finally Grams nodded. "I suppose you ought to know." She glanced toward the portrait over the fireplace. "When Cal approached me about renting the barn, I couldn't imagine how he'd live there. But he was willing to do all the work on the apartment himself. If you've seen it, you'll have to admit he's done a fine job, and he insisted on paying for everything that went into the renovation."

She'd misjudged him in that respect, at least. To her surprise, Andrea was relieved.

"He's certainly increased the value of the building," she admitted. "But even so, to lock yourself into a contract with that low a rent could be a problem." Cal's turning the lease against her still rankled.

"We agreed that as his business picked up, the rent would increase." Grams flushed, as if she found the discussion of money distasteful. "He insists on paying me more every month, more than he should. I don't want to feel as if I'm accepting charity."

No, Grams wouldn't like that feeling. She had always been the giver, not the recipient.

Andrea took a deep breath. "I'm sorry, Grams. I

shouldn't have gone to Cal without talking to you about it first."

"No. You shouldn't have." Grams gave her the look that suggested Andrea's manners weren't up to what was expected of an Unger. "Now I think we'll both see Cal and apologize."

"Both…"

Words failed her. Grams proposed to lead her by the hand and make sure she apologized properly, the way she had when Andrea had left the farm gate open and the Zook cows had gotten out.

"Grams, I can handle this myself. It's my mistake."

Her grandmother stood, every inch the lady. "It was my error, as well, in not telling you. We'll both go."

Apologizing to Cal alone would have been embarrassing. Doing it with Grams looking on was humiliating. It didn't help to know that she deserved it.

If she kept herself busy enough, maybe she could forget that awkward scene with Cal. At least that's what Andrea had been telling herself since Grams left to spend the evening with Rachel at the hospital. Unfortunately, it didn't seem to be working.

She shoved away from the desk in the library, blinking as she tried to focus her eyes on something other than the computer screen. It was getting dark, and she hadn't bothered to turn on any lights.

She stretched, rubbing at the tension in the back of her neck. She'd started entering data for the inn into the desktop hours ago. As far as she could tell, neither Grams nor Rachel had touched the computer since they'd bought it, supposedly for the business, and that increased her worries over their chances for success.

Running a B and B wasn't just about being a good cook or a good host. It was a business. She hadn't been kidding when she'd told Cal about Rachel's idea of a filing system.

And that brought her right back to Cal again. He'd been gracious when she'd apologized. Pleasant, even.

She frowned at Barney, who'd taken up residence on the hearth rug, seeming to transfer his allegiance to her when Grams wasn't around. "I'd be just as happy if he hadn't been so nice about it. You understand, don't you?"

Barney thumped his tail against the rug. The only thing he understood was that someone was talking to him. He rose, stretching very much as she had, and padded over to her. She patted the silky head that pressed against her leg.

"I'm being ridiculous, I suppose."

He didn't comment.

It had been a difficult situation, made worse by Grams accepting part of the responsibility for the misunderstanding. She'd actually admitted that she should have told Andrea the whole story.

That had hit her right in the heart. She didn't want her grandmother to feel any less in charge than she'd always been.

I don't know how to balance all this. The discovery that she was actually taking her problems to God startled her, but it felt right. Maybe Grams's quiet faith was having an impact on her. *Usually I think I can handle anything, but I can't. I need guidance. I have to know what I should do—about Grams, about the inn, even about Cal. Please guide me. Amen.*

Maybe it wasn't the most perfect of prayers, but

the admission that she couldn't see her way somehow made her feel a bit better.

And as for Cal having such an inside glimpse of their family dynamics—well, maybe she'd be lucky enough not to be alone with him for the next few days. Or ever.

Barney whined, his head coming up, and he let out a soft woof.

"What is it, boy? Do you hear Grams coming?" She peered out the side window, but there was no sign of a car turning into the drive.

The sheltie whined again, then paced to the door and nosed at it.

"You want to go out? I guess it has been a while." She opened the library door and then followed the dog through to the back hallway.

"Okay, out you go." The lights Cal had installed showed her the garden, the outbuildings, the barn, and beyond them, the dark, silent woods and pasture. All was quiet.

Barney bounded out, the screen door banging behind him. He'd be a few minutes at least, needing to investigate every shadow before coming back inside.

She leaned against the doorjamb, tiredness sinking in. Tomorrow was Sunday, and that meant church with Grams in the morning and an afternoon visit to Rachel. Probably she ought to try and find the rest of the receipts Rachel thought she had saved, just in case any of them required an explanation.

In typical Rachel fashion, the receipts had, her sister thought, been tucked away in one of Grandfather's ledgers, which she vaguely remembered putting on the top shelf of the closet which stored kitchen and dining room linens.

Of course. What a logical place to keep receipts they would need to produce come tax time, to say nothing of Grandfather's ledgers. Rachel hadn't inherited any of his organizational genes, that was clear. Obviously Andrea would either have to do the business taxes for them or hire someone locally who'd keep after them all year long.

She opened the closet, frowning at the creaking that came from the hinges. Sometimes it seemed everything in the house had its own sound, all of them together creating a symphony of creaks, cracks, whines and pops. Hopefully none of their guests would be the nervous sort.

The deep closet had shelves against its back wall, accessible only after she'd moved several metal pails, a corn broom and two mops. What the closet didn't have was a light, but the fixture in the hallway sent enough illumination to show her that there appeared to be a book of some sort on the top shelf, stuck between two roasting pans big enough to cook the largest turkey she could imagine. She'd need something to stand on in order to reach the shelf.

She propped the closet door open with one of the mops and retrieved a chair from the kitchen, glancing out the screen as she passed. No sign of Barney yet. She could only hope he hadn't found a rabbit to chase or worse, a skunk. She doubted they had enough tomato juice in the house to cope with that.

The very fact that she knew the remedy for a dog's encounter with a skunk gave her pause. That certainly wasn't part of her normal urban life. Since she'd been back in this house, all sorts of things were resurfacing from her early years.

Grasping the chair with both hands, she carried it into the closet and climbed onto it. She reached up to find that her fingertips fell inches short of the top shelf. That was what came of having twelve-foot ceilings. How on earth had her sister gotten the book up there to begin with? And why did she think that a logical place to put it?

She could go in search of a stepladder, but maybe if she put her foot on one of the lower shelves, she could boost herself up enough to reach the book.

She wedged her toe between two stacks of table linens that someone, probably Emma, had stored carefully in plastic bags. Bracing her left hand against the wall, she stretched upward, groping with her right. Her fingertips brushed the soft leather cover of the ledger. Memory took her back to Grandfather's desk, sitting on a high stool next to him, watching as he entered figures in a neat row.

This is the proper way to do it, Drea. If I keep the records myself, then I know they're accurate.

She blinked, willing away the childhood memory, and stretched until her hand closed on the edge of the book. Victory in her grasp, she started to pull it down. The palm that was braced against the wall slipped, the chair wobbled, then tipped. In an instant she was falling, tangled helplessly in chair legs and sliding linens, landing with a thud that would probably leave a bruise on her hip.

A board creaked out in the hallway, separate from the clatter of her fall. Before she could look the door slammed shut, leaving her in total darkness.

Her breath caught, and she pressed her lips together. *Don't panic. It's all right. All you have to do is get up and open the door. If you could cope with being trapped in the car and shoved into the toolshed, you can cope with this.*

She untangled herself, willing her heart to stop pounding, and fumbled with sweat-slicked hands for a knob. And realized there was none on the inside of the door.

Be calm. You're all right. Grams will be home soon.

But another voice was drowning out the calm, reasonable adult. It came welling up from someplace deep inside her, erupting with all the violence of a child's terror.

"Let me out!" She pounded on the door, unable to hold back the fear she didn't understand. "Let me out! Someone help me! Help!"

The child inside was crying, hot, helpless tears. *Someone help me. Father, please, help me.*

Cal rounded the corner of the toolshed, his sneakers making little sound on the damp grass. He could see the garage now, illuminated by one of the lights he'd installed, with the door still standing open. Katherine and Andrea must have gone to the hospital to see Rachel.

He frowned absently, coming to a halt and gazing around, probing the shadows, searching for anything that was not as it should be. It would be best if he got back to his own place before they returned. He and Andrea had already butted heads too many times today.

He wasn't sure whether it had been worse to bear her accusations or to listen to her apology. At least when she'd been throwing her fury toward him, he'd had the shield of his righteous anger.

It was only afterward that he began to wonder just how righteous that feeling had been. The hard lessons of the past had driven him to God, but he suspected he still had a lot to learn about living the way God expected.

Andrea had at least been furious with him on behalf of someone else. His feelings had been motivated entirely by something much more personal. He'd thought they'd been on the road to becoming friends. Now it was clear they'd never be that, and disappointment had fueled his anger. Maybe he hadn't expressed it, but he'd felt it, and that was just as bad.

He'd turned to head back to the barn when he saw Barney dash across the garden toward the inn door. Odd. Katherine wouldn't leave the dog outside when the place was empty. How had he gotten out of a locked house?

"Barney!" He took a few steps along the path toward the patio. "What are you doing out here?"

He expected the dog to turn and run to him with his usual exuberant greeting. Instead Barney pawed at the door, ignoring his voice.

The back of his neck prickled. Something wasn't right here. Apprehension pushed him into a trot that covered the rest of the way to the house in seconds.

Even so, by the time he reached Barney, the dog was howling, pawing at the door frantically. Cal grabbed for the collar even as he realized that the noise he heard was more than just the dog.

Somewhere in the house, someone cried for help.

He yanked open the unlocked door, scrambling into the back hall and stumbling over the eager dog. "Barney—"

He shoved the animal out of his way. Barney skidded, claws scrabbling on the bare floor, and then launched his body at the narrow, paneled door of the hall closet.

Dog and door collided with a thud that echoed the

pounding from inside. Cal's pulse thudded so loudly in his ears that it took a second to isolate the voice.

Andrea—but an Andrea who was a far cry from the brisk, efficient woman he knew. She sounded terrified. If someone had hurt her...

"It's okay," he shouted. Anything to dispel that panicky note in her voice. "Andrea, it's okay. I'm here. I'll get you out."

"Hurry." Her voice sounded muffled, as if she'd clamped her hand over her mouth.

He grabbed the small knob that released the catch, turned it, and Andrea tumbled into his arms. She grasped him, her fingers digging into his shoulders, her breath coming in harsh gasps.

He'd sensed her claustrophobia when she'd been closed in the toolshed for seconds. Now—now she was in the grip of a full-blown attack, as terrified as if she'd been faced with death instead of closed-in darkness.

"It's okay." He put his arm around her, feeling the tremors that coursed through her body. "Come with me." He piloted her toward the library, switching on lights as they went, sensing that nothing could be too bright for her at the moment. "You're safe now. Tell me what happened. Did someone hurt you?"

Her hand went up to her mouth as if to hold back sobs. She took one ragged breath and then another, seeming to gain a bit more control with each step they took away from the closet. Barney danced around them, trying to push his way between their legs, making little throaty sounds that sounded sympathetic.

"I'm all right." Andrea probably had to force the words out, and he felt the tension that still gripped her body.

"You're fine," he soothed. He switched on the lamp

next to the sofa and eased her to a sitting position. She still gripped his hand tightly, so he sat down next to her.

Barney, balked of his clear intent to take that space, had to be content with putting his head in Andrea's lap.

Cal smoothed his fingers over hers. "Did someone push you? Attack you?" He thought of the dark figure she'd seen out in the rain, and his alarm ratcheted upward. He should search the house, but he couldn't leave her in this state.

"No, nothing like that." She wiped away tears with her fingers. "At least—" She hesitated. "I don't think anyone was there. Probably the door just slammed shut when I lost my balance."

The slight shading of doubt in her voice had all his senses on alert. "Did you see someone? Hear someone?"

"I didn't see anyone."

Andrea straightened, putting up one hand to rub the back of her neck, as if tension had taken up residence there. Her usually precise blond hair tumbled about a face that was paler than usual, and her jeans and white shirt were smudged with dust. None of that was typical of Andrea, but it was somehow endearing.

Focus, he reminded himself. "You didn't see anyone. Did you hear something then?"

She shrugged, attempting a smile that was a mere twitch of her facial muscles. "You know how old houses are. This place makes all sorts of sounds even when it's empty."

"And it makes noises when someone is there. Someone who shouldn't be." His tone was grim. The back door had been standing open. Who knew how many other entrances had been just as accessible?

"I heard a creak that I thought came from the hallway, just before the door swung shut, but that doesn't mean anything. All the floors slant, and the door might swing shut on its own." She sounded as if she were trying to convince herself. "Besides, what could anyone gain by shutting me in a closet?"

Just saying the words put a tremor in her voice. The wave of protectiveness that swept over him startled him with its strength. He had no business feeling that way about Andrea.

He cleared his throat. "Maybe he wanted to keep you from seeing him. Or maybe—" Another, more disquieting thought hit him. "You're claustrophobic, aren't you? How many people know about that?"

"What do you mean?" Her fingers tightened, digging into his hand, and her voice rose. "Are you saying someone would do that deliberately to upset me?"

"Or to scare you off." He put his other hand over hers in a gesture of comfort and then frowned, groping for a rational thought that seemed to be lost in a sense of awareness of her.

"That's—that's ridiculous." But she didn't sound convinced.

"Look, Andrea, I'm beginning to think there's more going on here than we realize. First Rachel's accident, and then this business with the prowler—either the Hampton women are prey to a lot of bad luck all at once, or someone is willing to go to extremes to keep the inn from opening."

"Rachel." Her eyes darkened with fear as she zeroed in on the possibility of a threat to her sister. "But that was an accident. The police haven't found any evidence of anything else."

"I'm not trying to scare you." He raised a hand to

brush a strand of silky hair back from her face. His fingers lingered against the smooth skin of her cheek without his mind forming the intent.

"I'm not afraid." She attempted a smile that trembled on her lips. "In spite of the evidence to the contrary. But Grams, and Rachel—"

"I know. I don't like it, either." He wanted to wipe the worry from her face, but he wouldn't lie to her, pretending everything was all right when it so obviously wasn't. "Maybe I'm wrong. Maybe it's all a coincidence. But I don't like you being alone." Vulnerable, he wanted to add, but suspected she wouldn't appreciate it.

"I'm not alone. You're here. I appreciate—" She looked into his eyes and seemed to lose track of the rest of that sentence.

He understood. His rational thought processes had gone on vacation. All he could think was that she was very close, that her skin warmed to his touch, that he wanted to protect her, comfort her...

He closed the inches that separated them and found her lips. For an instant she held back, and then she leaned into the kiss, hands tightening on his arms, eyes closing. He drew her nearer, trying to deny the emotion that flooded through him, wiping out all his barricades in a rush of feeling.

"Andrea." He murmured her name against her lips, not trusting himself to say more. This shouldn't be happening, but it was. He'd probably regret it later, but now all he wanted was to hold her.

He'd told himself they couldn't be friends. Maybe they couldn't, but maybe they could be much more.

Chapter 9

Andrea wrapped her fingers around the coffee mug, absorbing its heat. The warmth generated by Cal's kiss had dissipated when he'd drawn back, looking as confused by what had happened as she was.

Maybe they'd both sensed the need to change the tempo a bit at that point. Cal had gone to search the house, leaving the dog with her. Barney had padded at her heels while she fixed coffee and carried a tray back to the library, apparently mindful of his duty to guard her. The journal, Rachel's receipts tucked inside, lay next to the computer, the innocent cause of her problems.

She stroked the sheltie's head. In spite of Cal's doubts about Barney's intelligence, the dog had seemed to know she was in trouble.

"Good boy," she told him. "If it hadn't been for you…" Well, she didn't want to think about that.

"If it hadn't been for Barney, you'd still have been all right." Cal came into the room as he spoke. "Your grandmother would have come home and found you soon, even if I hadn't heard the dog."

She knew he was trying to make her feel better, but she didn't want to think about what she'd have been like if she'd been closed in the closet all this time. Cal didn't understand the panic. No one did who hadn't experienced it.

"Did you find anything wrong anywhere?"

"No actual sign of an intruder, but there are far too many ways into a house this size." He frowned, looking as if he'd like to go around putting bars on the windows. "And I'm not saying that closet door couldn't have swung shut on its own, or even from the vibration when you fell, but it still seems pretty stable."

"Is that supposed to make me sleep well tonight?"

She watched as he took a mug, poured coffee and settled on the couch opposite her. She liked the neat economy of his movements.

"I'd put safety over a good night's sleep anytime." He looked toward the windows. "Your grandmother should be back soon, shouldn't she?"

She glanced at the grandfather clock in the corner and nodded. "I don't want her upset about this. It was just an accident. You agree?"

"Let's say I'm about eighty percent convinced of that. You're sure it wasn't a person you heard before you fell?"

He leaned toward her, propping his elbows on his well-worn jeans. As usual, he wore a flannel shirt, this time over a white tee, the sleeves folded back. Also as usual, his brown hair had fallen forward into his eyes.

"It was a creak. That's all. I told you—this house has a language all its own. Surely if someone had been there, I'd have heard him running away."

An image popped into her mind—the large, dark figure she'd seen outlined by the lightning. Her fingers tightened on the mug. If he'd been in the house, he would have made more noise than a gentle creak.

"Well, maybe. Unless he was smart enough to slip away the minute he heard you fall."

"You searched the house. You didn't find any signs someone had gotten in," she pointed out.

Lines crinkled around his eyes. "Does that mean you trust me?"

"Yes." The word came out so quickly that the sureness of it startled her. Maybe tomorrow she'd be back to being suspicious of him, but at the moment she was just glad he was here.

"Well…good." He seemed a little taken aback by her quick response. "Have you given any more thought to what I asked you? Does anyone else around here, other than family, know about your claustrophobia?"

She shook her head, wanting to reject the possibility. "I don't know. I suppose someone could. The Zook family probably knew." Levi popped into her mind, and she pushed him out again. He wouldn't remember something like that. "It was a lot worse when I was a child. I don't even remember what triggered it the first time, so I must have been pretty young."

"It didn't start when you left here, then."

She blinked, surprised at his linking the two things. "No. Why would you think that?"

The light from the Tiffany lamp on the end table brought out gold flecks in his eyes. "It's just that I've gathered it was a pretty traumatic time for all of you."

"Has my grandmother talked about our leaving?" She asked the question carefully, not sure she wanted to hear the answer.

"Only in a general way, saying how much it grieved her when you left."

"It wasn't our choice." Her voice was tart with remembered pain. "The adults in our lives didn't give Rachel and Caro and me any say in what happened."

"They don't, do they? My folks split up when I was twelve, and I always had the feeling that what happened to me was an afterthought. Did your parents—"

She nodded, her throat tight. "Our dad left. Not that he'd been around all that much to begin with." She frowned, trying to look at the past as an adult, not as the child she'd been. "He kept losing jobs, and Mom— well, she couldn't cope. That was why we moved in here, I suppose. Our grandparents were the stable element in our lives."

"And then you lost them, too." Setting his mug aside, he reached across the space between them to take her hands, warming her more than the coffee had.

"My mother quarreled with Grandfather." She shook her head. "I'm not sure what it was all about—maybe about Daddy leaving. It all happened around the same time. I just remember a lot of shouting. And then Mom telling us we were going away, hustling us out of the house before we even had time to pack everything."

"Where did you go?"

She shrugged. "Where *didn't* we go is more like it. Mom never seemed able to settle in one place at a time.

We moved constantly, usually one step ahead of the bill collectors."

Her hands were trembling. Silly to be so affected after all this time, but he grasped them tightly in his.

"I'm sorry," he said softly. "I shouldn't have brought it up."

"It's all right. We all grew up okay, in spite of it. And there was a trust fund from my grandparents to see us through college."

"Still, it can't have been easy, having your whole world change so quickly. Is your father a part of your life now?"

"No." Maybe it was odd that his absence didn't bother her more, but he'd never exactly been a hands-on father. "We haven't heard anything from him from that day to this."

"And your mother?"

"She died a couple of years ago. Driving under the influence, apparently. In Las Vegas." She pressed her lips together for a moment. "We hadn't seen much of her since we'd all been out on our own."

He moved his fingers over her hand, offering comfort. "Sounds as if your parents let the three of you down pretty badly."

She shook her head, the words seeming to press against her lips, demanding to be released. "It was Grandfather who let me down. Let us down, I mean. We counted on him. He could have stopped her. But he just stood and watched us leave and never said a word."

All the pain of that betrayal, held at bay over the years she'd been away, came sweeping back, threatening to drown her. That was why she so seldom came here, she knew it now. She didn't want to remember, and the memories were everywhere here.

"You really think your grandfather could have prevented what happened? Unless he was able to have her declared an unfit mother..."

She jerked her hands away. "I don't want to talk about it anymore." He didn't understand. Grandfather—he could do anything, couldn't he? Or was that a ten-year-old's view of the world?

Cal recaptured her hands. "I'm sorry," he said again. He brought her fingers to his lips so that she felt his breath with the words. "I wish I could make it better."

"Thank you." She whispered the words, shaken by the longing she felt to let him comfort her, to close the space between them and be in his arms again...

The sound of car wheels on gravel had her sitting up straight. She drew her hands from his, hoping he couldn't guess what her thoughts had been. She didn't know whether she was glad or sorry that Grams was home, ending this.

"Remember, not a word to Grams. About any of this."

He nodded. Then, too quickly for her to anticipate it, he leaned forward and touched her lips with his.

The organ was still playing behind them when Andrea and her grandmother stepped out into the May sunshine after worship. Andrea tucked her hand unobtrusively into Grams's arm as they went down the two shallow steps to the churchyard. She'd seen the sparkle of tears in Grams's eyes more than once during the service.

Actually, the minister's prayers for Rachel's recovery had made her own eyes damp. She'd expected to feel guilty, if anything, at going back to church after letting regular attendance slip out of her life over the past few years. Instead she'd felt welcomed, and not just by the congregation. The awareness of God's presence, growing in her heart since she'd returned, had intensified to the point that her heart seemed to swell. Grams had looked at her with a question in her eyes once or twice, as if she sensed what was happening.

"I see everyone still gathers out here after the service," she said as they reached the walk and moved away from the steps to allow others to come down. She wasn't ready yet to talk about this renewed sense of God in her life.

People clustered into small groups as they cleared the stairs, exchanging greetings, catching up on the news. A long folding table had been set up to one side, bearing pitchers of iced tea and lemonade. Several children had already started a game of tag among the tilted old gravestones. A few late tulips bloomed, bright red against gray markers.

Grams patted her hand. "Some things don't change. Once you and your sisters did that in your Sunday best."

"I remember. We didn't have any silly superstitions about cemeteries after playing here every Sunday."

The small church, built of the same stone as the inn, was almost completely surrounded by its graveyard, with burials dating back to the early 1700s. A low stone wall enclosed both church and churchyard. Even now, one little girl was emulating a tightrope walker on the top of it.

"Let me guess." Cal spoke from behind her, his low

voice sending a pleasurable shiver down her spine. "You used to be the daring young girl walking on the wall."

"Whenever my grandmother wasn't looking." She turned toward him as Grams began talking to the pastor. "I didn't realize you attended church. Here, I mean."

"If you're not House Amish or Mennonite, this is where you worship in Churchville, isn't it?" He glanced toward her grandmother. "Katherine didn't suspect anything last night?" he asked softly.

"She didn't seem to, but it's hard to be sure. When we were kids, we thought she had eyes in the back of her head and an antenna that detected mischief."

"There was probably plenty, with three girls so close in age."

She smiled, shaking her head. "Fights, mostly, over who took what from whom. Caroline, our youngest sister, was such a good actress that she could convince almost anybody of anything. Except Grams, who always seemed to know the truth. I just hope her antenna wasn't working last night."

"She'd probably have said something, if so. She's not one to keep still where people she cares about are concerned."

She nodded, but as her gaze sought her grandmother's erect figure, the smile slipped away. Grams had changed since Grandfather's death, and she hadn't even noticed it. The strength they'd always counted on was still there, but it was muted now. Or maybe Rachel's accident had made her vulnerable.

"I see now how much this place means to her." She pitched her voice low, under the animated chatter that was going on all around them. "I don't want anything that's going on to affect that."

His hand brushed hers in a mute gesture of support. "You can't always protect people, even though you care about them."

She glanced up at him, ready to argue, but maybe he had a point. She'd protected her little sisters during those years under their mother's erratic care, but eventually they'd been on their own. The situation was reversed now with Grams. She'd always been the strong one, and now she had to be protected, preferably without her realization.

Cal raised an eyebrow, lips quirking slightly. "Not going to disagree?"

"I would, but I see one of your favorite people coming. I'm sure you'll want to talk to her."

"Not Margaret." The hunted look in his eyes amused her. "It'll be tough to keep a Sunday state of mind with Margaret spreading her version of good cheer around."

She couldn't respond, because Margaret was swooping down on them. *Swooping* actually seemed the right word—the floating handkerchief sleeves of her print dress fluttered like a butterfly's wings.

"Cal. And Andrea. How nice to see the two of you together. Again. So lovely when young people find each other." Margaret put one hand on Cal's arm, and Andrea suspected it took all of his manners to keep from pulling away.

"We weren't lost," he said shortly. "We were just talking about the inn."

In a way, she supposed they had been, since that was what concerned Grams most at the moment. "Cal's been helping us with some of the repairs," she said. To say nothing of rescuing her from dark closets.

"You are such a sweet boy, to help a neighbor who's in distress."

The expression on Cal's face at being called a sweet boy suggested she'd better intervene before he was reduced to rudeness.

"Just about everyone has been very helpful in getting the inn ready to open." Except Margaret, she supposed. "It's coming together very well."

"Is it?" Shrewdness glinted in Margaret's eyes for an instant. "I was under the impression you're nowhere near ready to open for Memorial Day weekend. Sad, to have to cancel those reservations. It doesn't give the impression of a truly professional establishment. I'd be glad to take those guests, but naturally I'm completely full for that weekend."

"I don't know what makes you think that, but we're not canceling any of our reservations." She certainly hoped that was true. "You'll be pleased to know that we expect to open on schedule."

Margaret's eyes narrowed. "That's delightful. Of course, everyone won't be as happy for you as I am. Still, one has to break eggs to make an omelet." She turned away, sleeves fluttering. "Excuse me. I must go and talk to the dear reverend about the strawberry festival."

Andrea managed to hold back words until the woman was out of earshot. "What did she mean?" she muttered. "Who won't be glad to see us open on time?"

Cal cupped her elbow with his hand. "I think your grandmother's ready to leave."

She planted her feet, frowning at him. "Answer the question, please."

A quick jerk of his hand pulled her close to him, and he lowered his head to speak so no one could hear. "A few of the old-timers don't like the idea of another inn opening, increasing the tourist traffic in town."

"Nick mentioned something about that, but he really made light of their attitude." So light, in fact, that she hadn't considered it since.

"Did he?" He was probably wondering why she hadn't said anything to him. "Well, one of those people has your grandmother cornered at the moment, so I think we'd better go to the rescue."

Grams was talking with Herbert Rush, an old friend of Grandfather's. Or rather, it looked as if he was talking at her—and not about something pleasant, to judge by the color of his face and the way his white eyebrows beetled over snapping blue eyes.

Andrea hurried over, sliding her hand through Grams's arm. "Are you about ready to leave, Grams?" She fought to produce a polite smile. "How are you, Mr. Rush?"

The elderly man transferred his glare to her. "How am I? I'm unhappy, that's how I am. The last thing this village needs is another thing to draw tourists. I wouldn't have believed it of your grandmother. Turning a fine old showplace like Unger House into a tourist trap. Someone should do something about that. Your grandfather must be turning over in his grave."

"On the contrary, I'm sure my grandfather is proud of my grandmother, as he always was." She pinned a smile in place. Grams wouldn't appreciate it if she allowed anger to erupt. She turned toward the gate, grateful for Cal's presence on Grams's other side.

Apparently this place wasn't as idyllic as she'd been thinking, and Grams was getting the full picture of its less appealing side.

He seemed to be making one excuse after another to walk over to the inn these days. Cal rounded the tool-shed, checking the outbuildings automatically. Since sunset was still an hour away, he couldn't even tell himself that he was making his nightly rounds.

He wanted to see Andrea again. That was the truth of it. A moment's sensible thought told him that pursuing a relationship with her was a huge mistake, but that didn't seem to be stopping him from finding a reason to be where he might see her.

Well, that wish was going to be disappointed, because a quick glance told him the garage was empty. She and Katherine hadn't returned from their visit to Rachel.

But someone else was around the place, judging by the late-model compact that sat on the verge of the drive. Frowning, he quickened his steps. Probably nothing, but with all the odd things happening lately, it didn't do to take anything for granted.

His muscles tightened. A woman was on the side porch, shading her eyes as she peered through the glass in the door. He shot forward.

"What are you doing?"

He reached the bottom of the steps as she spun around, her mouth forming a silent O of surprise.

"I—you startled me." She grasped the railing. "I'm looking for Andrea Hampton. I knocked, but no one answered."

"She's out just now." The adrenaline ebbed, leaving him feeling he'd been too aggressive. She was younger than he'd thought at first glance, probably no more than twenty-two or three. Blond hair in a stylish, layered cut, a trim suit that looked too dressy for a Sunday afternoon in Churchville, a pair of big brown eyes that fixed on him as if asking for help. "Can I do anything for you?"

She came down the three steps so that they stood facing one another, looking up at him as if he could solve all her problems. "Is she going to be back soon? Ms. Hampton, I mean." Then, seeming to feel something else was called for, she added, "I'm Julie Michaels, her assistant."

He couldn't help the way his eyebrows lifted. So Andrea's office was following her here. "Cal Burke." He wasn't sure what to do with the woman. Telling her to go away certainly wasn't an option, though the urge to do so was strong. "I'm not sure when—"

The sound of tires on gravel took the decision out of his hands. "Here she is now."

At the sight of them, Andrea pulled to a stop in front of the woman's car. She slid out, frowning a little.

He reached Katherine's door and opened it, his gaze on Andrea as she came around the car. "I spotted her looking in the window. Is she really your assistant?"

"She is." There was a note in her voice he couldn't quite define.

Then she walked quickly toward the young woman. "Julie. I'm surprised to see you here."

Surprised and not particularly welcoming, if he read her correctly. Now what was that about? None of his business, of course, but still… He helped Katherine out and closed the door.

"I stopped by to pick up the report."

Andrea's brows lifted. "I said I'd email it in tomorrow. There was no need for you to come all this way."

"I was in the area anyway," she said. "I just thought it would be helpful. I didn't mean to be in the way." Her tone suggested a puppy that had received a swat instead of a pat.

"That was very thoughtful." Katherine stepped forward, holding out her hand. "I'm Andrea's grandmother, Katherine Unger." The glance she shot Andrea said that she was disappointed in her manners.

He was probably the only one who saw Andrea's lips tighten. "I'll get the file for you." She turned and went quickly into the house, leaving the three of them standing awkwardly.

Julie turned toward the patio, her hurt feelings, if that's what it had been, disappearing in a smile. "What a lovely place. You must be a wonderful gardener, Ms. Unger."

"I have a great deal of help. Come onto the patio where you can see the flowers."

He could go back to his workshop, but some instinct made him trail along behind them. Andrea hadn't expected this visit, and she didn't like it. Why?

"I'm sure Andrea must be a big help to you. It's great that she could take time off when you need her." Julie bent to touch the petals of a yellow rose that had just begun to open.

"Yes, yes, it is." Katherine's smile wavered a bit. "I don't know what I'd do without her at this time, with her sister in the hospital."

"I heard about the accident. I'm so sorry." The woman's words sounded sympathetic, but there was something watchful in those big eyes. "How long do you think you'll need to have Andrea stay?"

That seemed to be his cue. He spoke just as Katherine opened her mouth to respond. "Is that a Japanese beetle on the rosebush?"

Katherine turned away from the woman instantly, bending over to peer anxiously at the small leaves, brushing them with her fingers. "I don't see anything. Are you sure, Cal?"

He guided her a few steps away, keeping her focused on the flowers. "It was over here. I just caught a glimpse."

Knowing Katherine's devotion to her flowers, that should keep her occupied for a few minutes. And off the subject of Andrea's departure. That hadn't been a casual query, and the idea of the woman trying to pump Katherine raised his hackles.

The back door swung open. Andrea strode toward them, a manila folder in her hand. She held it out to Julie.

"Here you are. Please ask Mr. Walker to call me if he has any questions."

"I will." She tucked the folder under her arm. "You have such a lovely home here, Ms. Unger. Thank you for letting me see your garden." She glanced wistfully toward the house.

He took Katherine's arm before she could issue an invitation to a tour. "Let me give you a hand up the steps. Emma sent one of the grandkids over to mention potato salad and cold ham for a late supper if you came home hungry."

"She spoils me." Katherine took his arm, leaning on

it a bit more heavily than usual. "I guess I will go in, now. Goodbye, Ms. Michaels."

He shepherded her into the house and saw her settled in her favorite chair. When he got back outside, the Michaels woman was pulling out of the drive. Andrea sat on the stone wall at the edge of the patio, frowning.

"That wasn't exactly a disinterested call, was it?" He sat down next to her.

She glanced at him, eyebrows lifting. "What do you mean?"

"While you were inside, your assistant tried to pump your grandmother about how long you'd be away from work."

"I should have expected that." Her lips tightened. "Did she succeed?"

"I headed her off. How long has she been trying to look just like you?"

For an instant she stared at him, and then her face relaxed in a slight smile. "You don't miss much. Believe it or not, when I hired her, Julie was just out of college, with brown hair halfway down her back, glasses and a wardrobe that consisted of discount store polyester suits."

"She found a role model in you. I guess that's natural enough."

"At first it was flattering. It took me a while to realize that she didn't just want to emulate my style of clothing. She wants my job. And she sees my absence from the office as her golden opportunity to step right into my shoes."

"Your boss wouldn't be that stupid, would he?"

She shrugged, eyes worried. "The more days I'm gone, the easier it will be for her. If I stay too long, he may just decide he can do without me altogether." Her fingers clenched on her knees. "I can't let that happen. I can't lose everything I've worked for."

Something twisted inside him. She'd go, just like that. It was what he'd thought all along, but knowing he'd been right about her didn't make him feel any better.

"So that's it. Is your job really more important to you than your family?"

She swung toward him, anger sweeping the anxiety from her face. "I don't think you have the right to ask me that."

Matching anger rose. "Why? Because I'm an interfering outsider?"

"No." Green eyes darkened. "Because you expect me to spill my feelings and share my decisions when you're not willing to tell me a single thing about you."

Chapter 10

She shouldn't have said that. Andrea wanted to refute the words, to deny that she cared in the least about his secrets. But it was already too late. Whatever she did or said now, Cal would know that the imbalance in their relationship mattered to her.

She could feel the tension in him through the inches that separated them, could sense the pressure to shoot to his feet and walk away.

But he didn't. He sat, staring down at the edging stones along the patio, where the setting sun cast wavering shadows from the branches above. His profile was stern, the planes of his face looking as if they'd been carved from one of the planks of wood he used.

Doubt assailed her. Whatever it was that made him look that way—did she really want to know? She sensed that if he told her, that truth could change their relationship in incalculable ways.

He moved slightly, not looking at her—just the slightest shrug, as if he tried to ease the tension from his shoulders.

"You told me once I had too much of a corporate mind-set to be just a carpenter. Remember that?"

"Yes." *I don't want to know.* But she did. She did.

"I was a lawyer." He grimaced slightly. "Guess I still am, in a way, but I'll never practice again."

That was her cue to ask why, but she wasn't ready for that. She settled for an easier question. "Where? Not around here."

"Seattle." He leaned back, bracing his hands on the wall. The pose could have looked relaxed, but it didn't. "You wouldn't know the firm, but it's one of the big guns there."

"Prestigious." Her mind grappled to reconcile the informal country carpenter with a big-city lawyer. Difficult, but she'd always known there was something.

"You could say that. When I landed the position, I knew I had it made. Straight to the big leagues—not bad for an ordinary middle-class kid who didn't even know which fork to use." A thread of bitterness ran through the words. He shot her a sideways glance that questioned. "Can you understand how overwhelming that could be?"

"I think so." Cal had been young, ambitious, intelligent, and he'd gotten the break that ensured his future. She of all people knew what that felt like. "But something went wrong."

His hands clenched against the stone, the knuckles whitening. "Not for a long time. I threw everything into the job, and it paid off. I was on the fast track to partnership, and nothing else mattered."

He was circling the thing that caused him pain, getting closer and closer. She sensed it, and wanted, like a coward, to close her ears, but she couldn't.

"The senior partner called me in. Assigned me to the case of my career. One of our biggest clients was involved in a child custody dispute with his ex-wife. I was just the sort of aggressive bulldog he wanted to represent him. Win, and opportunities would open to me that I couldn't have imagined."

"You accepted." Of course he had. He wouldn't have evaded that challenge, any more than she would.

"Sure. I threw myself into the case, determined to do the best job any attorney could." He looked at her then, his brown eyes very dark. "I trusted the client. You have to believe that."

She nodded, throat tight. She thought she saw where this was going now, and already his tension infected her, so that her hands pressed tight against the stone, too.

He shrugged, mouth twisting. "I did a great job. Lived up to everyone's expectations. Demolished the opposition and won the case." He was silent for a moment, as if he had to steel himself to say the next thing. "Then I found out that my client had been lying. He really was molesting his six-year-old daughter."

She'd been prepared for it, she'd thought, but it still hit her like a blow to the heart. "The little girl—"

Dear Lord, could anything be worse?

"Yes. The child I gave back to her father."

"It wasn't just you," she said quickly. "It was a judge's decision, surely. And the mother must have had legal representation."

"I told myself that. All the arguments—that it wasn't just my responsibility, that I had a duty to represent my client, that our legal system is adversarial and everyone deserves representation. It didn't change anything. The bottom line was still the same."

"What did you do?" He'd have done something. She knew that about him.

"Went to the senior partner. He told me to forget it. I'd done my job, and it was out of my hands."

"You couldn't."

"No. Couldn't ignore it. Couldn't go to the mother without putting the whole firm in jeopardy. So I did the only thing open to me. I went to the client and told him either he relinquished custody to his ex-wife, or I blew the whistle on him. It would have meant disbarment or worse, but I'd do it."

He took a deep breath, and she had the sense he hadn't breathed in a long time. She hadn't, either.

"Did it work?"

He nodded. "Guess I was convincing enough, especially when I resigned from the firm." His voice roughened. "I saw the child back into her mother's care, but God alone knows how much damage was done to her in the meantime."

That was the guilt he carried, then. That was why he lived the way he did.

"Cal, you did everything you could. He was the criminal, not you."

He grimaced. "Nice of you to defend me. I spent months trying to tell myself that, until finally God forced me to face the truth. I'd been so ambitious, so determined to succeed, that I'd let myself get sucked into a life that didn't take into account any of the important things, like faith, honesty, other human beings.

I had to stop making excuses before I could repent and begin again."

That's what he was doing here, then. Starting over. Looking for peace in this quiet place where values still applied.

"You did the right thing." Maybe her opinion didn't matter, but she had to say it. She met his gaze. "You couldn't have done anything else."

Something in his eyes acknowledged her words. He didn't speak. They didn't touch. But they were closer than if they'd been in each other's arms. She seemed to be aware of everything about him—of every cell in his body, of the blood coursing through his veins.

She took a breath, letting the realization crystallize in her mind. She cared about him, far more than she'd known. She admired him more than she could say.

But what he'd just told her had shut out any possibility of a relationship between them, because the life she longed to keep was the very one he'd never go back to.

Emma, going up the attic steps ahead of Andrea, pushed the door open, letting a shaft of sunlight fall on the rough wooden stairs. Rough, but not dusty, Andrea noticed. Obviously Emma's cleaning fanaticism extended even to the attics of the old house.

"All of the quilts are packed away in trunks," Emma said. "It is good that they'll be useful again."

"I just hope they're still in decent shape after being in storage for so long." She emerged into the attic, which stretched out into the shadowy distance, marked by the looming shapes of discarded furniture.

Lots and lots of furniture. Cal had said the place was packed to the rafters, and he was right. Her unpracticed eye identified a dining room set that surely wasn't genuine Duncan Phyfe, was it?

Emma, weaving her way through odd pieces of furniture, let out an audible sniff. "I put them away proper. They'll just need a bit of airing, that's all."

If Emma had done it, of course it would have been done properly. She was the one who'd suggested the quilts when Andrea and Grams had been debating about drapes and bedcovers for the guest rooms.

"The English will like having Amish-made quilts in the rooms," she'd said matter-of-factly.

She was right. Their guests would come to Lancaster County to see the Amish, who ironically only wanted to be left alone, and they would be thrilled at the idea. So she and Emma were on a hunting expedition in the attic for quilts and anything else that would give the guest rooms a unique touch.

Concentrating on the decorating just might keep her mind from straying back, again and again, to that conversation with Cal the previous day. On second thought, nothing was strong enough to do that.

Cal. He'd wrung her heart with his story, and in the dark silence of the night, she'd found herself filling in all the things he hadn't said.

He'd given up everything—his career, his future, his friends—because it was the right thing to do. Plenty of people would have rationalized away their responsibility in the situation, but not Cal. He'd taken on even more than his share, and now seemed content that it was what God expected of him.

She approached that thought cautiously. Somehow it had never occurred to her, even when she was attending church regularly, that God might have a claim on one's business life. That God might require sacrifice, on occasion. That was an uncomfortable idea, but once planted, it didn't seem amenable to being dismissed.

Emma knelt in front of a carved wooden dower chest, one of several lined up near the window. Andrea hurried to join her, thinking that her jeans were more appropriate to kneeling on the wide-planked floor than Emma's dress.

Concentrate on the task at hand. The practical one was to choose the quilts for the bedrooms. The unspoken one was to use this opportunity to talk to Emma about Levi, to try and get a sense of whether he might have been the dark figure she'd seen the night of the storm.

Leave the theological considerations for later. And any thought of her feelings for Cal for later still.

Emma lifted the chest lid, exposing bundles wrapped in muslin sheets. She took out the first one, unwrapping it. Andrea grasped the sheet and spread it out so that the quilt wouldn't touch the floor.

"Squares in Bars," Emma said, naming the pattern as she unfolded it. "My mother made many quilts for your grandmother. This was one of hers."

Andrea's breath caught as the colors, rich and saturated, glowed like jewels in the sun streaming in the many-paned attic window. The quilt was bordered in a deep forest-green, with the squares done in the blues, maroons, pinks, purples and mauves of Amish clothing.

"It's beautiful." Drawn to touch, she stroked the colors. "Your mother was an artist."

Emma shook her head. "Just usual work. She was quick with the needle, I remember."

That was the closest thing to pride she'd ever heard from Emma.

"Here is one that belongs in your room." Emma pulled back the sheet on the second quilt. "Do you remember?"

Remember? She couldn't speak as the pattern came into view, myriads of diamonds expanding from the center in vivid and unexpected bursts of color. She touched it gently. How many nights had she fallen asleep trying to count the number of diamonds in the quilt?

"I remember," she said softly, her throat going tight. "Your mother made this one, too, didn't she?"

Emma nodded, her plain face softening a little at Andrea's reaction. "Sunshine and Shadow. It was her favorite pattern."

"Is that what it's called? I don't think I ever knew. I can see why—the alternating bands of dark and light are like the bands of sunlight and shadow made by the rails of a fence."

Emma traced a line of dark patches. "It's the pattern of life. Sometimes sun, sometimes shadow. Like Scripture says, 'To everything there is a season, and a time to every purpose under Heaven.' But always God is with us."

The words squeezed her heart. Would Emma consider Levi one of the dark bands? She never seemed to show disappointment or sorrow with him. Maybe this was the moment to ask, but Andrea couldn't seem to force the words out.

"I should put it in a guest room, though, not keep it for myself." But her hands clung to the quilt. Or maybe to the memory of how safe she'd felt, sleeping under it.

Emma shook her head in a decided way. "Your

grandmother ordered it from my mother just for you, when she knew you were coming to live here. It made her so happy to fix that room up for you, and how she smiled when it was all finished."

The image came clear in her mind, even from those few words. A younger Emma, a younger Grams, spreading the quilt on her bed, Grams's face lit with pleasure.

"Those were happy times, when we were here," she said, hoping her voice didn't sound as choked as it felt.

"Yes." Emma seemed to be looking back, too. "It was good, all of you children together, those days when the house was so full. We are in the *daadi haus,* now, Eli and Levi and me, and Samuel and his family have the farmhouse."

Andrea sat back on her heels, her arms filled with the quilt. "Does it grieve you, that Levi won't have a family of his own?"

Emma considered for a moment. "No, not grieve. He is as God chose to make him. I accept that as God's will."

The question she had to ask stuck in her throat, and she pushed it out. "I thought I saw Levi one night from my window. Does he go out after dark by himself?"

"No." The expression on Emma's face couldn't be disguised. Fear. Stark, unreasoning fear filled her face before she bent over the chest, hiding it. "No." Her voice was muffled. "Levi does not go out after nightfall. It would not be right."

Something cold closed around Andrea's heart. The unthinkable had happened. Emma was lying to her.

Cal walked into the hallway of the inn from the kitchen and paused, looking around. He hadn't been in since the painters finished, and he let out a low whistle. Katherine should be pleased. The Three Sisters Inn was a showplace, all right, with the parlors restored to their former grandeur. He might not know much about decorating, but he knew elegant when he saw it.

He put his hand on the newel post, sturdy now since he'd finished the repairs. Emma had said that Andrea needed some help moving things up in the guest rooms. He couldn't very well say no, but he wouldn't mind a little more time elapsing before seeing her again.

He'd told her things he hadn't told anyone else. He'd like to say he didn't know why, but that wouldn't be true. He knew. He cared about her. That was why.

It wouldn't go anywhere, that caring, and she knew that as well as he did. They were too different, and the life she prized was one that he'd never return to.

He started up the stairs. Well, she'd probably be as eager as he was to restore some barriers between them.

He reached the open center hallway on the second floor and glanced around. The doors stood open to the guest rooms—four on this floor, three more upstairs. Andrea was nowhere to be seen, so he went on up the narrower staircase to the third floor.

The rooms here were smaller and didn't seem quite finished. It looked as if Andrea had been putting most of her efforts into the second floor.

A loud thud sounded somewhere over his head, startling him. He yanked open the door to the attic stairway. "Andrea?" He bolted up the stairs.

"I'm all right." Her voice reassured him as he opened the second door at the top of the stairs.

"Good thing. I thought that was you. What are you

trying to do?" He picked his way through pieces of furniture to where she stood.

"I want to take this stand down to the blue bedroom." She tugged at the recalcitrant piece that lay fallen on its side, obviously the thud he'd heard. "It's heavier than it looks."

"It's solid mahogany." He bent to shift it upright, and then took a step back, looking at it. "Nice piece. What's that?" Something had fallen out when the door on the front of the stand swung open.

Andrea picked up several oversize green books. "Grandfather's ledgers." She dusted them off with the tail of her pale blue shirt and flipped one open. "Goodness, this dates back to before I was born."

"Seems like a funny place to store them."

She wrinkled her nose. "Rachel, getting the place ready to turn into an inn. Things that were in her way got stuck into the most unimaginable places. We really should do some serious sorting and organizing. These ledgers should be kept for their part in Unger house history, if nothing else."

She bent over the book. For a moment she was engrossed in her find, and he could watch her as closely as he wanted. With her blond hair pulled back in a ponytail and a streak of dirt on her cheek, she didn't look much like the sleek urban professional.

She glanced up, catching his grin before he could erase it. "What's funny?"

"Just thinking you look a little different, that's all."

"You try rummaging through this attic without getting dirty, in spite of Emma's ferocious cleaning," she said. "You certainly were right about this place. Grams could start selling things off to an antique dealer and fund the inn for the foreseeable future."

"Your grandmother mentioned some interest from one of the local antique dealers, but she's reluctant to part with anything. Or maybe the prospect of sorting seems overwhelming. Are you ready to start an inventory?"

"Don't tempt me." She glanced around as if she'd like to do just that. "You wouldn't believe the stash of hand-made quilts Emma and I found up here this morning."

Any potential embarrassment had evaporated in the face of Andrea's calm attitude. She'd found her way back to an easy friendliness, and that was for the best.

"Something you can use, I take it?"

She nodded, but the smile slid from her face. "I had a chance to sound her out about Levi. She insists that he's never out alone at night, so he couldn't be the person I saw."

"Did you believe her?"

She looked at him, distress filling her eyes. "I've known her most of my life. I'd have said she'd never lie. But no, I didn't believe her."

Her voice shook a little on the words, and he knew how much it hurt her.

"I'm sorry. Look, it may not mean anything. If it was Levi, he hasn't come back. Nothing's happened for a couple of days. Whoever he was, our prowler seems to be scared off."

She nodded. "And now that I've mentioned it, I'm sure Emma will make sure that Levi doesn't do any late-night wandering."

"Right." It was worth agreeing to see the concern

fade from her eyes. He just hoped they were right and the prowler was a thing of the past.

He seized the stand. "Well, shall we get this downstairs?"

"Yes, thanks. I appreciate the help. Rachel's coming home in a couple of days, and the opening is in less than a week." She tried to take the other side, but he pulled it away from her.

"I've got it. Just do the doors for me."

"Macho," she said, teasing, and went to open the door.

He muscled the stand down the stairs and around the bend at the bottom. Andrea closed the door while he leaned against the wall, trying not to breathe hard.

"Let's leave it here until I have a chance to clean it."

He nodded and started down the next flight of stairs. "Anytime you want heavy moving done, you know who to call."

She followed him. "But—did you want something, before I waylaid you with the stand?"

"Emma sent me upstairs. Guess she thought you could use an extra hand."

"My thanks to both of you." She paused as they approached the landing. "That sounded like the side door." She passed him and hurried on down the stairs.

When they reached the bottom, no one was there. She glanced into the library. "Margaret." She didn't sound especially welcoming. He couldn't say he blamed her.

Margaret scurried across the room, holding out an armload of peonies. "I just brought these in for your sister. I hope you don't mind—I thought they might cheer her long recuperation. Hello, Cal. You're here again, I see."

He nodded. It was probably best to ignore the comment.

"Of course I don't mind." Andrea took the flowers. "But why did you come in the side? Wasn't the front door open?"

"I didn't." Margaret looked surprised. "I came in the front."

He'd have said the sound had been from the side door, too. Odd.

There was a rap at the front door, and James Bendick popped his head in. "Andrea—oh, there you are. And Margaret." He came in, holding a bouquet of pink roses. "I heard Rachel is coming home, so I brought her these, but someone beat me to it. Margaret, those must be straight from your beautiful borders."

Margaret batted her eyes at him. "You're such a flatterer, James."

"This was sweet of you, Uncle Nick." Andrea took the flowers, putting the ledgers down on the drop leaf table in the hallway to do so.

Bendick seemed to be determined to ignore him. Perversely, Cal leaned against the newel post, wondering how long it would take for the man to acknowledge his presence.

"Those look like some of your grandfather's old ledgers." Bendick flipped one open. "Dating back to the Dark Ages, I see."

"Cal and I found them in the attic. I thought Grams might enjoy seeing them."

Having Cal forced on his attention, Bendick nodded. "Burke. Helping out, are you?"

"Just doing the heavy moving." Cal pushed away

from the post. "I'll be going, Andrea. Give me a call if you need anything else brought down."

"I will. And thank you, Cal."

If her smile was anything to go by, Andrea must have bought his suggestion that they'd seen the last of their prowler. He just hoped he was right.

He went quickly past the parlors to the side door, reached for it, and then stopped.

The side door was the only one where someone entering wasn't likely to be seen, either from the kitchen or the library. It had been locked when he'd come over. He'd tried it first before entering through the kitchen.

Now the door stood ajar. Someone had come in. Or gone out.

Chapter 11

Andrea sank down in a kitchen chair, grateful for the mug of coffee Emma set in front of her. The morning was only half over, but she'd been working nonstop. It was time to take a break.

Grams sat at the end of the table with her usual cup of tea. "Do you think the bedroom for Rachel is all right? I hate the idea of putting her in the maid's room."

"It's fine," she said quickly, before Grams could get the idea of making a change after all the work they'd already done to prepare a ground floor room for Rachel's homecoming. "She has to be on this floor because of the wheelchair, and that room is perfect. It has its own bath."

"She will be close to the kitchen," Emma added, stirring something in the large yellow mixing bowl. "She will like that, she will."

Obviously Emma was on her side in this. Neither of them wanted to start rearranging furniture at this point.

"Once she's home, we can see if there's anything else we can do to make her more comfortable," Andrea pointed out.

"I suppose you're right." Grams still looked a bit doubtful, probably over the idea of a daughter of the house being relegated to the maid's room. Rachel had certainly lived in worse when she was in culinary school, but Grams wouldn't want to hear that.

"What are you making, Emma?" A change of subject was in order.

"Rachel's favorite cake. Banana walnut." She emptied a cup of walnuts into the mixture. "Black walnuts from our own tree will make it extra good."

She inhaled the scent of bananas and walnuts. "Smells wonderful. I'd best stay away while it's baking, or I might be tempted to get into it before Rach gets home tomorrow."

Rachel home tomorrow, and the grand opening on the weekend. That would go well—it had to. Of course it would be a shame that Rachel couldn't make her special breakfasts, but Emma would serve hearty Amish meals instead and the guests would be delighted.

And once that was over, she could make plans to get back to work. They would need more help after she left, of course, but Emma's daughter-in-law seemed eager for the work, and she'd pay the salary herself, if necessary.

She glanced at Grams, wondering how she'd feel if Andrea inquired more closely into her finances. She'd opened up a little, but Andrea still didn't feel she had a good handle on how secure Grams was.

And then there was the other regret. Cal. Her mind

drifted toward the night they'd kissed, and she pulled it firmly back. There was no sense in thinking about what might have been. They both recognized the attraction and the caring, but the differences between them were just too great.

Still, she couldn't ignore that sense of loss.

"I'm just relieved we've had no further problems with prowlers," Grams said. "I'd hate to have our guests upset. Those lights were a fine idea."

Grams didn't know, of course, about the other incidents, and Andrea had no intention of telling her. There were too many possibilities for troublemakers—Levi, sneak thieves, teenagers intent on vandalism, even the holdouts in the community who were opposed to the decision to open the inn. It didn't really matter who it was, as long as it stopped.

"Andrea?" Grams was looking at her questioningly.

"Yes, I'm sure you're right. There's nothing more to worry about."

Grams reached across the table to touch her hand lightly. "Thanks to you. I don't know what we'd have done without you."

Andrea clasped her grandmother's hand, the fragility of fine bones under the skin making her aware again that Grams needed taking care of. "I loved doing it."

"You have so much business sense." Grams's eyes grew misty. "Just like your grandfather."

She wasn't sure she wanted to be compared to her grandfather, but she knew that to Grams it was a high compliment. "Thank you."

"I'm thinking it's time I turned my business affairs over to you. Nick has been very helpful, of course, but he's not family. You'll do it, won't you?"

For a moment she couldn't speak. If she'd needed anything to assure her that Grams thought of her as a competent adult, this would do it.

"Of course I will." She blinked back surprising moisture in her eyes. "I'd be honored."

"That is good." Emma used a spatula to get the last bit of batter into the pan and then smoothed the surface with a practiced swirl. "'There is a time to every purpose under Heaven.'" She quoted again the words she'd said earlier, and they seemed to resonate. "A time to turn things over to the younger generation. Eli and me, we still have plenty to do, but now it's our son's turn to manage."

"The Amish know how to do it right," Grams said, smiling. "They build the *daadi haus* for the older couple and turn the farm over to the next generation. Everyone has a role to fill."

"*Ja.*" Emma carried the oblong pan over to the old gas range that took up half of one wall. "It is good to know where you belong."

She bent over, cake pan in one hand, and pulled open the oven door with the other.

There was a loud whooshing sound. Before Andrea could move, flames shot out of the oven, right in Emma's face.

Cal sat beside Andrea on the patio wall, waiting. The paramedics were in the kitchen with Emma. So was her husband, Eli. He and Andrea had been relegated to the outside as unnecessary.

Levi stood next to the gray buggy that was pulled up in the driveway. He'd buried his face in the horse's mane, and once in a while his shoulders shook.

"Do you think I should attempt to comfort him?" Andrea said softly.

He shook his head. "I tried, just before you came out. It seemed to make him worse, so I gave up. He'll be all right as soon as he knows his mother is fine."

"Is she?" Andrea's lips trembled, and she pressed them together in a firm line.

He covered her hand with his where it lay on the stone wall between them, and the irrelevant thought passed through his mind that when she was gone, he wouldn't be able to look at this wall in the same way.

"I'm sure she will be." He hoped he sounded positive.

Her fingers moved slightly under his. "You didn't see. It was awful. Thank goodness Grams knew what to do. She had a wet towel on Emma's face before I'd even figured out what happened."

"I don't suppose you ever saw a gas oven blow out. She probably has. It used to be a fairly common accident, years ago. Since most of the Amish cook with gas, it still happens—did while I was staying out at the Zimmerman place, but luckily no one was hurt."

What about this time? He wasn't sure what he thought, not yet. He didn't want to believe someone had tampered with the stove, but it didn't do to take anything for granted.

"Tell me what happened."

Andrea's face tightened. "I don't want to go over it again."

"I don't suppose you do, but we have to figure out what caused this."

Her eyes met his, startled. "You think it wasn't an accident?"

"I don't know what I think, yet. That's why I want

to ask you a few questions." He was surprised to hear that lawyer's voice coming out of his mouth.

She took a breath, seeming to compose herself. "Emma was baking a cake. For Rachel's homecoming. I guess she'd been preheating the oven. Yes, I'm sure she had, because I remember seeing her turn it on." She shrugged. "There isn't anything else to tell. She opened the oven door to put the cake in, and the flames came out in her face." She shivered. "I hate to sound stupid, but what made it do that?"

"The pilot light was blown out—it had to be. The gas built up in the oven, and when the door was opened, that was all it took to ignite."

"It could have happened accidentally." She sounded as if she were trying to convince herself.

"I suppose so," he agreed. "When was the last time the oven was used?"

"Last night—no, I take that back, we didn't use it last night. It would have been in the morning yesterday, when Emma baked."

Something tingled at the back of his mind. "Why did you say last night?"

"Well, it's silly, really. Grams and I were laughing about it. Emma insists on leaving something cooked for our supper, and then I put it in the oven to heat. And she always asks, so I don't even dare to heat it in the microwave. Emma doesn't hold with microwaves."

"It might have been safer, this time."

She nodded. "Anyway, neither of us was very hungry last night, so we just had sandwiches. We were joking about who had to confess to Emma." Her voice shook again, and she turned her hand so that her palm was against his, clasping it tightly. "Cal, it had to be an accident. No one would do that deliberately."

"Maybe. But too many odd things have been happening for me to write them all off as coincidence."

The back door opened. The paramedics came out, carrying their gear, and headed for their truck. Then Eli emerged, supporting Emma, who held a wet dressing to her face. Levi gave an inarticulate cry and shambled toward them.

Eli caught him before he could grasp Emma in a bear hug, talking to him softly and urgently in the low German the Amish used among themselves. Levi nodded, touched his mother's sleeve, and then went to unhitch the horse.

Andrea approached, holding her hand out tentatively. "Emma, I'm so sorry. Are you all right?"

"Ja." Eli answered for her. "The glasses protected her eyes, praise God. Her face is painful, but it will heal."

Emma came from behind the dressing for a moment, her skin red and shiny. "You take care of your grandmother, now. And my cake—"

"Don't start worrying about the cake. You can make another one for Rachel when you're completely recovered."

They watched as Eli and Levi handed her up carefully into the buggy. Levi took the reins.

"I'll come by later to see how you are," Andrea called as the buggy creaked slowly away.

She looked as if she wanted to go after them, do something to make this better. He touched her arm.

"Maybe we'd better check on Katherine."

"Yes, of course." She ran her fingers through her

hair. "I'm beginning to think I'm not very good in an emergency."

"You'll do." He followed her into the house, wondering. If this had been deliberate—but there wouldn't be any way to prove it. Still, he wanted a look at the stove.

He got his chance almost immediately, when Andrea, seeing how shaken Katherine was, took her grandmother upstairs to lie down. He waited until they'd disappeared up the steps and then opened the oven door.

When Andrea came back a few minutes later, he was still bending over the open door.

"Did you find anything?"

He shrugged. "Only how easy it would be to blow out the pilot. You'd better have someone come from the gas company to check it out, but I don't think he'll find anything wrong."

He closed the door. Andrea sagged against the kitchen counter, as if her bones had gone limp.

"Rachel comes home tomorrow. The first guests arrive on Saturday, and now Emma is out of action. What could anyone have to gain by tampering with the stove?"

He shrugged. "Someone might have thought it would delay the opening."

"Who would care?" She flung her hands out in frustration.

"Margaret cares. She doesn't want the competition. And there are those who don't want anything to draw more tourists here."

She shook her head at that. "I can't believe anyone would hurt Emma for such a reason."

He hesitated, but she had to know. "It might not have been aimed at Emma."

She blinked. "What do you mean?"

"If anyone knew that you usually heated up supper, the target might have been you."

"But—how would they know? And even if one of us mentioned it, how could they be sure Emma wouldn't take it into her head to bake something?"

He frowned. "That's the thing. Yesterday afternoon, when I came in, I tried the side door, but it was locked. When we came down from the attic, Emma had already gone, but she always uses the back door. I found the side door was not only unlocked, but ajar."

"You mean someone might have come in then and tampered with the stove."

He couldn't tell whether she accepted it or not. "Could have. Could have had a good idea you'd be the next to use it. Could have been a lot of things, but there's no proof."

"No." Her face was pale. "There's not remotely enough to take to the police."

"Maybe I'm being overly suspicious. I hope so. But I don't like it."

"Neither do I." She rubbed her forehead. "It has to be just an accident. There's an innocent explanation for all of this, surely."

"I hope so." He wanted to say he'd protect her, but he didn't know if he could. And he certainly didn't have that right. He reached out to touch her cheek, the caress lingering longer than he intended.

"Take care of yourself, Andrea. Call me if anything, anything at all, strikes you as odd."

"I will."

But she was probably thinking the same thing he was. How did you protect yourself against something as amorphous as this?

"No, thank you, it's wonderful, but I can't eat another bite." Andrea tried to soften the refusal with a smile. Nancy Zook, wife of Eli and Emma's son Samuel, held a cherry pie in one hand and a peach pie in the other. After the huge serving of Schnitz un Knepp— ham hock, dried apples and dumplings—she'd thought she'd never eat again, but Nancy had urged a sliver of pie on her.

"Ah, it's nothing. Soon it will be time to make the strawberry preserves. We will send some over to you." Nancy put the pies down on the table and turned to offer seconds to the rest of the Zook family—Eli, Samuel, their five children and Levi.

Emma was keeping to her bed for the evening, but when Andrea had slipped over to the attached *daadi haus* to see her, she'd been insistent that she'd be back at work soon. Given the painful-looking blisters on her face, Andrea doubted it.

She'd walked over to the Zook farm late in the afternoon to bring get-well wishes and roses from her grandmother. The insistence that she stay to supper had been so strong that she couldn't have refused without insult, especially after they learned that Grams was having supper at the hospital with Rachel.

The room looked much like any farmhouse kitchen, with its wooden cabinets and linoleum floor. A wooden china closet held special dishes. One difference was that the only wall decoration was a large calendar featuring a picture of kittens in a basket. In most Old Order

Amish communities, only such a useful picture could be placed on the wall.

She sipped strong coffee, glancing around the long, rectangular table with its covering of checkered oil-cloth. The children chattered amongst themselves softly, mindful of having an English guest. With their round blue eyes and blond hair, the girls in braids, the boys bowl-cut, they looked very alike.

Eli and Samuel talked about the next day's work. Levi sat silent, looking down at his pie. His clean-shaven face was unusual for an Amish adult male, but the beard was a sign of marriage. His soft round cheeks were like those of the children.

Had the figure in the rain had a beard? She wasn't sure. She didn't want to think it, but nothing that had been done would be beyond Levi's capabilities.

She glanced at the gas range. He'd know about the pilot light. But he'd never hurt his mother. That was a ridiculous thought.

A small voice at the back of her mind commented that he might have expected it to be her. All of the Zook family would know about the supper arrangements.

She wanted to reject the idea, but she couldn't. Levi seemed so uneasy with her presence at the table. He'd sent her only one startled glance when she first sat down, his blue eyes as wide as those of a frightened deer, and since then he'd kept his gaze fixed firmly on his plate, showing her only the top of his blond head.

A low rumble of thunder had all of them looking to-ward the windows.

"Ach, a storm is coming yet." Eli pushed his chair back. "We must get the outside chores done quickly."

The children scurried from the table, diving toward the door in their eagerness to be first out.

"I'd better leave if I don't want to get soaked on the way home." Andrea rose and held out her hand to Nancy. "Thank you so much for the wonderful meal."

"It's nothing." Nancy bobbed her head in a formal little gesture. "Would you be wanting Levi to walk you back?"

"No." That came too quickly. "I'm sure he has work to do. I'll be fine, but I'd better run."

She hurried out the back door, waving to the children as she headed for the path that went around the pond and through a small woodlot before coming out behind the barn where Cal had his shop.

Thunder rumbled again, closer now. It had been foolish not to bring a jacket, with afternoon thunderstorms forecast. Still, if she hurried, she could probably beat the rain home.

The breeze picked up, ruffling the surface of the pond and making the tall ferns that bordered it sway and dance. The scent of rain was in the air, and lightning flashed along the horizon. The distant farms, each marked by twin silos, seemed to wait for the rain.

She scurried past the pond with a fleeting memory of sailing homemade boats on it with the Zook children. The path plunged between the trees, and it was suddenly dark. She slowed, watching the path, having no desire to trip on a tree root and go sprawling.

A trailing blackberry bramble caught at her slacks, then tugged the laces of her sneakers, pulling one free of its knot. She bent, quickly retying it. Quiet—it was so quiet here. Even the birds must have taken shelter from the coming storm.

But as she rose, a sound froze her in place. Was that a footstep, somewhere behind her?

She looked back, seeing nothing, but the undergrowth was thick enough to hide a figure unless it was close. Too close.

That thought got her feet moving again. Hurry. Don't think about the possibility of someone behind you. Think about the fact that the last thing Cal told you was to be careful. Is this being careful?

Cal. She yanked out her cell phone. Better to risk feeling foolish than get into trouble. She could still feel those strong hands that pushed her into the toolshed.

Cal answered almost at once.

"It's Andrea. I'm on the path coming back from Zook's farm. Maybe I'm being silly, but I thought I heard someone behind me."

"I'm on my way." The connection clicked off.

She'd stopped long enough to make the call, and now the sound was closer. The bushes rustled as if a body forced its way through them.

Could be a deer. But even as she thought the words she started to run, feet thudding on the path, instinct telling her to flee like a frightened animal.

Around the twists in the path, careful, careful, don't trip. If you fall, he could be on you in a moment.

The sounds behind her were louder now, as if the follower had given up any need for secrecy. She didn't dare look behind her. To lose even a second could allow him to catch up.

Lightning flashed, close now, and the boom of thunder assaulted her ears. She was nearly out of the woods, just a little farther...

She spurted into the open like a cork from a bottle,

and as she did the heavens opened. In an instant she was drenched and gasping as if she'd been shoved into a cold shower.

Don't stop, don't stop...

And then she saw Cal running toward her. Relief swept over her. She was safe.

Chapter 12

Cal put another small log on the fire he'd started in his fireplace and watched flames shoot up around it. Maybe the fire would warm and comfort Andrea. It was probably better than putting his arms around her, which was his instinctive reaction.

He put the poker back in the rack, glancing toward her. She sat on the sofa, wearing one of his flannel shirts, towel-drying her hair. She looked vulnerable, which made it even harder to keep his distance.

He had to find a way to help her, but he had to do it without wrecking the hard-won peace he'd found since he'd come here. Getting emotionally involved with a woman who couldn't wait to get away from this life would be a mistake. So would reverting to acting and thinking like a lawyer.

"Thanks." Andrea looked up at him, producing a

faint smile. "For the fire and the hot chocolate. I've already had enough coffee to keep me up half the night."

He sat down in the armchair, a careful distance from her. "Can you tell me about it now?"

"There's not much to tell." She frowned, absently toweling the damp hair that clung to her neck. "I'd gone over to see how Emma was, and Nancy insisted I stay for supper. When we noticed the storm coming up, they all scattered to do their chores, and I headed down the path. I'd just reached the woods when I thought I heard someone behind me."

"Back up a little. Did you see where Levi was when you left?"

"I'm not sure. Nancy offered to have him walk me back, but I said no." Her gaze met his. "I'm a little ashamed of that. I'm letting suspicion make a difference in how I treat people. That's not right."

"Maybe so, but it's probably unavoidable. So you don't know where he went at that point?"

"I think he headed for the barn with the boys, but I'm not positive, but just because I was at Zook's farm, that doesn't mean Levi was the one who followed me."

"No, but it's more probable than that someone else was hanging around, watching you."

He could see the shiver that went through her at the suggestion, and regretted it. But somehow they had to get to the bottom of this.

"So you never actually saw the person who followed you."

"No. Just heard him. At first I thought it was an animal, but once I started to run—" She wrapped her arms around her, as if comforting herself, and the too-long sleeves of the shirt flopped over her hands. "I'm sure what I heard was a person."

"I didn't see him, either." He frowned. What could anyone hope to gain by such a stunt?

Andrea shoved her hair back from her face. "That doesn't mean he wasn't there." Her voice was tart.

"I didn't mean that. I'm trying not to think like a lawyer, but old habits die hard." He'd thought he had it licked before Andrea came, involving him in her problems.

That wasn't fair. The trouble had already been here, but something about Andrea's arrival seemed to have brought it out.

"It's not that bad to think like an attorney, is it? After all, you are one."

"I'm a carpenter," he said. "Any resemblance to the person I used to be is a mistake."

A slight frown wrinkled her brows. "I can understand your grief and guilt. But do you think that necessarily means you can't be an attorney?"

His turn to frown. "You think I'm wasting my life here. Is that it? Believe me, I've gained far more than I lost in making the change. Peace. A new relationship with God." He paused, his momentary irritation dissolving. "In my old life, I'd have been embarrassed if someone brought up God in conversation. Am I embarrassing you?"

"No." Her face softened. "Maybe it's the impact of this place. I've thought more about faith since I came back than I had in the past year. Feeling—I don't know. Tugged back, I guess."

"I'm glad." He reached across the space between them to take her hand. Her fingers were cold, and he tried to warm them with his. "Even when you go away…"

He stopped. He didn't want her to leave. That was the truth, however irrational it might be. She wouldn't stay. Her life was elsewhere.

"When I leave—"

Her eyes met his, and he saw in them exactly what he felt. Longing. Tenderness. Regret.

Be careful. You're not going to kiss her again. It would be a mistake, getting entangled with someone who is determined to leave.

He rose, moving to the fireplace and leaning on the mantel. Take himself out of range.

"As far as this incident is concerned…" He frowned, trying to concentrate on the problem. "Most likely the person who followed you was Levi, simply because no one else could have known you were there. But if stopping the inn from opening is the object of all this harassment, why would he care?"

"I suppose that must be the motive—at least I can't think of any other reasonable hypothesis." She frowned. "It still seems overly dramatic to think that any of these solid, law-abiding Pennsylvania Dutchmen would resort to trying to scare me away just to eliminate another B and B."

"None of it is very logical." He had to get a handle on some aspect of the situation. He might have a better chance of doing that if his heart didn't perform such peculiar acrobatics whenever he looked at Andrea.

"There's still nothing to take to the police. I can just imagine their reaction to my story of being followed coming back from the Zook farm."

"They wouldn't be impressed, I'm afraid." They'd

be polite, of course, but what could they do? It wasn't as if she'd been attacked. That thought sent a coldness settling deep inside him. The incident with the stove was an attack, but he couldn't prove it, or that she had been the target.

Andrea glanced at her watch and then shot to her feet. "Look at the time. I have to get home before Grams. I can't let her see me like this."

"You look pretty good to me." He pushed away from the mantel. "Sort of casually disheveled."

"I look as if I've been dragged through a knothole," she said tartly. She started for the door.

He followed her. "I'll walk you back."

"You don't need—"

"I'll walk you back," he repeated firmly, opening the door. "No more wandering around alone, okay?"

He thought she'd flare up at that, but she just nodded. "I'll take the dog with me everywhere I go. He might not be the brightest of creatures, but at least he'll make noise."

He wanted to offer himself instead of the dog, but that wouldn't be wise, not when just being within six feet of her made him want to kiss her. Like now.

He yanked the door open. The rain had subsided to a faint drizzle. "You're right. We'd better go."

Before he gave in to the powerful need to have her in his arms.

"Just grate the cheese." Laughter filled Rachel's voice as she sat in her wheelchair in the kitchen, the table pushed aside to give her more room. "Go on, use the grater. It won't bite you."

"I'm not so sure." Andrea gingerly lifted the metal

grater, wary of its sharp teeth. Still, anything that had Rachel laughing had to be good.

Afternoon sun streamed through the kitchen windows, but she was making a breakfast frittata. At least, she was attempting to. She began grating the cheese into the earthenware bowl Rachel had chosen, trying to keep her fingers out of reach of the grater's teeth.

"You really think I can prepare a breakfast that will satisfy the guests." She frowned. "Make that three breakfasts, if Emma doesn't come back until next week."

"Look at it this way," Rachel said. "You're not so much cooking as being my hands. I'm really cooking. You're following directions."

The cheese stuck on the grater, and she gave it a shove. The bowl tipped, the grater flew up, and cheese sprinkled like snowflakes over the tile floor.

She looked at Rachel. "Your hands just made a mess."

Rachel's lips twitched. Then, as if she couldn't hold it back, she began to laugh.

Andrea glared, but an irrepressible chuckle rose in her throat.

"Go ahead, laugh. I never claimed to be able to cook. That's your department. I eat out or open a frozen dinner, and my cheese comes already grated in a bag."

"I'm sorry." Rachel's green eyes, so like her own, brimmed with laughter. "It's just that you're so competent on the computer and all thumbs in the kitchen."

"It's a good thing there's one area of my life that's under control."

But was it? The computer represented the business world to her, and how could she know what was happening back at the office when she was stuck here? Emailing her assistant wasn't the same as being there, especially when that assistant had her eyes on Andrea's job.

"I'd be just as out of place in your office," Rachel said. "Here, hand me the bowl. Maybe I can set it in my lap and do the grating."

"No, I'm determined now. I will learn how to do this." She began again, careful to keep the bowl steady. "After all, you'll have to learn how to keep the reservations on the computer after I leave. I'll get to laugh at you then."

"Did you really get all that computerized?" Rachel shook her head. "I kept putting off trying, because it looked so hard."

"It'll be much easier once you get used to it. Much of your traffic will come from the Web site I started, especially when we get some more pictures up. Right now I just have the basics." That was one good thing accomplished, and the computer really would make running the inn easier, if she could get Rachel in the habit of using it.

"I'm astonished. You've done more in two weeks than I did in six months."

She must be getting more sensitive, because she detected immediately the note in Rachel's voice that said she was comparing herself unfavorably with her big sister.

"That's nonsense," she said firmly. "The renovations are all credited to you, and as for the garden…" She glanced out the kitchen window at the borders filled with color. "The guests will love looking at that while they have their breakfast. Always assuming I manage to make anything edible."

"You'll be fine," Rachel said. "You just have to do one main hot dish for each day. We'll serve fresh fruit cups, that special Amish-recipe granola that Grams gets from the farmer's market, and the breads and coffee cakes that Nancy offered to make. It'll be fine."

"Thank goodness for Nancy. She promised us Moravian Sugar Cakes for the first morning. I'll gain a pound just smelling them." She looked down in surprise, realizing she'd actually grated the entire block of cheese without getting any bloody knuckles. "We have to remember to bring flowers in to put on the tables, too."

Rachel nodded, turning the chair so that she could see out the screen door toward the garden. "I wish I'd been able to get the gazebo moved. That was one thing I intended that I didn't get to."

"Move the gazebo?" Andrea glanced out at the white wooden structure with its lacy gingerbread trim. "Why?"

Rachel shook her head. "You really don't have an eye for a garden, do you? It's in quite the wrong place, where it doesn't have a view. It makes the garden look crowded, instead of serving as an accent piece."

"I'll take your word for it." She wiped her hands on a tea towel. "What do I do next?"

Before Rachel could answer, the telephone rang.

Rachel picked it up. "Three Sisters Inn," she said, a note of pride in her voice. But a moment later her face had paled, and she looked at Andrea with panic in her eyes.

"Just a moment, please." She covered the receiver with her hand. "It's Mr. Elliot—has a reservation for the weekend, an anniversary surprise for his wife. He claims he received an e-mail from us, canceling, saying we aren't going to be open yet. You didn't—"

"Of course not." For a moment she stared at her sister, speculations running wildly through her mind. Then she reached for the phone. Redeem the situation first, if she could, and figure out where the blame lay later.

"Mr. Elliot?" It was her businesswoman voice, calm, assured, in control. "I'm terribly sorry about this misunderstanding, but we certainly didn't cancel your reservation."

"You didn't send this email?" He sounded suspicious.

"No, sir, we didn't. My sister has been hospitalized, and perhaps something went out without our knowledge." That made it sound as if they had a vast staff capable of making such an error.

"Seems a sloppy way to run an inn," he muttered, but the anger had gone out of his voice. "So we're still on for the weekend."

"Yes, indeed." She infused her voice with warmth, even as her mind seethed with possibilities. "And we'll provide a very special anniversary cake to surprise your wife. Don't worry about a thing."

When she finally hung up, her hand was shaking.

Rachel stared at her. "They're still coming?"

"Yes. But it's a good thing he was angry enough to want to blow up at us, or we'd never have known."

"The other guests—" Rachel's eyes darkened with concern.

"I'll get the list and call them right away." She hurried into the library, headed for the computer, hearing the wheels of Rachel's chair behind her.

"Maybe we can reach them before they have a chance

to make other plans." Rachel sounded as if she were clinging hard to hope.

"Cross your fingers." Andrea paused. "The person who planned this overreached herself. If she'd waited until the last minute, we'd probably have been sitting high and dry with no guests."

"She?"

"She. I can't prove it, but I know perfectly well who did this."

"It had to be Margaret. She was in the library the other day with access to the computer. She even said something to me Sunday about hearing we wouldn't be able to open in time. But what can I do? There's no way to prove it."

Andrea had spotted Cal making his nightly rounds with a flashlight and called him in. Grams and Rachel had gone to bed early, and the house was quiet.

They sat on the sofa in the old summer kitchen that still bore remnants of the playroom it had been when she and her sisters had lived in the house. Games were stacked on the shelves to the right of the fireplace, and if she opened the closet, she'd find a few toys that Grams hadn't wanted to give away.

Cal frowned, staring absently at the cavernous fireplace. "You could bring a civil suit against her, but that would be using a bazooka to rid the house of mosquitoes."

"Not worthwhile, obviously, but I hate letting her get away with it. And the nerve of her—she just walked in the library when we were upstairs, calmly accessed the reservation records on my computer, and sent the emails."

He glanced at her. "The computer was on?"

"Don't remind me of how easy I made it for her. I not only had it on, it was open to the reservations. Well, it's password protected now, but it certainly got us off to a bad start."

"Did you lose any of the reservations?"

"Only one. The others consented to rebook after I'd groveled a bit."

That surprised a smile out of him. "I didn't think you knew how to do that."

"That's a lesson I learned early in my career. If there's a problem, don't waste time defending yourself. Just fix it."

"Not a bad philosophy. I'll bet you didn't know running a B and B would have so much in common with your real life."

His words were a reminder that her time here was coming to an end. She fought to ignore the hollow feeling in the pit of her stomach.

"Anyway, I'm absolutely certain Margaret's guilty of monkeying with the computer, but would she prowl around at night or dress up in Amish clothes to stand out in the rain? I don't think so."

"Anyone with such a fund of insincerity can't be trusted, but I'm inclined to agree with you about that. She'd be afraid of being caught in an embarrassing position."

"I'd like to catch her at something." She shook her head. "That sounds vengeful, doesn't it? Grams would be ashamed of me. It's just that we've all worked so hard—"

"I know." He squeezed her hand. "Are you ready for guests to arrive on Saturday?"

"I think we're in good shape, but I'm certainly glad Grams didn't tell them they could arrive Friday night. Rachel's been walking me through cooking the breakfast meals. We actually ate my artichoke and sausage frittata for supper, and it wasn't half-bad. And Nancy Zook is providing all the baked goods we need."

He nodded. "I heard from Eli that she's agreed to help out some, at least until Rachel's on her feet again."

"I expect I'll be coming back on weekends, at least through the busy season."

Did that sound as if she were asking for something—some hint of where they stood? She hated having things unresolved.

"I'm glad we'll still get to see you." His tone was as neutral and friendly as if he spoke to Eli Zook.

Maybe that answered the question in her mind. Cal recognized, as she did, that the differences between them were too fundamental. The hole in her midsection seemed to deepen.

Ridiculous. She'd only known him for weeks. But when she looked at him, she realized that wasn't true. Maybe in chronological terms they hadn't known each other long, but she'd met him at a time when her emotions were stretched to the limit and her normal barriers suspended.

And since then she'd relied on him in a way that startled her when she looked at it rationally. Did she have anyone else, even back in Philadelphia, that she would turn to for help as naturally as she'd turned to him?

No. She didn't. And that was a sad commentary on the quality of her life.

Cal apparently wasn't engaging in any deep thoughts

over the prospect of her leaving. He was frowning toward the small window in the side wall.

"Shouldn't we be able to see the reflection of the garden lights from here?"

She followed the direction of his gaze, vague unease stirring. "Yes. I'm sure I could see the glow the last time I looked that way."

Cal rose, walking quickly toward the hallway and the back door. She followed. They stopped at the door, peering out at the garden, which was perfectly dark.

"Something's happened to the lights." She couldn't erase the apprehension in her voice.

"It may not be anything major." Cal opened the door, switching on his flashlight. "I connected the new lights to the fuse box in the toolshed. Could have blown a fuse, I guess. I'll go check." He stepped out onto the patio.

"Be careful."

Already at the edge of the patio, he turned to smile at her. "I always am." He lifted the flashlight in a little salute, and then stepped off the flagstones. In an instant he was swallowed up by the dark.

She clutched the door frame, hands cold. Irrational, to be worried over something so simple, but then, plenty of irrational things had been happening. She yanked open the door and stepped outside, driven by some inner compulsion.

The beam of his flashlight was the only clue to Cal's location, halfway to the toolshed. She should have gone with him. She could have held the light while he checked the fuses.

The stillness was shattered by an engine's roar. Lights blazed, slicing through the darkness. She whirled. Something barreled from behind the garage—

something that surged across the grass, sound and light paralyzing her.

Cal. Cal was pinned in the powerful twin headlight beams. Before she could move the massive shape rocketed across the garden, straight toward Cal.

Screaming his name, she darted forward. The vehicle cut between them with a deafening roar. She couldn't see—the light from Cal's torch was gone. Where was he?

Chapter 13

Cal dived away from the oncoming lights, instinct taking over from thought. The roar of the motor deafened him. Something struck his head, and he slammed into the ground.

He couldn't breathe, couldn't think, facedown in the damp grass. He gasped in a gulp of cool air, shaking his head and wincing at the pain.

Think. Look. Try to identify the car.

No, truck—a four-by-four, by the sound of it. He shoved up onto his knees. The vehicle careened through the garden, ripping up flower beds, smashing the birdbath.

He forced his brain to work. It would be gone in an instant. He had to try and identify it. No license plate to be seen—the rear lights were blacked out. He fought the urge to sink back down on the grass, trying to clear his head. It didn't seem to work. Someone was shouting his name.

Andrea. She flew toward him, barreled into him. He winced and would have toppled over but for the hard grasp of her hands.

"You're all right—I thought you were hit." Her fingers clutched at him, and her voice caught on a sob.

He touched his forehead and felt the stickiness of blood, warm on his palm. He leaned on her, aware of the roar of the truck's engine. If he could get a good look at it before it disappeared around the building...

The dark shape had reached the pond. It turned, wheels spinning in the mud left from yesterday's rain. He could make out the shape, not the color. The driver would cut off down the lane....

He didn't. He spun, straightened, and bucketed straight toward them.

He clutched Andrea. Closest shelter, no time—

"Run! The patio—"

Clutching each other, stumbling a little, they ran toward the patio. He forced his feet to slog as if through quicksand, the truck was coming fast, they weren't going to make it, Andrea—

He shoved her with every bit of strength, flinging her toward the stone patio wall. Threw himself forward, the truck so close he felt the breath of the engine. Landed hard again, pain ricocheting through his body.

Metal shrieked as the truck sideswiped the patio wall, scattering stones. He struggled, trying to get to his feet, dazed, left wrist throbbing. Strength knocked out of him. If the truck came back, he was a sitting duck....

Then Andrea grabbed him, pulling him onto the patio, dragging him to safety. The truck made a last defiant pass through the flower beds, charged past the garage, clipping it, and roared off down the dark country road, disappearing into the trees.

Andrea clutched him, her breath coming in ragged gasps. "Are you hurt?"

He shook his head, wincing at the pain. "You…"

It was more important than anything to know that she was safe, but he couldn't seem to form a question.

He tried to focus on her face, white and strained in the circle of light from the door. Katherine stood in the doorway, saying something he couldn't make out, Rachel behind her in the chair.

He had to reassure them. He staggered a step toward them and collapsed onto the flagstones.

"I'm not going to the hospital. I'm fine." Cal might look pale and shaken, but his voice was as firm as always.

Andrea found she could breathe. He'd be all right. That terrible moment when she thought the truck had hit him—she could stop thinking about it now.

But she couldn't kid herself about her feelings for him any longer. That brief instant when she'd thought he was gone had been a lightning flash that seared heart and soul, showing her exactly how much she cared.

The paramedic leaned on the back of a kitchen chair, looking at him doubtfully. "Might be a good idea to let the docs check out that wrist."

"It's a sprain." He cradled his left wrist in his other hand. "The wrap is all I need."

She'd urge him to let them take him to the hospital, but she knew that was futile. She wrapped her fingers around the mug of coffee someone had thrust into her hands, wondering how long it would take for the shaking to stop.

Grams's kitchen was crowded with paramedics and police, but for the first time in her memory, Grams seemed to have given up the reins of hospitality. She sat at the end of the table, robe knotted tightly around her, her face gray and drawn.

Love and fear clutched at Andrea's heart. Grams had to be protected, and she was doing a lousy job of it.

Please, Father, show me what to do. I have to take care of them, and I'm afraid I can't.

The paramedics, apparently giving up on Cal, began packing up their kits, leaving the field to the police.

There were two of them this time. The young patrolman who'd come before stood awkwardly by the door, and the township chief sat at the table. Obviously the authorities took this seriously. As they should. Cal could have been killed.

The chief cleared his throat, gathering their attention. Zachary Burkhalter, he'd introduced himself—tall, lean, with sandy hair and a stolid, strong-boned face. He must be about Cal's age, but he wore an air that said he'd seen it all and nothing could surprise him.

"Maybe you could just go over the whole thing for me, Mr. Burke. Anything you saw or heard might help."

Cal shoved his good hand through his hair, disturbing a tuft of grass that fluttered to the table. She probably had her own share of debris, and she thought longingly of a hot shower.

"I didn't see much. Seemed like it took forever, but it probably wasn't more than a couple of minutes at most. We noticed the outside lights had gone off. I thought it was a fuse, started across toward the toolshed where the box is. The four-by-four was behind the garage, out of sight."

She nodded, agreeing, and the chief's gaze turned to her instantly. Gray eyes, cold as flint.

"You agree with that, Ms. Hampton?"

"Yes. I saw the truck come out from behind the garage. To be exact, I heard it, saw the lights. It crossed the back lawn to the pond, turned around and came back, went past the garage again and down Crossings Road. It took less than five minutes, certainly."

And they'd fought for their lives the whole time.

"Can you identify the driver?" His gaze swiveled back to Cal.

"Too dark without the security lights. As Ms. Hampton said, they'd just gone off."

"That ever happen before?"

"No." Cal's voice was level. "It hadn't."

She knew what he was thinking. Someone could have tampered with the fuse box. Would they have had time to do that and get back to the truck before she and Cal went outside? She wasn't sure, but she couldn't say how long the lights had been off.

"And the truck?" Burkhalter obviously wanted a description they couldn't give.

"The rear lights of the vehicle had been blacked out somehow. It was a four-by-four, some dark color—that's about all I could see." Cal was probably berating himself that he didn't get a better look.

Burkhalter nodded. "We've found it, as a matter of fact."

Cal's brows shot up. "That was fast work, Chief."

"Abandoned down Crossings Road, keys missing,

scrapes along the fender from hitting the wall. The back lights had been broken."

"Whose is it?" The question burst out of her mouth. If they knew who was responsible...

Burkhalter's gaze gave nothing away. "Belongs to Bob Duckett. Easy enough for someone to take it— he leaves the garage door standing open and the keys hanging on a hook."

Of course he would. Half the township did that, probably, thinking this place was as safe as it had been fifty years ago.

"Bob Duckett wouldn't do anything like this." Grams finally spoke, her voice thin and reedy.

"No, we're sure he didn't." Burkhalter's tone softened for Grams. Then he looked back at her, and the softness disappeared. "You reported an earlier incident, Ms. Hampton?"

"Yes." She glanced toward the patrolman. "We had a prowler."

"This was considerably uglier than prowling."

She glanced toward Rachel, shaken by the bereft look on her face. Rachel had expended hours of work and loving care on the garden, only to have it devastated in a matter of minutes.

"You have any idea who might want to do this?" He glanced around the table, aiming the question at all of them.

Grams straightened, clasping her hands together. "No one could possibly have anything against us, Chief Burkhalter."

Andrea moved slightly, and Burkhalter was on to it at once. "You don't agree?"

She was conscious of her grandmother's strong will,

demanding that she be silent. Well, this once, Grams wouldn't get her way.

"There are people who are opposed to another bed-and-breakfast opening here," she said carefully.

"What people?" Burkhalter wouldn't be content with evasion.

She had to ignore Grams's frown. "Margaret Allen, for one. And I understand Herbert Rush and some of the other old-timers don't like the idea."

"It's ridiculous to think they'd do this."

Grams's tone told her she'd be hearing about this for a while. Grams couldn't imagine anyone she knew stealing a four-by-four to drive it through the grounds, but someone had.

She shivered a little, her gaze meeting Cal's. *Do I say anything about Levi? Surely he couldn't be involved. He doesn't drive, for one thing.*

Cal cradled his left hand, his expression giving nothing away. A bruise was darkening on his forehead. Her heart twisted.

"Could have been teenagers," Burkhalter said. "Hearing their elders talk about the inn, deciding to do something about it. Clever enough, though, for him, or them, to put the vehicle behind the garage while they tampered with the lights. No one would see it there unless they were driving down Crossings Road, and likely enough not even then."

And no one was likely to be going down Crossings Road at this hour. It led to several Amish farms, but they were probably dark and quiet by this time.

"I trust you're not going to just dismiss this as casual vandalism." Rachel spoke for the first time.

"No, ma'am." Burkhalter's gaze lingered on Rachel for a moment, but Andrea found it impossible to read. "We won't do that." His glance shifted, sweeping around the table. "Anyone have anything else to add?"

Someone stood outside the house one night. Someone might have pushed me into a closet. Someone probably followed me back from the Zook farm yesterday. Someone—Margaret, for choice—tampered with our reservations. There were good reasons for saying none of those things.

"We don't know anything else." Grams's voice had regained some of its command. "Thank you for coming."

Burkhalter rose. "We'll be in touch." He jerked his head to the patrolman, who followed him out the door.

Grams waited until the outer door closed behind them. She stood, pulling her dignity around her like a robe. "Cal, you must stay in the house tonight. Come along, I'll show you to a room. Andrea, please help Rachel back to bed."

She was too tired to argue. Besides, if she did have a chance to speak to Cal privately, what could she say? Her feelings were rubbed too raw to have a hope of hiding them. Maybe it was better this way.

Andrea walked into the breakfast room the next morning, wincing as the bright sunlight hit her face. The French doors stood open, and Rachel sat in her wheelchair on the patio.

She walked outside and put her hand on her sister's shoulder in mute sympathy. Rachel reached up to squeeze it.

"Stupid to cry over a garden." Rachel dashed tears away with the back of her hand. "It's just—"

"It was beautiful, and you and Grams made it." Andrea finished the thought, her stomach twisting as she looked at the damage. Dead or dying flowers lay with their roots exposed, and deep ruts cut through the lawn. The birdbath was nothing but scattered pieces, and the patio wall where she and Cal had sat bore a raw, jagged scar where stones had been knocked out. The only thing that hadn't been hit was the gazebo, probably because it stood off to one side.

"It's hard to believe that much damage could be done in a few minutes." Something quivered inside her. It could have been worse, much worse. It could have been Cal or her lying broken on the lawn.

"I am so furious." Rachel pounded her fists against the arms of the wheelchair. "If I could get my hands on the person who did this, I'd show him how it feels to be torn up by the roots."

The fury was so counter to Rachel's personality that Andrea was almost surprised into a laugh. Rachel was a nurturer, yet when something under her care was hurt, she could turn into a mother lion. "Maybe it's a good thing we don't know, then. I'd hate to see my little sister arrested for assault."

"It might be better," Rachel said darkly. "Then I wouldn't have to see the guests' faces. They'll be here the day after tomorrow, Dree. What are we going to do?" The last words came out almost as a wail.

"We're not going to waste time on anger." She had to give Rachel something to focus on other than the fury that could give way, too easily, to helplessness. "You make a list of what you want, and I'll head out to the nursery first thing. I'll spend the rest of the day putting new plants in. They'll at least last while the guests are here."

Rachel's brows lifted. "You? When was the last time you dug in the dirt?"

"Probably when I left the sandbox stage, but you'll tell me what to do. Look, I know it won't be the same—"

"What about the wall? And the lawn, and the birdbath? It would take an army to get things in shape by Saturday."

Andrea grabbed the chair and turned Rachel to face her. "Look, this is no time to give up. Now stop acting like a baby and go make that list."

"You stop being so bossy." Rachel glared at her for an instant, and then her lips began to quiver. "Um, remind me how old we are again?"

Laughter bubbled up, erasing her annoyance. "About ten and twelve, I think." She gave the chair a shove. "Go on, write the list. We'll make this work. I promise."

Smiling, Rachel wheeled herself through the doorway.

"Rach?"

She turned.

"Has anyone checked on Cal this morning?" She forced the question to sound casual.

"Grams said he was dressed and gone an hour ago," Rachel said. "I'll get some coffee started while I make up the list." At least she looked more herself as she wheeled toward the kitchen.

Andrea walked to the patio wall and surveyed the damage. She might be able to plant flowers, given enough instruction, but this she couldn't fix. Disappointment filtered through her at Cal's absence. She'd expected that today, of all times, he'd be here to help.

Well, he had a business to run. Once that would have been a guaranteed excuse, at least from her perspective. She'd changed, if all she could think was that he should be here.

Stepping over the patio wall, she began to gather the stones that were scattered across the grass. Maybe she couldn't fix the wall, but she could make the area look a little neater.

The stones proved far heavier than she expected. She straightened her back, frowning at one particularly stubborn one.

"Take it easy." Cal's voice spun her around. "I'll do that." The bag he carried in one arm thudded against the wall.

"I thought you left." Did she sound accusing?

"I went to get cement mix to repair the wall." He lifted his eyebrows. "Not very complimentary that you thought I'd desert you this morning."

She wasn't sure what to say to that. "Well, you do have a business to take care of."

"Friends come first," he said shortly.

Are we friends, Cal? What would he say if she blurted that out? She wasn't sure she even wanted to hear the answer.

Movement beyond him on the lane distracted her. "What on earth…?"

Cal turned. "Looks like the Zook family think friends come first, too."

Her breath caught, and tears welled in her eyes. Three buggies came down the lane, packed with people, and a large farm wagon bore so many flowers that it looked like a float in the homecoming parade.

She could only stand and stare for a moment. And then she bolted toward the house.

"Rachel! Rachel, come here this minute! You're not going to believe this!"

Andrea sat back on her heels, admiring the snapdragons she'd just succeeded in planting with Nancy's help.

"Looks good already." Nancy, Emma's daughter-in-law, smiled, brushing a strand of dark hair back into the neat coil under her prayer cap. "We brought enough flowers, I think."

She nodded. They'd certainly brought enough help. Eli and Cal fitted the last stone into place on the wall, while Nancy's small son stood by holding the bucket with cement. Nancy's husband and another Amish man, their red shirts a bright contrast to black trousers, used a lawn roller to smooth out the ruts. The grass seemed to spring into place in their wake. And the flowers...

"You must have gotten up at dawn to dig all of these plants to bring. We can't thank you enough for this."

"We always get up at dawn," Nancy said. "This is just being neighborly."

All along the flower border figures knelt, setting out new plants to replace the ruined ones. Children ran back and forth, fetching and carrying, the girls with bonnet strings streaming, the boys small replicas of the men.

Funny. When she'd spread the Sunshine and Shadows quilt over her bed this morning, she'd felt that they were locked into a dark stripe. Now the sun had come out. She glanced at Cal, who seemed to be keeping himself busy well away from her. Or maybe it would be more accurate to say that the dark was interwoven with the bright.

A time to plant and a time to pluck up that which is planted.

A clatter of spoon against pan sounded. Emma stood in the doorway. Her face was still red and painful-looking, but she'd arrived with the others and marched into the kitchen. "Breakfast when you are finished. The flowers must be in before the sun is high." She vanished back inside.

The comment seemed to inspire a fresh burst of industry. Nancy handed her another flat of blooms. "Impatiens," she said. "Along where it's shady."

Andrea nodded. The move brought her next to Levi, who was setting out clumps of coralbells. When he saw her, his round blue eyes became even rounder.

"Hi, Levi. Thanks for helping." In the light of day, her suspicions of him seemed silly. Levi was, as he'd always been, an innocent child at heart.

He ducked his head, coloring a little. "Help is good." He seemed to struggle with the words, and she realized he'd be far more comfortable with the language of the home. Unfortunately, she'd forgotten whatever German she'd learned as a child.

"Yes. You're good neighbors."

He stared at her, and she saw to her horror that his eyes were filling with tears. "Sorry. Sorry."

He scrambled to his feet, arms flailing awkwardly, and ran toward the barn.

She was still staring after him when Nancy knelt next to her, picking up the trowel he'd dropped and finishing the planting in a few deft movements. "It makes no trouble. Levi will be fine. One of the children will get him when it's time to eat."

"I didn't mean to upset him."

"He's been—" she paused, seeming to search for a word "—funny, just lately. He'll be all right."

"You don't know what's causing it?"

Nancy shrugged. "He doesn't talk so much. Sooner or later he will tell his mother, and she will make it right. Some simple thing, most likely."

Nancy was probably right. She certainly knew Levi better than Andrea did.

Still, she couldn't help but wonder. Why had Levi begun to cry at the sight of her? And why had he said he was sorry?

Chapter 14

Cal pulled into the driveway and stopped close to the back garden. He'd seen Rachel mourning over the pieces of the birdbath earlier. The one he'd found at the garden store out toward Lancaster should be a decent replacement.

He got the wheelbarrow from the utility shed in the garage, struggling to manage it. Even with his wrist taped, using that hand was awkward. Lucky it wasn't the right, or he'd be out of work until it healed.

Andrea emerged onto the patio, carrying a watering can. She checked at the sight of him, then waved and began sprinkling the potted plants along the edge of the patio.

Maybe Andrea hadn't quite figured out what had changed between them last night, either. He hefted the birdbath onto the wheelbarrow with one hand. They were both trying to look busy, which probably meant they were both confused.

During those moments when they'd fought for their lives, there hadn't been time to think, only to act and feel. Trouble was, he felt too much.

Lord, does it make any sense at all for me to fall for someone like Andrea? If You've taught me anything in the past year, isn't it that this is the life that's right for me? Andrea could never be content with that. She's itching to race back to the city the minute she's free.

If he told her what he felt—but that could only lead to pain and awkwardness between them.

He was maneuvering the birdbath into place when Andrea caught the opposite side and helped him.

"This is lovely. Where did you find it?"

"Little place over toward Lancaster." If he looked at her, he might weaken, so it was better to concentrate on getting the birdbath into exactly the right spot. "I thought it would please Rachel."

"She'll be delighted." Her tone had cooled in response to his.

He hated that. But wasn't it better for both of them in the long run? Why start something that could only end badly?

Andrea touched a scalloped edge. "About last night…"

He tensed, but before she could say anything else, a buggy came down the drive, the horse driven at a fast trot. "It's Eli." He went to meet the buggy, aware of Andrea hurrying beside him.

Eli pulled up. "Have you seen our Levi since this morning?"

"No, not since we were working on the lawn." He

glanced at Andrea, and she shook her head. "Is something wrong?"

"No one has seen him all day." The lines of his face deepened. "That's not like him. He never goes far, and he always tells his mother. We are starting a search."

Cal glanced at his watch. Nearly five. Levi had been missing for something like seven hours.

"What can we do to help?" Andrea said.

"Search all your buildings. And pray."

"We'll do both," he said quickly. "If we spot him, we'll ring the bell." He nodded toward the old-fashioned dinner bell that hung next to the kitchen door.

"I must tell the other neighbors." Eli was already turning the buggy, and he rolled off without another word. The Amish habit of leaving off the niceties of conversation could seem abrupt, but it was certainly understandable now.

Andrea glanced toward the house. "Grams and Rachel are resting, and they wouldn't be much help in any event."

He headed for the garage. "They don't need to know yet. We can start at this end and work our way out toward the barn."

While he checked the cars and the garage loft, Andrea opened the door to the attached utility shed.

By the time he came back down, she was dusting her hands off. "Nothing in there but a lot of spiderwebs." She hesitated a moment, as if something was on her mind. "You know, Levi was a little odd this morning."

"Odd in what way?" He headed for the old brooder coop, which stood next in the line of outbuildings.

"He was upset when he realized I was working next to him." She seemed to be choosing her words carefully.

"I tried to talk to him, but all he'd say was that he was sorry. Then he ran off, almost in tears."

"You didn't get a sense of what it was all about?"

She shook her head. "When I mentioned it to Nancy, she said he'd been withdrawn lately, but she didn't take it seriously."

"What could he have been sorry for? For what happened last night?"

"I don't know." She brushed her hair free of the collar of her shirt with an irritated movement. "Does that seem very likely? He doesn't know how to drive, does he?"

He flung open the door of the brooder coop. It was packed solidly with furniture. "A mouse couldn't hide in here." He closed the door again. "I wouldn't think Levi could drive, but a surprising number of Amish people can. Learn when they are teens, most of them. What direction did Levi head when he ran off?"

"Toward the barn—yours, not the old one. But wouldn't you have seen him if he were there?"

"I haven't been in all day. Too much else to do. Maybe we'd better check there next."

She nodded, trotting beside him as he quickened his pace. It wasn't the first time Levi had wandered off, but he didn't generally go farther than the Unger place. Levi could have decided to take refuge in the barn, he supposed, hiding from some imagined misdeed.

They hurried up the earthen ramp, and he pulled the door open.

"Levi! Levi, are you in here?" The words echoed in the barn's lofty spaces.

Andrea grabbed his arm. "The trapdoor to the lower level. It's open."

He swung around, following the direction of her

pointing finger. The hatch, used long ago to throw hay down to the stalls in the lower level, was always kept closed and bolted. Now it yawned open.

He was there in an instant, bending to peer down into the shadowy depths. His heart jolted into overtime.

Levi lay on the floor below, arms outstretched, blood darkening the straw beneath his head. His hands were open, palm up, and next to his right hand, glinting in the shaft of sunlight that pierced the dimness, lay a ring of car keys.

Andrea sat on the plastic chair in the hospital waiting room. She glanced at her watch. How much longer? Surely the doctors knew something by now. At least they'd been given this secluded room in which to wait, rather than sitting out in the open where others could stare at the quaintly dressed Amish.

Grams sat bolt upright on her chair, as if to show any sign of weakness would be a betrayal. She had her arm around Emma, who wept softly into a handkerchief. Nancy sat on Emma's other side, having left the children with Rachel, who'd been quick to say she'd be more trouble than she was worth at the hospital.

Men clustered in a group in the far corner, drinking coffee and talking in low voices. Every now and then the door opened and more Amish appeared, quickly segregating themselves by sexes. A carryover from their separation in church or simply a male desire to be as far away as possible from female tears.

The men's black jackets, the women's black bonnets seemed almost a sign of mourning. She shook off that thought. Levi would be all right. He'd been breathing on his own when they brought him in. That was a good sign, wasn't it?

Each time the door opened, all eyes went to it. Each time, Emma sobbed a bit more.

"I don't understand." Emma's wail was loud enough to startle even the men. "Why did Levi go to the barn? How did he fall?"

Grams took the twisting hands in hers. "We'll know when he's well enough to tell you," she said firmly.

Eli came to his wife and patted her awkwardly on the shoulder. "We must accept," he said. "It is God's will."

Was it? The questions that had hovered at the back of Andrea's mind since she and Cal found Levi forced their way to the front. Her eyes sought out Cal. He was filling his foam cup at the coffee urn, but, as if he felt her gaze on him, he looked up and brought the cup to her.

"Have some. I know it's awful, but at least it's hot."

She took the cup, rising and moving toward the window, where they had the illusion of privacy. "Do you really believe Levi could have driven that truck?" She kept her voice low.

He glanced toward the group around Eli before answering. "It's starting to look that way. Samuel admits that Levi was fascinated by cars. He thinks some of the local teenagers might have thought it was funny to show him." He shook his head. "I just can't figure out how he'd get away from home last night. Emma has been keeping pretty close tabs on him."

"She has, but she was probably exhausted. I don't see how he'd have gotten the keys if he didn't do it. Unless the driver dropped them someplace and he picked them up. And assuming they're the keys to the truck."

"Maybe we're going to find out."

The door had swung open again. This time it was Chief Burkhalter. He glanced around the room, seeming surprised to find it so crowded.

"Any word yet on the boy's condition?" He directed the question to Eli.

Eli shook his head. His normally ruddy face was gray with pain. "The doctor will come when they've finished, he said."

"In that case…" His gaze singled out the two of them. "Maybe you'd step outside so we can have a word, since you found him."

She was grateful for Cal's hand on her back as they followed Burkhalter out into the hallway, knowing everyone watched them go. In the corridor, he gestured them into a room a few doors away.

It was a replica of the other waiting room with its pale green walls and generic landscapes. The chairs looked just as uncomfortable. Burkhalter jerked three of them into a circle. At his commanding look, they sat.

She had nothing to feel guilty about, did she? So why did she feel as if she wanted to look anywhere except into Burkhalter's face?

"Tell me about finding him."

Cal nodded. "Eli came over to tell us he was missing and asked us to search the property. Ms. Hampton and I happened to be out in the garden at the time. We started searching the outbuildings."

"It didn't occur to you to look in the inn first?"

Andrea blinked. "I suppose I knew it was unlikely Levi would go inside. He's—well, skittish around strangers." She thought of the rabbits that looked askance when she came out onto the lawn and hopped quickly away.

"So you started searching. What took you to the barn?"

"I remembered that he had gone that way when he left the group that was repairing the damage from last night." She closed her mouth, reluctant to say anything that might contribute to his suspicion.

"Did you talk to him at all this morning?" The man seemed to have radar for evasions.

"Yes, a little. He seemed upset." She darted a glance toward Cal, but he couldn't help her. "He said he was sorry."

"Sorry about what?" Burkhalter's response was like the crack of a whip.

"He didn't say. He ran off." She shook her head to forestall any questions. "There's no point in asking me anything else. That's all I know. I remembered he went toward the barn, so we went there. We saw the trapdoor open." Her voice shook a little, and Cal's hand closed hard over hers. "We found him."

Burkhalter transferred his gaze to Cal. "That trapdoor. You always leave it open?"

"No. I always keep it closed and bolted."

"What did you do after you spotted him?"

"Called paramedics. Went down to see if we could help him." Cal had apparently decided he could be as laconic as Burkhalter.

"I ran back to the house to ring the dinner bell," she said. "We'd agreed that's what we'd do if we found him."

Burkhalter nodded, his gaze fixed on her face. "You know, Ms. Hampton, whenever the police get called in, people get choosy about what they say. Mostly it's innocent enough, but they don't want to say more than they have to. Wouldn't you agree, Counselor?"

If Cal was surprised that the chief knew about his past, he didn't betray it. "Maybe so, if they think it's unimportant."

"Cops get so they have a sense when someone's hiding something." He turned on Andrea. "How about it, Ms. Hampton? What aren't you telling me?"

She blinked. He really did have radar. "It's nothing."

"Tell me anyway, and let me decide if it's nothing."

She brushed the hair back from her face. She had no choice, and surely nothing she said could make matters any worse now.

"There was another incident, after the prowler call. I was locked in the downstairs pantry. I thought it was an accident—maybe I bumped the door myself."

"And what else?"

"One night when it was storming, I went to close the windows. I saw someone standing out on the lawn, watching the house." She hesitated. "It appeared to be a man in Amish clothing. I couldn't identify him any further."

"She called me," Cal said. "I came over—didn't catch him, but I found the place where he'd been standing. Judging by the way the grass was trampled, he'd been there for quite a while."

Burkhalter made a show of consulting a small notebook. "I understand your housekeeper had an accident with the stove."

"Yes." Levi wouldn't do anything to hurt his own mother. Surely Burkhalter could see that. "The repairman couldn't say whether someone had tampered with it or not. It could have been an accident."

"Quite a string of bad luck you folks have been having," he observed.

She waited for him to probe more deeply, but to her surprise, he rose.

"You can join the others, if you like."

"Chief." Cal's voice stopped him at the doorway. "Those keys—were they the keys to the stolen truck?"

He didn't move for a moment. Would he answer?

"Yes," he said. "They were."

The stack of green ledgers in the middle of the library desk gave Andrea pause. Rachel, searching in the lower kitchen cabinets for a bundt cake pan, had unearthed yet another batch of Grandfather's records that she'd put away in an unlikely place. Andrea had delivered a lecture on organization, but doubted whether it would do any good.

Andrea pushed the ledgers to one side and switched on the computer, feeling too tired to deal with much of anything this morning. The doctors had come out at last and announced that Levi had a severe concussion and several broken ribs, but would mend. Emma's tears had turned to rejoicing, and the bishop, a local farmer named Christian Lapp, led a lengthy prayer of thanksgiving.

Finally she'd persuaded Grams to come home. It had been nearly one before the house was quiet, and then she'd lain awake, unable to turn off the questions in her mind.

They'd all come down to one, in the end. Why? Why would Levi do such a thing? Until he told them, no one would know.

Guests were arriving tomorrow. She shoved her hair back and called up the reservations on the computer screen. Were they ready? Aside from a sense that all of them would have difficulty playing the genial host, she thought so.

The front door opened. "Hello?"

"In the library." She shoved her chair back, but the visitor came in even as she rose.

Betty. For a moment it seemed odd, seeing the woman anywhere but behind her desk at Unger and Bendick.

"Betty." She gave what she hoped was a welcoming smile. "What brings you to see us?"

There was no returning smile. Betty marched to the desk and set down a stack of file folders and several computer disks. "Mr. Bendick asked me to bring these to you."

Andrea stared at them blankly. "I'm sorry?"

Betty's lips pressed together in an offended line. "Mrs. Unger informed him that you would be handling all her finances in the future."

With everything else that had been happening, she'd forgotten that vote of confidence from Grams. "I see. I didn't intend for you to bring those over. I'd have come in to talk with Uncle Nick."

"He thought this would be best." Even Betty's hair, piled in some sort of complicated knot on her head, seemed to quiver with indignation.

It looked as if she'd have to mend some fences. "My grandmother didn't intend any lack of confidence in Uncle Nick. She appreciates everything he's done, but she thought she'd have me do it rather than to take advantage of him, as busy as he is."

Betty leaned over to flip open the top folder. "There are forms here that Mrs. Unger must sign. Please have her do so."

Obviously Betty was offended on Nick's behalf. She found it hard to believe that Nick cared all that much. Surely managing Grams's affairs was an extra burden he didn't need.

"I'll have her sign them when she gets back from the hospital."

Betty paused, and Andrea could see her need to hold on to the grudge battling her curiosity. The curiosity won.

"Is she visiting that Zook boy who caused all the trouble?" Incredulity filled her voice.

"My grandmother is good friends with the Zook family." Andrea stood. "Thank you for dropping these off. I'll take care of them."

Betty glared at her for a moment. Then she turned and stalked out. The front door slammed.

"She isn't too happy with you." Cal walked in from the kitchen as she sat down.

She felt the little jolt to her heart that seemed to come with his presence. "Did you bring my grandmother back from the hospital?"

"She wanted to stay a while longer, so Emma arranged for someone to pick them both up. I told Katherine I'd stop by and update you."

"How is Levi?"

He came and perched on the corner of the desk. "The doctors seem satisfied. He should come home in a few days, if all continues to go well."

That was good news, but where did they go from there? "Has he said anything? Explained?"

He shook his head. "He's conscious, but he doesn't seem to remember much about his injury. Burkhalter tried to question him, but Levi got so upset he gave up." He shrugged, clearly not happy with the situation. "Levi had the vehicle keys, so there doesn't seem to be much doubt that he did it."

"Why?" She shoved the desk chair back. "That's what kept me up half the night. What could Levi possibly have against us?"

"Emma was afraid she had the answer to that. It seems the Zooks got worried that if the inn was successful, your grandmother might decide she wanted to use the property they lease from her. She thinks Levi heard them talking and misunderstood. Got some foolish idea he was helping them. And Emma finally said that he does get out at night sometimes."

Her throat tightened. "Poor Emma. It would be hard for her to admit that."

"Well, your grandmother assured her the land is theirs to use as long as they want it, and when I left they were holding each other and crying, so I think they're going to be all right."

He shifted position, not looking at her. "You know, I have an offer to go out to the Zimmerman farm and work on a cabinetry job. I kept putting it off because of everything that's been going on here, but now that it's resolved, I should go."

"I see." She sensed he was saying more than the words indicated. "When will you leave?"

"This afternoon. It'll take a few days, so I suppose you'll be gone by the time I get back."

For a moment she couldn't speak. This was it, then. Cal was letting her know, in the nicest possible way, that he didn't want a relationship with her.

Well, that was for the best, wasn't it? They were committed to completely different values. This wasn't about the distance between Churchville and Philadelphia. It was a question of what they wanted from life. Since that couldn't be reconciled, it was better to make a clear break before anyone got hurt.

She managed to smile, forced herself to hold out her hand. "Thank you again for everything you've done to help us get under way. I'm sure I'll see you when I come back from time to time."

He nodded, holding her hand for a moment as if there was something else he wanted to say. Then he turned quickly and was gone.

She sank back in the chair. She'd been wrong about one thing. It was already too late to keep from getting hurt.

Chapter 15

Barney whined, lifting his head from the library carpet to look at Andrea. He probably wondered why she was still at the computer when everyone else in the house was asleep. Over the past week, she'd gotten into the habit of keeping the dog downstairs with her after Grams went to bed, letting him out for one last time and then putting him into Grams's room when she went up.

"It's all right, boy." She leaned back in the desk chair, covering her eyes with her hands for a moment. The figures on the computer screen had begun to blur, particularly when she tried to compare them with the cramped writing in Grandfather's last couple of ledgers.

Maybe it would be better to take all of the financial records back to the city with her on Monday, so that she could go over them at her leisure. She'd begun to find discrepancies. It looked as if Grandfather had been failing more than she'd imagined in his final years.

She studied the portrait above the mantel, her grandfather's painted features staring back at her. Was that what happened? Had he really lost that sharp business sense of his and been too proud to admit it? She was startled to realize it hurt to think of him that way.

Aware of the dog whining again, she closed down the program and stacked the ledgers on the edge of the desk. "All right, Barney. You can go out, and then we'd both better get some sleep."

Barney, understanding the words *go out,* trotted toward the back door. When she opened it, he darted outside with a sharp woof.

She leaned against the door, trying not to look in the direction of the barn. Of Cal's empty apartment.

Working on the financial records had, for a few hours, absorbed her mind completely. She could get lost in the rows of figures as easily as other people got lost in a good book.

Now the pain came rushing back. Cal had shut the door on whatever might have been between them. She understood his reasons, but he could have given her some say in the matter. At least, he could have if he felt what she did.

Maybe she was wrong about that. Maybe those close moments between them, those kisses, had been merely attraction to him, with nothing more solid behind it.

Her mind fumbled with an unaccustomed prayer. *I'm trying to find my way back to You, Lord. For a while, I thought Cal was going to be part of that, but I was wrong. Still, no matter how much it hurts to lose him, knowing him has helped me look at things more clearly. Please, guide me to live the way You want.*

No lightning flashed. She didn't have a burst of insight. But peace seeped into her heart, easing the pain and giving her comfort.

Barney barked, the sound muted. Frowning, she stepped outside and called, "Barney! Here, boy!"

Nothing moved anywhere in the lighted area of the yard. He must have gone farther afield while she stood there lost in thought.

Everything looked perfectly peaceful, but somewhere beyond the fringe of outbuildings, the dog yipped.

She reached back inside to slip the flashlight off its hook. She'd have to get him—if she went up to bed without him, Grams would have a fit. And he'd probably wake the house with his barking.

At least, with Levi in the hospital, she didn't have to worry about encountering any prowlers. Poor Levi. Would charges be brought against him? Surely not, if Grams had anything to say about it.

She crossed to the toolshed, shining the light around. Beyond the range of the security lights it was pitch-black, the sliver of a new moon providing little illumination.

She called again, her voice sharp. This time the answer was a whining cry that sounded distressed, and her fingers tightened on the flashlight. Was Barney hurt? Trapped in some way? She hurried toward the sound, behind the row of outbuildings, into the blackness.

Yards ahead of her, across the overgrown lane, loomed the dark bulk of the old barn. A shiver went down her spine. The sound seemed to be coming from there.

The building had been kept in repair, but it hadn't been used for anything in years. Still, there might be something that Barney's collar could have become hooked on.

That must be it.

She trotted toward the earthen ramp to the upper level, flicking the flashlight around as she went, hoping she wouldn't spot any night creatures larger than a mouse. But the dog's presence had probably frightened away any other animals.

One of the big double doors stood ajar just enough for Barney to get through. She'd have to see that it was secured—something else to add to her to-do list. They couldn't have inn guests wandering around where they might get hurt.

She entered, swinging the light. The space was empty, an oil mark on the floor mute testimony to the farm vehicle that had once been parked there. Grandfather must have had the barn cleared out when it was no longer in use.

Her flashlight beam picked up a small door opposite the entrance. The dog's now-frantic barking came from there.

She hurried across the dusty floorboards and grabbed the door, yanking it open. A foul, metallic aroma rushed out at her. Memory stirred. They'd kept fertilizers and pesticides in here long ago. Her light bounced off floor-to-ceiling shelves, still laden with rusty cans. The place looked like a toxic waste dump. Her grandfather's care of the building hadn't extended to clearing this out, apparently.

Barney's eyes shone in the light, and he wiggled with impatience. "Barney." She was embarrassed at the slight tremor in her voice, even though there was no one but the dog to hear. "What happened, baby? Are you stuck?"

Sure enough, the dog's collar was caught in the prongs of an old harrow that lay on the floor. She hurried to kneel beside him. When she patted him, she had to try to quiet his excited leaps and attempts to lick her face.

"Hold still, you silly thing. I can't release you when you're doing that." She put the flashlight down, fumbling with the collar, the dog's jumps nearly knocking her over. The flashlight rolled, illuminating what lay in the corner.

Nick Bendick. Uncle Nick. He sprawled against the wall, unconscious. Alive? Her heart seemed to stop.

"Uncle Nick?" She hurried to him, dropping to her knees next to the inert form.

She groped for his wrist, breathing again when she felt a pulse—weak, but at least he was alive. She grabbed the flashlight, trying to focus with hands that were shaking. It looked as if he'd stumbled on the harrow, hitting his head against the wall. But what on earth was he doing here?

The circle of light wavered, and she forced herself to steady it. It touched Nick's hand, lying lax on the barn floor. Her breath caught, and the world seemed to spin.

In Nick's hand was a dog leash, next to it a torn paper bag, dog biscuits spilling from it.

She couldn't seem to move. Barney hadn't gotten tangled up on his own. Nick had been waiting, knowing she always let the dog out the last thing at night. Had trapped Barney, apparently intending to use him to lure her here.

Her mind struggled to the obvious conclusion. The

financial records. Anger swept through her. This was about her interest in the financial records. Grandfather hadn't been losing his touch. Nick had been cheating him.

She had to get help. Run to the house, call the paramedics and the police, let them sort it out. She hurried back to the dog, struggled with the collar for another moment, and finally got it free.

Uncle Nick. It was impossible to believe. Could he really have intended to hurt her? Surely he'd never hurt anyone in his life.

Except Levi. Her mind seemed to leap from one understanding to another. Levi, lying on the floor with the keys planted next to him. How much of what had been happening had been caused by Nick's frantic efforts to keep her from looking into the financial records? He must have realized she was the one person who would understand what he'd done.

The authorities would figure it out. Barney beside her, she hurried toward the door. Cool night air hit her like a slap in the face. Get help. That was all she could do now.

She darted toward the distant house, the circle of light bouncing ahead of her, and Barney woofed at the unexpected excitement. If Grams heard him, came out—well, she'd have to know the truth about the man she'd trusted soon, in any event.

If Cal were at the barn, she'd call on him for help. But he wasn't. He'd left. Ridiculous, to feel that she needed him.

She rounded the corner of the toolshed and flew straight into someone.

She stumbled back, gasping. The security light

showed her Betty, of all people. Another surprise in a night of surprises. She grasped the woman's arm.

"You have to help me. It's Nick—he's hurt. He—"

"I'll help."

Betty patted her reassuringly with one hand. The other lifted something. Light reflected from a long, silvery shaft. It swung down, pain exploded in her head, and the ground came up to meet her.

Andrea struggled to open her eyes, but her head spun and ached. She'd just lie here another minute...

Then consciousness came rolling back. Nick. And Betty. Betty had hit her with a golf club. Impossible, but it had happened. Nick and Betty must be doing this together.

A warm, furry body next to her, a rough wet tongue washing her face. "Barney," she whispered, coughing on the word.

She moved, aware of hard wooden boards beneath her, of the acrid smell that made her want to gag. She was back in the tiny storage room in the old barn. Barney was with her.

Something hard poked into her ribs. She rolled, feeling for it, and pulled out the flashlight. Fumbled for the switch, thinking if she had to stay in the dark another instant she'd start screaming...

The light came on. Maybe this was worse. She could see the tall shelves on either side of her, enclosing her with their load of poison. She sucked in a breath and was instantly sorry when the air burned her throat.

Then she saw what still lay against the wall. Nick. Her mind spun.

Get out. She had to get out. She stumbled to the door,

groping for the handle. Locked. Incredibly, Betty had locked her in here. Betty. How could she even have gotten her here? It was impossible.

Then she identified the sound that rumbled from beyond the door. A car's engine. Betty must have driven up the overgrown lane behind the outbuildings and hauled her in here.

She pounded on the door. "Betty! Let me out of here. You can't get away with this."

"Can't I?" Betty's voice was muffled by the thick door, but she must be standing close to it on the other side. "I think I can. You've always underestimated me, all of you. My plans have been made for a long time, my money safely salted away under another name. I knew Nick would break down at some point. He always had such a soft spot for your grandmother."

She sounded like an indulgent mother, admitting a failing in her child.

"You were stealing from the firm." Hard to think it through, with the fumes fogging her brain. "But Nick— was he in it with you? Is that what this was all about?"

"Nick had a little gambling problem, you see. Borrowed some money from the accounts. He wasn't very good at it. Your grandfather would have found him out in a week if it hadn't been for me." There was a trace of pride in her voice.

"Betty, think about what you're doing." She forced herself to be calm. Rational. One of them should be. "Just let me out, and we'll go to the police together. I'll get you a lawyer—"

Betty chuckled. "Dear Andrea, always so sure you know what's best. I have no intention of going to the police. You and Nick are going to have an unfortunate accident, and I'm going to be far away by the time it's sorted out and they start to look for me."

"Accident..." She tried to move, but her muscles didn't obey. She could lie down, just rest for a moment; it would be all right....

Shock sent her upright. Her mental fog wasn't just from the closed room and the cans of chemicals. The car was running because Betty was pumping carbon monoxide into the room.

She dropped to her knees, fingers fumbling along the bottom of the door. Yes, there was the mouth of a hose, thrust under the corner of the door.

Please, Lord, please, Lord, help me know what to do. If I can just block it...

She swung the light around, picking up an old feed sack shoved onto a shelf. Grab it, twist a piece small enough to fit into the hose, stuff it in, coughing and choking, pray it blocked enough to give them a few more precious moments to live....

A few moments. Not enough. No one would look for her until morning, probably. How long would it take until they searched here?

She slumped back, trying to force her numbed wits to move. The walls were closing in. She couldn't stop them, and she felt the familiar panic, blurred by her fogged mind, but there, creeping in, loosening her control.

Father, help me hold on. If I panic, I'll die. Forgive me for drifting away from You. Hold me in Your hands, living or dying.

Hands. Hands reaching out to her, pulling her free. She shook her head, knowing it was a memory, but a memory of what?

It wouldn't come. Think. What else could she do?

Noises outside the door. A car door opening and closing. The car driving away. Betty was gone.

She was still alive, and so was Nick from what she could tell. But not for long unless she could think of something. She swung the light around. Metal shone for an instant on the shelf—she reached, hand closing on a bar about the size of a tire iron.

Excitement flooded her, clearing her mind. If she could get the door open...

But a moment's effort showed her that was impossible. The door was solid, resisting her feeble efforts to open it.

Think. Think. If you can't get out, maybe you can get air in. The wall behind her was solid stone, the end wall of the barn. Nothing there, but the wall to her right must be an outside wall.

She crawled over to it, dragging the bar. Barney, whimpering a little, struggled to her side. Was it her imagination, or was the air a little better here? The dog seemed to think so. He put his nose at the base of the wall, right where the siding boards came down to meet the floor.

Nick. She crawled back to him, grabbed his arms, and dragged him toward the wall. No time now to worry that she was injuring him further. If she didn't get them some air, they would die.

Adrenaline pulsing, she ran her hand along the joint, feeling the slightest crack between the boards. Big enough to wedge the bar in? Her fingers seemed to have grown stupid along with her brain. It took three tries before she forced the bar in.

Wiggle it, shove it, find something to hit it with— but there she ran out of luck. There was nothing loose in the room sturdy enough to hit the bar. She'd have to keep wiggling it, trying to force it through to the outside, but her mind was fogging again.

Ironic. She'd filled up the slight crack with the pry bar, cutting off whatever air might come through.

Give me strength, Lord. Help me. I know You're here with me. I know whatever You intend is right. But I can't stop trying, can't stop fighting....

"To everything there is a season, and a time for every purpose under Heaven. A time to live and a time to die..."

Barney slumped to the floor. Poor boy. He'd go first. She and Nick were bigger, so they'd last longer. Push, keep pushing, a little farther...

"A little farther, Drea." Her grandfather's voice. He was the only one who'd ever called her that. "Just a little farther. Don't stop now. Another inch, and you'll reach my hands."

Another inch. A vague dream of Grandfather's strong hands, tight on hers, lifting her out into the cool air, holding her close. Safe. She'd always been safe with him.

Safe in God's hands. Living or dying...

Another inch. She pushed the bar, felt the resistance give way as it slid through. Befuddled. Taking a moment to realize she had to pull the bar back out.

Feel the cool air on her face, rushing in through the hole she'd made. Drinking in long gasps of it. Drag Nick's limp form, then Barney, up to the opening, feeling the dog stir.

But tired. So tired. She slumped down, head on Barney's fur.

Chapter 16

Cal eased off on the accelerator when he hit the outskirts of Churchville. He was making a fool of himself, rushing back at this hour, but the urge to see Andrea again, to clear the air between them, had been too strong to ignore.

He'd tried hiding from life, and it hadn't worked. He couldn't hide. Life kept finding him.

And beneath that urge to see Andrea had been something he couldn't explain, a sense that all was not right. An urgent feeling that he was needed.

Well, he was here, and how he'd explain arriving at this late hour, he didn't know. They'd all be asleep, probably, and he'd have to wait until morning to see Andrea anyway.

But as he turned into the drive at the inn, he saw the glow of lights in the library. It had to be Andrea, sitting up late at the computer. Relief flooded through him, making him realize just how tense he'd been.

A glimpse of movement drew his attention. From beyond the outbuildings, a dark car spurted out, hit the winding country road and raced away.

Cal jammed on the brakes and slid out, leaving the motor running, all his instincts crying out. That was wrong, very wrong. He ran toward the back door, and the minute he saw it, he knew his instincts were on target. The door stood open, light pooling out onto the patio, and no one was there.

His feet thudded across the patio. None of them would go off and leave the door standing open at this hour. He bolted inside and ran for the library. Lights on, computer on, desk chair pushed back. It looked as if Andrea had just walked away.

Some rational part of his mind kept insisting that there could be a logical explanation, but he didn't believe it. Rachel—Rachel was sleeping on this floor now, in the little room off the kitchen.

He saw the light go on as he ran to it. He was probably scaring her to death.

"Rachel, it's Cal. Is Andrea with you?"

"No. What's happening?" Fear laced her voice.

He flung open the door. Rachel sat up in bed, pulling a robe around her.

"The back door is standing open, and I can't find Andrea."

"If she took the dog out—"

He felt as if he'd been doused with cold water. "That must be it. Sorry. I'll just check."

Logical explanation, see? But the fear drove him

back out to the patio. "Andrea! Andrea, are you out here?"

A light went on overhead, and he heard footsteps on the stairs. Katherine. She hurried toward him.

"Cal, what are you doing back? Why are you calling for Andrea?"

"Is she upstairs?"

"No." She glanced toward the library and paled. "She and Barney were still down here. She must have taken him out. But why didn't she hear you call?"

"I'll look for her. Where's a flashlight?"

She pulled a drawer open and thrust a heavy torch into his hand. "I'm calling the police."

He jerked a nod and hurried out the door. Better a false alarm than a tragedy. He'd never been one to go on instinct, but this sense was stronger than he'd ever experienced.

Is it You, Lord? If it is, help me to listen. Show me where to go. Please, keep her safe.

He ran across the lawn toward the outbuildings. The car that had no possible reason for being there—it had come from behind the outbuildings. He swung the light around.

"Andrea! Where are you?"

Nothing. The buildings were dark and silent, the security lights reflecting from them, mocking him. They hadn't kept Andrea safe.

And the dog—the dog must be with her. "Barney!" he yelled. "Here, boy. Barney!"

Not even an answering woof. He paused by the tool-shed, the urgency pounding along his veins like a power in his blood, telling him to hurry, hurry. But where?

Lord, help me. If this is from You, help me.

He took a breath. Think. The car came down the disused lane behind the outbuildings—the lane that led only to the old barn. He ran, heart thudding in his ears. Behind him, from the house, the bell began clanging insistently. Katherine, trying to rouse the Zook family to come and help.

The circle of light bounced. He rounded the corner, saw the barn doors, and knew the instinct that drove him was right. Both doors stood open, and the grass leading to them was bent down from the passage of a car.

He thudded inside. A car had been in here—he could smell the fumes. Strong, too strong. He swung the light around. Empty, nothing...

The light flashed on a door—solid as the barn, the old-fashioned latch dropped down into its pocket, securing it. He ran toward it, stumbling on a length of hose, righting himself, reaching the door.

Flung it open and staggered back from the fumes. Andrea. He took a deep breath and threw himself through the door. Woman and dog lay together against the outer wall. Another figure—a man. Bendick. Still, too still.

He grabbed Andrea, stumbled back out, through the barn, out into the cold night air. Think, remember your CPR training, but even as he thought it she coughed, choked and gasped in a gulp of air.

Tears filled his eyes. *Please, God, please, God.* He knelt in the damp grass, holding her against him. "Andrea, wake up. Say something. Breathe."

She stirred, murmured something, then sank limply against him. But she was breathing. Her eyelids fluttered.

"I've found her!" he shouted at the top of his lungs. "Call the paramedics." Poor Katherine must be terrified, but he couldn't do anything else. He'd have to go back in for Bendick....

Lights bobbing toward him—Eli, his son and the oldest grandson with him, running with trousers pulled on over nightshirts.

"In the barn, the back room. Bendick and the dog. Mind the fumes." Samuel nodded and pelted into the barn with the boy, while Eli knelt beside him.

"Will she be all right, then?"

"She's breathing." He looked at the older man, not ashamed of the tears that spilled over. "She's alive."

"Thank the Lord," Eli said.

The wail of a siren split the night.

Yes, thank You, Father. Thank You.

Andrea toyed with the piece of dry toast that was all she thought she could get down. They sat around the breakfast table in various stages of exhaustion. Emma kept pressing food on people, as if that were the only cure for the night they'd been through.

Since she'd missed most of it, either through being unconscious or at the hospital, she tried to concentrate on what Chief Burkhalter was saying, but her gaze kept straying to Cal.

His face was drawn, the skin pulled tight against the bone, as if he'd been in battle and wasn't sure it was over. She'd had no chance to talk with him alone, and still didn't know what had brought him back. She only knew he'd come in time to save her. That was enough.

Barney padded around the table from Grams to her,

sighed, and thudded heavily to the floor next to her, as if he'd decided that she needed his protection.

"…caught up with the woman the other side of Harrisburg," Burkhalter was saying. "She tried to bluff it out. Might have gotten away if Burke hadn't gotten to you in time." He eyed her soberly. "Just glad you're okay."

She nodded, not sure she trusted herself to speak. The memory was too fresh.

"I don't understand." Grams seemed to have aged overnight. "I'd believe anything of Betty, but Nick—we've known him and trusted him for thirty years."

"Are they talking?" Cal asked.

Burkhalter shrugged. "The woman clammed up tight and asked for a lawyer. Bendick is still in the hospital, but he's babbling like Conestoga Creek." He turned to Grams. "Might make you feel a little better to know that apparently Bendick never intended to steal from the company. He had gambling losses he was ashamed to admit to your husband, took money to pay them off intending to replace it, he says, but the secretary found out and started blackmailing him. I imagine a thorough look into the books will prove she helped herself to quite a bit. Whether you'll ever get it back again is another question. The lawyers will have to sort that out."

"I still don't understand," Rachel said. "What was the point of all of the tricks they pulled? Was that Uncle Nick or Betty?"

"According to Bendick, they figured Andrea was the one person who might make sense of their doctored records, especially if she got hold of her grandfather's ledgers. The secretary was pulling the strings, blackmailing him to try and scare Andrea away. He claims he couldn't take it anymore, was coming here to tell you the truth when she attacked him."

The timing suddenly made sense. "I had the ledgers on my desk in the afternoon, when Betty stopped in. She must have thought I was on to them."

"We found the ledgers in her car," Burkhalter said. "Looks like they had some hope of locating them before you did. And he thought if Mrs. Unger gave up the idea of the inn, you'd go back to the city and leave things alone."

"Levi saw him." Emma spoke unexpectedly, her hands holding tight to the back of Grams's chair. "He finally told us. He saw Mr. Bendick here when he shouldn't of been. He wanted to tell Andrea, but he was too shy. Mr. Bendick said to meet him in Cal's place, so he could explain. Instead he pushed him."

"Levi—he was trying to tell me that night when he stood outside the house. And he followed me when I left the farm."

Emma nodded. "He meant to help. He didn't know how."

It was all starting to fall into place. "What about Rachel, the hit-and-run? Did they do that?"

"Bendick claims not," Burkhalter said. "We'll keep looking, but we may never know the truth about that."

Grams reached up to clasp Emma's hand. "At least Levi and Rachel are going to be all right."

"And Ms. Hampton," Burkhalter added. "The secretary hoped we'd think Bendick was guilty, at least long enough to let her get away." He shifted his gaze to Cal. "What made you come back, Burke? Did you suspect it was something to do with the books?"

Her breath stopped. *Why, Cal? How did you know?*

"No, not at all." He looked as if he were blaming himself. "I just…" He hesitated. "I just had a feeling."

Grams glanced at the clock and got to her feet. "Goodness, we'll be having guests here before you know it. We have to get ready." She bustled around the table, making shooing motions with her hands. "Andrea, you go and rest before you fall over. We'll take care of everything. Go on now."

People began to scatter. If Cal intended to tell her anything, it would have to wait.

The final guests left on Monday afternoon, heaping delighted praise on Three Sisters Inn. Andrea looked at Grams and Rachel. They wore grins just as goofy as hers probably was.

"We actually did it," she said. "I'm not sure I believed it would work."

"I did." Rachel patted her arm. "Thanks to you, and Grams, and Emma, and Nancy, and everyone else who helped out."

"They all said they'd be back." Grams sounded a little surprised. "Two couples have already booked for a second visit."

"You know, Grams, if you're able to recover the money Betty stole, you might not have to run the inn." She was fairly certain she knew the answer to that, but they may as well get it out in the open.

Grams looked astonished. "Not run the inn? Of course we will. This is the most fun I've had in years."

Andrea hugged her. It looked as if she'd been wrong about a lot of things, but this was one time when she didn't mind that.

Grams patted her. "You should go and rest. You both should."

"Sounds good." Rachel stifled a yawn.

"I think I'll go out back and get some fresh air first." Andrea whistled to Barney, who scurried to her side. She patted his head. "You're my self-appointed watchdog, aren't you?" So maybe he wasn't the brightest dog in the world, but he was loyal.

Afternoon sun slanted across the lawn, filtering through the trees to touch the brilliant colors of the flowers. The sandstone patio wall glowed golden. Cal sat, just where she thought she might find him.

The dog padded quietly at her heels as she stepped off the patio and went to sit beside him.

He gave her a questioning look. "You're not turned off by the view out here after what happened to you?"

That was a nice, safe way to start what they had to say to each other. "It's still beautiful." She managed to look at the dark bulk of the old barn where it lifted above the outbuildings. "I guess there's something about nearly dying that makes you appreciate life."

"I should have been here," he said abruptly, emotion roughening his voice. "I shouldn't have left until I was sure everything was all right."

Sorrow deepened. It would have been better if he'd said he shouldn't have left at all, but he hadn't. She'd have to accept that.

"You came back in time, that's all that counts." It took an effort to keep her voice even. "What made you come back, Cal? I need to know."

He touched her hand lightly, and that touch seemed to reverberate through her. "I kept thinking I'd been unfair, leaving the way I did without talking to you. I tried telling myself I'd done it for the best, but I wasn't very convincing." He looked at her then. "I'm sorry."

She nodded, trying to dispel the lump in her throat. "That's why you came back last night? Because you'd been wrong to leave without talking to me?"

"Not exactly." His brow furrowed. "I don't know if I can explain. I just felt an overwhelming pressure to come, not to wait for morning, not to delay, just to come." His fingers wrapped around hers. "I think God was giving me the push I needed. That's the only explanation I have."

"It's all you need." The feelings she'd had when she was trapped came flooding back—the assurance of God's presence, the half-remembered dream about Grandfather. "Remember when you asked me what brought on my claustrophobia?"

He looked startled by the change of subject, but nodded.

"I found out. Some of it I remembered, some Grams told me. When I was five, I fell into an abandoned well behind the old barn."

"That would certainly do it."

She nodded. "Grandfather was out in the field with Eli and some of the men. They heard me cry. My grandfather had the men hold his legs and lower him down so that I could reach his hands. He pulled me out."

"And you didn't remember it?"

"No. I asked Grams why they didn't tell me, but apparently they thought it was better forgotten. Last night—last night I remembered, some of it at least. When I was digging the airhole, I could feel God's presence with me. Somehow I'd lost that certainty of His presence, but now it's back. And I remembered my grandfather's voice, telling me to reach farther so I could take his hand. It kept me going."

Cal held her hand between his palms, and his touch comforted her. "You feel differently about your grandfather than you did when you came."

She nodded, wanting to articulate it. He needed to understand how she'd changed. "I can see him more clearly now, and look at the situation like an adult instead of a child. He was a strong, stubborn, fallible human being, not a superhero. He loved and he made mistakes, like we all do. But the loving—that was the important part."

"I'm glad," he said simply.

She turned to face him. "Understanding that made me see that I want things to be straight between us. No long silences or things left unsaid."

"That's asking a lot. I'm not sure I'm brave enough for that."

"I think you are." She had to give him the choice. Either they could take the risk of loving each other, or he could go back to hiding from the world in his safe, peaceful sanctuary.

He looked down at their clasped hands. "You know why I left. I'd started to care about you too much. I knew the kind of life you want, and I couldn't ask you to change. It seemed better—safer, I guess—if we parted before it became too difficult." The corner of his lips curled slightly. "I was wrong. It was more than difficult. It was impossible. Andrea, I know that hiding isn't the answer for me. I choose this life because it's right for me, but I don't want it to come between us."

Something lifted inside her, and she wanted to laugh. They'd been so foolish, trying to protect themselves from falling in love. God had known better than they had.

"Funny thing about that." She couldn't help the lilt to her voice. "Being here with family again, seeing how unreasonable my boss is and how cutthroat my colleagues, made me take a serious look at what I want out of life. Maybe that security I was looking for doesn't mean I have to have the biggest office, or make the most money."

He was looking at her with so much love shining in his eyes that she didn't know whether she should laugh or cry.

"I was thinking I might start a little bookkeeping business of my own, where I could be my own boss. You know any small towns that might need a business like that?"

He slid his arm around her and drew her close. "I think we might be able to find the right place. And I know a carpenter who'll give you a good price on office furniture."

She leaned into him, feeling his strength, knowing his character and his faith. She'd been looking for security in the wrong place, just as Cal had been looking for peace in the wrong place. God was calling them to love and to dare, not to hide and be safe.

She lifted her face, meeting his lips, and knew this time she was home to stay.

* * * * *

Debby Giusti is an award-winning Christian author who met and married her military husband at Fort Knox, Kentucky. Together they traveled the world, raised three wonderful children and have now settled in Atlanta, Georgia, where Debby spins tales of mystery and suspense that touch the heart and soul. Visit Debby online at debbygiusti.com, blog with her at seekerville.blogspot.com and craftieladiesofromance.blogspot.com, and email her at Debby@DebbyGiusti.com.

Books by Debby Giusti

Love Inspired Suspense

Her Forgotten Amish Past
Dangerous Amish Inheritance
Amish Christmas Search

Amish Witness Protection

Amish Safe House

Amish Protectors

Amish Refuge
Undercover Amish
Amish Rescue
Amish Christmas Secrets

Visit the Author Profile page
at Harlequin.com for more titles.

AMISH RESCUE

Debby Giusti

Then spake Jesus again unto them, saying, I am the light
of the world: he that followeth me shall not walk
in darkness, but shall have the light of life.
—*John* 8:12

This story is dedicated to children at risk. Please join me in praying for their protection and well-being so the forces of darkness will not prevail against them.

Chapter 1

Sarah Miller's heart pounded in sync with the foot-steps that echoed up the stairway leading to the third story of the old antebellum home. Rats scurried in the attic as she crouched in the closet, pulled her knees to her chest and fought back tears that burned her eyes. The rats didn't frighten her, but Victor Thomin did.

The shuffle of his feet on the landing signaled his approach. Keys rattled as he unlocked the door, send-ing another wave of panic to ricochet along her spine. The locks—all three of them—were to protect her from those who hoped to do her harm…or so Victor claimed.

"Sarah?"

Her lungs constricted at the sound of his voice. She gasped, struggled for air and wished she could be any-where except in his mother's house, where he said she was safe.

The door creaked open.

In her mind's eye, she could see his pallid skin, deep-set eyes and shock of red hair as he glanced around the room.

"Where are you, Sarah?" Anger rose in his voice. "Are you hiding from me?"

He knew too much about her, about being left alone as a child, about the fire and the fear that continued to eat at her even though she should know better. Why had she told him so much in her drugged stupor? At least he no longer forced her to take the pills.

"You can't hide from me, Sarah." His voice made her tremble all the more.

The closet door flew open. She startled, gasped for air and wanted to run but was too frightened to move.

He grabbed her arm.

"Don't hurt me." She struggled to pull free. "It was the dream that made me hide."

"Did you dream of being dragged from the car along with Miriam?" he asked, seemingly concerned. His hold eased. "Tell me about it, Sarah."

His voice was syrupy sweet now. How could he be such a Jekyll and Hyde? Hateful one minute, feigning compassion the next.

If only she could remember all the details of the car-jacking instead of hazy flashes that clouded her mind.

He leaned closer. "I told you about the bad men, Sarah, the men in your dreams. They captured your sister, but I'm working to get Miriam back before she's transported so far away that you'll never find her again."

Sarah's stomach roiled, sickened by the horrific thought of her sister gone forever. All her life, Sarah had relied on Miriam in times of need. But it wasn't just Miriam she could count on. Even her eldest sister, Hannah, had offered support, though the two of them had not been as close.

"If Miriam can't help me, then Hannah will."

He clicked his tongue. "She left you years ago. Remember, you told me how you cried after Hannah was gone."

Frustrated that he had manipulated even that information from her, she raised her chin in defiance. "I don't believe what you said about Miriam. You're wrong, Victor. She hasn't been taken away. She'll save me."

Sarah eyed the open door to the hallway. Without thinking, she shoved past him and ran toward the stairs.

He chased after her, grabbed her arm and threw her down.

Her shoulder crashed against the floor. She groaned, then scrambled to her feet. He caught her hair and yanked so hard she thought her scalp would rip from her skull.

His other hand wrapped around her neck; all the while he pulled her hair until her face pointed to the ceiling, exposing her throat, where his fingers tightened, constricting her airway.

She clawed at his arm and kicked, her lungs on fire. She couldn't swallow, couldn't scream.

"Don't ever doubt me, Sarah."

Hot tears seared her eyes. She tried to nod, but the movement caused more pain along her scalp.

Her ears rang, something gurgled in her throat, blackness swirled around her. Her knees gave way. In the split second before she would have slipped into unconsciousness, he released his hold. She fell to the floor, gasped for air and clawed her way back to reality.

"Are you going to obey me?" he demanded, standing over her, hands on his hips and eyes glaring.

She opened her mouth, hoping he hadn't seriously damaged her vocal cords. A raspy "Yes" filtered out along with a whimper.

"That's my good Sarah."

She wasn't good and she wasn't his. She never would be. After her mother's transgressions, she would never belong to any man, and especially not a crazed lunatic who had suddenly become abusive. His verbal threats had unnerved her and made her tremble, but until today, he had never touched her inappropriately or raised his hand in anger. Seemingly in the blink of an eye, all that had changed. She couldn't fathom why. The only thing she did know was she needed to escape from Victor's control.

Not that she'd had an opportunity to elude him in the past. He kept close watch on her during the day and made sure she was locked away each night.

With a huff, he yanked her to her feet. "Mother has been asking for you."

"She wants Naomi." From what Sarah could tell, Naomi was a local Amish woman who had taken care of Ms. Hazel before Victor had brought Sarah here. Ms. Hazel repeatedly asked for her.

"You're taking Naomi's place."

Something in his tone chilled Sarah to the core. "Wh-what happened to Naomi?"

His gaze turned somber. "She disappeared, leaving Mother brokenhearted."

More likely, Victor had arranged for Naomi's disappearance.

He touched Sarah's cheek. She turned her head away.

"Listen to me." He grabbed her jaw and forced her to look at him. "A man is bringing your sister here in a day or two. I'll pay George off. Then you and Miriam can take care of Mother together. If you want to see your sister, do as I say."

His thin lips twisted into a hateful smirk. "But if you disobey me, if you try to escape, I'll—"

He let the threat hang.

She uttered the first question that came to mind. "Then will I disappear like Naomi did?"

He bristled.

Evidently, she had struck a chord that rang a little too true.

"I'm not afraid of you, Victor." Could he hear the tremble in her voice?

He leaned closer. "What if I turn off the power and use candles to light the house? Remember what you told me about the fire when you were a little girl?"

Her chest constricted. She struggled to pull air into her lungs.

"Do everything I say, Sarah, so you and Miriam can be together again, and so you can be safe. Do you understand?"

She cocked her head and furrowed her brow as if listening to a rustling sound coming from the unfinished portion of the attic.

He bristled. "What's wrong?"

"Do you hear them?" she asked, feigning an unfounded confidence in her voice.

His face blanched.

"Rats, Victor. They're in the attic."

"I don't believe you."

The fear that flashed from his eyes proved what Sarah had assumed was true.

"Feed Mother her breakfast," he ordered as he hurried out of the room.

From the open doorway, Sarah watched him race down the stairs to save himself from the rats. If she could only escape as easily.

Her momentary euphoria at having unsettled him was short-lived. Exhausted from lack of sleep and weeks of confinement, Sarah dropped her head in her hands. Hot tears burned her eyes. Would she ever be free again?

"Send someone to help me, Lord," she pleaded, her heart breaking at the hopelessness of her plight. "I don't want to die trapped in this old house."

Joachim Burkholder guided the buggy along the mountain road. He had come home like the prodigal son. Except he had not squandered money or lived a life of debauchery. He was, instead, coming home to reconcile with his father. At least that was his plan.

Metanoia, some called it, a conversion or transformation, which was what Joachim had started to experience. Now, he needed to piece his broken life back together. He had tried to live *Englisch*. His heart remained Amish.

Jostling the reins, he encouraged the mare forward. Together he and Belle had traveled from farm to farm to farm. Joachim had worked odd jobs and saved his earnings until his yearning to come home had caused him to slowly retrace his steps.

Belle increased her speed as Joachim took in the rolling hills and lush valleys. How deeply he had missed the beauty of this land and the serenity of the Amish way of life.

Gott, he silently prayed, *forgive my obstinate pride that forced me away from family and faith when I sought to place my will above Thy own.*

The tranquil setting soothed Joachim's troubled soul. He breathed in the loamy scent of Georgia clay mixed with fresh pine from the trees that dotted the side of the roadway. The cool morning air tugged at his black jacket and lulled him into a sense of peaceful calm that dissipated as soon at the buggy rounded the bend. At the bottom of the incline, a level plain stretched out in front of him. His gut tightened as he recognized this particular section of the road home he had inadvertently taken.

Was he trying to add more burden to his already guilt-laden shoulders? Why had he guided Belle to the very spot he had never wanted to pass through again? Some memories were too hard to bear.

He glanced back, debating whether to turn around, retrace his journey and take the longer route that would circumvent this place of pain.

Joachim squared his shoulders, refusing to cower. He needed to face the past to heal. He felt sure that was the advice the bishop would provide when and if he sought to return fully to his Amish faith.

As he turned his gaze to the intersection ahead, Joachim's chest constricted. The morning sunlight filtered through the gray sky overhead, yet for a moment, he stepped back in time as the memory of that night assailed him. He heard the rhythmic clip-clop of horses' hooves against the pavement and the creak of the two buggies as they strained along the ill-fated path.

In his mind's eyes, he saw Eli turn and laugh at

Joachim, who followed close behind in the second buggy. The ongoing competition between the two brothers had taken a tragic turn that night.

At eighteen, Joachim should have known better than to go along with the seemingly innocent challenge. He did not blame his brother. Nor had his *datt* blamed Eli. Instead, his father had blamed Joachim.

Once again, he remembered how Eli had egged him on, ignoring the roar of the oncoming vehicle and the headlights speeding too fast.

Joachim had raised his voice in warning. "A car approaches on the road." But Eli had not heard and had not reacted.

The crash of metal and splintering wood echoed in Joachim's memory, along with the horrific cry that had come from his own throat as he screamed his brother's name.

Five years had passed, yet Joachim's grief was still so raw. "*Gott*, forgive me," he whispered as he hurried Belle through the intersection.

Perhaps coming home to the mountains had been a mistake. What had happened could not be undone. No matter how Joachim tried to reconcile the past.

He needed longer to decide if he was ready to contact his father. Work would help. Using his hands and carpentry skills to transform disrepair into integrity would allow him to see more clearly. If he could hole up somewhere, he might be able to stem the figurative bleeding of his wounded heart and come to terms with his future and the way he wanted to live his life.

Belle flicked her head.

"You want to go home, girl. I know. But I need more time."

The turnoff to the old Thomin homestead appeared in the distance. The house had needed work five years ago. If Hazel Thomin were still alive, the elderly lady might hire Joachim to do odd jobs around the property while he tried to decide how he was going to piece his life together.

He pulled back on the reins to slow Belle's pace, then nudged the mare onto the path that led to the grand home. The property had been in Mrs. Thomin's family for generations, but what he saw made his spirits plummet even more. The house that had been regal in its day—some called it a mansion—now appeared wasted from neglect.

Joachim grimaced, noting the peeling paint and the sagging facade. The stately beauty had come under hard times and was in need of a steady hand that could restore her original beauty as well as her once-sturdy understructure.

He guided the buggy toward the front of the house and glanced up to see a young woman near Joachim's age peering from a second-story window. Blond hair hung around her slender face. She stared at him, wide-eyed, for a long moment. His chest tightened in response to the need he recognized, even at this distance, in her pensive gaze. Before he could acknowledge her presence, she stepped away, leaving him confused by the tangle of emotion that wrapped around his heart.

Joachim pulled the horse to a stop and jumped to the ground as the front door opened. Victor Thomin stepped outside, coffee mug in hand. Tall and skinny with unkempt red hair, Hazel Thomin's only child had not improved in looks—or, it seemed, in temperament—over the last five years.

With a surly grunt, Victor raised the mug to his lips and drank deeply, his beady eyes intent on Joachim, even as he wiped the back of his hand over his thin lips. A cut festered that had spattered his knuckles with dried blood.

Recalling the baleful glance of the woman at the window, Joachim made a connection that caused his eyes to widen in horror—though he immediately reminded himself that it could be wild speculation and not credible in the least. He had no proof of abuse, yet Joachim could not and would not ignore his instincts. Victor had been a scoundrel in his youth, and from the downward pull on his drawn lips, there was no reason to think he had changed.

Extending his hand, Joachim introduced himself. Instinctively, he knew from Victor's menacing expression that the red-haired man had failed to recognize him.

Victor reluctantly accepted the handshake. "Is there something you want?"

"I'm looking for work." Joachim glanced again at the overhead window, feeling a sense of loss at finding it empty. "Carpentry, painting or any handyman jobs you might need done. I can provide references."

Victor pursed his lips. "You're from around here?"

Joachim would not lie, but he saw no reason to provide more than a minimum of information. "I worked in North Carolina for a number of years. Folks said there might be jobs in this area of North Georgia."

He studied the once-beautiful home, pausing to gaze at each window, hoping for another sign of the illusive woman. "Looks like they were right. Your house could use a bit of upkeep."

Victor shrugged. "I doubt this old place is worth the effort."

"A few repairs will make a big difference," Joachim assured him. He touched the dry rot around the front door and peered inside the house through the sidelight. His heart skittered in his chest.

The woman he had seen moments earlier now stood poised on the landing. She raised her index finger to her lips as if pleading for him to remain silent about her whereabouts. The furtive look on her oval face made him even more concerned about her wellbeing.

Joachim turned back to Victor. "I can do as little or as much as you want. But you should know that the value of your property would improve with the repairs, in case you decide to sell any time soon."

Victor arched a brow. Seemingly, the mention of financial gain brought interest. "You think I could find a buyer?"

Joachim nodded. "*Yah*, if you are willing to fix some of the problems."

"I've got rot around the back porch, too," Victor volunteered. "Plus, the kitchen door is warped and won't close easily."

"Let me have a look," Joachim suggested. He motioned Victor to take the lead and then glanced again into the house. The woman had disappeared.

Joachim sighed at his own foolishness. He knew better than to play hide-and-seek with an *Englisch* woman. He needed employment, not involvement in a domestic dispute. Although she and Victor seemed an unlikely match. Perhaps she was a caregiver for his mother. Still, something did not seem right. Whether she was there as an employee, a spouse or a guest...no woman should look so afraid.

After rounding the house, Joachim climbed to the back porch. Quickly he inspected the sagging roof and rotting soffits, trying to get his mind off the woman who continued to tug at his heart.

His gaze turned to the kitchen window. He stepped closer in pretense of examining the sill, all the while peering through the glass, searching the kitchen and hallway beyond for some sign of the woman.

Victor stood to the side. "If I do hire you," he warned, scratching his chin, "I won't stand for laziness or slipshod work."

Movement caught Joachim's eye. Something or someone hurried across the entrance hallway to the front door.

"I understand your concern, but you will not find me to be lazy or my work slipshod," Joachim said, hoping to keep Victor's attention on the disrepair instead of what was happening inside the house.

Feeling the need to provide a distraction, Joachim tapped the sill and pushed on the wood before moving to the next window and repeating his assessment.

"Yah," he finally said. "There is much work to be done. I could start tomorrow. Pay me only if you are satisfied with the completed job."

"I'll think it over." Victor took another slug of his coffee. "Stop by tomorrow, and I'll let you know."

Joachim nodded. "Sounds *gut*."

Leaving Victor on the porch, Joachim returned to the front of the house. He glanced at the outbuildings and barn in the distance. Had the woman left the house?

Was she now hiding close at hand, or was he making more out of that which was innocent?

"Sarah?" Victor's voice sounded as he entered the house.

Joachim climbed into the buggy and flicked the reins. Thankfully, Belle responded with a brisk trot.

Although Joachim kept his eyes on the road, he knew he was not alone. He had seen the tarp—which had been neatly folded and stowed away earlier—strewed over the back of the buggy. Someone was hiding under the thick covering.

He hurried the mare along the driveway and felt a sense of relief as he guided Belle onto the main road.

A sports car raced by, going much too fast. The woman in the passenger's seat turned to stare at Joachim as if she had never seen an Amish man.

Too soon, the sound of another vehicle filled the air.

Joachim looked back, seeing a red pickup truck turn out of the Thomin driveway. Victor sat behind the wheel. The tires squealed as he gunned the engine.

Would he pass by as the other car had done or stop and demand to know who or what was hiding under the tarp in Joachim's buggy?

Coming home had been a mistake. More than reconciling with his father, Joachim needed to reconcile with himself as to why he was so eager to help an *Englisch* woman on the run.

Chapter 2

Sarah blinked back tears and tried to calm her heart before it ricocheted out of her chest. She had been a fool to think she could escape. The squeal of tires and the whine of a vehicle approaching the buggy made her realize the full extent of her mistake.

She curled into an even smaller ball and prayed the tarp would keep her hidden. After two months of captivity, she shuddered at the thought of what her punishment might be if Victor found her. Plus, she had put the Amish man in danger, and now he would be subject to Victor's wrath, as well. The man driving the buggy was innocent of any wrongdoing and had stepped, quite literally, into a perfect storm that was getting worse by the moment.

That she had grabbed the opportunity to run away from Victor still stunned her. An action she never would have taken if not for his abuse earlier this morning. She had planned to escape with Miriam after they were re-united. Her sister would have known what to do and where to go. Miriam had saved Sarah from the fire. She would have saved her from Victor, as well.

Instead, the Amish man with the broad shoulders and understanding gaze had been the catalyst that had Sarah running for her life. Even when peering down at him from the window, she had felt an instant surge of hope when their eyes met, as if he knew she was in danger and had come to her rescue.

The hope evaporated with the deafening roar of the motor vehicle. She fisted her hands and bit down on her lip, willing herself to remain still while internally she wanted to kick her feet and wail like a small child who didn't want to be punished for some misdeed. Yet she had done nothing wrong.

Victor was the one at fault, a fact she needed to re-member. How thoroughly he had filled her mind with lies so that she sometimes confused her innocence with guilt.

"You're the reason, Sarah, that we have to hide from the police," Victor had complained on more than one occasion. "If I didn't need to protect you, I would be free to come and go. Instead, we must hole up and hide out so the corrupt cops won't find you and sell you into slavery along with your sister."

He had brainwashed her with his constant badger-ing about her guilt. Fear, fatigue and her dulled senses, caused by the drugs he forced on her, had added to her confusion.

Thankfully, today, she was able to think rationally enough to seize the opportunity to escape. Pulling in a fortifying breath, she smelled the musty scent of the tarp mixed with the damp cool air of the encroaching storm. If dark clouds hung overhead, hopefully, they weren't a harbinger of what would happen to her in the next few moments.

Instead of the weather, she focused on the clip-clop of the horse's hooves on the pavement and tried to ignore the blast of a horn and the revved acceleration of the vehicle that forced the buggy to the side of the road.

"Hold up there, Belle." The deep voice of the Amish man quieting his horse should have calmed her unease, but knowing Victor was the reason brought another volley of fear to wrap around her spine and underscored the seriousness of her situation as the buggy came to a stop.

God help me, she silently prayed. *Help the Amish man. Save both of us from Victor.*

"Hey, Amish." Victor's voice. "Did you see a woman leave my house?"

"Your *mudder*?"

"Not my mother." Victor's sharp retort reminded Sarah of the caustic tone he often used with her. "A twenty-one-year-old woman wearing jeans and a sweater."

"She is your *schweschder*?" The Amish voice was deep and calming.

"What?" Victor didn't understand.

"Your *schweschder*," the Amish man repeated. "Is your sister the woman for whom you are searching?"

"I don't have a sister," Victor spat. "I'm looking for the woman who works for us, helping my mother. Did you see anyone?"

"A car passed by, heading toward Petersville. A

woman sat in the passenger seat. The man driving had a bald head."

"What color was the woman's hair?"

"Blond. This is perhaps the woman you are seeking?"

Victor grumbled. A car door slammed and tires squealed as he drove away. Sarah held her breath and listened to the sound of the engine disappearing into the distance.

"He's gone." The Amish man's voice was low and reassuring. "You can come out now."

He had known she was under the tarp?

She raised the edge of the covering and stared up at a square jaw, furrowed brow and deep-set eyes filled with question.

"Did he hurt you?" he asked.

She hadn't expected his concern or the tears that filled her eyes. "Not until today."

"He will return soon. Plus, a storm is approaching."

She looked at the darkening sky.

"I will take you someplace safe. Do you have family in the area?"

She glanced at a nearby road sign—Petersville 5 miles, Willkommen 30 miles—and shook her head. "My sister will be here tomorrow or the day after. She'll make sure I'm safe once she arrives."

"But today you need lodging," he said, calmly stating the obvious. "Stay under the tarp in case Victor returns."

Without further discussion, he turned his gaze to the road and clicked his tongue. The buggy jerked as the horse responded. Sarah found the sound of the horse's hooves on the pavement and the sway of the carriage mildly soothing.

She didn't know anything about the Amish man, yet he had helped her escape. She had to trust him, at least for the moment. From what she knew about the Amish, they kept to themselves and had little to do with law enforcement. If so, the man in the buggy might help her elude the crooked cops who had hijacked Miriam's car and were searching for both sisters even now. He might also help her reconnect with Miriam and take both of them to safety. But where would that be?

Sarah had moved from town to town her entire life with no place to call home except the short-term rentals where she and her mother and sisters had lived for a month or two at most, before moving on to the next temporary lodging. How foolish she was to think her life in the future would be different, no matter how much she longed for stability and a home of her own.

Relieved though Sarah was to be free of Victor, she worried about his mother now left home alone with her crazed son. Over the last few weeks, Ms. Hazel's condition had deteriorated much too quickly, making Sarah wonder if Victor was doing something to speed up her decline.

Concern for the older woman weighed heavily on Sarah's shoulders, but she couldn't do anything to help Ms. Hazel at the moment. Right now, she needed to close her eyes and rest. Sarah had escaped, although she felt anything but free while hiding under the tarp with Victor prowling the area in search of her.

Should Victor return to question her rescuer again, would the Amish man whose faith embraced peaceful nonresistance be able to save her? Or would Victor find her? She shuddered at the thought, knowing that if he got his hands on her once more, Victor would ensure Sarah never escaped again.

The dark sky mirrored Joachim's inner struggle. Passing through the intersection where Eli died had been Joachim's undoing earlier. Now he was hiding a woman he did not know. The added complication only made him more conflicted.

All too clearly, he had recognized the pain on the woman's face as she glanced down at him from the window and again as she stood on the stairway inside the Thomin house, her finger to her lips and her eyes pleading for mercy. Her expression had reminded Joachim of his own sense of hopelessness and despair that had overwhelmed him following his brother's death.

Was that what had drawn Joachim to the woman and made him long to protect her?

He glanced at the rear of the buggy, where she lay under the tarp. By the steady rise and fall of the heavy covering, he presumed she had fallen asleep, which was probably for the best. Fatigue had lined her face along with fear that made him grateful he had come to her rescue.

The wind picked up, and the temperature dropped as dark clouds billowed overhead. Joachim needed to find shelter before the storm brought more chaos to this already confusing day.

He flicked the reins, hurrying Belle. Instinctively, she knew the route he had chosen to take.

The woman needed a place to hole up for a day or two until she could connect with her sister. Petersville was the nearest town, but that was the direction Victor had gone. When he failed to find her there, he would more than likely retrace his route to search more thoroughly in the local area.

The Burkholder farm adjoined the Thomin property, but the road connecting the two homes took a circuitous route around the fields and pastures. Glancing at the sky, Joachim wondered if Belle would get them to shelter in time.

If his father was tilling the soil in the distant acreage, Joachim might be able to signal his sister, Rebecca, especially if she was working in the garden. She had written him faithfully while he was away, telling him about the family. In spite of the breezy news she shared, Joachim had read between the lines, all too aware of the emotional anguish Eli's death had caused his family.

More than anything, Joachim longed to see *Mamm* again, yet his mother would abide by the rules his father established. Having to watch her turn her back on him would be almost too hard to bear.

And the woman hiding in the back of his buggy? If his father forbid Joachim entry into the house, he would hole up in the barn and give the woman as long as she needed to decide where she wanted to go. Until that time, Joachim would stand guard, ensuring Victor did not find her.

But would she want Joachim's help?

He shook his head. An *Englisch* woman was not in his future, yet whether he liked it or not, she was very much in his present. More than anything, Joachim wanted to keep her safe from Victor and from anyone else who might cause her harm.

Chapter 3

In her dream, Sarah watched Victor raise his hand to strike her. She screamed, then flailed her arms and tried to free herself from the shroud that covered her.

"You are safe." Hands reached for her, removed the heavy covering and pulled her into an embrace.

Not Victor, but the Amish man.

"Shh," he soothed, cradling her like a child.

It was the first comfort she had felt in far too long. She buried her head against his neck, wanting to remain forever enveloped in his warm and protective hold.

Tears filled her eyes and spilled down her cheeks, wetting his cotton shirt. Hearing the rain, she was more than grateful to be under cover and out of the storm, and even more grateful for the human contact.

The rapid thump of his heart proved the Amish man wasn't a figment of her imagination. She nestled closer, not wanting to open her eyes or leave the security of his embrace for which she had hungered too long.

Thunder crashed overhead.

"Joachim?" A woman's voice said the name, her tone filled with surprise.

Another clap of thunder.

Her Amish protector tensed and pulled back ever so slightly.

Sarah clung to him for a moment before her eyes fluttered open.

His head was turned. She followed his gaze to the woman dressed in a calf-length blue dress, white apron and bonnet, who stood just inside the open barn door.

Outside, rain pummeled the earth. The day had turned dark as night. Or was it night already? She wasn't sure how much time had passed. The woman's questioning frown seemed equally dark. Perhaps she was the man's wife. The thought cut through Sarah's heart. She had been such a fool.

Embarrassed by her neediness and the way she had reached out to the man, she untangled her arms from where they had wrapped around him.

He glanced down at her, a glint of confusion flashing from his dark eyes.

Was he upset that his wife had found him giving comfort to a woman who wanted nothing more than to return to his embrace?

"I—I'm sorry," she stammered, trying to make sense of what had happened. "I was asleep. I didn't realize…"

"Who are you?" the Amish woman demanded, glancing first at Sarah and then turning her frosty gaze to the man. "Joachim, is there something you did not tell me in your letters?"

"She needs help, Rebecca."

"*Yah*, and it looks like you need help as well from the way you clutched the *Englischer* to your heart."

"Father is in the house?" he asked, seemingly sidetracking the issue at hand.

Rebecca shook her head. "He and *Mamm* are visiting Aunt Mildred and Uncle Frank in Kentucky. They will be gone for a few more days. Had you written that you were coming home, they might not have left."

Sarah was trying to follow the conversation and understand the undercurrent of what was really being said. The man had mentioned his father. No, his tone implied that it was *their* father. Was the woman not his wife?

"Excuse me," Sarah said, pulling away from him and peering at both of them. "You're not married?"

The woman huffed. "Why do you think this?"

Evidently, Sarah had jumped to the wrong conclusion. She held up her hand. "I'm sorry. I don't want to offend either of you."

She turned to Joachim. "Thank you for bringing me here. If I could stay in the barn until the storm passes, I would appreciate it."

His brow furrowed. "You plan to leave?" He shook his head. "This cannot be."

He climbed from the buggy and motioned to the Amish woman. "We must take our guest into the house."

Glancing back, his gaze burrowed into hers. "Your name is Sarah?"

She nodded. "Sarah Miller."

"I'm Joachim Burkholder." He pointed to the other woman. "My sister, Rebecca."

The weight on Sarah's shoulders lifted ever so slightly. Sister. Not wife. Tears again stung her eyes.

"She needs food and lodging, Rebecca."

The Amish woman stepped closer. Her earlier scowl softened but she seemed hesitant to offer Sarah a hearty welcome.

"We must hurry," Joachim said. "Before Victor returns."

Rebecca grasped her brother's arm. "Victor Thomin?"

"*Yah*. He is staying at his mother's house."

"*Ach,*" his sister groaned, with a shake of her head. "Naomi said he is not a good man."

"You know Naomi?" Sarah asked. "Victor's mother kept asking for her."

Rebecca nodded. "Naomi lived nearby. She cared for Ms. Hazel while Victor was away."

Joachim pointed to the open barn door. "The rain eases. We must go inside."

He reached for Sarah and helped her from the buggy. Taking her hand, he hurried her out of the barn.

Dark clouds rolled overhead. Another storm was approaching, but Sarah breathed in the cleansing air, feeling a sense of relief. She had escaped Victor. She had a place to stay. At least for now, she was free.

A bolt of lightning pierced the sky and struck nearby. The almost-immediate crash made Sarah realize everything could change in an instant.

She would never be free of Victor, not until the hateful man was stopped.

The rain intensified just before Joachim and Sarah reached the porch. Another sound was discernable over the rain. He glanced at the drive and tensed. A horse and buggy scurried along the main road. For a long moment, Joachim stared after the buggy and then let out a deep breath.

"You thought it was Victor, didn't you?" she pressed.

He squeezed Sarah's hand, hoping to provide reassurance and bring comfort to her seemingly still-anxious heart. "Victor will not find you here."

At least that was Joachim's hope.

Together they climbed the steps to the porch. He opened the door and motioned her inside. She wiped her feet on the latched rug and hurried into the kitchen.

A sense of calm and right order enveloped Joachim as he stepped over the threshold and stopped to take in the peacefulness that pervaded the space. Glancing at the familiar furnishings—the table and chairs, dry sink and cabinets—his *datt* had made, Joachim soaked in the aura of home and family he had missed for the last five years.

"Rebecca can brew coffee," he said, hoping his voice did not reveal the mix of emotions that had welled up within him upon entering the house. He turned to the newcomer. "Perhaps you would prefer tea?"

Sarah glanced at Rebecca, who hurried in behind them.

"I have cold cuts and cheese and fresh baked bread if you are hungry."

"Thank you both," Sarah said. "But first, I need to wash my hands and face, if you don't mind."

"Of course." Rebecca pointed to the stairs. "I will take you to the room where you will stay the night. Joachim must tend his mare. We will eat after he returns from the barn."

His sister turned as if to shoo him outside. But despite her prompting, he was slow to head to the door.

He did not want to leave the home to which he had only now returned. He also did not want to leave Sarah.

He gently touched her shoulder. "So much has happened, but you are not to worry. Victor is in town, searching for you there."

"And if he comes here?" she asked.

"I will not let him into the house."

Belle needed to be groomed and fed. Rebecca would take care of Sarah until he returned. Still, leaving the house this time was almost as hard as leaving the mountains had been five years ago.

How could he have grown so attached to a woman—an *Englisch* woman—in such a short period of time? He knew nothing about her except that she needed a safe place to stay for a day or two. He and Rebecca would open their home to her, but Joachim needed to be careful. As taken as he was by her in such a short time, he feared what might happen in the days ahead. He must guard not only Sarah, but also his heart.

Chapter 4

Joachim had said that he would keep her safe. As much as Sarah wanted to believe him, she was worried. Victor was unpredictable, and his mood swings had grown progressively more extreme. He had warned her never to leave him, but she'd done just that. Given how angry he'd been before over smaller infractions, what would his response be to this?

Rebecca filled a pitcher with water and motioned for Sarah to follow her. "A diesel pump runs our well, so we always have water in the house," the Amish woman explained as they climbed the stairs. "Propane heats our water for washing and bathing. Later I will fill a tub for you."

On the second floor, she ushered Sarah into a small but spotlessly clean bedroom. A beige patchwork quilt pieced with blue triangles covered the single bed. A chest of drawers, table and straight-back chair filled the room.

Rebecca placed the pitcher on the chest next to a large porcelain bowl. She opened the bottom drawer and pulled out a thick terry-cloth towel, a bar of soap and a glass bottle.

"I made the soap and shampoo and added natural oils to both products. I hope you will find them to your liking."

"Thank you, Rebecca. You and your brother have been so thoughtful."

Rebecca seemed to appreciate the compliment that hopefully would wash away her earlier concern about Sarah. The Amish woman offered a weak smile. Her cheeks glowed pink with a mix of embarrassment and appreciation. "Come downstairs when you are ready to eat."

Sarah glanced at the inviting bed, wishing she could hide under the covers and curl into a ball. Maybe then she wouldn't worry about Victor finding her again. Was she safe here? Sarah needed to learn more about Joachim Burkholder and his Amish family. Thanks to them, she had a place to stay, at least for now.

She scrubbed her face and hands and dabbed water through her hair, appreciating the clean, fresh scent of the bar soap and eyeing the liquid shampoo. Using the bath products Rebecca had made would be a welcome treat, although so much could happen in the hours ahead. Sarah needed to focus on figuring out what she needed to do to remain free from Victor instead of on creature comforts like having a long soak in a hot tub.

After patting her face and hands dry, she returned to the kitchen.

"The coffee is hot," Rebecca said in greeting. "Or as Joachim mentioned, I could make tea."

"He's still in the barn?" Sarah asked, knowing nothing about farm life and feeling somewhat awkward around his sister.

"*Yah.* Joachim feeds his horse before he feeds himself."

"You seemed surprised to see him."

The Amish woman nodded. "He has been gone from our home for a number of years. It is *gut* to have him back again."

"Do you have other siblings?"

"A brother, Eli, died a few years ago."

"I'm sorry."

"It was *Gott*'s will."

Sarah didn't want to think about a loving God taking anyone's life. At the moment, she longed for something to keep her mind on anything other than death. "May I help you prepare the lunch?"

"You can slice the bread. It is cooling on the counter." Rebecca pointed to the raised loaf. A knife lay next to a cutting board.

"It's homemade?" Sarah asked, admiring the plumpness of the loaf and the golden brown crust.

"*Yah.*" Rebecca arranged the meat and cheese on a platter. "I always make extra bread and sell it to tourists who stop at our driveway."

Sarah looked out the window, suspicion growing within her. "Do people often come to your house?"

"It is not something that should worry you," Rebecca assured her.

In spite of Rebecca's comment, Sarah couldn't shake off her concern about strangers visiting the Burkholder farm while she stayed there. She continued to peer from the window, hoping for some sign of Joachim—and for no sign of anyone else. The door to the barn hung open, and the interior looked dark and foreboding.

Rebecca claimed Joachim was caring for his horse, but what if she was wrong? Victor could have returned and overpowered Joachim when he wasn't looking. Perhaps Victor was ready to barge into the house and capture Sarah again.

Minutes ticked by, only increasing her worry. "Why is Joachim taking so long?" she finally asked, unable to calm her unease.

"You could go to the barn and ask him yourself," Rebecca suggested. "Or you could join me in the main room where I have my mending. Joachim will come inside shortly."

Joachim had assured Sarah earlier that she was safe, but it felt to her as if too much time had elapsed since he had left the house. Rebecca moved into the main room and started humming. The tune, a childhood favorite, should have calmed Sarah's unease. Instead, it only added to her concern. What was she doing in a strange house with people she didn't know?

She glanced at the oil lamps on the wall, the candles on the sideboard and the matches on the table. Her chest constricted and her pulse raced. A ringing sounded in her ears that failed to overpower the voice screaming through her mind.

Fire!

She wrung her hands. The memory of that night so long ago returned, constricting her lungs and leaving her gasping for air, overcome by the same panic that filled her every time she even thought about flames.

She had to leave. Now.

Ever so quietly, she opened the kitchen door and gulped in the damp air, all the while the voice continued to warn her.

While in the buggy, she had seen a sign for Willkommen. Victor had mentioned Miriam was being held somewhere in that area. Their aunt lived in Willkommen, as well. At least that's what their mother had told them. If Sarah could get to Willkommen, she might find her aunt, and together they could search for Miriam.

She pulled in a fortifying breath and then raced down the steps and scurried past the barn, heading toward the pasture and a line of trees on the far side of the field. She would hide there until the roadway looked clear. Then she would cross to the opposite side where a thick patch of trees flanked the road. Hidden by dense underbrush, she would make her way to the narrow two-lane that veered off from the main road, where she had spotted the sign for Willkommen.

As much as Sarah had appreciated Joachim's help, she couldn't rely on him to keep her safe. He was Victor's neighbor.

She checked the road for cars, saw that it was clear and crossed the pavement. The approach of a vehicle sounded in the distance. Her pulse raced. She turned to glance over her shoulder.

Her heart stopped as a red pickup crested the nearby hill. Victor!

She ran toward the trees, needing to disappear in the brush. She wouldn't let him capture her again.

The truck accelerated.

She ran faster.

The screech of brakes made her heart lurch.

Victor had seen her.

Footfalls pounded the pavement. He was coming after her.

She'd been so foolish. Victor was more of a threat to her safety than the matches and candles and oil lamps. She never should have traded the security of Joachim's house for the outdoors, where she was so vulnerable.

"Sarah!" Victor screamed her name.

She hesitated for a fraction of a second, then chastised herself for being so easily swayed.

Fighting against the pull of his voice, she forced herself forward, remembering how he had choked her this morning until she couldn't breathe.

She pushed through the bushes, needing to escape his voice, his control. To escape him.

"You won't get away, Sarah," he called, as if reading her mind. "I'll follow you. You can't escape from me."

The branches scraped her arms and pulled at her sweater, but she kept going, ignoring the cuts to her flesh. She couldn't listen to her body. She had to listen to her mind, warning her to run fast, run hard, run away.

She made a sharp turn to the right and ran all the faster. The only sound she heard was her own raspy breath and pounding heart. For an instant, she thought she had eluded him until the sound of his footfalls returned along with the rustle of leaves.

If only she had stayed at Joachim's house. He would have protected her.

"Sarah!" He was close. Too close.

She tripped.

He grabbed her.

She fought to free herself from his hold.

No! She tried to scream, but his hand clamped around her mouth.

"Sarah?" Victor called again. This time, he was farther away and moving in an opposite direction.

If Victor wasn't holding her, then who was?

Soft. Her skin was so very soft.

Joachim dropped his hand, releasing Sarah from his hold.

She stood ever so still, as if afraid to move.

"He's heading back to his truck," Joachim whispered. "You lost him when you made that sharp turn to the right. I saw you cross the street when I left the barn, but it took me a while to catch up to you."

"Oh, Joachim," she said, pulling in a deep breath. "Victor was following close behind me."

"But you outsmarted him, Sarah."

She turned to gaze up at Joachim with blue eyes that were crystal clear and filled with sorrow. His heart tripped in his chest, making him want to move even closer.

"I never should have left your house," she said, seemingly oblivious to the way her nearness affected him. "It wasn't because of any distrust for you or your sister. It was me. I didn't want to cause you any problems. If Victor found me at your house, I'm not sure what he would have done. Plus, I need to get to Willkommen. My sister Miriam—"

She shook her head. "I haven't mentioned my aunt. My sister, my mother and I came here to find her, but dirty cops hijacked our car. Miriam and I were taken and our mother was killed. Victor said he bought me so

I could take care of his mother. I'm still so confused."
She pulled in a ragged breath. "It was crazy of me to
think I could have found my way to Willkommen, yet
it seemed like the best choice I had in that moment. I
don't have any place else to go."

"You have my house. Victor will not find you there.
I will protect you."

At least Joachim hoped he could keep her safe.
"Willkommen is a two-hour buggy ride from Petersville," he tried to explain. "Even if you were strong, the
trip would be difficult for you to manage on foot. You
have been held captive. You must gain your strength
first. I will take you when you are ready."

"I wasn't thinking." Sarah tugged at a strand of her
golden hair. "Or maybe I was thinking too much about
getting away from Victor."

Joachim held out his hand. She placed hers in his, her
touch light, but she was trembling and her pale face gave
him even more cause for concern. She needed time to
rest and gain her strength. Good food and lots of sleep
would help build up Sarah's reserve. Then they could
think about traveling to Willkommen.

"Rebecca will wonder where we are," he said. "We
will go now and take a path that leads through the
woods. The spot where we will cross the road is thick
with trees on both sides of the pavement. We will move
slowly and keep watch lest Victor be close at hand."

"I'm all right, Joachim. You don't have to worry
about me."

But he *was* worried. He was worried about the fatigue written so plainly across her sweet face. She was
too thin and too pale, and no matter how strong she tried
to appear, she needed rest and nourishment.

He had to get Sarah to his house to keep her safe. Hopefully, she wouldn't run away again because next time he might not be able to save her.

Once they arrived back at the Burkholder house, Joachim held the kitchen door open for Sarah and motioned her inside.

"Rebecca has lunch ready," he said, as they stepped over the threshold and into the warmth of the Amish home. "A good meal is what we both need."

His eyes were filled with understanding as he looked at her and smiled. "Is that not right?"

"I am hungry," Sarah admitted, grateful for Joachim's focus on food instead of mentioning her foolish mistake of thinking she could outwit Victor.

Just as Joachim had mentioned, she needed to gain strength before she journeyed to Willkommen. Besides, Victor said Miriam might be arriving at his house in a day or two. This wasn't the time for Sarah to run scared.

"Joachim, you are ready for a cup of coffee?" Rebecca asked as she entered the kitchen, her needlework still in her hands. From her casual gait and nonchalance, she evidently had not realized what had transpired after Sarah left the house.

"Yah," Joachim said with a nod. "I will wash my hands, and then I will also be ready for the meats and cheeses you have placed on the table."

He and Sarah both washed at the sink. Rebecca filled mugs with coffee and motioned Sarah to sit next to her at the table.

Joachim sat across from both women and bowed his head.

Sarah and Rebecca followed suit, with each person praying silently.

Thank You, Lord, Sarah mentally intoned, *for Joachim rescuing me in the woods, and thank You for providing this place of shelter from the storm. Send Miriam and let me help her escape whoever is holding her captive so she and I can be together again.*

She glanced up to find Joachim staring at her. Her chest tightened, and a warmth tingled her neck. Glancing away, she reached for the meats and cheeses and placed a slice of each on a piece of bread.

Hungry though she was, Sarah kept thinking of Victor's mother, knowing Ms. Hazel was at the mercy of her son. What would become of the frail woman if Victor left the area for good?

"You are thinking of Victor?" Joachim asked.

"His mother. She's bedridden. A sweet lady who is too infirm to help herself."

"Victor is not to be trusted." Rebecca said with a decisive nod.

Sarah reached for her coffee, not willing to let her expression reveal her own struggle, knowing she had wanted to believe Victor when he'd first taken her from the cabin where she and Miriam had been held. He had told her he would keep her safe from the men who planned to traffic both sisters across state lines. Had it been the drugs that made Sarah believe—at least for a day or two—that he would protect her?

Joachim placed his mug on the table and cocked his head. "A vehicle approaches."

Sarah recognized the sound. Her stomach tightened, and she clutched her hands. "What if it's Victor?"

"Stay inside." Joachim left the table. "Do not let anyone see you."

He opened the door and stepped onto the porch. Rebecca ran to open the window over the sink.

"It is a pickup truck," she relayed to Sarah. "A man is driving. Red hair."

She glanced back at Sarah. "*Yah*, it is Victor."

Sarah wanted to find a closet and hide.

"The pantry." Rebecca pointed to the walk-in alcove. "He will not see you there."

Sarah's heart nearly pounded out of her chest. She hurried into the pantry. Peering around the curtain that divided the cupboard area from the kitchen, she watched the truck pull to a stop.

"Hey, Amish." Victor's raised voice floated through the partially open window. "I spotted the woman I told you about. She disappeared in the woods. If you see her, let me know."

"Why do you need to find this woman?" Joachim asked, his voice calm and rational in contrast to Victor's nervous high pitch.

"Sarah worked for my mother. Now she's gone. In fact, if you know of an Amish girl who wants a job, I need to hire someone."

"Dependable help is hard to find," Joachim said.

"As sickly as my mother has become, I doubt she'll live long. I plan to get the house ready to sell. Come over tomorrow. I have work for you, and remember to let me know if you see that woman."

Victor turned his truck around and drove off.

Sarah's heart hammered in her chest. If she had been outside on the porch, or even standing next to a window, Victor would have spotted her.

Joachim entered the kitchen and hurried to where she stood, her eyes wide and back to the wall.

"He is gone," Joachim assured her.

Sarah was too frightened to move. Victor had found her once. He could find her again no matter what Joachim did to try to stop him.

Fear. Joachim had seen it in Sarah's pretty blue eyes when he had come back inside the house after Victor had driven away.

"He is gone," Joachim assured her again. From the look on her face, he knew his words did little to quell her upset.

A knock sounded at the front door. Sarah took a step back and gasped.

Joachim glanced at Rebecca. "You are expecting someone?"

"Levi Plank has been helping me while *Mamm* and *Datt* are away." She peered from the kitchen window. "*Yah*, it is Levi."

Her voice took on a lilt Joachim had not heard, and the blush to her cheeks made him pause.

"Levi is a friend," Rebecca assured Sarah. "You do not need to be afraid."

But her words did little to change the concern written so plainly on Sarah's face. She backed even farther into the pantry and covered her mouth with her hand; all the while her eyes sought out Joachim. He nodded his encouragement before he stepped toward the door.

Years before, the young Amish man had been his brother Eli's friend. Both the same age, Levi had been the quiet, pensive one whose personality contrasted sharply with Eli's charisma.

Rebecca opened the door, her eyes twinkling with interest, a warm and welcoming smile on her face as she invited Levi inside. "I have a surprise that I did not expect. Joachim has come home."

In the five years that Joachim had been away, the quiet youth had grown into a muscular man whose grip was strong and firm when the two men shook hands.

"This is a *gut* surprise," Levi said. Then as if overcome with enthusiasm, he pulled Joachim close and slapped his back. "You have been missed."

The sincerity of his welcome touched Joachim. "It is good to see you, my friend."

"Our parting was difficult. I trust you have been well. It was time for you to come home, *yah*?"

Joachim nodded. "It was time."

Levi's gaze turned to the alcove where Sarah peered with wide eyes at the gathering.

"You have brought someone home with you?" Levi asked, a hint of confusion evident in his tone.

Sarah took a step forward as Joachim introduced her to Levi. "Sarah needed a place to stay," Rebecca quickly volunteered. "She will remain with us for a day or two."

"You have found a good house," Levi said with a nod. "Plus, Rebecca is known for her pies and cakes."

He rubbed his stomach. "Often she asks me to taste her baked items after the chores." He smiled at the young Amish woman. "Perhaps today we will all be able to enjoy a slice or two of pie."

Rebecca laughed. "*Yah*, that is possible after the animals are watered and fed. You know I cannot resist you, Levi, with all the help you have provided."

"Then I will hurry to the chores as my mouth waters for the special treat that awaits."

Joachim nodded. "I, too, am grateful for your help, Levi. We will go together."

"I will bake something while you both work," Rebecca assured them. She glanced at Sarah. "We will both remain in the house and watch for Victor."

"Victor Thomin?" Levi asked.

"Yah." Rebecca nodded. "He is a dangerous man. I do not know how Naomi could work so long in his house."

"My sister helped Ms. Hazel, but she had nothing to do with Victor. Ms. Hazel lived alone back then."

Sarah stepped from the alcove. "Your sister was the Amish woman Ms. Hazel mentioned? She misses Naomi."

"We all miss her," Levi admitted.

"I don't understand," Sarah said.

Levi pursed his lips and thought for a moment before responding. "Victor came home. She did not like being around him, but we fear something else could have happened because she left not only the job but also the area. We have not heard from Naomi since then."

Sarah's brow furrowed. "Did you go to the police?"

"The Amish in this community do not trust the Petersville police. It is commonly known that they can be bribed and bought. My *datt* would not have gone to them, except for his concern for Naomi's welfare." Levi's voice took on an angry edge as he continued. "They were no help and said Naomi must have left for a better life among the *Englisch*."

Rebecca patted his shoulder, offering support.

He nodded his thanks and then continued. "It was not what my father wanted to hear. We will not go to the police again. They do not understand our ways. Some say they are only interested in their own gain."

"Victor told me the police were corrupt," Sarah shared. "Although he is corrupt as well, so I don't know if I can believe what he said. Still, my sister's car was hijacked by men claiming to be police." She quickly explained being sold to Victor and how Joachim had helped her escape today.

Levi was right, Joachim thought. The Amish did not trust the police, but Victor needed to be stopped by law enforcement. Perhaps Sarah would change her mind about notifying the authorities if she knew them to be honorable. Right now, she was exhausted and still traumatized by what had happened. Joachim would broach the subject again later. In the meantime he would do everything possible to keep her safe.

Chapter 5

Sarah appreciated the bath Rebecca drew while the men worked outdoors. The fragrance of the sweet-smelling soap she provided filled the air like a spring bouquet. Sarah stepped from the tub feeling rejuvenated and grateful as she slipped into the Amish dress Rebecca had provided.

"With a clean body, you must also have fresh clothes," Rebecca stated as she instructed Sarah on how to pin the fabric and then adjust the apron around her waist.

"What about the bonnet?" Sarah asked.

"It is a prayer *kapp*. Amish women cover their heads when they pray."

"But you wear it all the time?"

"This is true. We are always ready to pray when our head is covered."

"I pray but perhaps not often enough," Sarah admitted.

"The *kapp* will remind you to do so."

Sarah thought of being in the closet as a child. The smoke had seeped under the door, making her even more afraid. God hadn't saved her even though Sarah had prayed. Thankfully, Miriam had come to her rescue.

"Did you ever pray for something that didn't come about so that you felt God refused your prayer?" Sarah asked.

"*Gott* does not refuse prayer, but sometimes that which we desire is not according to His will." Rebecca sighed. "I told you that Joachim and I had a younger brother named Eli, who died in a buggy accident. My *mamm* prayed for him to live."

"I'm so sorry about your brother."

"As I mentioned earlier, it was *Gott*'s will." Rebecca smiled ruefully. "This is what my *mamm* believes."

"And your father?"

Rebecca's face clouded. "My father does not blame *Gott*." She hesitated as if weighing whether to say something else, then shrugging, she added, "He blames Joachim."

Before Sarah could question her further, Rebecca picked up the white bonnet from where she had placed it on the dresser and handed it to Sarah. Earlier, she had pulled her towel-dried hair into a bun, and she now placed the bonnet on her head.

Rebecca stood back and nodded her approval. "You look like an Amish woman. Victor will not recognize you if he returns to talk to Joachim."

Sarah's stomach roiled thinking again of the hateful man who had held her against her will for too long. How could his mother, who seemed sweet and unassuming, birth a baby who would grow to be so vicious?

What had caused Victor to turn out so bad? She shook her head at the issues within families. Sarah's oldest sister, Hannah, had left three years ago. Sarah had pleaded for her to stay, but Hannah said she had to leave. Sarah hadn't understood her reasoning or why Hannah had never contacted them again.

When she begged her mother to reach out to Hannah and ask her to return home, her mother had shoved the request aside, just as she ignored anything that didn't suit her. Sarah never understood how she could turn her back on her own child. Although too many times her mother had turned her back on Miriam and Sarah. At least Sarah had always had Miriam, but where was she now and would the two women ever be reunited?

The rain returned. Fat drops pounded the barnyard, and thunder rumbled overhead. Joachim and Levi hurried to finish the chores.

Glancing at the upstairs window, Joachim thought of when he had first seen Sarah. Had it been only a few hours since their eyes had connected at the Thomin home?

He followed Levi into the barn. The two men spoke little as they worked, but the silence was comfortable, and the physical labor relaxed the tension in Joachim's shoulders. Some of his earlier concern about Sarah evaporated, and instead of confusion, he felt a sense of purpose and right order.

"Your father is a *gut* farmer, but he is getting old," Levi confided as he paused for a moment to wipe his brow.

"*Datt* planned for Eli and me to work the land with him," Joachim admitted. "Now he needs to find help. You are good to aid him, Levi."

"I help only when he is not in town. He is too proud to take on another person the rest of the time."

Joachim nodded. "*Yah*, he is proud."

"He will be glad to see you."

"You are good to give me comfort by your hopeful words, but I do not think my *datt* will welcome me home."

Levi narrowed his gaze. "You come asking forgiveness, *yah*?"

"I do, but my father and I must both bridge the divide between us. I will walk halfway. I hope he will walk halfway, as well."

"Sometimes the son must walk farther, especially if the father believes he is right."

Joachim pondered Levi's words while he added feed to the troughs and watched the horses eat the newly offered grain.

Levi might think his father would be open to Joachim coming home, but what if his homecoming brought back too many memories of what had happened? Maybe when he faced his father again, Joachim would discover that he had been foolish to think reconciliation was possible.

Once the horses were fed, the two men rolled up their sleeves and washed their hands and arms at the water pump, and then ran to the house as lightning split the sky.

Joachim opened the door and hurried into the kitchen ahead of Levi.

Rebecca stood at the stove, holding a pie that she had just pulled from the oven.

"The storm comes again," he said as he crossed the kitchen to the towel hanging on a hook.

He dried his hands, then glanced up as Rebecca turned to face him. His heart lurched in his chest, sending a new wave of confusion over him. He stared open-mouthed at the Amish woman.

Not Rebecca. The face he saw beneath the white *kapp* made his breath catch in his throat.

Sarah.

"Rebecca provided the clothes." Sarah's hand wrapped through the fabric of the skirt. "Your sister said Victor would not recognize me like this."

"My sister is right." Joachim struggled to find his voice. "I did not recognize you at first glance."

"You think I look like Rebecca?"

Her blue eyes reached into his heart. She was beautiful. Not because she was in the Amish dress or because her hair was pulled into a bun but because some of the pain she had worn earlier had eased. The lines that tugged at her face had lifted, and the open honesty of her gaze hit him anew.

"Joachim, you haven't answered me," she said, her eyes filled with concern. "Is something wrong?"

"Nothing is wrong and you do not look like Rebecca, but I am surprised to see you as an Amish woman."

"Am I offending you?"

He shook his head. "You could never offend me."

Levi hurried inside and stopped by the door to wipe his feet. Bewilderment washed over his face as he glanced first at Sarah and then at Rebecca, who stepped back into the kitchen.

"You are both staring as if you have never seen a woman in an Amish dress," Rebecca said with a laugh.

Levi pointed to the stove. "I was wondering if you could spare a cup of coffee and a slice of pie for a hungry man."

"*Yah*, of course." Rebecca's cheeks glowed with a hint of embarrassment. "But I have ham and cheese on the table, along with fresh baked bread. You need to eat something substantial before you have your pie."

Levi smiled as he accepted the cup of coffee she offered. "You know what I need even before I do."

The twinkle in her eyes warmed Joachim's heart. Rebecca's interest in the young man was more than evident, and Levi seemed taken with her, as well. Joachim was happy for his *schweschder* and hoped Levi would start the courting process soon. Perhaps Joachim could chaperone and take them for rides in the country. He would occupy his mind with thoughts of pretty Sarah in her blue dress and white apron while Rebecca and Levi chatted with each other.

If only Sarah was wearing the Amish dress as a woman of their faith instead of as an *Englischer* who needed to hide her identity and had nothing else to wear.

Joachim and Sarah sipped coffee as Levi ate the lunch Rebecca had provided. Although Sarah said little, her eyes took in the conversation he and Levi had about the farm and what could be done if his *datt* were open to accepting help to make the fields more productive.

"The Amish Market in Willkommen is a fine place to sell produce and baked goods," Levi shared. "My uncle goes twice a week as do many of the other Amish farmers. The *Englisch* come from as far away as Atlanta. They buy handcrafted items, too—including woodwork. You could do well in this area, Joachim, if you opened a shop in town."

He shook his head and laughed. "I am a carpenter, Levi, not a store clerk."

"Yet you charge for your labor when you go house to house. How different would that be from selling chairs and tables and lawn furniture to walk-in customers?"

Although Levi had a point, Joachim saw only the

folly in his comment. Once his father returned home and Joachim had a chance to talk to his parents, he doubted they would want him to remain at home. In fact, Rebecca would probably be chastised for allowing Joachim to stay in the house while their parents were out of town. There would be no point in Joachim staying in the area and opening a shop if he was shunned by his family.

Suddenly, his mood dampened, and the coffee tasted bitter in his mouth.

"You will have pie?" Sarah asked as she and Rebecca cleared the table once Levi had eaten.

Joachim nodded. "Only a small slice. There is much yet to be done. The fences need repair. The barn, as well. Tomorrow I will go to Victor's house. Today, I will work here."

"I'm sure your father will appreciate your help."

If only that would be so, yet Joachim suspected his *datt* would be hard-pressed to appreciate anything his son did.

Sarah accepted a small piece of pie from Rebecca and carried it to table.

"Denki," Joachim said as he took the plate from her.

She glanced at Levi. "I'm sure you would like pie."

"Yah, but a much larger slice than Joachim," the younger man said with a grin. He glanced at Joachim. "I must work for my father this afternoon, and tomorrow is the barn raising. Did Rebecca tell you?"

Joachim shook his head.

"The Byler barn burned," Levi continued. "Samuel had wood delivered, and he has asked us to arrive in the morning. We could use your help, Joachim."

"Of course. Samuel is a *gut* man. If he needs help, I will be there."

As Joachim and Levi ate the pie, Rebecca wrapped cheesecloth around a second pie and tied the edges together. "I baked extra for your *mamm*. Tell her thank-you for the onions she sent yesterday. They were sweet and will keep in the root cellar."

Levi smiled. "She will like to hear that her gift was well received."

"*Yah*, of course, it was."

"She always asks about you, Rebecca. You should come to visit."

"Perhaps when *Mamm* and *Datt* return."

"They will not be gone much longer?" Joachim posed.

"Only a few more days," Rebecca responded. "But, Levi, I will see your *mamm* tomorrow at the barn raising. She will be there, *yah*?"

"Probably not. Her arthritis is bad, especially when it rains."

Levi bid Joachim and Sarah farewell and accepted the pie from Rebecca. She walked outside with him, and the couple stood talking on the porch.

Joachim glanced at Sarah. She rinsed dishes in a bucket of water at the sink. "You will be all right here in the house with Rebecca if I am working in the barn?" he asked.

"Of course, I'll be fine. Don't worry."

"I was not worried."

"Then you were concerned."

"Perhaps," he said with a shrug. "I know you were frightened when Victor drove onto the property earlier."

"You should tell him to stay off your land."

"*Yah*, this I could do. But that is not how a good neighbor acts."

She narrowed her gaze. "Is it necessary to be a good neighbor to a man who is so hateful?"

"If I want him to think I have nothing against him." Before he could explain what he meant, the back door opened and Rebecca returned to the kitchen.

"I am interrupting something?" she asked.

"No," Sarah insisted. "But I am tired and would like to rest."

Joachim peered through the window at the darkening sky. "Black clouds roll overhead. The storm may turn the day to night. Perhaps you will need a candle in your room."

Sarah's face tightened. She shook her head. "There's still plenty of daylight. Besides, I don't like candles."

Joachim didn't understand her comment, nor did he understand the fear that returned to her face and the way she clasped her hands together. Something about candles had set her off, but what? And why?

"Perhaps the oil lamp would be better," Rebecca offered.

"I'll be fine," Sarah insisted. "The room has a window. I will awake before nightfall, if I can even sleep."

Sarah grabbed her skirts and hurried upstairs. Her footfalls echoed in the house and made Joachim's heart ache.

He had to let her go, but he wondered what the *Englischer* was hiding. Sarah feared Victor, but there was something else she feared.

Chapter 6

Sarah hadn't realized how exhausted she was until she removed the bonnet and apron and lay on the bed. She draped the quilt over her legs and turned her head away from the diffused light coming from the windows. In less than a minute, she was sound asleep.

Sometime later, a noise startled her awake. She turned to glance out the window, seeing the failing light. The steady rhythmic pitter-patter of raindrops on the roof made her want to close her eyes again.

She began to drift back into a light slumber when someone pounded on the downstairs door. She sat up, slipped her feet into her shoes and hurried to the window. She peered around the curtain, but all she could see was the barn, not the drive where a car or buggy, undoubtedly, sat parked.

Not a red pickup truck.

But what if it was Victor?

Her breath caught in her throat as the banging started again.

Where were Joachim and Rebecca?

And what if the person at the door *was* Victor?

Sarah's hand rose to her throat. She glanced around the room, searching for a closet in which to hide, but the Amish bedroom had no closets and only one door that led to the hallway. She backed into the corner beyond the bed, as far as she could get from the window, her pulse racing.

She spied the prayer *kapp* on the dresser where she had placed it. Rebecca's mention of an Amish woman always being prepared to pray circled through her mind.

"Lord, he-help me," she stuttered. The words stuck in her throat.

A voice sounded outside. Joachim's voice.

Slowly, she approached the window, making sure she was not visible from below.

Joachim stood at the doorway of the barn talking to someone. Her stomach churned. She rubbed her hand across the waistband of her dress, hoping to calm her internal unrest, all the while she silently beseeched Joachim not to reveal her whereabouts if he was talking to Victor.

A sinking feeling settled over her. If she'd trusted the wrong man and Joachim and Victor were actually friends, she could end up back in the attic, being held under lock and key, which was the last thing she wanted.

"Help me, Lord," she mumbled as she tied the apron around her waist, settled the bonnet onto her head and hurried downstairs in hopes of seeing for herself who had come knocking at the door.

* * *

Joachim did not expect to be just as broadsided when he saw Sarah for the second time dressed in Amish clothing. Maybe it was her flushed cheeks or the question he read in her gaze that made him stop as he entered the kitchen and stared at her until she seemed ready to flee up the stairs again.

"Who was at the door?" she asked, her eyes hooded. "I heard knocking. It was Victor, wasn't it?"

"It was a man from town who came to buy fresh eggs. He has come often in the past and did not realize Rebecca had taken down the sign about having eggs and baked goods for sale. I told him none were for sale today."

"But—" She shook her head.

"But you thought it was Victor," Joachim said.

"I don't know what I thought. The pounding woke me. I couldn't see the drive—"

"I told you I would keep you safe." But she had not believed him. Joachim let out a frustrated breath, knowing too well that Sarah's trust would be hard earned.

"You're going to his house tomorrow," she said as if to justify the assumption she had incorrectly made.

"I need the work, Sarah. Plus, what better way to keep my eye on Victor? He held you against your will. What if he does the same thing to the next woman he brings home to care for his mother? The police need to be notified so he can be stopped from hurting anyone else."

"No." Her voice was firm. "The police are already too involved."

"Involved in capturing you?"

She turned her back on him and hung her head.

Joachim mentally chastised himself. He had caused her upset, which was the last thing he wanted. "I do not understand," he finally admitted. "Perhaps you can explain everything."

She stepped toward the kitchen table and slipped into a chair. Her face was tight with emotion.

"It is difficult to talk about, *yah*?" he said, following her to the table and sitting across from her.

She offered him a weak smile as if to acknowledge what he said was true. "Until recently, my sister Miriam and I lived outside Knoxville with our mother. She had shown signs of dementia over the last year or so. A few months ago, she started talking about a long-lost sister with whom she wanted to reconnect. Her name is Annie Miller." Sarah stared at him expectantly. "I believe my aunt lives in Willkommen."

Joachim nodded. "The next town."

"A road sign said it is thirty miles from here."

"*Yah*, that is right."

"On the way to find my aunt, we got lost. It was night. A police car pulled us over. At first I was relieved, thinking they would help us, but then—"

She clasped her hands and held them tight against her heart.

"Something happened," he prompted, knowing the retelling must be difficult.

"There were two police officers, although I wonder if they truly were law enforcement. One of them grabbed Miriam and pulled her from the car. My mother became agitated and opened the passenger door. She wanted to protect my sister, but a second man—he was in the police car."

She hung her head and blinked back tears that filled her eyes. Joachim reached for her hand.

"I can't remember everything, but a second man—the one in the police car—shot my mother."

Joachim hadn't expected her comment. "*Gott* help you, Sarah, for what you had to endure."

"They took Miriam and me to a cabin and held us in separate rooms. Everything after that was a blur. Victor hauled me away at some point. I know he forced me to take drugs that he said would help me. I stashed them in the corner of my mouth and spit them out whenever I could. But I couldn't get rid of all of them. I was in a drugged stupor for too long. Eventually he took me to his mother's home. All told, he held me against my will for two months. When I saw your buggy, I knew I needed to get away. I hadn't taken the pills he offered for a few days so I was clearheaded and able to think for myself." She glanced up at Joachim. "You came at the right time."

Joachim had been drawn home for some reason. He had thought it was to reconcile with his father. Maybe it was because of Sarah's need.

"Now," she continued, "I'm not sure what I should do. Perhaps I should leave."

"Leave?" Had he or his sister done something to upset her? "Surely Rebecca said nothing that caused you concern."

"No, Joachim, your sister has been very helpful and welcoming."

"Then you think I do not want you here? That is not true."

"Victor is your neighbor. Perhaps he's a friend, although I cannot see how you would want anything to do with such a hateful man." She glanced down at the dress she wore. "You were kind to invite me to stay, and I'm grateful for the clean clothing Rebecca has provided. I'll remain here tonight and leave in the morning."

Joachim could not believe what she was saying. The fact that she thought he would have anything to do with Victor was unsettling.

"Victor is not the type of man I would ever call friend. It troubles me, Sarah, to have you think that I would not see with clear vision who he really is. But you have been through so much, and often our minds jump to incorrect conclusions."

His own father had done exactly that. "I told Victor I would start work tomorrow, not because I like the man but because I want to ensure Victor does not cause more harm. When I work at his house, I can see what he is doing and hopefully keep him from harming any other woman. Plus, you were concerned about his mother. I am, as well. I will find a way to check on her."

Sarah stared at him for a long moment. "I want to trust you, Joachim."

He took her hand. "And you can. If I was a friend to Victor, I would have told him where to find you. He never would have left my father's farm alone if he thought you were here."

She sighed as if weighing his words. "I want to believe you."

"Then *do* believe me, Sarah. It is that easy. You are safe here. Victor will not enter this house, I will make certain of that. You must decide what you want to do and where you want to go. If you want to go to Willkommen, I will take you, but that would be in a few days. First you must get stronger."

Sarah had been held captive for too long. Rebecca's cooking and the peace that even Joachim could feel in the Amish house would replenish Sarah's strength and her health.

That night when they sat at the table, Sarah had little to eat, and the sadness in her eyes worried him even more than her hesitancy to enter into a conversation.

After they finished eating, she started to clear the dishes, but Joachim took her hand. "I will help Rebecca. You need to rest."

"Joachim is right," Rebecca encouraged. "You do not need to help me tonight. You need to sleep."

"But—"

Joachim took her plate and placed it near the sink. "It is dark. You'll need a candle to go upstairs."

Her eyes widened, and she shook her head. "I don't want a candle."

"Perhaps the gas lamp then. You can adjust the wick so only a small flame will light the room all night if you do not want to remain in the dark."

"The dark doesn't frighten me," she insisted.

But something frightened her.

"I have a flashlight in my buggy. Wait here and I will get it."

"You are Amish, yet you can use a flashlight?"

Rebecca nodded. "We do not run electric wiring into our homes, but flashlights, which are battery powered, are allowed."

Joachim hurried outside and returned soon thereafter with a flashlight in hand. He turned it on. "You will be safe tonight."

She took the flashlight and nodded. "Thank you, Joachim."

Glancing at Rebecca, she added, "Thank you for dinner. Don't let me sleep too late in the morning."

Joachim watched as Sarah slowly climbed the stairs, her footsteps heavy as if she had little or no energy. Would she be able to get over the pain she had experienced?

He thought of her future and wondered where she would go once she gained her strength. To Willkommen to find her aunt and perhaps track down her sister? Or farther away where Joachim would never be able to see her again?

She was *Englisch*. He was Amish.

Whether he liked it or not, the two could never mix.

Chapter 7

Sarah woke the next morning to the smell of bacon and eggs. Her mouth watered, making her realize how hungry she was. Last night with Joachim sitting across the table from her, she had eaten little. Thankfully, she had slept well and now hurried to dress and go downstairs.

Rebecca was clearing the table and turned as Sarah entered the kitchen. "What is wrong this morning? You look worried."

Sarah glanced around the room, seeing the empty skillet on the wood-burning stove. Dirty dishes were piled in the sink, and the butter and jelly sat on the counter.

"I missed breakfast?" *And Joachim*, she wanted to add.

Rebecca motioned her toward the table. "I have kept a plate of bacon warm in the oven. Your place is still set at the table, and eggs will not take long to fry. I can toast the bread or you can eat it as is."

"Thank you, Rebecca, but I hate for you to go to all that trouble."

"It is no trouble. Joachim has already eaten."

Sarah stepped to the window and peered toward the barn. "Is he hitching the horse to the buggy?"

"He is in the east pasture, repairing a fence. One of our cows got out. Thankfully, he got her back, but now he must fix the breach."

Sarah felt a sinking in her stomach. The nervousness she had felt last night returned, and her appetite left her. "Maybe I don't need breakfast."

"You must start the day with food," Rebecca insisted. "I will fetch more eggs from the chicken house."

"Let me. It's the least I can do."

"If you insist." Rebecca handed her a basket. "The nests are just inside the coop. You will see them. There should be plenty of eggs."

Sarah hurried outside, relieved to be of help, and inhaled the fresh country air, enjoying the sense of freedom with the open spaces all around her. For too long, she had been locked in the old Thomin house, which smelled of dust and mildew.

She looked for Joachim, but couldn't see him. She did, however, see a barking dog, which ran from one of the fields, wagging his tail and warming her heart. She bent to pat his head and scratch under his neck. "Aren't you a cute Yorkshire terrier. I'll have to ask Rebecca your name. I'm glad you want to be friends."

The dog licked her hand. "You're what Victor needs. Did you know your ancestors were bred to hunt rats?"

The playful terrier wiggled all the more. His antics

made her laugh, which she hadn't done in so long. Even before Victor she couldn't remember the feeling of acceptance that flowed over her with the playful dog so eager for her attention.

She laughed again as the dog danced at her feet. "I need to get the eggs before Rebecca comes looking for me." Sarah scratched the dog's head and then hurried to the hen house with the pup scampering along beside her.

"Don't scare the hens," she warned playfully.

The clucking coming from the hen house assured her she would find eggs, which she quickly did. After filling the small basket Rebecca had given her, Sarah started back to the house.

The sound of a vehicle caused her to turn toward the main road. Her heart stopped.

A car sped by going much too fast. A tan sedan.

She let out the breath she had been holding and hurried to the porch, the pup at her feet.

Rebecca met her at the door, holding a large bag of dog food in one hand. "I see you have met Angelo. He is lovable, *yah*? Maybe too much so at times."

"Angelo?" Sarah smiled down at the dog. "That doesn't sound like an Amish name."

Rebecca chuckled. "He belonged to a local man named DeCaro. When he moved away, he could not take Angelo so we agreed to keep him. The dog is a wanderer. He visits lots of farms and comes back when he's hungry."

She handed Sarah the bag. "We will make a trade. I will begin cooking your eggs if you fill Angelo's bowls. You will find his dishes at the side of the porch."

Sarah enjoyed being useful, and Angelo seemed to appreciate the attention she showered on him as she filled his food dish and a second bowl with fresh water.

Hurrying back inside, she ate the eggs Rebecca had prepared along with the crisp bacon and a thick slice of bread slathered with butter.

"I'm so full," Sarah admitted. "Breakfast was delicious." She stood and carried her empty plate to the sink.

A buggy turned onto the drive. Rebecca hurried to the window and peered outside. "It is Levi. He will take us to the barn raising."

"What about Joachim?" Sarah asked, feeling a knot form in her stomach.

"He will join us later at the Byler home."

"I'll wait for him here."

"Joachim did not want you alone in the house, Sarah. You are to go with us."

"But what if we pass Victor on the road?"

Rebecca smiled. "You will sit in the back of the buggy. Victor will not see you there. Besides, being dressed as an Amish woman protects you from Victor even if he still searches the area. He would not think to look for you among us, and he would not be able to spot you just from passing the barn. The women work in the kitchen getting the lunch ready. He might drive by on the road, but he will not come into the Amish home."

Sarah bit her lip, trying to weigh the pros and cons of leaving the protection of Joachim's home. She had made an almost disastrous mistake by leaving yesterday and didn't want to repeat her error.

"What about the other women?" she asked. "They'll realize I'm not Amish and Victor might find out."

"*Ach*, this is not something that should cause you worry. After what happened with Naomi, the Amish give Victor a wide birth. His true self is known and not admired, to say the least. The Amish ladies you will meet today will not talk to Victor, of this you can be certain."

"But won't they ask questions about where I came from and why I'm with you?"

"We will tell them the truth. You are visiting from Tennessee. We will not mention anything more. You are used to *Englischer* gatherings where perhaps people are inquisitive. The Amish do not pry." She tilted her head. Her eyes twinkled. "At least most of us try not to pry, but there are busybodies even among the Amish. I will make certain you stay away from anyone like this today."

Sarah had to smile at Rebecca's insights. Human nature was human nature no matter the culture. Some people thrived on knowing everything about everyone else.

"You're sure Joachim will join us later?" she asked again.

"*Yah*, I am certain." Rebecca picked up a basket from the table and handed it to Sarah. "Carry this potato salad to the buggy. Levi will tuck it in the rear where it will not turn over. I will bring the pies."

Sarah pulled in a fortifying breath and grabbed the wicker basket. "Did you make the basket?"

"*Yah*, I did. In the winter I weave, and sell my baskets in the warm weather along with the produce from the garden, fresh eggs and my baked items to the people from town."

She handed Sarah a black bonnet with a wide bill, and a lightweight black cape. Once both women were properly attired, they grabbed the baskets and hurried outside to where Levi waited with the buggy.

He arranged the food in the rear and then helped Sarah onto the back seat. Rebecca sat in front next to him.

Sarah peered from the buggy, hoping she was hidden from roving eyes, especially if Victor happened by. She rubbed her right hand over her stomach to still the unrest within her. If only Joachim were at her side.

Levi flicked the reins, and his mare headed to the road. Thankfully, both directions were clear. Sarah settled back in the seat, soothed by the side-to-side sway of the buggy and the clip-clop of the horse's hooves on the pavement as Levi turned the mare onto the main road.

The crisp morning air mixed with the musky scent of the still-damp earth. She turned her gaze to the distant pastures, hoping to catch sight of Joachim. All she saw were a few horses on the hillside and newly tilled fields waiting for planting.

The repetitive cycle of tilling, planting, harvesting year after year had to bring satisfaction to the farmers who worked the soil and depended on God's providence to provide an abundant harvest.

Thinking back on her own life, she saw little fruit, no matter how hard she worked to be productive. She had tried to be a dutiful daughter and sought ways to help her mother, although her efforts always fell short of her mother's expectations. Yet she had continued to try to prove herself.

It had started with the fire that was never talked about, never forgiven. Outrage from her mother would have been better than the silence. At least then the issue could have been discussed and resolved. Instead, it remained a gaping hole in their relationship. A hole that never closed and always festered.

"You are all right?" Rebecca turned to ask, probably hearing another of Sarah's sighs.

"I'm fine. The air is refreshing and the scenery is so picturesque. I'm glad you invited me to join you today."

"We will be there soon. The barn is to be built on the Byler land. As you probably heard Levi mention yesterday, Samuel and Ester lost their barn in a recent fire."

Sarah tugged the cape tight around her neck, trying to push aside the memories from the past.

"Did...did a candle overturn?" she finally asked.

"Lightning caused the fire," Rebecca shared.

"I'm sorry."

"*Yah*, but it is a reason to gather today. The men will work to build the barn, and the women will work in the kitchen so the men have food when their stomachs grumble."

"My stomach is grumbling now for a slice of your pie," Levi joined in with a laugh.

Rebecca poked his arm playfully and turned back to face the road. Levi leaned a bit closer to her, and Rebecca's laughter carried an even stronger lilt.

Sarah's heart warmed to the attraction between them that was so obvious. For half a second she longed for someone in her own life who could make her laugh and take away the pall that hung across her shoulders.

She was being foolish. Such a relationship was not in her future. Her mother had made mistakes in the men she chose. Sarah had learned wisely to guard her feelings lest she, too, succumb to a man who would break her heart or her spirit. Love was not for everyone. Her mother was proof of that.

The ride to the farm took a little more than twenty minutes. Levi helped Sarah climb down from the buggy and then handed her the same basket she had carried earlier.

A two-story Amish house stood nearby with small outbuildings directly behind the main structure. A stream of women climbed the porch steps and entered the house carrying baskets and bowls and boxes. Sarah imagined the delightful offerings loaded within the containers—cakes and cookies and freshly baked bread.

In the distance, lumber was neatly piled in stacks on the ground. Giant frames lay waiting to be raised. Beyond the location for the new barn, she saw the charred remains of a former structure, now little more than burned rubble. The acrid smell of smoke wafted past her and made her turn from the destruction and focus on the men milling close to the woodpiles. They chatted amicably among themselves, and laughter punctuated their conversation.

Sarah had read somewhere that the barn and house raisings combined neighborly help with social time and were important mainstays of the Amish life. Even as an outsider, she could sense the excitement and an energy that was almost palpable.

Although buoyed by what she saw, thoughts of Victor returned and brought Sarah back to her own predicament. Longing for the protection of the house, she hurried in that direction, unwilling to be out in the open for long, especially with Joachim nowhere in sight.

Levi joined the other men while Rebecca fell in step next to Sarah.

"The women will know I am not Amish." Sarah repeated her earlier concern. Surrounded by the Amish, she realized how much she stood out, in spite of the clothing she wore. Surely the women would recognize her attempt to be something she wasn't.

"Do not worry," Rebecca said. "I told you before,

all you must say is that you are a friend visiting from Tennessee. This is true. You do not need to enter into long conversations with the other women. Just smile and nod."

Which sounded so easy when Rebecca said it, but as Sarah stepped into the house overflowing with women, she felt totally out of place. Following Rebecca's lead, she removed her cape and black bonnet and hung them on a peg by the door.

Lowering her gaze, she walked behind Rebecca into the kitchen and was relieved when someone handed her a whisk and a half-filled mixing bowl.

"The cream needs to be whipped," the woman instructed before she moved to the stove to stir a pot of what looked like homemade noodles.

Complying with the woman's wishes, Sarah stood in the corner, beating the cream with a steady motion. Thankfully, the women were so busy preparing the meal that they paid little attention to the newcomer.

Once the cream was whipped, Sarah helped grate cabbage for the slaw and clean carrots and kale fresh from the Bylers' garden.

The smells of succulent meats and vegetable casseroles, mixed with the warm scent of baked goods, made her look forward to the luncheon in spite of the hearty breakfast she had eaten this morning.

Glancing through the window, she smiled at the young children playing close to the house, watched over by older girls who hauled food to the long tables set up in the shade of the mighty oaks.

"You will help me?" Rebecca asked as she lifted a large container of lemonade from the sink. "We will use a small wagon to take this to the men."

Sarah wiped her hands on a nearby towel and followed Rebecca outside. Together, they pulled the wagon to where the men worked. The frame had been raised while the women were busy in the kitchen. Now the barn had a sturdy outer structure upon which men climbed.

The steady tap of their hammers filled the air, along with the grinding of hand drills and the grating rasp of saws, cutting through the four-by-fours. The smell of fresh wood overpowered the earlier scent of the fire, and Sarah breathed in the clean aroma as she scanned the structure.

Her heart leaped in her chest when she spied Joachim, big and strong, perched high atop the massive support frame. He hammered a crossbeam into place, seemingly oblivious to the danger of being so precariously poised.

"Joachim doesn't fear heights, it seems," she said, her eyes focused on his long legs and strong arms.

Rebecca followed her gaze. "My brother has been a climber since he was a boy. *Yah*, he fears little."

Once the beam was nailed in place, he glanced down, finding Sarah in the swarm of people as if he had eyes only for her.

Her spine tingled and a smile parted her lips. Joachim waved in response, filling her with a sense of well-being.

Rebecca poured lemonade into glasses, and Sarah distributed them to the men who eagerly accepted the refreshing drink.

Grabbing Sarah's arm, Rebecca pointed to the road.

Sarah's breath caught. Victor's pickup pulled into the drive and braked to a stop near the house.

He stepped out and stood for a long moment, staring at the gathering of workers.

Sarah clutched Rebecca's hand in fear. Victor was near the porch, blocking her path to the kitchen. Her pulse raced. Exposed and in danger of being discovered, she searched for a hiding spot.

Her only recourse were the outbuildings. Trying not to be obvious, she wove her way between the men.

A barking dog drew her attention to the open field. Angelo appeared in the distance racing toward her, his tail wagging.

She glanced back. Victor turned in her direction at the same moment. His eyes widened, and he pushed through the children playing on the lawn.

Sarah ran. Skirting the first shed, she edged around a second building to where another structure stood.

If only the door was unlocked. She climbed the stairs, grabbed the knob and pushed on the door, relieved that it opened. Slipping inside, she saw the pile of sawdust in the corner and the various woodworking machines. She pulled in a deep breath and closed the door behind her.

From the window, she caught sight of Victor. He glanced again at the house and then walked with determined steps toward the workshop.

A dog barked. She peered through the window. Angelo stood at the door, demanding entry. Victor rounded the second outbuilding and was heading straight for her.

She climbed behind a pile of plywood.

Her heart pounded. A roar filled her ears. Her pulse raced so that she was sure the entire workshop must be shaking in sync with her trembling body.

Angelo continued to bark. He wanted to be let in, right now.

Footsteps sounded outside. The door creaked open.

She held her breath. Sawdust tickled her nose so that she wanted to sneeze but she managed to stay silent.

"What's going on, you stupid mutt?" Victor demanded, his voice gravelly and laced with anger. "Did someone come in here?"

She envisioned Angelo clawing at the plywood, drawing Victor's attention to where she hid.

If the dog didn't reveal her presence, the unbridled pounding of her heart would alert him for sure.

Angelo barked again.

Please, Lord.

"What'd you find, boy?" Victor drew closer. "What's behind that pile of plywood?"

"Is there something you need?" Joachim's voice as he entered the workshop.

Victor growled. "I saw that woman who cared for my mother. She came in here."

Joachim laughed. "You are seeing things unless she is Amish. No *Englischer* is here."

Victor stepped closer to the plywood. Angelo sniffed at the opening to where she huddled.

"The dog's found something, Amish. The woman's hiding."

Something scurried across the floor. Angelo chased after it.

Victor gasped.

"It was only a mouse," Joachim assured him.

Sarah held her breath. Victor hated rats. Hopefully, his dislike of rodents included mice.

"I saw the commotion from the road and wondered if I would find you here. Why aren't you at my house?" Victor groused.

"This morning I must help with the barn. Perhaps

you will stay and eat with the Amish? The women have been cooking for days. Later, I will come to your house."

Victor huffed. "I need to go to town this afternoon so don't keep me waiting."

"And the lunch?" Joachim asked.

"I don't want your food." Victor stomped out of the workshop. The door slammed behind him.

"Sarah?" Joachim was moving the wood.

A flurry of fine wood particles filled the air. Then his arms were around her, pulling her from her hiding spot.

"Are you all right?"

"Oh, Joachim." She let out the breath she had been holding. "Victor almost found me. If you hadn't—"

Joachim pulled her closer. "Angelo is the one who saved you by scaring that mouse out of its hiding spot."

"Angleo may have saved me, but he also caused the initial hoopla that drew Victor's attention. By the way, I don't like mice," she admitted, "but anything to keep Victor away."

Rebecca opened the door and peered inside. "He is gone."

Joachim stepped away from Sarah, leaving her feeling vulnerable. She wanted to be back in his arms, but she resisted the urge to move closer.

Why was she letting down her guard around Joachim? Sarah was an *Englisch* woman who had no place in his Amish world.

Chapter 8

Joachim hated the disrepair he found in the Thomin home. Sagging gutters, peeling paint, broken shutters, but the worst problem was the dry rot. When Victor's father, Mr. Thomin, was alive, he had kept the house in tip-top shape. A woodworker by hobby, he had taken pride in ensuring the house was well maintained. The father had died when Victor was a teen. Ms. Hazel had maintained the home until her health started to fail. In her declining years, she struggled to care for the inside of the house and did little for the exterior. Joachim could work on the house for weeks and still not shore up all of the more deep-seated structural problems that would require even more extensive work.

He glanced at the drive and wondered how long Victor would be gone. A niggling voice kept playing Sarah's words in his head, especially her concern for Victor's mother. Joachim needed to check on the elderly woman. He would never forgive himself if something happened to her.

He placed his tools on the porch, wiped his hands on a rag and stamped his feet, not wanting to track dirt into the home. After peering again at the driveway, he reached for the kitchen doorknob.

"Joachim?"

He turned, surprised to see Sarah running toward him from the path through the woods. Concern clutched his heart.

"What are you doing here? Is something wrong at the farm?" Instantly he regretted the harshness of his tone when he saw the grimace on her face as if she had been offended by his question.

"Did Rebecca send you?" he asked.

She shook her head. "But she told me about the short-cut through the woods. I thought it would be safe to come because Victor said he would be gone this afternoon. I'm worried about my sister. He promised me Miriam would join me either today or tomorrow. I should have mentioned it this morning, but after what happened at the barn raising, I wasn't thinking straight. Did you see anyone? Miriam's tall with brown hair."

"You need to go home, Sarah. Victor left for town, but who knows when he will be back. I was going inside the house to see about Victor's mother when I heard you call my name. I will check on her and see if any other woman is being held inside, but first, you must return to my house."

"No, Joachim. Victor will be gone for a while. I need to see how Ms. Hazel is with my own eyes. Maybe she'll know something about Miriam."

"It is too dangerous," he insisted.

Sarah pushed past him and opened the door.

As frightened as she was of Victor, Sarah seemed determined to see his mother for herself.

"You are making a mistake," he warned.

"Guard the door and let me know if you see Victor."

Joachim shook his head. "You are not going anywhere without me. Besides, we will have a better view of the road from the upstairs window. I will keep watch from there."

Sarah hurried up the stairs, and Joachim followed. At the top of the landing, she tuned left and opened the door to a large bedroom. Mahogany furniture filled the room. Ms. Hazel lay on a king-size bed, looking tiny and frail against the large pillows and down comforter.

Sarah hurried to the bed and touched the woman's arm.

Joachim stepped to the window, relieved that he could see the roadway in the distance and the route Victor would take home.

"She's asleep, and I can't wake her," Sarah said, her voice filled with concern. "Ms. Hazel, can you hear me?"

Finally, the woman groaned. Her eyes fluttered open for a minute, long enough for a sweet smile to cover her lips before she drifted to sleep again.

A tray sat on a small table near the bed with the remains of a piece of toast and a soft-boiled egg. "It looks like she had something to eat not too long ago," Joachim said. "Maybe Victor is taking better care of her than you thought he would."

"If only that were true. He left her alone in this big house."

"I was working outside."

"And would you have heard her cry out if she needed help? Plus, you weren't here this morning when he stopped by the Bylers' farm."

Sarah moved to the dresser, pulled open the top drawer and took out a pill bottle. "The label is made out to Hazel Thomin, but the bottle is empty. It's for Cardoxin, which sounds like it might be a heart medicine. All the while I've been here, Victor has never refilled her prescription."

She pulled out another bottle. "This one has remained empty, too. It's Lasix. Mother took that. It's a diuretic to eliminate fluid buildup within the body."

"Perhaps Victor keeps the filled bottles of pills in his own room."

Sarah flashed him a look of frustration and opened a second drawer. Her eyes widened as she held up a third bottle. "Over-the-counter sleeping medication. Half the pills are gone."

She looked at Joachim. "Do you know what this means?"

"That Victor needs to refill her medication?"

Sarah frowned. "The sleeping pills are one way to ensure an infirmed woman doesn't try to get out of bed or wander around the house. If Victor is sedating his mother, he's despicable. Even more so than I had initially thought."

Joachim flicked his glance back to the road and his stomach soured. "His truck, Sarah. He is turning into the driveway. Hurry. You must leave the house now."

She returned the pills to the drawers and then raced from the room and down the stairs.

Joachim followed her. On the first floor, she peered

through a window. Victor parked his truck and then stepped out of the vehicle onto the driveway with a scowl on his face.

"You have to hide," Joachim warned.

But where?

She opened the door to the basement and scurried down the steps. He closed the door behind her.

"What are you doing?" Victor's voice.

He burst into the kitchen, his eyes filled with fury as if ready to lambast anyone who stood in his way.

Victor stopped short, seeing Joachim at the sink, holding a glass of water to his lips. He drank it down in one large gulp, then smiled at Victor. "I trust you had a good trip?"

"What are you doing inside the house?"

"I did not think you would mind me getting a drink of water. If this is a problem, I will bring a jug of water with me tomorrow."

Victor flicked his gaze around the kitchen as if to make certain nothing was disturbed. "Did you go anywhere else?"

"I told you I needed a drink of water. Is this a problem?"

"No, of course not. Did anyone stop by the house?"

"You are expecting someone, perhaps?"

"No one. I just thought—"

He let the sentence hang.

Joachim pushed past him. "I must return to my work, but first you should see what I found on the opposite side of the house. You have time for me to show you now?"

"More problems that will cost more money?"

"I believe you have spare wood in one of the sheds outside. I saw this, *yah*?"

"My father's shop. You can use anything from there."

"That was my hope." He motioned Victor forward. "Come, let us walk to the front of the house. I will show you the problem."

Joachim had been digging out dry rot all afternoon, never thinking he would be able to use the disrepair as a decoy for Sarah.

He squared his shoulders, knowing he needed to distract Victor long enough for Sarah to escape.

If he only could.

The basement was dank and smelled of mildew. Light from a small window allowed Sarah to make her way down the stairs and then to the far corner of the basement where she stood, listening for any sign of Victor opening the kitchen door and descending to where she hid. She had been foolish to enter the house, even if she'd wanted to ensure Ms. Hazel was all right.

Muffled voices came from the kitchen, followed by footfalls as the two men walked through the house and left through the front door. She hurried to that side of the basement and peered through a mud-splattered window. Joachim was talking to Victor and pointing to the house.

If Joachim could distract Victor long enough, Sarah could leave through the kitchen and pick up the path just beyond the barn.

She started for the stairs and then stopped. A scratching sound came from the other side of the basement. She had little time to waste but paused as the scratching repeated.

Moving even farther into the rear of the basement, Sarah noticed a small alcove and a padlocked door. The scratching came again.

Sarah tapped on the door. The scratching continued.

Her heart stopped. Was someone signaling from behind the door?

She searched for keys to open the locks but found none.

Knowing she had to be careful, she put her mouth to the door and whispered, "My name's Sarah. I'll come back to help you. Can you hear me?"

Silence.

She glanced back at the window. Joachim couldn't keep Victor occupied much longer. Sarah would be of no help to anyone if she fell into Victor's control again.

She hurried up the stairs and slowly opened the kitchen door. The muffled sounds of the men's voices filtered through the house.

"Thanks for showing me the problem, Joachim." The front door opened. "Right now, I need to check on my mother."

Sarah stepped back into the basement and pulled the door closed behind her.

Hovering on the top step, her heart nearly pounded out of her chest.

Footsteps sounded in the hallway. Was Victor heading up the stairs or coming into the kitchen?

Sarah clutched her stomach to still its rumblings.

He entered the kitchen. Glasses clinked. Water ran in the sink. She heard movement below and glanced down, seeing a small, brown creature with a long tail run across the floor. Sarah pretended rats didn't bother her when she was with Victor, but she didn't like rodents of any kind, especially ones with beady eyes and long tails. Her gaze landed on something else that troubled her—an old tin of rat poison sat open on a workbench. Victor must have used the poison to control the rats in the house.

She thought of Ms. Hazel's lethargy and rapid decline. The woman's shallow complexion was troubling, as well.

Was Victor poisoning the rats…and his mother?

Sarah gripped the basement handrail as a wave of vertigo swept over her. The rapid pounding of her heart and her accelerated pulse were probably making her feel woozy. The walls started to cave in around her in a sweep of claustrophobia.

She closed her eyes, hoping that might calm her anxiety, but it only made the symptoms worse. She gripped the handrail more tightly and opened her eyes to get her bearings.

Victor's footsteps came again. This time, he neared the basement door. She glanced down, seeing the doorknob turn.

No! she silently screamed.

The phone rang. A landline. Victor hurried into the front parlor to answer the phone.

Sarah had only a minute or two. Opening the door, she crossed the kitchen and slipped outside. She didn't look back to see if she could find Joachim. She had to get away, back to the path before Victor returned to the kitchen.

The memory of being held captive flashed through her mind. The attic room, the dark nights she lay hearing the rodents running through the attic. The candle

Victor would bring to light the room, knowing she was terrified of the open flame.

She couldn't and wouldn't go back again. No matter what happened, she needed to remain free.

What about the scratching in the basement? Brushing it off as rats would make everything so much easier. But she had been held against her will. What if Victor were holding another person? A chill scurried down her spine. What if the sounds were a call for help from someone beyond the padlocked door? Sarah couldn't ignore her gut feelings nor the sounds. She had to find a way to learn where that door led. Maybe then she'd know if another woman was being held captive.

Chapter 9

The day could not pass fast enough for Joachim. He had watched Sarah run out of Victor's house and scurry back to the path. Just as she disappeared into the woods, Victor had stepped onto the porch, demanding to know why Joachim was not working.

He had welcomed the chastisement. It showed that Victor had no idea who had been in the house. Sarah had made it safely to the path and, hopefully, had made it home, as well.

A storm blew in later in the afternoon, which provided a good reason for Joachim to pack up his tools earlier than he would have normally. Victor had grumbled, but the dark billowing clouds and flashes of lightning that ripped across the sky overrode his discontent.

Belle was skittish on the way home as thunder clashed overhead. A car raced by much too fast, throwing water against the buggy. If only the *Englisch* realized how their cars could unsettle a horse, they might be a bit more cautious. Too many accidents happened on back roads even in good weather; add water to the mix and the situation got even more risky.

Joachim thought again of the fateful night his brother had died so tragically. Had the driver of the other vehicle been tried for recklessness? Probably not. The Amish with their slower moving buggies usually bore the blame, and the cases rarely went to court.

His spirits were bolstered when he turned onto his father's property. He leaped from the buggy and hurried to the back door, needing to assure himself that Sarah was there before he tended to his mare.

He pushed open the door.

She stood at the dry sink, kneading dough. His unexpected entrance startled her. A gasp escaped her lips, but when she turned and recognized him, her fear disappeared and was replaced with an awareness that connected them just as had happened that first time she had glanced at him from inside the Thomin home. Joachim's chest constricted, and the world stood still for one electrifying moment.

Sarah was on an emotional roller coaster. Hearing movement behind her, she feared Victor had entered the Burkholder kitchen. When she turned, her eyes locked on Joachim, standing there baring his soul in the intensity of his gaze. Her heart stopped beating for one brief second as if both of them were suspended in time and had gone someplace far away from the fear and confusion that had existed in her life for too long.

"Joachim, I thought you were someone else." She

raised her hand and patted her chest as if to start her heart beating again. "You scared me."

He seemed to search for words, and then shook his head and headed back outside to his buggy. Had she said something wrong?

Hurrying to the window, she watched him lead his mare into the barn. Knowing Joachim, he would remain there caring for his horse while she wondered what had transpired. The moment of connection had taken her to a special place only to have his rejection topple her back to the reality of the moment. She was foolish to give her feelings such free rein. After her mother's less than wise choices in male companions, Sarah had shielded her heart. Now here in this Amish home, she had let down her guard and was making another huge mistake.

She turned from the window and picked up the dough only to slam it down on the dry sink and pound her fists into the plump flour mix. Over and over again, she pushed and folded and stretched the dough until her arms ached from the strain. Kneading the dough eased her frustration until the door opened again. This time she could sense Joachim's presence even without seeing him, as if there had been a trigger within her body signaling his nearness. How could she hide her true feelings if even her body gave her away?

She dropped the dough into a greased mixing bowl, covered it with a dish towel and placed it on the back of the stove, where the warmth could help the yeast to rise.

She turned and tried to smile in spite of the tangle of confusion that swirled within her.

"Let me wash my hands, and then we'll have coffee." She struggled to hide her inner turmoil. "Rebecca is gathering potatoes from the root cellar. Although she also planned to clean the shelves and rearrange the canned goods. She said the task would take quite some time. While she is gone, we need to talk. But first I must tell you what I heard while I was in Victor's basement."

Talk? Joachim wondered what Sarah wanted to discuss and what she had heard. He took a seat at the table and watched as she filled two mugs and placed one in front of him.

"You take yours black?" she asked.

He nodded and waited as she added cream from the pitcher to her own cup and a teaspoon of sugar. After stirring the hot brew, she reached for a plate of cookies on the counter and placed both the plate and her cup on the table as she slid effortlessly into the chair across from him.

"I apologize for startling you earlier," he said. "I hurried inside to ensure you were home and all right. The last I saw, you were running toward the path. I stood by the door ready to distract Victor in case he came outside."

"He remained on the phone?"

"For only a minute or two, talking to someone named George."

Sarah's eye widened. "George is the man who is supposed to bring Miriam here. Did you hear him mention my sister's name?"

"I only heard a bit of the conversation and nothing about Miriam. Victor disconnected and stepped outside just as you disappeared into the woods. I feared he had seen you, but his only concern was my need to get back to work. Thankfully, the storm came up this afternoon so I could come home early."

She touched his sleeve. "You are wet from the rain."

"*Yah*, and from the cars that sped around the buggy, never realizing the water their tires stir up."

"Perhaps you should change into something dry."

He shook his head. "You said we should talk. What do you want to discuss?"

She leaned in closer. "What I heard in the basement."

"You heard Victor talking to me, no doubt."

"Only your muffled voices. I ran to the far end of the basement, needing to hide in case Victor came downstairs. I thought he might have heard the basement door close. Thankfully, the water ran in the sink. The sound must have drowned out the closing door."

"I was sure he would not believe that my only reason for being inside was to draw water into a glass. As hateful as Victor seems, he can be a bit of a *dummkopf*, as we say."

Sarah wrinkled her brow. "I need a translation."

"Stupid. A dummy who lacks common sense. His father was a learned man, well-thought-of in the local community. His mother was known for her big heart and sweet disposition. Somehow Victor missed out on the fine qualities seen in both parents."

"Children do not always take after their parents, which is a relief to me," Sarah said. "I never wanted to be like my mother."

"She was an authoritarian and demanding of you?" he asked.

"Not really. I longed for structure and stability, but she could never settle down. We were nomads traveling from one rental property to another across the United States. Two or three months in one place was the norm. Then my mother would become dissatisfied and decide it was time to move. Often the bills she couldn't pay would mount up, and she'd wake us in the middle of the night so we could sneak out of town undetected."

"I left this area five years ago," he shared. "Before that, this house was the only home I had known."

Sarah smiled. "We're both so different."

"Yet sometimes opposites are attracted to one another."

She glanced down as if unsure of how to reply, perhaps even unsure what he was alluding to with the comment. Joachim understood her confusion. An Amish man and an *Englisch* woman were as extreme opposites as two people could be. They had found each other because of her need to escape and his willingness to come to her aid. Otherwise, it was unlikely their paths would ever have crossed.

"We have gotten off the topic," she quickly added. "I wanted to tell you what I heard in the basement other than your mumbling voices."

He raised his cup to his lips and took a long pull while she gathered her thoughts.

"I have been in the basement before," Sarah began, "but Victor has always gone with me. Ms. Hazel kept extra canned goods there, so I would help Victor carry the items upstairs. One day we saw a rodent. He was especially unsettled by the small creature."

"This is what happened today. The mouse frightened him."

Sarah nodded. "His house is infested with rodents, so he has reason to be anxious. Ms. Hazel kept old rusted tins of rat poison in the basement. The kind that contains arsenic, although I'm not sure how effective it might be as old as the cans look. Today the poison sat open on a basement workbench."

"Which means he is trying to solve his rat problem."

"Probably. I went to the very back of the basement where I hadn't been before. That's when I heard the noise."

"A rat?"

"Maybe, but I don't think so. It was a scratching sound. I found a corner alcove and a doorway."

"You opened the door?"

"I couldn't. A metal bar ran from one side of the wall to the other and was padlocked. I looked but couldn't find a key."

"A secret room perhaps?"

"I'm not sure. Could it be a door that leads outside?"

Joachim shook his head. "I have been all around the house, checking for damage, and have not found a door from the basement level. The only entrances appear to be the one that leads to the kitchen and the other into the main foyer. Besides, the basement sits almost entirely belowground. Stairs would be needed, or a ramp to climb from the basement to ground level. I have seen nothing like that which you have mentioned."

"It's an old house, Joachim. Perhaps the stairway has been filled in."

"This could be, but then the door would lead nowhere. Are you sure the scratching sounds came from behind the door? The basement is large. A sound on one side could echo in another area. Besides, a scratching sound does not mean a human being is involved, especially when rats and other rodents seem to have taken up residence in the house."

She sighed. "It sounds crazy, doesn't it? You probably think I'm a *dummkopf*, like Victor."

Joachim laughed. "You could never be like Victor, nor do I think you are being foolish. Maybe you heard exactly what you think. Victor is an evil man, and it would not be surprising if there are other victims of his cruelty. But it is also possible that your fear is causing you to jump to conclusions. You were held captive for a period of time. Perhaps you heard a sound, but your imagination took it to the extreme. You have a big heart, Sarah, and would not want another human to be held against his or her will. I will check the outside of the house tomorrow and will look for anything that could have been filled in or a door that could have been walled off. If I see something, I will let you know."

He hesitated. "The Amish are not prone to calling in law enforcement, but so much has happened. I understand you want to avoid the police, but…"

"I can't and I won't trust the local law enforcement. Victor said the police were involved. They might tell Victor where to find me."

"Suppose Victor captures someone else?"

"Perhaps he already has, if the sound I heard in the basement was caused by another person."

"Then all the more reason to involve the police."

"Maybe when I'm ready to leave and return to Tennessee."

"You are not leaving any time soon?"

"I can't stay here much longer, Joachim. I need to find my sister Miriam, if she's even alive. I also have an older sister, Hannah, who left the family three years ago. She was going to Atlanta. I might find her there."

"Atlanta is a big city. A person could get lost in such a place."

"Are you saying I shouldn't try to find Hannah?"

"I would think involving law enforcement might be the best way to find both your sisters."

"Corrupt law enforcement won't help me, Joachim. I would have to trust the person I tell."

"You have told me, which must mean you trust me."

She smiled. "You saved me, Joachim. You could have revealed my whereabouts to Victor a number of times, and instead you've chosen to keep me safe. I have to trust you. At least for now."

She scooped up the empty mugs and took them to the sink just as Rebecca entered the house, carrying a basket filled with potatoes. Her face was flushed. Levi followed her inside. He was laughing as if he did not have a care in the world. Would Sarah ever be able to laugh with such abandonment, or would she carry the weight of all that had happened on her shoulders forever?

Chapter 10

"Is something wrong, Joachim?"

Rebecca stood staring at him. Her smile was gone, and she looked concerned as she glanced from him to Sarah. "Did something else happen? Did Victor come to the house again?"

He shook his head. "I left Victor at his mother's house."

"Yet you look as if something is very wrong."

He glanced at Sarah, giving her the opportunity to share what was troubling her.

"The coffee is hot," she said, as if to deflect the tension that filled the room.

Levi grabbed a cup from the cabinet and headed to the stove. Sarah filled his cup, refilled hers and Joachim's, and then poured coffee for Rebecca.

His sister seemed surprised to be the one served for

a change. "You should sit at the table, Sarah, and let me pour the coffee," Rebecca said. "I am not used to being waited on."

Sarah smiled and appeared to appreciate Rebecca's comment. "You and Joachim have done so much for me. It is the least I can do."

When everyone was at the table, sipping coffee, Sarah joined them and waited for a lull in the conversation before asking, "Do you remember seeing a basement door at the Thomin house?"

She looked at Levi. "Did your sister ever mention the basement?"

He shook his head. "I cannot remember Naomi saying anything about the basement. Why do you ask?"

"Joachim and I wanted to ensure Victor's mother was all right. Victor was away, so we went to check on her. We found her empty prescription bottles that Victor has not refilled. We also found sleeping pills. As lethargic as his mother has been, I fear he might be sedating her."

Rebecca sighed and shook her head. "Victor is not to be trusted, that is for certain. It troubles me deeply that he might not be providing adequate care for his mother."

"It troubles me, as well. But there is something else." Sarah recounted hiding in the basement and the scratching sounds she heard.

"Surely it was the rats that you say have nested in the house," Levi suggested. "Perhaps Victor needs a few cats to scare the rodents away."

"It sounds as if more than one cat would be needed," Rebecca added.

Sarah nodded and then continued, "The barricaded door could lead to a storage closet, but it could, at one time, have been an outside exit from the cellar. Do either of you recall hearing of a basement door on the exterior of the house in years past?"

Levi shook his head. "I have not seen a basement exit, although I do not recall ever walking around the house. A few times, I took the buggy and picked up Naomi after she finished working. She always came out of the kitchen door."

Rebecca nodded in agreement. "I have been to the kitchen entrance, but have not walked around the house either. Nor would I have had any need to look for an old door. But I do know someone who might provide information."

Joachim leaned closer. "Someone in the area?"

"*Yah*, that is so. Do you remember Mamie Carver, the *Englisch* woman who used to buy eggs from me?"

"The Carver family lived in a small house that sat back from the road. As I recall, they rented a tract of land from the Koenigs and grew vegetables that Mamie's mother canned."

Rebecca nodded. "That is right. Her mother died a few years ago, and Mamie's eyesight is failing, but she is still able to tend her garden. You must visit her, Joachim."

"How would she be able to help us?" Sarah asked.

"Her mother worked for Ms. Hazel's parents, who owned the home before Ms. Hazel married. Miss Carver's grandmother worked there, as well."

Sarah's face brightened. "So she might recall information about the basement."

"Perhaps she visited the house. It was customary for the owners of the big houses to provide for their staffs at Christmastime. Often there would be a day of celebration with food and activities. The children of those employed on the property would take part. Miss Carver may have been involved, or she might recall her mother or grandmother talking about the event."

Sarah glanced at Joachim. "We must find Mamie and talk to her."

"Tomorrow. If the rain continues, Victor will not expect me to work."

"And if the sun shines?" Sarah asked.

"I will work in the morning and tell him I must tend to my father's farm in the afternoon."

He glanced at Levi. "You will be here?"

"*Yah*, I told your *datt* that I would help Rebecca with the chores until he returns with your *mamm*. He knows that day after tomorrow I must go to Willkommen to help my uncle at the Amish Market."

Joachim's heart sunk. "Day after tomorrow? Our *datt* is returning home that soon?"

"This I do not know for sure," Levi admitted. "I only told him when I would be gone."

"You know our parents," Rebecca added. "They only schedule when they will go on their visits. They rarely plan their return."

Joachim nodded. What his sister had said was true. His parents could stay away longer...but perhaps not. Which meant it might be no more than forty-eight hours until Joachim would have to talk to his father. If their meeting did not go well, Joachim might be forced to leave home again. He glanced at Sarah, knowing he was not ready to leave her.

He would hold on to each precious hour. There was so little time. Would it be enough time to tell Sarah how he felt? Or would he leave never sharing how special she was to him?

Chapter 11

The deep rumble of thunder woke Sarah before the first light of dawn. Rain fell in torrents, but she was grateful for the downpour. The storm would provide a reason Joachim would not be able to work for Victor today.

She and Joachim needed to visit Miss Carver and learn more about the padlocked doorway. Sarah thought again about yesterday when she heard the scratching noise. Could the sound have been made by a mouse or a rat or some other creature?

Throwing back the quilt and sheet, she dropped her feet to the floor and reached for the flashlight, grateful again for Joachim's thoughtfulness. She hadn't wanted to tell him about her childhood and the fear that still troubled her.

The fact that her mother had never again mentioned the incident had made it even more difficult to bear.

She longed to be forgiven, but forgiveness had never been provided.

Once she had mustered the courage to mention the fire to Miriam. Even her sister had shoved aside her comment. "That was the past," Miriam had told Sarah. "We need to focus on the present."

But the guilt she carried had followed Sarah into the present and remained a weight around her neck. No matter how hard she tried, Sarah would never be rid of the memory.

Footsteps sounded in the hallway. From the lightness of the step, Rebecca was hurrying downstairs to add wood to the stove and begin her day of cooking. Sarah dressed quickly and followed her to the kitchen.

The tin coffeepot sat on the burner. Water dripped through the grounds and filled the house with the rich scent of the morning brew.

"You are up early," Rebecca said in greeting. Her eyes were bright and her smile welcoming. Levi had stayed after dinner last night, and the two of them had sat on the front porch until well after sundown. Sarah envied the relationship they had, an easy and familiar connection even when they weren't conversing. A bond connected them as surely as if their hearts were actually tied together with a ribbon.

As much as Sarah longed to have someone in her life to lean on, she couldn't trust her instincts. She had seen the destruction caused by love wrongly given. That was one of the reasons she had encouraged her mother and Miriam to drive to Willkommen. Sarah had wanted to find her long-lost aunt, her mother's sister, but she had also wanted to breathe new life into her own daily routine. Secretly, she had dreamed of remaining with her aunt when her mother and Miriam returned home. Foolish though it seemed, she had hoped the rural mountain community would provide an opportunity for her to start fresh without the constant shadow of her mother's disapproval.

She poured coffee into a mug and sighed as she reached for the pitcher and added a dollop of the rich cream and a teaspoon of sugar.

Now she wondered if she would have stayed in Willkommen if Miriam and her mother returned home to Tennessee. Sarah had relied on Miriam to guide her through the first twenty-one years of her life. It was doubtful to think Sarah would have become more independent in Willkommen.

"You seem pensive this morning." Rebecca's statement pulled her from her thoughts.

"I'm still tired," Sarah admitted.

"You should have slept longer."

"I wanted to help you with breakfast, yet here I am pining over my coffee. What can I do?"

"We have bread from yesterday. Joachim likes it with butter and jelly. Could you fetch the butter from outside? It sits in a jar in the cool tub of water near the pump. You'll find a bottle of milk there, too. Bring both inside, if you do not mind."

Sarah glanced out the window. The pitter-patter of rain on the tin roof of the kitchen had eased, although the sky remained gray and overcast. She opened the door and stepped into the damp morning air, relishing the clear freshness of a new day washed clean by the earlier storm.

She hurried down the steps and followed the well-worn path to the pump. To the side was a tin tub half filled with cold water, as Rebecca had mentioned. The butter sat in a half-submerged glass jar next to the milk jug. She lifted both from the tub, shook off the excess moisture and turned back to the house.

The sound of a car's engine made her heart lurch. She hurried for the protection of the porch and ducked behind the railing, her eyes straining to see the vehicle on the road this early. Surely it wasn't a red pickup.

Peering through the gaps between the fence posts, she realized her folly. If Victor was on the road and turned his truck into the Burkholder farm, she would be seen instantly.

She held her breath and stared at the road as the sound of the engine grew louder.

"Please," she whispered.

A black sedan zipped along the roadway and passed the farm.

She let out the air she was holding and clutched the two jars close to her heart.

"Sarah?"

She jumped, nearly dropping the milk and butter. Hands reached to grab them and locked around her arms. When she looked up, she stared into Joachim's questioning eyes.

"I have startled you again," he said, contrition evident in his tone.

She tried to cover her surprise. "I thought you were still asleep."

"The Amish rise early. Animals must be fed and watered. Stalls mucked."

"You haven't forgotten about visiting Mamie Carver, have you?"

He smiled. "I have not forgotten. It appears more

storms are brewing in the distant sky, which provide the excuse I need for Victor. He will not expect me this morning. After breakfast I will take the buggy to Miss Carver's home."

"I'll go with you," Sarah insisted.

"Storms may continue throughout the entire morning. You should remain here and stay dry."

"I'm not made of sugar, Joachim."

He laughed and his eyes glanced down at her shoes, wet from the rain. "You have not melted yet, that is true. You can go with me, but we must be careful in case Victor is on the road."

"He sleeps late and doesn't like to get his truck dirty when the roads are wet. I don't think we'll run into him."

"You know him well."

Sarah hesitated. Joachim was right. After weeks of being held captive, she knew Victor's idiosyncrasies, of which he had many. Somehow all that knowledge hadn't helped her escape until Joachim came into her life. She owed him her gratitude.

"I don't know if I ever thanked you for saving me. If you hadn't come along—"

"As I recall, Sarah, you were the one who snuck from the house and hid in the buggy. You saved yourself. The only thing I did was drive my buggy off Victor's property."

"Did you know I was hiding there?"

A smile twitched his lips. "I saw that the tarp had been moved. You had raised your finger to your lips when I glanced through the window. It was easy to realize you did not belong with Victor."

"He had grown increasingly antagonistic," she

shared. "That particular morning, we were in the attic. I mentioned the rats, which probably added to his agitation. He choked me until I could not catch my breath. I knew then that I had to escape."

"Then I arrived at the perfect time."

She nodded, feeling the pull between them that made her want to step closer. Instead, the clip-clop of horses' hooves on the road caused her to draw back. She was too visible, especially with the sun rising in the east. She would be safer inside. And her heart would be safer if she put some distance between herself and Joachim. But was safety what she really wanted when it came to him? He had saved her. Was she letting down her guard because of what he had done? She would forever be grateful, but she could not confuse gratitude with affection.

"Rebecca is fixing breakfast," she said. "You must eat, then we will find Miss Carver and learn what we can about the Thomin basement."

"You still believe a person made the scratching sound?"

"I don't know, but I won't have peace until I ensure that no one else is being held captive."

She hurried up the stairs to the porch, relieved to have Joachim follow close behind her. For a moment, she thought of Rebecca and Levi entering the kitchen last night with that special bond between them so evident.

Would Rebecca be aware of a connection between Joachim and Sarah? She sighed at her foolishness. She was putting too much emphasis on a moment in the early morning before she had a chance to think clearly. Joachim was Amish. His faith intrigued her, and if truth be known, he intrigued her as well, but the handsome carpenter needed to look for someone within his own community to capture his heart.

Sarah stamped her feet on the rug as she entered the sweet-smelling kitchen. She was acting like a *dummkopf.* Better to guard her heart and her head until she could get safely away—from Victor and perhaps from the handsome handyman, as well.

In a moment of weakness, Joachim had agreed to Sarah accompanying him to visit Miss Carver. Hopefully, he had not allowed his heart to override his head. Even if Victor usually slept late and kept his truck off the road during wet weather, the man's actions had become more erratic according to Sarah.

Joachim would never forgive himself if his moment of weakness, giving in to her pleading to come with him, put Sarah at risk. He blamed it on her crystal-blue eyes, which shimmered like a placid lake, reflecting the sun's bright rays. One glance at her and he was lost in another world, a world without the restrictions that came from an Amish man having interest in an *Englisch* woman. As much as Joachim needed to be Amish, he longed to be with Sarah.

Their time together was passing much too quickly. His father would be home soon. Joachim had moments of despondence when he was convinced he had been a fool to think reconciliation could be achieved. At other times he had hope that his father would accept him back. Pride was the wall that stood between them. At the present moment, Joachim believed his *datt* would not change his mind or his heart.

He sighed, pondering whether he had been foolish in coming home. Yet if he had not, he never would have met Sarah. The thought that she would still have been under Victor's control made Joachim grateful that he had journeyed back to his Amish roots. He only wished Sarah could embrace that which gave meaning to his own life. But a *fancy* woman could never embrace the *plain* life. Of this, he was sure.

Chapter 12

"I do not think this is a good idea," Rebecca told Sarah. Both women stood at the sink filled with breakfast dishes and peered through the kitchen window as Joachim disappeared into the barn to hitch Belle to the buggy.

"The sky is dark," Rebecca cautioned. "More rain will fall, and there will be lightning and thunder. Belle spooks in storms. You are tired and still healing from what you have endured. The seat of the buggy is not what you are used to. Stay here and let Joachim go alone to talk to Miss Carver."

Sarah appreciated Rebecca's concern, but she would not be content to stand at the window and watch for Joachim's return.

"Didn't you tell me that Miss Carver lives close?" Sarah asked. "Surely a short trip won't be a problem.

Joachim was worried about me getting wet. You are concerned that I will not be comfortable in the buggy."

Her frustration mounted the more she thought about Rebecca's and Joachim's desires to coddle her.

"I was not comfortable locked in an attic room or being tied up in the passenger seat of Victor's truck," she said. "The drugs didn't help my comfort either, especially when I didn't have any food and reacted to the heavy medication on an empty stomach."

She hadn't intended to be so adamant, but she wasn't a prima donna. She had endured a lot over the last few weeks and none of it good.

Rebecca turned, her gaze filled with compassion. "I was thinking only of your well-being, Sarah, but you are right. You have endured so much. I am not sure I would have survived. You are a strong woman and independent. I was wrong to want to hold you back."

Independent?

No one had called her that before. "But I'm not strong," she countered. "I've always relied on my sister Miriam."

"Your sister was not with you at the Thomin house, *yah*? You escaped by yourself."

"I escaped because of Joachim."

Rebecca tilted her head. "You worked together to escape Victor. I want you to remain safe so that you and Joachim can share more moments in the future."

Sarah took a step back. "I can't think of the future, Rebecca. I can only think of today. Plus, I have to focus on the sound I heard. Suppose a person is being held captive? That's what's most important, not whether I am comfortable or dry."

"*Yah*, you are right. I will pray Victor is holding no

other women against their will, and I will pray he does not find you again."

Rebecca grabbed the cape hanging on one of the pegs by the door and draped it over Sarah's shoulders. Reaching for the black bonnet, she smiled. "The wide bill will offer protection from buffeting winds. It will also keep you hidden from view should Victor be on the road." After tying the bonnet securely under Sarah's chin, Rebecca nodded her approval.

"It limits my vision." Sarah adjusted the bonnet, still mildly upset by Rebecca's somewhat overly protective nature. Then she felt embarrassed by her curt tone. Rebecca was merely concerned for her safety.

"I'm sorry, Rebecca. You're kind to let me wear your cape and bonnet. I'll get used to the wide bill, even if it limits my vision."

Rebecca chuckled. "A woman can sometimes hide her feelings within the hat."

"I doubt you want to hide your feelings from Levi." Sarah couldn't help but counter.

Rebecca's cheeks turned pink. "Levi is a good friend and a good man, but he has many women who are interested in him."

Sarah raised her brow. "Yet he comes here every day."

"Coming here is a job. My *datt* hired him."

"Your father did not tell him to have a twinkle in his eye or laughter on his lips. I've seen the way he looks at you."

"Do you mean he is laughing at me?" Rebecca's own eyes sparked with mischief.

"You know exactly what I mean."

"I see something in Joachim's gaze as well, when

he looks at you. He has been away for five years, yet I know my *bruder*."

Sarah held up her hand. "Your *bruder*, as you say, came home to talk to your father. Anything you see in his gaze is his concern about how that meeting will turn out."

Rebecca lowered her eyes. "I worry about that meeting, as well. My *datt* is a strong man who has been deeply hurt by the death of his younger son." She glanced up. "He has also been hurt by the absence of his oldest son."

"Have you told Joachim?"

"Some things he must find out on his own. Besides, I see through my own eyes. Perhaps I do not see as Joachim would."

The sound of the buggy caused both women to glance outside. "It is time to go." Sarah pulled the cape tight across her neck.

"I almost forgot." Rebecca ran to the pantry and returned with a basket draped with a dark blue cloth. "This is for Miss Carver. There is bread and cheese, eggs, butter, and a pie. She does not have anyone to help her with her baking."

"She'll enjoy the food, I'm sure. I'll tell Mamie you were thinking of her."

"Perhaps she can come for supper after my parents return. They would like to see her."

"Be careful while we are gone, Rebecca. I worry about your safety with Victor so close."

"I will lock the door. Do not worry about me. Take care yourself." She readjusted the bonnet around Sarah's face.

Her thoughtfulness touched Sarah. Without forethought, she hugged Rebecca. "Be on guard lest Victor comes searching for me. You must remain safe."

"*Gott* will provide," Rebecca said as the two women parted.

Sarah opened the kitchen door and stepped onto the porch, thinking of Rebecca's words. God hadn't provided protection for her mother or Miriam or herself when they had been carjacked. Would He protect Rebecca today? What about Joachim?

All of them were in danger, and it was because of Sarah. She had brought danger to this peaceful Amish farm. She had been thinking only about herself and her own well-being. She hadn't truly considered Rebecca's or Joachim's safety.

The last thing she wanted was to have anything harmful happen to either of them. Rebecca was a lovely woman who had a full life ahead of her with Levi, even if she wasn't ready to admit that. And Joachim?

He had so much to offer a woman. The right woman. An Amish woman to whom he could give his heart.

If only Sarah could be part of his future, but that was a silly thought that needed to be erased from her mind.

Joachim helped Sarah into the buggy and climbed in next to her. He spread a protective throw over her legs.

"The rain won't hurt me, Joachim," she politely informed him.

"*Yah*, but you have not ridden in the front of an Amish buggy when so much moisture covers the road. The cars do not understand how their wheels throw the water. I do not want you drowning before we talk to Miss Carver."

She laughed. Not what he had expected.

"You think my words are funny?" he asked.

She shook her head and touched his arm. He liked the feel of her fingers and the way she leaned into him. Perhaps riding together was a good idea after all.

"I wasn't making fun, Joachim. I was laughing about the seriousness of your expression. You are always so concerned about my safety."

He relaxed a bit and allowed his mouth to turn up in a responsive smile. "I have never found anyone else in the back of my buggy, Sarah Miller. There is a certain amount of responsibility I must take to ensure you remain safe and protected. Do you consider this a bad thing or an inconvenience?"

Her fingers rubbed his arm, making a ripple of current flow along his spine. She had too much of an effect on him, especially sitting so close.

"I've never had anyone concerned about me before, Joachim." Suddenly, her face was serious, and her words struck an even deeper chord within him. He stared into her eyes and lost all sense of time and space and where they were to go and why they were going there. Instead, all he could focus on was her beauty and the pureness of her gaze and the way his heart lurched whenever she smiled.

Rebecca opened the kitchen door and pulled him back to reality. "Sarah, you forgot the basket."

She seemed equally as confused as she pulled her eyes away from Joachim and glanced at Rebecca. "Oh yes, I'm sorry. I wasn't thinking."

Joachim hoped she *had* been thinking, thinking about him.

He took the basket from his sister's outstretched hand and placed it on the floor of the buggy behind them.

After waving farewell to Rebecca, he reached for the reins and with a flick of his wrist, Belle trotted along the drive. He pulled her up a bit at the edge of the road to check traffic in both directions before the buggy turned onto the main road.

"We will hope the rain will keep the *Englischers* with their big cars at home," Joachim said, steering the conversation to practical matters of the head instead of the heart.

"Rebecca said Miss Carver's house is not far."

"Not far in miles, but the drive will take time. You are used to vehicles with engines. We have only Belle."

"She'll get us there," Sarah said with confidence.

Joachim liked her optimism. He smiled again and flicked the reins. Belle increased her speed to a steady trot and ambled along the roadway, heading away from Petersville and the Thomin home toward the cluster of Amish farms. Would Sarah appreciate the beauty of the land and the bounty of *Gott*'s providence for providing such a fertile area to farm?

Joachim hoped she would. He wanted her to like everything about the Amish and their way of life. The truth was he wanted her to like him, as well.

Chapter 13

The Amish farms rolled by one after another, each picturesque in its simplicity. Young children stood on their front porches and watched, wide-eyed as the buggy passed.

Sarah inhaled the country air and the musky smell of the red Georgia clay. Joachim seemed lost in thought, so she kept her gaze on the homes they passed. She wondered about the women working in the kitchens or helping the farmers in the field. Had they been raised Amish or had some of them lived the life she knew? If so, how had they decided to embrace the *plain* life? Surely the transition would be a challenge, yet she had found nothing difficult about being in the Burkholder home. She would have liked a mirror to check that her bonnet was on straight, but she could see enough of her reflection in the windowpane. She had never worn makeup or done much with her hair, so that wasn't a problem.

Sometimes she caught Joachim looking at her, and his gaze made her realize she must have done something right concerning her grooming, even without a mirror.

"The farms are lovely, Joachim. You will have one someday like your father?"

"*Yah*, although I like working with wood so I would have fewer fields and a larger workshop for my carpentry."

"You did carpentry work while you were away?"

"I did. There was more than enough work."

"Do you plan to stay here in the Petersville area or return to the Carolinas?"

"It depends upon my father. If he will have me in his house again, then I will stay."

"And if not?" she asked.

"Then I will find my own way and a new place to live."

"But you will remain Amish?"

"*Yah*, Amish is who I am."

For some reason, his response took the joy she had been feeling out of her heart.

Joachim turned the buggy onto a dirt side road and encouraged Belle onward. The path was pockmarked, and the ride became bumpy. Sarah bounced from side to side and began to understand Rebecca's concern about the buggy ride.

When the back wheel dropped into an especially large hole, she gasped and reached for the handle on the seat to steady herself.

"Do people ever fall off?" she asked in all seriousness.

Joachim put his arm around her and drew her closer. "I will not let you fall."

His words and the strength of his touch relieved her

concern. She settled against him. In spite of the bumpy road, she liked sitting close to Joachim.

The ride soon came to an end at a small house. A tin roof hug over the raised porch and cast the door and two windows in shadow. A wooden rocking chair sat idle as Joachim helped Sarah climb from the buggy.

"The house could use some repair." Joachim kept his voice low. "I will come back with my tools once I have finished at the Thomin home."

He rapped on the door. "Miss Carver, it is Joachim Burkholder and a friend. We have brought food from my sister, Rebecca."

Silence greeted them. Joachim knocked again. He glanced at Sarah and then over his shoulder, eyeing the road they had just traveled. "I will check the barn. You stay here."

"I'll go with you."

He nodded, but before they left the porch, the sound of footsteps caused them to glance at the corner of the house. A wizened woman appeared, stooped with age; her white hair contrasted sharply with her brown skin. She carried firewood and seemed out of breath with the effort. Seeing that she had company, her eyes widened and a smile pulled across her full face.

"Don't know if my eyes are making a fool of me, but I see Joachim Burkholder standing on my front porch big as life."

Sarah smiled at the humor in the woman's tone.

"Your eyes have not fooled you," Joachim responded as he flashed an equally warm smile back at the sweet woman. "I have come home."

Mamie nodded. Her gaze fell to Sarah. "And you have brought a pretty girlfriend to brighten my day."

Joachim hurried to where Mamie stood and took the wood from her hands. "You have a heavy load. Allow me the pleasure of helping you."

Mamie laughed. "You can help me any time, Joachim. Any time at all."

She climbed the stairs and held out her hand to Sarah. "Mamie Carver, ma'am."

"My name is Sarah," she replied, feeling strength in the woman's handshake and seeing the twinkle in her eyes. Miss Carver might be advanced in years, but she still had a spring in her step and a charisma that made Sarah feel instantly at home.

"Come inside. The coffee is hot. Joachim, you can set that firewood by the stove. Don't mind Butch. He's old, but friendly."

Sarah bent to pet the beagle who ambled toward them after Mamie opened the door.

"You would like Angelo," Sarah told the pup. "He's small, but friendly."

"Butch used to be a good hunter," Mamie bragged. "Now his nose doesn't smell much. Same as mine. Although I'd be interested to know what's in that basket you're carrying."

Sarah laughed. "Rebecca's pie and fresh baked bread, cheese and butter. Also some eggs."

"Which I appreciate. You folks come in and sit a spell."

She motioned them into the small but tidy house. The kitchen was to the left. A table and four chairs sat in the middle of the room with a stone fireplace to the right. Close to the hearth was a second rocking chair with a straight-back chair positioned nearby.

Peering through an open door, Sarah noticed a small

bedroom. The single bed was covered with a quilt, and a latched rug covered the floor.

Sarah slipped out of her cape and took off her bonnet.

"Sit at the table, please." Mamie pointed her toward a chair. "I'll pour coffee."

"May I help?" Sarah asked.

"I'd like that. Milk's in the refrigerator. There's sugar on the counter. Why don't you slice that bread Rebecca made? I haven't had breakfast, and I'm hungry. Surely you and Joachim would like something to eat, as well."

"I'm still full from breakfast," Sarah and Joachim said in unison and then laughed.

Sarah opened a cabinet and found a plate and a serrated knife in the drawer next to the sink. She cut a thick slice of bread and slathered it with butter and strawberry preserves Rebecca had thoughtfully included.

As Mamie poured three cups of coffee, Sarah peered into the pantry and noticed the near-empty shelves, making a mental note to share the information with Rebecca.

Once Mamie finished eating her bread, she took a long drink from her coffee and wiped her hand over her mouth.

"Joachim, your sister makes pies like my mama and grandmamma used to make. Mama always said it was the lard that made her crust so flakey. Now the doctors tell us lard is bad for our health."

"Do you have any brothers or sisters?" Sarah inquired.

"I've got a younger brother. He and his wife live near Willkommen. I don't see much of them these days. His wife has rheumatism and stays close to home."

Sarah perked up at the mention of Willkommen. "Do you know of anyone named Annie Miller in that town?"

"Not that I recall, although I don't know many folks on that side of the mountains. Next time I see my brother, I could ask him. Is she a friend of yours?"

"My mother's sister."

"Yet you don't know her, child?"

"My mother left home at a young age. She never returned to this area. In fact, she never told us that she even had a sister until not long ago."

"Sometimes we stay away for a number of reasons." Mamie glanced knowingly at Joachim.

"And sometimes we return home seeking to mend any broken fences," Joachim added.

"Which is a very good thing," Mamie stated with a nod. "The good Lord says not to focus on the speck in another's eye, but rather to recognize the plank in our own. My brother and I had a tiff some years back. Can't remember what it was about. One day, I drove to his house. Even before he could say hello, I told him I was sorry. I wanted the divide between us to end."

"What happened?" Sarah leaned closer. She noticed Joachim was focused on the old woman's story, as well.

"My brother just stood there looking at me. In fact, he paused so long I was ready to turn around and get back in my car. Before I did, he stepped toward me, looked deep into my eyes and said he was sorry for the time we had wasted with the anger. He said it was time for healing. Then he pulled me into a bear hug, and we both laughed until tears ran from our eyes."

She stared at Joachim for a long moment, then turned her gaze to Sarah. "Your mama would do well to reconnect with her family."

Sadness flitted over Sarah. "She was killed not long ago."

"Oh, child, I'm so sorry. I saw pain in your eyes. I didn't know the reason. You need to find your aunt and be that conduit of peace and unity in the family. You can bridge the gap even after all those years."

"But suppose I can't find her?"

"Have you asked the Lord's help? He listens and responds when the request is for our good. I'll ask Him to help you."

Warmth swept over Sarah. A feeling of being loved, which was something she always had hoped to feel from her own mother. Miriam and Hannah had loved her but not in the same way as a parent, and she'd always felt the lack. Mamie, a sweet woman who had only just come into Sarah's life, had shown her how to fill the hole in her heart. Sarah needed to put her trust in the Lord.

Mamie covered Sarah's hand with her own and squeezed ever so gently. "You turn to God with your needs, child. He'll make everything right. I know what I'm talking about."

She glanced at Joachim. "Your father made a mistake. You reacted because you were young and hurt by Eli's death and your own confusion. I'm glad you've come home."

"*Yah*, but my *datt* is visiting relatives. He and my *mamm* return home in a day or two. I am not sure how he will react to seeing me again."

"In his heart, he loves you. Remember that, Joachim. You are his son."

"But you know my father is a proud man."

"What does scripture tell us? *Pride goeth before a fall*." She nodded as if appreciating her own wisdom.

"You ask the Lord to make you the better man, Joachim. You can do that. But first, you must erase any pride in your own heart."

As Mamie took another drink from her cup, Sarah scooted closer. "There is something else we need to ask you, Miss Carver. Rebecca and Joachim told me that your grandmother and mother worked for Ms. Hazel Thomin's parents. Perhaps you went to the house as a girl?"

She nodded. "Sometimes I helped to move furniture or polish shoes or the silver. A house that big takes constant care. After Mr. Thomin passed, Ms. Hazel needed even more help. My brother and I were there often." She rubbed her cheek. "If you see Ms. Hazel, you tell her I said hello. She's a good woman."

"Her health has declined and she's bedridden," Sarah said.

"I'm so sorry about her failing health. I heard Naomi Plank was caring for her."

"Naomi left the area almost a year ago."

"Then who's taking care of Ms. Hazel?" Mamie narrowed her gaze. "Don't tell me that son of hers is back."

"That's the problem," Sarah said. "He *is* back, and I worry that he's not giving her good enough care."

"I'd like to give him a piece of my mind."

Sarah smiled, knowing Mamie would not mince words with Victor about his lack of concern for his mother. "We need your help on something else, Mamie, that involves Ms. Hazel's home."

Joachim leaned closer. "I am making repairs to the Thomin house. There is a boarded-up doorway in the basement, but I cannot see an opening on the outside of the structure. Do you recall a door leading from the basement?"

Mamie shook her head. "The only doors to the outside that I knew about were the one leading into the main hallway and the kitchen door. I've been in the basement enough to know I had to leave the house by the back door."

"Was there a closet or cubbyhole, perhaps?" Sarah asked.

"I wish I could help you, but nothing comes to mind."

Discouraged, Sarah glanced at Joachim. He nodded as if it was time for them to head back to the farm.

"Is there anything we can do for you before we leave?" Sarah asked, grabbing her mug and Joachim's off the table.

"You can pour me another cup of coffee and bring me my Bible." Mamie pointed to a small table near the rocker by the fireplace. "And my glasses. I always take time to read the Lord's word each day. My eyes may be bad, but not so bad that I can't read my scripture. The Lord always has something to tell me."

"I wish He would tell us about the basement," Sarah admitted as she quickly washed the mugs at the sink and placed them in the strainer. After drying her hands, she poured Miss Carver a fresh cup of coffee and placed it on the table, along with the Bible and glasses.

"Don't forget to take that basket back to Rebecca," Mamie added. "Hopefully, she will take pity on an old woman and bring me another pie in a week or so." Her eyes twinkled.

"I'll be sure to let Rebecca know how much you enjoyed what she provided. I'll also tell her that her pie rivaled your mother's. I'm sure Ms. Hazel loved your mother's pies, too."

Mamie chuckled. "You've got that right. Ms. Hazel

would come to the kitchen house in the summer just to check on when the pies would be pulled from the oven. Course I'd be waiting on them, too."

"The kitchen house?" Sarah asked.

Mamie nodded. "It sat about thirty yards from the big house. Stoves gave off too much heat in summer before air-conditioning to be attached to the main house. The old homes all had a free-standing kitchen used in the summer. The root cellar was there. My mama used to send me down to get the apples for the pies. Mighty nice to have an excuse to visit a cool spot in the heat of the summer."

"Where exactly was the kitchen house located?" Joachim pressed.

Mamie thought for a moment. "To the rear of the house, but more to the east side so the hot afternoon sun wouldn't shine on it. The cool of the shade trees would help, too."

Joachim glanced at Sarah. She shook her head. "I'm not good at understanding distances, but it seems that was a long way to carry food back to the house. What happened if it rained?"

"Why, they used the tunnel when it rained," Mamie was quick to reply.

Sarah looked at Joachim. "A tunnel? From the root cellar?"

Mamie nodded. "Sure enough. It led to the big house so when the rain came, the food could be carried to the dining room without getting wet."

"But the tunnel didn't lead to the dining room," Sarah said.

"No." Mamie shook her head. "The tunnel led to the basement."

Chapter 14

After saying goodbye to Mamie Carver, Joachim helped Sarah into the buggy and guided Belle along the dirt path to the main road. More rain had fallen while they were inside, and a thin layer of water lay across the asphalt once they turned onto the main road.

"The barricaded door has to lead to the tunnel," Sarah said as she adjusted the bonnet on her head and pulled the cape tight around her neck. "But I never noticed a kitchen house."

"Mamie talked about it sitting in the shade under trees. Perhaps the woods have grown around the old structure. Or maybe it was torn down when air-conditioning was installed and they did not need it anymore. The only buildings I know of are the barn and the few outbuildings located on that side of the house. Mr. Thomin was an expert carpenter. There is a wood shed nearby and also another small building that houses garden tools."

"Look around the grounds the next time you're there."

He nodded. "*Yah*, that I will do for certain."

The rain started again and the wind gusted, sending a sheet of water against the buggy. Sarah lowered her head against the pummeling rain.

Thunder rumbled overhead. Joachim hurried Belle. He needed to get Sarah home and out of the storm.

In the distance, the sound of an approaching car made his pulse quicken. *Please,* Gott.

Sarah lifted her gaze. Her face was lined with worry. "Surely it can't be Victor."

"It is probably someone else on the road, but no matter who it is, lower your head as the car passes," Joachim cautioned.

He flicked the reins to encourage Belle. The buggy creaked as the horse trotted up the small hill.

The approaching car crested the rise, taking up more than half of its lane. Joachim steered Belle to the edge of the road as the car zoomed past. It was a big, boxy SUV painted white, with tinted windows that made it impossible to see the driver or passengers.

The car was going much too fast for the narrow road. The wheels splashed a wave of water against the buggy, soaking both of them.

The SUV screeched to a stop. Joachim glanced back. Had the driver realized his mistake and stopped to offer an apology?

The SUV backed up and pulled next to the buggy. The driver's window rolled down partially, and a man peered through the opening. He had a full face and small eyes, which glared at Joachim from under bushy brows. A scar ran along his cheek and disappeared under his jaw.

From the frustration written so plainly across his face, rather than the remorse Joachim had hoped to see, the guy was probably not going to ask forgiveness for his negligent driving. Someone huddled in the back seat. Joachim could not see the person's features through the tinted glass, although the person did appear to have long hair.

"You folks know of a man name Victor Thomin?" the bushy browed guy asked. "I thought he lived along this road, but I can't find the turnoff to his house."

Sarah bristled at the mention of Victor's name.

"You must turn your vehicle around and head back toward Petersville, the way you came," Joachim replied. "You will see a brick mailbox on the left about two miles ahead. Turn onto that driveway. His house sits back from the main road."

The guy nodded but failed to offer thanks. Instead, he pulled his car into a nearby drive, backed onto the road and then gunned his engine and squealed past Joachim and Sarah, sending more water to splash over them. The close proximity of the massive car as it barreled past made Belle skittish. She pranced and shook her head, causing the buggy to edge off the road. The back wheel angled up a small rise.

The whole carriage tilted. Sarah screamed.

Joachim reached for her. Before he could grab her arm, she slipped through his hands and flew out of the buggy.

"Sarah." His heart lurched. He leaped to the pavement and knelt next to where she lay. Her eyes were closed, her mouth open ever so slightly.

"Sarah, are you all right?"

She moaned. Her eyelids fluttered open.

Relief swept over him. He touched her hand. "Tell me you can raise your hand."

She wrinkled her brow. "My hand...why?"

"Just do as I ask."

She raised one hand and then the other.

"What about your neck? Does anything hurt?"

"Everything hurts, but I didn't break anything—at least I don't think I did." She rolled to her side and started to raise herself.

"Go slowly. You had a bad fall." Joachim grabbed her arm and helped her stand.

She wobbled for a second and then brushed the dirt from her dress. "Rebecca's pretty outfit is ruined."

"It will wash. Are you sure you are all right?"

"Yes, but I'm getting cold. Who was that man?"

"One of Victor's friends perhaps. You have seen him before?"

She shook her head. "Never. Did you notice someone in the back seat with long hair? I couldn't see clearly through the windows. Do you think it was Miriam?"

"I do not know, but we must get you home now."

Joachim lifted her into the buggy, overwhelmed with gratitude that Sarah had not been badly injured. Much as he did not want to think of another buggy accident, he could not help but remember what had happened five years earlier. Eli had lain on the road in almost the same way Sarah had fallen. Only Eli had remained where he was, unable to move and struggling for air as the life ebbed from him.

"Are you sure you are not badly hurt?" Joachim asked again as he spread the blanket over her legs and crawled into the buggy next to her.

"I'm still shaking inside, but I'll be fine once we get back to your house."

"The rain has eased. That is good." He moved the reins, signaling Belle to start walking. The buggy creaked as the wheel came free from the mud, and the buggy moved back onto the roadway. Joachim made a sound with his mouth to encourage Belle. The mare increased her gait.

Holding the reins with one hand, Joachim wrapped his other around Sarah, pulling her close. The thought of what could have happened made his stomach sour.

She had mentioned her shaking insides. His felt no better. The shock of watching helplessly as she fell to the ground made him want to take out his frustration on Victor's friend, who had caused the mishap. If Joachim ever saw him again, he would explain the importance of giving a horse and buggy a wide berth. But would an explanation even have a small effect on the man? He seemed to be absorbed by his own needs and uncaring about the consequences of his actions to anyone else, including beautiful Sarah.

Joachim thought again of the person slumped in the rear of the car. All his instincts told him something was not right, but he did not want to alarm Sarah.

No other cars passed them on the way home, for which Joachim was grateful. He pulled Belle to a stop by the back porch and then hurried around the buggy to help Sarah down. Rebecca came out to greet them.

"I have been worried with the storm." Her frown

grew more pronounced as she looked at Sarah. "Something has happened."

"Sarah fell from the buggy," he said.

"*Ach!* No!"

"A car passed us going too fast. Belle got skittish and moved off the road. There was an upward incline that caused the buggy to tilt."

"I was anything but graceful." Sarah smile ruefully.

"Did you hit your head? Perhaps you should take her to the doctor, Joachim."

Sarah held up her hand. "No to the doctor. I'm not seriously injured, just cold and a little bruised. I want to get dry and pretend that I didn't slide off a buggy seat." She glanced at Rebecca. "You were right to warn me. Riding in a buggy is not easy, especially in the rain."

"Or when cars drive too close and too fast," Rebecca added.

"The driver of the car knows Victor." Sarah touched Joachim's arm. "I keep thinking about that person sitting in the back seat. I couldn't see her through the glass. What if it *was* Miriam?"

"I am going to Victor's now. Hopefully, I will learn more about this man and his passenger."

Sarah grabbed his hand. "Be careful, Joachim. The man had an evil look in his eyes. I don't want anything to happen to you."

He wrapped his fingers through hers and stepped closer. Sarah had an effect on him that made his head swim and sent everything else into oblivion so that all he saw was her.

"I will be fine," he assured her. "Victor will wonder where I am since the rain has stopped. Besides, if he has houseguests, he will be less interested in the handyman doing repairs."

"Victor sees more than you would think. He has ways of appearing when you don't suspect him of being anywhere in the area. Be cautious, Joachim. And remember that Victor is not to be trusted."

"I will remember."

He did not want to leave Sarah, but he needed to get to the Thomin home before the next volley of rain started. If the storms continued, he would come home after working for a bit under the overhang of the porch to escape the rain.

Stepping away from her was difficult.

"Get dry and stay warm," he told her. "I will return soon."

Rebecca stood on the porch, her face drawn and looking as forlorn as Sarah. He was aware of the danger of going back to the Thomin home, but he needed to see what was happening there for himself. As Sarah had mentioned, Victor was not to be trusted. The arrival of the second man and the passenger in his car made Joachim even more concerned.

Sarah was worried about what Victor could do to Joachim. She was also worried about the man in the SUV, as well as his passenger. Could the woman be Miriam? Would her arrival at the Thomin home be a good thing or would it place her sister in even more danger? The last time Sarah had seen Miriam had been in the cabin where they had been held captive after the carjacking. Victor had claimed that a man named George had her now. If only Sarah had more information.

Rebecca and Joachim had cautioned Sarah to keep

her head down, which was what she had done when the man pulled his SUV to a stop beside the buggy, yet that hadn't kept her from catching a glimpse of the guy at the wheel. He looked menacing and evil. Just like Victor. Which made her all the more concerned about her sister and worried about Joachim's safety.

Could the newcomer be George, the man who was supposed to deliver Miriam? Sarah shivered at the thought of her sister being considered a delivery, like property or chattel. This was the twenty-first century. Women weren't supposed to be owned or controlled by anyone. But life in this part of Georgia was a free-for-all with corruption run amuck. That was why she couldn't go to the police. They were corrupt, as well.

At least she had found Joachim, a man of virtue and integrity. She appreciated all he had done for her, but she worried about his safety. *Protect him, Lord*, she prayed, hoping her prayer would be heard. *And protect Miriam.*

Chapter 15

The ride to the Thomin property seemed especially long today, no doubt because Joachim was thinking of the way Sarah had gripped his arm and the plea he had heard in her voice.

Eventually he turned onto the Thomin driveway and guided Belle toward the barn, where she would stay while he dug through the decaying wood and replaced the rotten areas on the back porch. Once the rain stopped and the wood dried, he would paint the new patches to make them identical to the old.

The white SUV that had caused problems earlier sat parked at the front porch. Joachim stared into the rear seat, seeing nothing of interest. On the porch, he noticed a large duffel bag leaning against the side of the door frame. The arms of a man's brown dress shirt poked from the drawstring closure. Would the filled bag, if propped up in the back seat, have given the appearance of a person with long hair? He shook his head and sighed, suddenly not sure of what he had seen through the tinted windows. He flicked the reins and guided Belle around the vehicle and into the barn. After unpacking his tools from the buggy, he hurried to the back porch.

The kitchen door opened. Victor sneered. "Where have you been? I thought you *plain* people got up early in the morning?"

As much as Joachim did not like Victor's tone, he steeled himself and gave a brief nod as he set his tools on the porch. "The storm was severe. It is dangerous to be on the road when lightning strikes so close."

"That's a lame excuse," Victor said with a wave of his hand.

"I do not offer it as an excuse" Joachim was quick to point out. "I have provided the reason I was delayed arriving. Would you prefer that I leave you now?"

Victor shook his head. "No need to get huffy."

Joachim was not huffy, but he was concerned about what might be happening inside the house. The television was tuned to a sporting channel and cheers from the crowd filtered through the back door.

"Victor, bring me a beer," a male voice demanded.

"You have guests today?" Joachim asked, glancing around Victor in hopes of seeing into the house.

"Get to work," Victor growled before he disappeared back into the kitchen.

Joachim glanced through the windows on the side of the house, searching for some sign of a woman. Seeing nothing except empty rooms, he glanced into the wooded area where Mamie mentioned the kitchen house had been located. Over the years, a thick forest had encroached within twenty feet of the Thomin home. If the kitchen house had been left standing, the woods would have surrounded the small outbuilding by now.

The sounds of the game on the television and the cheers of the onlookers bolstered Joachim's determination to continue searching. Convinced the men would remain focused on the TV, he hurried to the rear of the house.

Victor found him there. "I'm a little miffed at you, Burkholder," he said, his voice raised. "What didn't you understand about doing a day's work?"

Joachim placed his hand on his forehead as if to shade his eyes from the sun, which had only just peered through the dark clouds.

"I wanted to see the rotting areas on the second and third stories of the house. To do so, I must stand here at the back of the structure." He eyed the upper floors and nodded. "*Yah*, there is more work to be done on the second and third floors. I can see the rot. I must go inside and open the windows to check the sills."

"Not today," Victor insisted. "We'll do it another time. Now get back to work."

Joachim complied with Victor's wishes, but he continued to peer through the windows, hoping to catch sight of the newcomer and whomever might have ridden in the rear seat. Joachim also studied the forested area in hopes of spotting some sign of the kitchen house. Victor kept appearing at the kitchen door—no doubt, checking on him. Tomorrow would be a better day. At least that was Joachim's hope.

Sarah fretted all day about Joachim and whether Miriam was at the Thomin home. Rebecca was worried as well, and both women spoke little. Instead, they busied themselves with sewing. Rebecca was piecing a quilt and taught Sarah how to cut the squares and sew them together on a treadle sewing machine. The rhythmic cadence of the machine filled the house. Sarah enjoyed the repetitive work, but the hours still dragged by too slowly, and her concerns failed to ease.

Late in the afternoon, they put away the sewing and turned to cooking the evening meal. Sarah chopped onions for a stew and almost cried, not from the acrid sting of the onions but from her own worry.

"When will Joachim get home?" she finally asked, no longer able to hold in her emotion.

"Victor will want Joachim to work until five o'clock at least," Rebecca said as she peeled carrots. "He might demand Joachim make up the hours he missed this morning due to the rain."

"Which means Joachim won't be home until after dark," Sarah said with a sigh.

A dog barked near the barn. Sarah peered from the window. "It's Angelo. He's back from his day's escapades."

"And probably hungry," Rebecca added. "Would you mind feeding him?"

"Does he ever come inside?"

Rebecca shook her head. "Dogs are creatures *Gott* created for the outdoors." She lowered her voice and looked stern as she recited the statement. Then she smiled at Sarah and returned to her usual tone of voice as she explained, "That's what my *datt* says."

"He is a gruff man?" Sarah asked.

"On the outside, *yah*, but—" Rebecca patted her heart. "On the inside, where it really matters, he is softer, although you must not tell him I said that. I think he enjoys having people think he is stern."

"And your mother?"

"*Mamm* does not let his caustic tone bother her. She is strong, but in a loving way. You will like her, Sarah."

"And what will she think of having an *Englisch* woman in the house?"

"It is not what *Mamm* thinks that concerns me. My *datt* is the one who will have questions."

"Perhaps it would be best if I leave before he and your mother return home."

"And where would you go? You said your mother has died. Your sister Miriam has disappeared, and you have lost touch with your eldest sister, Hannah. You have nowhere to call home."

"I have an aunt who supposedly lives in Willkommen. At least that's what my mother claimed, but her mind had become addled and I'm not sure if she knew what she was saying."

"I hope you can find your aunt someday."

Which seemed highly unlikely at the present time. Whether she wanted to admit it or not, Rebecca was right. Sarah had no place to call home.

She thought of the sound she had heard in the basement and wondered again if Victor was holding someone else captive. Perhaps someone who had a home and loved ones who were worried about her.

"Have you heard of anyone who has gone missing in the area?" Sarah asked.

Rebecca looked up from the carrots. "Naomi is gone if that is what you mean."

"What about other Amish women? Do you know anyone who disappeared without explanation?"

"Once, about a year ago, a man came to this house. He said he was a policeman, but he was in an unmarked vehicle and asked if we had seen a young woman named

Rosie. I do not remember her last name. She was Amish and lived near Willkommen. He claimed the authorities were looking for her."

"Had Rosie done something wrong?"

"I asked, but the man said he could not say anything more." Rebecca shook her head. "He mentioned that she was Amish and had gotten mixed up with the wrong people."

Victor would fit the wrong people category. "Did you ever see her?"

"I saw a woman once at the Thomin house after Naomi was gone. That day, I had baked a cake and took it to Ms. Hazel, thinking she would be lonely without Naomi."

"That's when you saw the Amish woman?"

"*Yah*, at an upstairs window. She turned away when she saw me. I knocked on the door, but she either did not hear me or chose not to answer my knock."

"You think she could have been the missing Amish girl?"

"I wondered if she could be. Not long after that, a policeman stopped by our roadside stand and bought some of our homegrown tomatoes. I told him about the girl I had seen, but he did not seem concerned. I am not even sure if he inquired at the Thomin home. He bought three pounds of tomatoes and then did not have enough money to pay for them. He said he would come back and bring the rest of the money. I was foolish to believe him."

"You never saw him again?"

"Never."

"Joachim says I need to talk to the police."

"I do not know if that is wise," Rebecca said with a shake of her head. "The Amish do not involve law enforcement when there is a problem. We handle things ourselves. But even if we accepted the idea of contacting law enforcement, I do not believe I would trust these policemen. The Petersville police have not helped the Amish in the past."

"Victor told me the police are not to be trusted, but then that's coming from Victor."

"Yet Victor must be stopped from repeating what he did to you," Rebecca said.

"If I go back to Knoxville, I'll tell the authorities there."

Rebecca's brow raised. "Will they care what happened in the mountains of Georgia?"

"I don't know. My mother always ran from the police. When they came looking for us, it meant we had too many bills that hadn't been paid. Even before I met Victor and he told me I couldn't trust the police around here, I had a fear of anyone in law enforcement."

Rebecca patted her hand. "You have had a hard life, *yah*?"

Sarah shrugged. "I never thought of it as hard. It was my life and the only way to live that I knew. Although seeing the peace in this house shows me another way, a way I would like to follow."

"You would like to be Amish?"

"What I want is to sink roots down somewhere and have a home to call my own."

Rebecca nodded her approval. "And a good man to share that home with you as your husband?"

"You're getting ahead of me, Rebecca."

"You do not want a husband?"

"I don't want to be my mother. She made bad choices with men."

"But you are not your mother," Rebecca assured her. "You are your own person."

"A person who can't seem to stand on her own. I need to be more independent, to take care of myself and to be able to make my way in life."

Rebecca nodded. "Perhaps you yearn for a life in the world you left, instead of being holed up in an Amish house."

"The world is not what I want. I want this." She looked around her. "I want the peace and love I feel in this house. I want to work hard and have a sense of accomplishment at the end of the day."

"You have worked hard before, I can tell by the way you always help me and the way you learned to use the sewing machine so quickly today."

"But it wasn't the same in Knoxville. There was always an undercurrent of unease. I never knew if my mother would get upset and become volatile. Maybe it was the yearning for her affection, for words of acceptance that made me a hard worker—even if it never paid off. Growing up, I wanted to please her, but I always seemed to miss the mark, as the saying goes. If I tried to coax her into affirming me, she would ridicule my attempt or walk away as if she had never heard me."

"Mothers are not all the same. Some have big hearts. Others have small hearts. Hopefully, their hearts, no matter the size, are filled with love for their children."

"Yet shouldn't a mother with even a small heart, let her child know the loves she feels for that child?"

"*Yah*, it is so, but *Gott* loves you, Sarah. You are a *gut* person. You should open your heart more to Him and see if you find that acceptance for which you are searching."

Sarah wished it would be as easy as Rebecca implied.

At that moment, she heard the welcome sound of a buggy turning onto the drive and ran to the window. She smiled when she saw Joachim. She threw open the kitchen door and stepped onto the porch.

He looked tired and worried as if he carried too much on his shoulders. Sarah's heart skipped a beat as she was confronted once more with the truth. She had brought pain and struggle into Joachim's life. Anything good that she sensed in this house was there in spite of her. Yet anything that brought concern and even danger was *because* of her.

Joachim and his family had lived their years in this home and on this farm situated next to Victor's parents. All families had problems, but as far as she knew during that time, nothing had happened to upset the harmony between the Thomins and the Burkholders. Her seeing Joachim through the window at Victor's home had changed everything.

He looked at her from the buggy. Her knees became weak, and she felt light-headed. Silly reactions that didn't do anything to help Joachim. She had to control her emotions and her inner feelings. She had to guard her mind and her heart. She needed to leave the area as soon as possible because staying here, staying close to Joachim, would ruin his life.

Her spirits plummeted as she accepted the truth— leaving the peace and security she felt in this home would be the worst thing to happen to her. She had found something here. Something she wanted to hold on to, but something that didn't belong to her. Something she would only ruin if she stayed.

Her mistake. She had to leave, but leaving would break her heart.

Chapter 16

Joachim had not wanted to stay so late at Victor's home. He had wanted to come back to Sarah. Thoughts of her had carried him through the afternoon. Now that he was home, his heart nearly burst with joy seeing her on the porch waiting for him. If only Sarah were an Amish woman instead of a woman of the world.

Some things were not meant to be. His mother had told him that years ago when he had a crush on a non-Amish girl he had met at the lake where the teens sometimes gathered. The girl was visiting her Amish uncle and aunt, but all too soon she had returned to Atlanta, back to the life she knew. She had promised to write. He had waited for the mailman every day that summer, his heart becoming more and more saddened with each passing day he did not hear from her.

His mother's words back then brought no comfort,

but they had provided the wisdom he held on to when he was on his own in North Carolina.

He had come home to find where he was meant to be, but now that he was here, all he could think about was a woman who would soon leave him. Sarah, like that young teen so long ago, would not write, and once her life returned to normal, she would probably not even remember the Amish man who had helped her escape.

"You stayed so long," Sarah said in greeting. "I was worried."

"Victor was insistent that I finish the back porch. He and the man with the scar were drinking beer as they watched sports on television all day."

"Did you see a woman with long hair?"

"I saw no one else. Now I wonder if the form in the back seat was a figment of my imagination."

Sarah furrowed her brow. "Meaning what?"

He explained about the puffy duffel bag he could have mistaken for a person.

"Oh, Joachim, I thought it could have been Miriam."

He shook his head. "I do not think there was anyone else in the house, Sarah. I am sorry."

"Did you search the woods for the kitchen house?"

"I tried, but Victor spotted me through the window and came running outside to call me back."

"Maybe he didn't want you discovering something in the woods."

"I thought he was more concerned about the work not getting done."

"What about the man with the scar?" she asked. "Did you see him?"

"*Yah*, each time he pulled another beer from the refrigerator. I wrote his license plate number on a scrap of paper. We will give it to the police."

"Not the Petersville Police—they can't be trusted. But there should be law enforcement in Willkommen. We could go there. I need to find my aunt. She may have news of Miriam."

"Yet all you know is your aunt's name."

"Isn't that enough?" Sarah asked.

"People move. They get old. She could be infirmed and receiving medical care someplace."

"Then I'll check the nursing homes. Surely there's one in the area."

"We will wait until my parents return. With Victor and the strange man next door, I do not want to leave Rebecca alone. Then I will take you."

"What about Ms. Hazel?" she asked.

"Through the kitchen window, I watched Victor fix a tray and carry it upstairs. It was probably for his mother."

"Did you see a can of rat poison in the kitchen?"

"What are you saying, Sarah?"

"I'm worried about his mother."

"You think he would poison his own mother?"

"The old rat poisons contained arsenic, which can cause lethargy, confusion. Those are all symptoms that Ms. Hazel had."

"Yet you said yourself, she is old and infirmed. She would not have to be poisoned to appear confused or dazed."

"Except she was caring for herself while Naomi was there if what Levi said is true. I got the impression Naomi was more of a housekeeper than a caregiver."

"I do not doubt Levi."

"Nor do I, but it seems suspicious to me that Ms. Hazel's health would fail so quickly."

"Naomi has been gone for almost a year. Many things can change in a year. Ms. Hazel could have had a stroke. She could have gotten pneumonia, which would cause serious complications and setbacks."

"And she could be ingesting small doses of arsenic," Sarah said again.

"What about the sleeping pills we found in her dresser drawer?"

"I'm not counting those out either. Victor might give her sleeping pills so she will stay in bed while he drives round the countryside looking for women."

"And if he had someone holed up in the basement, why would he not use that person to help with his mother?"

From the look on her face, Joachim's statement had stopped Sarah like a brick wall. Surely she realized he was right.

"Why would Victor lock someone in an underground cellar if he needed care for his infirmed mother?" Joachim asked again.

Sarah raked her hand through her hair, nearly knocking off her bonnet. She caught it before it dropped to the ground. Strands of her hair pulled loose and fell over her cheek. He reached out his hand to weave them back in place.

"I don't seem to be getting the hang of this Amish thing, Joachim."

She was being truthful, and he knew it. Sarah was not suited for the Amish life. She needed her world and not his.

"Sometimes we want what cannot be."

She stared into his eyes for a long moment. "The problem is, Joachim, I'm not sure what I want."

With a heavy sigh, she walked to the door, pushed it open and slipped back inside.

Joachim felt as confused as Sarah seemed to be. Surely she realized they were not meant for each other. No matter how much he wanted what could never be.

Sarah entered the kitchen and washed her hands, then seeing the pot of boiled potatoes in the sink, she grabbed the potato masher and took out her frustration on the spuds. By the time Joachim stepped inside, the pot was filled with creamy mashed potatoes that would be a perfect side dish to the roast Rebecca was cooking in the oven. The rich aromas filled the kitchen and made Sarah's mouth water.

She refused to look at Joachim and then hated herself for being so petty. He was thinking of her safety and was trying to be cautious. If the Amish didn't trust the Petersville police, there had to be a good reason, but Joachim was right. They needed law enforcement somewhere to run the license plate and then investigate whether the man with the scar had anything to do with Miriam.

Ever since Victor had turned against her in the attic the day she had escaped, Sarah had wondered if she would ever see her sister again. For all she knew, Miriam might be dead. Something Sarah was not able to admit aloud.

Tears sprang to her eyes, but she blinked them aside. She had to be strong and hold on to the hope that Miriam was alive. If so, Sarah had to find her.

Again she thought of the scratching sound in the

basement. Suppose Miriam was being held captive in some other place and had tried to alert others to her whereabouts. What if her signal for help had been ignored? Miriam wasn't in Victor's basement, but if some other woman was being held captive, Sarah had to act.

Joachim entered the kitchen and stood for a long moment just inside the door, staring at her.

Sarah's heart ached. "I have to find the kitchen house. If my sister was being held in a place like that, I'd want someone to try to save her. I can't stay here in safety when someone might be locked away in an underground cellar."

"I will go tonight," Joachim said. "When it is dark and when Victor's friend is gone or has passed out from his drinking. You will stay here with Rebecca."

"No, Joachim. I'm going with you. I have to go. I can't save my sister, but maybe I can save someone else. Sometimes we have to sacrifice for another. Isn't that what your faith teaches you? It's what I believe. Christ gave up his life so we might be saved. Surely you believe that, too. So you have to understand why I need to go with you."

"What if I don't go?" he asked.

"Then I will go alone. Either way, I have to make sure no one else is trapped in Victor's snare."

"And if something happens to you, Sarah. What will happen to me?"

"The same thing that will happen when I leave here. You will go on with your life." She glanced around the kitchen. "Your future is here with your family. I have to make a new life for myself, but I would not be able to go on if I didn't find that root cellar and determine if someone is being held there."

She looked at him. "Can you understand?"

He nodded. "*Yah*, I understand. But it puts you in more danger, which is not what I want. I want something more for you, Sarah."

"Then go with me, Joachim. We'll find the kitchen house and search for someone held against her will. Then when I leave Petersville, I'll know I did the right thing."

"What about Ms. Hazel?"

"I'll alert the authorities in Willkommem or the next town or Atlanta if need be. I'll keep talking to law enforcement until someone listens to me. That's what Miriam would do." She grabbed the pitcher of milk and poured some into the potatoes, then mixed in a large scoop of butter.

As good as the mashed potatoes appeared and as wonderful as the smells were in the kitchen, Sarah suddenly wasn't hungry. Everything was about to change. Joachim's parents would return soon, and they wouldn't want an *Englisch* woman underfoot, which made Sarah sad.

For all her bluster, she didn't want to leave this Amish home. Even more important, she didn't want to leave Joachim.

Chapter 17

Joachim tapped on Sarah's bedroom door. "It is time," he whispered, hearing her stir. He turned on the flashlight as she opened the door.

"I fell asleep," she admitted, rubbing her face.

"Are you sure you want to do this?"

"We discussed it earlier. I have to, Joachim. I appreciate you going with me."

"I told you that I would go alone. I had hoped to search the woods today, but Victor kept too close of a watch. He seemed nervous, like a skittish colt."

"Maybe his friend frightens him. The guy looked like he was used to pushing his weight around."

"He is a big man, *yah*. I do not even want to think what happened that caused his scar."

"Perhaps too many beers in a bar someplace."

Joachim held his laughter in check so as not to wake

Rebecca. "Let's hope both he and Victor are sleeping off their beers and will not arise from their slumber."

"I'd like to feed both men those sleeping pills we found in Ms. Hazel's room. Then they wouldn't hear us as we search the property."

"We will find the kitchen house tonight," Joachim assured her. "Tomorrow we can determine how to help Ms. Hazel."

She glanced at the small arch of light. "You brought a flashlight instead of a candle. Thank you, Joachim."

"The flashlight will help us find the root cellar."

He stretched out his hand and was grateful when she placed hers in his. Her skin was soft and smooth, and her nearness made his heart skip a beat. He needed to control his emotions tonight lest he do something foolish that might alert someone in the Thomin house.

Sarah's safety was the most important thing to him. Actually, if truth be known, it was all that mattered.

"We will take the path through the woods on foot," Joachim whispered when they left the house and headed along the drive. "The buggy would make too much noise. Stay behind me on the trail. I must turn off the flashlight so Victor does not see us. The trees will block the light from the stars, forcing us to move slowly."

They made their way along the narrow path. Joachim had traveled it many times in daylight. Tonight, the sounds of the forest seemed especially ominous. Leaves rustled, perhaps from a squirrel or some night creature crawling through the underbrush. Snakes were common, but he would not mention that complication to Sarah.

"Wait, Joachim," she whispered. "My skirt caught on a bush."

She tugged it free and then headed on. "It's so dark."

He squeezed her hand. "We are almost there."

Except the trail seemed to stretch forever.

Eventually, they came to the edge of the tree line, where Joachim stopped. He put his finger to his lips as a reminder for them to remain quiet.

For a long moment he studied the house and surrounding area, then motioned Sarah to follow him. Slowly they wove behind the outbuildings and the barn.

"We will cut through the trees until we get to the area where the kitchen house should be located."

Sarah glanced at the Thomin home. "All the windows are dark. Victor used to leave a small light on in Ms. Hazel's room. When I took breakfast to her in the morning, it would still be on."

Joachim squeezed her hand again, hoping to provide reassurance. "We must stay focused. Tonight we will find the kitchen house and determine what caused the sound you heard. As I mentioned, we will decide how to help Ms. Hazel tomorrow."

She nodded. Even with the darkness, he could see her eyes, wide with worry.

"Do you see the SUV that belongs to the man with the scar?" she asked.

"No, but it was parked in front of the house earlier. We would not be able to see it from here. As much as he drank today, I hope he did not try to drive home."

"He's probably staying in one of the guest bedrooms on the second floor. Victor's bedroom faces the front of the house, but the windows in the guest room overlook the back lawn. We need to be careful in case he happens to wake."

"He won't see us, Sarah."

Joachim took the lead. Without a path to follow, he had to pick his way through the underbrush.

"Be careful," he cautioned as he navigated an especially thick area of bramble.

If only he had been able to search the woods in the light of day. Tonight, everything lay in shadows so that even the most common tree or shrub took on a strange appearance.

At long last they arrived in the area where the kitchen house most likely would have been located. Joachim stared into the darkness, seeing nothing.

"What do we do now?" Sarah asked, leaning closer.

"We start searching and walk in a grid fashion so we cover all the ground to make sure we don't miss any trace of it. Remember, it might have been torn down, or fallen apart due to disrepair. But hopefully, we will find some sign of an older structure."

"And if we don't?" Sarah asked.

"Then we will return home without any answer to your question about the noise in the basement."

"I don't want to give up, Joachim."

"I do not want that either. Let us walk next to each other so we can cover two times the amount of area," he suggested.

She glanced over her shoulder at the large Thomin house. "The windows in one of the guest bedrooms are open. That may be where Victor's friend is staying."

Joachim put his finger to his lips. "Then we will be quiet so he has nothing to hear."

He grabbed her hand. "Come, we must walk."

Traversing the area in the dark was a challenge. The smallest bush or tree root caused Sarah to stumble. Joachim caught her each time and helped her regain her balance.

"I'm beginning to think this is impossible," she admitted.

"We will keep looking. Do not get discouraged."

"It's not that."

"You are tired."

She nodded. "You must be, too. I keep thinking about the scratching sound and whether Miriam is being held someplace far from here."

"We can go home and return tomorrow," Joachim offered.

"No. I want to keep searching."

They walked in silence for the next fifteen minutes.

Sarah stopped to lean against a tree. "I'm sorry, Joachim. You would do better without me."

"We will leave now."

Her shoulders slumped. "I feel like a failure."

"You are no such thing. You are tired and still not strong enough. Do not be discouraged."

"Maybe just another ten minutes," she suggested.

He nodded, and they set out again. A break in the trees surprised them. The clear area was easier to navigate with the stars visible overhead, which shed light on the ground.

Joachim pointed to a raised area just a few steps away. They hurried forward and then stopped to stare at what appeared to be stacked bricks.

"It looks like part of an old chimney," he said. "We have found the kitchen house—or at least what remains of it."

He glanced around, searching for some sign of a root cellar or opening for a tunnel. If only they had more light. Glancing over his shoulder, he saw the big house through the trees. They were close to finding what they came searching for, but would the remains of the old structure reveal anything about the scratching sounds Sarah had heard, namely whether a person was being held captive?

Sarah's heart pounded with excitement and anticipation. They'd found at least a portion of the old kitchen house. And even though the building was mostly gone, surely the tunnel had remained. Now they needed to find what was buried belowground.

"No telling how much dirt and debris has settled over this area," she said, glancing around.

"We will walk a few steps away from the chimney," Joachim suggested. "Perhaps ten or twelve feet, and then walk around the periphery of what would have been the outbuilding."

"That sounds like a good plan." They paced off the steps, and then each turned in opposite directions. Sarah walked to the left and took tiny steps, her gaze on the ground. Knowing they had discovered the location of the actual kitchen house gave her confidence. Her foot stumbled over a raised area. She bent and touched the rock that had caught her foot.

"I've found the foundation for a wall," she whispered to Joachim.

He hurried to join her. "*Gut*. We will keep walking, hopefully around the outer wall of the old structure."

Together, they slowly moved forward. Sometimes the stone wall disappeared, but they continued on until they found another section of the old wall.

When they were almost three-quarters of the way

around, Sarah stopped. "What's that?" she asked, pointing to a metal slab on the ground.

Joachim bent and worked his hands over the flat surface then down the edge of the covering. "I have found a padlock."

Sarah's heart raced. "It's the door to the cellar."

Joachim nodded. "You are right."

He glanced at the house that sat less than fifty feet away. "If only the windows in the house were not opened. If we are going to explore the tunnel, then I will need to break the lock, which will make noise."

"We don't have a choice, Joachim. We can't turn back now."

"*Yah*, it is true. We must continue our search." He pulled a hammer from his waistband and knelt on the ground next to the metal slab.

Hammer in hand, he glanced up at her. "If you hear anyone coming, run through the woods and angle around, keeping the barn as a point of reference. It will be dark so you will need to be careful, but you should find the path back to my farm on the far side of the barn."

"You're worrying me."

"That is because I am worried, Sarah."

"If Victor and his buddy are sleeping off all the beer they drank, the sound of the hammer might not wake them."

"This we can only hope to be true. Let me know if you see anything change at the house."

She stared at the windows, dark and devoid of life.

Joachim raised the hammer.

She held her breath.

Her heart jerked as his hammer hit the padlock. The

clank of metal striking metal echoed through the forest, shattering the night and the stillness.

Sarah continued to stare at the windows. Would she be able to see anyone as dark as it was?

She glanced down. The padlock was still attached. Joachim raised his hammer and struck again.

A light went on in the house.

"Joachim?" She pointed to the window.

He fiddled with the padlock and then held it up triumphantly. Quickly, he stepped aside, grabbed the edge of the metal door and lifted it open.

They both stared into a dark hole.

"Watch the house," Joachim whispered. "Run if someone comes outside, but warn me first. I am going down into the cellar."

She grabbed his arm. "Be careful."

He nodded. Pulling out his flashlight, he stepped onto the wooden stairway that led into the darkness.

Sarah's heart lurched. She wrung her hands, wishing she and Joachim could be anyplace else except at this root cellar in the middle of the night.

She focused her eyes on the light in the window. The minutes passed too slowly. Leaves rustled behind her. She glanced back, half expecting to see Victor. Relieved when he didn't appear, she bent and stared into the darkness.

"Joachim?" she whispered.

Her heart pounded. The sound of her pulse roared in her ears. Where was Joachim and what had he found?

From out of the darkness down the tunnel, a face appeared. Not Joachim's, but a young woman.

Slender, pale, wide-eyed.

Sarah stretched out her hand and helped the woman

up the stairs. Tears glistened on her dirt-smudged cheeks. She pulled in a ragged breath. Sarah's heart broke thinking of what she had endured.

"I'm Sarah." She opened her arms and pulled the woman into her embrace.

"My...my name is Rosie Glick."

Sarah smiled. "You're safe now. Victor won't hurt you again."

Rosie gripped her tightly for a long moment and then turned as Joachim climbed from the cellar.

He held a pile of blankets in his arms. Rosie hurried forward and took the blankets from him, a look of relief on her slender face.

Sarah stepped closer. Her heart bursting with wonder and surprise as she stared down, seeing the tiny newborn infant in Rosie's arms.

Chapter 18

"We must hurry," Joachim warned both women. He lowered the metal covering into place and motioned them to head deeper into the woods, away from the house.

A door slammed.

"Victor?"

A man stood in the backyard, the big guy they had seen in the car. He called out for Victor a second time and then started jogging toward them.

"Hurry," Joachim whispered.

Rosie clutched the baby and tried to keep up. Joachim grabbed Rosie's arm. Together, he and Sarah helped the young woman move faster.

Joachim glanced over his shoulder.

The darkness prevented him from seeing the man, but he heard his heavy footfalls.

Again the visitor called out for Victor.

Joachim would not let Rosie be captured again, especially with the baby.

The barn appeared on the right. If only they could clear the outbuildings and find the path.

A kitchen light flicked on in the house, and a person stepped onto the back porch. Shoulder-length brown hair, medium height, slender build.

Sarah stopped and stared at the figure. Her eyes narrowed. "Miriam?"

Joachim turned just as Sarah started to run, not away from the big house, but toward it.

He pointed out the barn to Rosie. "Wait there with the baby."

Joachim hurried to cut Sarah off before Victor's friend saw her. Thankfully, he caught up to her and grabbed her arm.

She turned on him, anger flashing from her eyes. "It's my sister. I have to save her."

"Look again, Sarah. What you see is a man with shoulder-length hair. Your eyes are playing tricks on you."

She shook her head and glanced again at the slender, but very masculine, figure on the porch. "Oh no," she groaned, realizing her mistake.

Joachim took her hand. "Come. We must hurry."

They started to run, but not toward the barn. Joachim did not want to lead the men to Rosie. Instead, he turned back the way they had come.

Victor's friend chased after them. The long-haired man, as well. Sarah gasped for air. Her foot caught and she stumbled. Joachim helped her up. She was winded and frightened. The big man with the scar was gaining on them, his friend lagging some steps behind.

Joachim's heart pounded, fearing Sarah would be captured again. He would rather die himself than let that happen, but she could run no farther, which meant they had to hide. But where?

Think! Think!

"Go on without me, Joachim."

He wrapped his arm around her shoulders and guided her deeper into the underbrush. Both men followed too close behind them.

"It's no use," Sarah gasped.

She was right. Running would not work.

The clearing appeared ahead. "Hurry, Sarah. Just a little farther."

Gott, help us, he prayed.

Dark clouds filled the night sky, blocking the star-light and making the clearing even more difficult to tra-verse. They were close. He knew it, but the men were close, too, gaining on them.

Joachim stumbled. He stopped short and dropped to the ground.

"What's wrong?" Sarah cried.

His fingers found what he had been looking for. He lifted the metal slab, exposing the black void.

"Hurry, Sarah, crawl into the cellar."

"No, I can't."

"You have to. Now." He took her hand and ushered her forward. "I will not leave you. We will hide together until the men return to the house."

"But—"

"Now, Sarah." The men's footfalls echoed in the night. They were close. So. Very. Close.

With a faint whimper, Sarah climbed down the wooden stairs and disappeared into the darkness. Joachim followed her. He lowered the slab over them. The musty scent of the damp earth filled his nostrils. Sarah grabbed his arm. He pulled her close, feeling her body tremble as the men ran across the clearing, searching for them.

"I will not leave you." Sarah kept playing Joachim's words over in her head as they waited silently for Victor's friends to give up their search and return to the house. Her head rested against Joachim's chest. She heard his heartbeat, which calmed her racing pulse and helped her endure the time they remained underground.

Finally, Joachim stirred. "I'm going to raise the covering ever so slightly. Do not make a sound."

He moved away from her. A lump filled her throat, and she blinked back tears that burned her eyes. She had to be brave and remain still. At least she was with Joachim. Her heart went out to Rosie, who was alone with her baby. Just so the men wouldn't find her.

A gust of fresh air floated over Sarah as Joachim pushed up on the metal slab. She could see the outline of his profile as he stared motionless through the opening.

Finally, he nodded and reached for her hand. "The house is dark. I trust they have gone back to bed."

Together they climbed from the cellar. Sarah sucked in a deep breath of fresh cool air, grateful to be free. Joachim replaced the covering over the root cellar and pointed toward the barn.

Slowly, they moved away from the house. If they only would find Rosie and her baby waiting for them.

Sarah glanced back at the house that stood black against the night. She recalled the men who had chased them—the large, scarred man they had met on the road, and the other man who she had mistaken for her sister. The slender man with shoulder-length brown hair had been the passenger in the SUV and not Miriam.

Just as Joachim had said, her eyes had played tricks on her. Another mistake. She had made so many.

Joachim squeezed her hand as if he could read her mind. He pointed to a path through the woods that allowed them to move more quickly.

Her heart pounded as they approached the barn and entered through a side door.

"Rosie?" Joachim called, his voice little more than a whisper.

Silence.

He walked by the stalls and peered into the nooks and crevices. Had Victor or one of the other men found her and taken her back to the house?

Sarah wanted to scream with frustration and anger at herself. If she hadn't made the mistake about Miriam, Rosie and her baby would have escaped.

Oh, God, help her!

A soft mewing made Sarah turn. She glanced through the open doorway to a second outbuilding. There on the ground, with her back against the wall, sat Rosie, holding the baby in her arms.

Rosie was exhausted, and the trip back to Joachim's house sapped what little strength she had.

"Only a little farther," Sarah whispered, taking the baby and cuddling the infant close. Joachim picked Rosie up in his arms and carried her back to his house.

Sarah knocked on the kitchen door and Rebecca let them in. "Where have you been? I heard you leave the house, and I have been so worried not knowing what happened."

Joachim carried Rosie inside. Rebecca guided him to the rocker by the fire. "It is warm here. I will make tea."

She hurried to the kitchen and passed Sarah, only now noticing the bundle in her arms. Rebecca stopped short.

"Oh my, Sarah. Do you have what I think you have?"

She nodded. "Rosie's baby."

Rebecca turned to look at her brother. "Victor was holding her captive?"

Joachim nodded. "In the morning, I will go to Petersville. The police need to be told. If one officer is corrupt and not interested in getting involved, then I will find another one who will listen. And if not Petersville, then I will drive to Willkommen. Victor must be stopped. He must be stopped now."

Sarah's heart soared with emotion as she rocked the baby who slept in her arms. She had never held a baby so small or so beautiful.

Rebecca prepared food for Rosie, who ate and then asked for more. She kept looking at Sarah and making sure her baby was still sleeping.

No one asked her questions. There would be time for that later. Right now, she appeared too tired and had been through so much.

"There's a spare room upstairs and a bed," Sarah said. "We'll care for the baby down here while you get some sleep."

"Are you sure?" Rosie asked.

Sarah nodded. "Tell me his name."

"Joseph. My baby's name is Joseph."

"Don't worry about your little one," Sarah assured her. "Get the rest you need. Tomorrow we can talk."

Rosie gave a weak smile. "Thank you for saving Joseph and me."

"I heard scratching on the wall when I was in the basement of the big house. That was you, wasn't it?"

Rosie nodded, her face still so pale. "Victor locked me in the root cellar, but he did not remember the tunnel."

"How did you find it?"

"I searched for some way to get out and found the doorway. Dirt had piled up around it. Before the baby came, I cleared the dirt and pried open the door."

"You went into the tunnel?"

Rosie nodded. "Victor left a candle for me. I used that to see my way. I thought it would lead to an exit. When I got to the end and found it blocked, I cried." She glanced at the baby. "That night, my pains started."

"You went into labor and delivered the baby by yourself?"

Rosie nodded, then closed her eyes.

The memory was either too difficult or the young woman too fatigued to go on.

"You need to rest," Sarah insisted. "Tomorrow we will decide what to do next. You are from around here?"

"My parents live near Willkommen."

Sarah glanced at Joachim. If he took Rosie and her baby home to her parents, perhaps Sarah could go with them and make inquiries about her aunt.

Before she could mention her plan to Joachim, he headed to the door.

"Stay here with Rebecca and Rosie," he told Sarah. "I will go back along the path and make certain we were not followed."

Her heart lurched. "Oh, Joachim, be careful. Victor is a terrible man, and his friends seem equally as bad. I'm afraid of what could happen to you if they see you. Please, don't go," she pleaded.

"It is important to stay on guard, Sarah. This is what I must do."

"But suppose you find them. You don't have a weapon. Your faith does not allow you to respond to their violence."

"Sometimes a man must do what he knows he must do."

"Which means you could get hurt."

"When I was working in North Carolina, I was forced to confront two men who thought being Amish meant being weak. They had no love for *Gott* in their hearts, Sarah, and they left me no alternative but to protect that which was mine."

"What do you mean?"

"I had to show them the fallacy of their ways. Did not Christ drive the money changers from the temple?"

She nodded. "Would your minister approve of your actions?"

"We do not have a minister, Sarah. A bishop leads us and he, more than likely, did not approve of me leaving my home. For a period of time, I had my feet in both worlds, trying to be both Amish and *Englisch*. For that, I must ask forgiveness."

Sarah didn't understand how one man could hold so much power over Joachim. "And what if the bishop says you cannot stay in the area?"

"If I ask forgiveness of *Gott* and of my Amish community, he will not deny my request. He wants what *Gott* wants, and that is for me to live by the *Ordnung*, the rules established for our community."

"What does the *Ordnung* say about matters of the heart?"

His brow furrowed. "A man takes a wife and the two become one. This is the way we have lived through the years. Perhaps I do not understand your question?"

"What if the woman is not a member of the Amish faith?"

Joachim lowered his gaze and sighed. "Then the relationship could not continue. An Amish man marries an Amish woman. Marriage to someone outside the faith is not allowed."

"Isn't that narrow-minded, Joachim?"

He shook his head. "It is the way we keep our faith and our way of life. As much as I tried, I could not walk on both sides of the fence. The choice must be made, either to fully embrace the Amish faith or to leave it altogether. A person must decide which way he or she is to live life." He smiled weakly. "Sometimes that is a hard choice."

Then he turned and walked to the door. After grabbing his hat off the wall peg, he reached for the knob.

Cool nighttime air blew into the kitchen as the door opened, making Sarah shiver. Joachim had clearly explained the choices available to a person drawn to the Amish way of life. Where did Sarah stand?

She was attracted to Joachim and, as she suddenly realized, to his faith, as well. Although she wasn't ready to fully embrace the *plain* life. She needed longer to consider her options, but she was running out of time. Remain *Englisch* and say goodbye to Joachim, or embrace his Amish faith and remain in the area. If only she knew what the future would hold.

She glanced though the window, seeing Joachim hurry toward the pathway. She was running out of time.

Amish or *Englisch*? The decision was one she wasn't able to make. At least not tonight.

Chapter 19

Less than three hours later, the first rays of dawn pulled Sarah from a light slumber. The baby was still asleep in her arms. She glanced around the room, hoping to find Joachim in one of the chairs. Instead, she realized, with a heaviness in her heart, that she was alone.

Too much time had passed since he had left the house. Thoughts of what could have happened stabbed her like a knife. A tiny cry escaped her lips, making the infant stir.

She rocked the little one and tried to force the vision of Joachim being locked in the attic room from her mind. Even worse were visions of him thrown into the dark, dank root cellar.

If Victor was holding him captive, then she couldn't let him remain there. She had to do something to set him free. But what and how?

The baby stretched, then wrinkled his precious face and started to root for a feeding. She patted and rocked, hoping to soothe him back to sleep, yet little Joseph continued to search for nourishment. A shrill cry escaped his thin lips.

As much as she didn't want to wake Rosie, the baby was hungry and needed to be fed. His cries quickly became inconsolable. Sarah carried him upstairs. The door to the extra bedroom jerked open, and Rosie stretched out her arms to take the child. The baby nestled against his mother. She nodded her thanks to Sarah and then retreated into the bedroom and closed the door behind her.

Sarah stood in the hallway and longed to hold the baby in her arms again. The unconditional love she had felt for the small infant surprised her. A love without reservation. The little one had accepted her love unconditionally as well, and had slept in her arms with absolute trust.

Sarah had always wanted that type of love from her own mother. Instead, she had received criticism and scolding and had grown up sensing she was unwanted. If Sarah ever had children, she would ensure they knew how much she loved each of them and how special they were to her.

She sighed and shook her head, surprised by thoughts of children when she had never allowed herself to consider marriage and family. Surely it was this house with the love and acceptance she had found here that was changing her mind.

But Joachim had told her without hesitation that he could not be interested in an *Englisch* woman. She did not need to be told twice. He had made his feelings on the matter perfectly clear. With all that had happened and as confused as her life had been, she wasn't ready to commit to the Amish faith. At least, not yet.

A swell of melancholy filled her as she headed back downstairs. She walked slowly through the house, seeing the simple beauty of the rockers by the wood stove, the calendar hanging on the wall in the kitchen, and the gas lights sitting on stands in front of aluminum disks that magnified the light and helped to brighten the rooms. She still had an aversion to matches, but the long-necked fireplace lighters and the gas lights with tall hurricane chimneys that encircled the flames were no longer threatening.

She ran her hand over the silky smooth wood of the dry sink and marveled at the workmanship. Had Joachim made the piece for his mother perhaps? Or had his father, who Joachim claimed was a farmer at heart, crafted the kitchen work area long ago for his new bride?

She stepped to the window, seeing the warm glow of the first light on the horizon. The barnyard came into view. As she watched, a small animal bounded along the drive and raced toward the house. Sarah hurried onto the porch and bent to welcome Angelo home.

"Oh, it's good to see you, boy." She scratched his neck. The pup nosed at Sarah's hands and jumped to lick her face. She laughed at his excitement and attention, and again, she was filled with a sense of acceptance and love.

Footsteps sounded. Her heart skidded to a halt. She stood, ready to flee into the house, but before she did so, her eyes caught sight of the man walking toward her.

Her heart went from a standstill to an erratic thumping that warmed her neck and made her want to run to welcome this man home.

"Oh, Joachim," she said as he drew closer. "I was so worried about you."

He opened his arms and reached for her. She stepped into his embrace, the thoughts of their differences fleeing so that all that mattered was being with him.

"The night is over, Sarah, and we are both safe."

She lifted her face to his, longing to remain forever in his arms. He lowered his lips to hers, but before they kissed, a car turned into the drive and captured both of them in the arc of its headlights.

Sarah raised her hand to her forehead, shielding her eyes from the glare as the vehicle pulled to a stop.

A man stepped to the ground. "Joachim Burkholder?"

Sarah felt Joachim tense. *"Yah?"*

The man moved to the front of the car, his dark blue uniform now visible in the headlights.

Sarah blinked and saw the logo for the Petersville Police Department on the side of the car.

"I'm here to take you into headquarters for questioning," the officer said. "You're wanted in connection with the death of Eli Burkholder."

"What?" Sarah looked from the policeman to Joachim.

Shock registered on his face. "Eli died five years ago."

"Did you not flee the area immediately after his death without leaving the statement that law enforcement specifically requested?"

"I do not remember being told to do that."

"Maybe you'll remember more clearly if you come down to headquarters."

"This is not something I want to do."

"Are you resisting arrest, sir?"

Resisting arrest? Everything was going from bad to worse. At first the policeman had mentioned questioning Joachim. Now he talked about making an arrest.

"You've made a mistake," Sarah insisted. "Joachim has done nothing wrong. You need to question Victor Thomin. He's at his mother's house. It's the next property on the road to Petersville. The turn is about a mile and a half from here."

"Ma'am, the Thomins are one of the oldest and most respected families in this area."

"I'm not disparaging the family, I'm talking about their son, Victor. He—"

Joachim grabbed her hand. "Sarah, be quiet. This is not the time."

Rebecca stepped onto the porch. "Joachim, what is happening?"

"Go inside," Joachim insisted. He glanced at Sarah. "Both of you."

"Why do you want to question him?" Sarah demanded of the officer.

"Lady, we received a tip that Mr. Burkholder was in town. We've been wanting to talk to him for years about that old investigation. And now that he's back, he has also been incriminated in illegal operations happening in this local area that involves human trafficking."

"If you're investigating human trafficking, then you definitely have the wrong man. I told you to question Victor Thomin," Sarah insisted, but the officer ignored her and moved to handcuff Joachim.

"I will go peacefully," he told the cop.

The officer ushered him to the squad car, where he frisked him and then clicked the handcuffs into place.

Seeing Joachim handled like a common criminal made Sarah shake inwardly. What was happening? Her world was falling apart. Victor was the kind of man who should be taken in for questioning, not Joachim.

Rebecca hurried from the porch to stand next to Sarah. Both women watched the officer open the rear door of the squad car and shove Joachim into the back seat. The door slammed shut, sending a shiver down Sarah's spine.

The officer climbed behind the wheel, started his car and backed onto the main road. The police sedan turned toward Petersville and drove off.

The stillness was overpowering. Sarah stared at the road as the taillights disappeared from sight.

Angelo nuzzled Sarah's leg and then started to howl.

Joachim glanced back through the window of the police squad car and caught a last glimpse of Sarah standing in the drive, her eyes wide and fear wrapped around her slender face.

After what she had just heard, he was certain she thought he was a killer, just like the heinous man who had killed her mother.

Any chance of convincing her that the Amish way of life—and particularly life with him—would be something she should consider had disappeared the moment the police officer had clasped the cuffs around his wrists.

The night of the buggy accident, Joachim's world had fallen apart. In the years since, he had tried to rebuild it, but all his efforts had fallen apart in the last few moments. He felt vile and unwanted, like a snake that needed to be squashed underfoot lest its deadly venom strike someone down. He had looked into Sarah's eyes and seen her gaze go from one of affection to disgust.

Moments earlier, he had come so close to kissing her that he could almost feel her sweet lips on his. His heart had soared as high as the eagle flies, and he had thought of nothing else except holding her close and keeping her safely protected and with him for the rest of his life.

Then everything had plummeted and his future, the one he had envisioned with Sarah at his side, disappeared with the click of the cuffs.

Thoughts of going to prison and all the humiliation that accompanied incarceration ate at his gut. Surely he would be exonerated of guilt, yet even the accusation of wrongdoing would mark him. He shook his head, seeing another option, one that was also troubling. He envisioned the loneliness of a vagabond carpenter traveling from job to job, never with a place to call home and never with a *gut* woman like Sarah—no, not a *gut* woman, an amazing woman—to walk with him through life.

The officer was talking on the radio, unaware of the pain Joachim was experiencing. Would he realize his mistake, or would Joachim be held behind bars and forced to face a trial where he would be accused of being responsible for his brother's death?

Perhaps his father had been right. Joachim did not deserve to remain part of the family. He had been shunned and rightfully so.

Gott, forgive my transgressions. I came home to reconcile with my datt. That reconciliation will never be.

He turned again to glance back at the farm where he had grown up and where he and Sarah had shared such a short period of time. He now knew what he wanted in life. He wanted his Amish faith, and he wanted Sarah walking through life next to him.

This morning, riding in the back of the police car, Joachim realized he had wanted too much.

Chapter 20

Sarah's heart was heavy as she returned to the house and climbed the stairs without saying anything to Rebecca. Joachim, with his concern for others and his willingness to help those in need, was not a man who would take a person's life. Nor did he have anything to do with trafficking. Sarah couldn't believe such nonsense, yet she herself had watched as he had been handcuffed and locked in the back of a patrol car.

Joachim, who had come to her rescue, who had saved her from Victor, who looked at her and made her knees weak and her stomach turn to jelly, was the most wonderful man she had ever known, yet she couldn't stay around and hope there was a chance for them. Joachim had said as much himself when he had discussed the differences between them.

Sarah was an *Englischer*.

Joachim was Amish.

And never the two shall meet or mix or fall in love or declare their love or get married and have a family.

His arrest had nothing to do with her upset. Even if the police officer had not appeared, Sarah would still be struggling to make levelheaded decisions about what to do next. How foolish she had been to have given her heart to Joachim. He wasn't meant for her. After all the legal problems were ironed out, Joachim would find a wonderful Amish woman who would cook his food and sew his clothes and help him in the fields and with milking the cows and slaughtering the pigs. All the things about which Sarah knew nothing. Although she was willing to learn.

She lightened her footsteps when she passed Rosie's room and headed to her own chamber. Pushing open the door, she stepped inside and then quietly closed the door behind her.

The tension that had welled up within her since she had been in Joachim's arms burst loose. Tears fell from her eyes. She stumbled to the bed and collapsed onto the thick quilt as she struggled to control her outburst. She didn't want to concern Rosie or Rebecca with her tears. Hopefully, they wouldn't hear her when she left the house. She could no longer stay here, where everything reminded her of Joachim.

But where would she go and what would she do? A trip to Willkommen to inquire about her aunt? Yes, that made sense as a first step. If the woman couldn't be found, Sarah would board a bus and return to Knoxville.

She wiped the tears from her eyes, and in spite of the heaviness of her heart, she eventually fell asleep. Awakening a few hours later, Sarah headed downstairs and hurried into the kitchen. Rosie sat at the table sipping from a mug of coffee.

"Did you sleep?" Sarah asked.

"Not with the baby in bed with me. I had slept earlier, but after he nursed, I kept wondering how I would face my parents."

"They love you, Rosie. They want you home with them." At least that's what Sarah hoped.

She poured a cup of coffee, weighing how she would leave this wonderful Amish home and how she would get to Willkommen to find her aunt.

"Joachim had said he would take me home," Rosie said. "Now I'm not sure how I will get there."

Sarah nodded. "Perhaps I will go with you, Rosie. I need to find an aunt who may live in Willkommen."

"You are not staying here with Rebecca and Joachim?"

Joachim isn't here, Sarah wanted to remind her. Instead, she asked, "How long did you help Ms. Hazel?"

"More than seven months."

"You didn't try to escape?"

"Where would I go? I was an unwed mother. I could not go home. I could not go anywhere."

"What about Joseph's father?"

"His name was William." Rosie lowered her eyes. "William is dead."

"I'm so sorry." Sarah's heart went out to the young woman. "For those reasons you never tried to escape?"

"That is true, although if I had known that Victor would lock me in the root cellar close to my delivery time, I would have tried to escape. He was not abusive except with his words, but I was foolish to think he was a better man than he proved himself to be."

"What led to him forcing you into the cellar?"

"I told him the baby was due, and that I needed help. He did not want to bring in a midwife. It was easier to lock me away than to have a doctor or midwife find out he was holding me in his mother's house."

"How did Ms. Hazel seem when you first arrived?"

"She was sick, and her condition grew worse. I told Victor she needed to see a doctor. He refused to take her. Instead, he gave her sleeping pills."

"You saw him give her pills?"

"*Yah*, many times."

"You need to tell the police."

Rosie shook her head. "I do not want to talk to the police. They cannot be trusted. You must know this for yourself. After all, they have Joachim. From the window, I watched as the officer put him in the police car."

Sarah's heart ached, thinking of Joachim in custody. She had run away from law enforcement as a child each time her mother woke her in the middle of the night, saying they must leave town before the police came knocking at their door.

She had vowed to never live like that again. She didn't trust law enforcement, but she wouldn't do anything to be under suspicion again, and tying herself to Joachim would do just that. He had helped her escape Victor and had provided a safe place for her to stay until she gained her strength and was ready to move on with her life, but he wasn't the man with whom she wanted to spend the rest of her life, especially if he had problems with the law.

Tears burned her eyes. Tears for Joachim and his plight, but also for herself. She had made another mistake. She needed Miriam. What would her sister advise? After considering the matter, Sarah decided that Miriam would say to leave the area and to forget about Joachim, that he wasn't the man for her.

Sarah had to find a way to take Rosie and the baby home, alert the authorities and then find her aunt. If her aunt couldn't be found, Sarah would have to find a way to earn enough money for a bus ticket. She had to go somewhere. Home to Knoxville or south to Atlanta or maybe to Birmingham or Montgomery. She had to leave the area to get free of Victor and find a place where she could start over.

In that new spot, she would try to forget Joachim, although she doubted he would ever be erased from her memory or her heart.

Joachim peered through the bars of the jail cell. His life had gotten more complicated. Officer Nelson had hauled him into police headquarters, fingerprinted him and then ushered him quickly into a holding cell.

No telling how long Joachim would remain behind bars. His mind returned to Sarah with her crystal-blue eyes, silky skin and lips that begged to be touched. If only he could go home.

"What're you in for?" a guy asked from an adjoining cell.

"The officer mentioned manslaughter. Actually, it was a buggy accident that killed my brother five years ago."

The guy nodded. "Ask to talk to Sergeant Evans. He's the only sane cop in the bunch."

Joachim appreciated the tip. He would try to talk to

Sergeant Evans, but as the minutes ticked by too slowly, all Joachim could think about was Sarah and whether she would still be at his house when and if he was released from jail.

Rebecca hurried into the kitchen and pulled biscuits from the oven. "Where is Rosie? I heard her talking to you?"

"She's upstairs with the baby."

"I'm worried about her."

"I am, too. That's why we need to hitch Belle to the buggy and drive Rosie and Joseph home."

"What are you saying?"

"This is our chance to get help for Ms. Hazel. We will take Rosie and her baby home and then find Levi in Willkommen. He said he would be working with his uncle at the Amish Market. Levi will know how to locate the police, a law-abiding officer we can trust. The good cops will save Ms. Hazel and arrest Victor and insist that Joachim be released."

"I'm not sure that is the best idea," Rebecca reasoned. "Rosie is weak and her face is flushed. I fear she has a fever. If so, she must stay here and rest."

"Then I'll go to Willkommen alone."

"You are a smart woman, Sarah, but you do not know about horses or how to guide the buggy." Rebecca wiped her hands on a towel. "Let me give Rosie something to eat, then I will get the buggy ready. We will go together."

Relief swept over Sarah. "We'll locate Levi. He'll help us."

"*Yah*, he goes often with his uncle to the market there. He will know about the police and who we can trust. I am frightfully worried about Joachim with the Petersville police, especially if Victor was the informant who called them. Think of how many lies he will tell them about Joachim."

Sarah took a tray with biscuits and ham upstairs to Rosie and quickly explained that she and Rebecca were leaving to get help and that Rosie needed to remain inside with the doors locked.

"Are you sure my baby will be safe here? I am not worried about myself, but I am worried for my child."

"You'll both be safe."

But would they be? *Please, God, let nothing happen to this young woman and her precious infant.*

Sarah hurried to the kitchen. She grabbed the cape off the peg and put the bonnet on her head and tied it under her chin. Looking around the kitchen one more time, Sarah saw the chair where Joachim had sat and the towel where he wiped his hands. Mentally revisiting the past few days, she saw his warm smile and the acceptance and understanding in his brown eyes. She had to say goodbye to his memory and to this home where she had found something she had never experienced in her life. She had found love and acceptance and the true meaning of Christian charity and a heartfelt concern for others. She would carry that memory with her forever.

Rebecca led Belle, now hitched to the buggy, out of the barn. With no time to spare, Sarah opened the door and hurried outside. Dark clouds covered the sky and blocked the warming rays of the sun, as if all of nature was mourning Joachim's arrest and the hateful crimes that had happened in the house next door.

Sarah needed to get help for Ms. Hazel and Rosie

and the baby, and yes, Joachim, too. Then, unless she could find her aunt, she would leave the area never to return again.

She climbed into the back of the buggy, missing Joachim's strong arms to lift her onto the seat. She could no longer rely on him. She had to rely on her own wherewithal.

Rebecca had called her strong, although she felt weak and unsure of the future. What would it bring? All she saw was loneliness and sorrow in the days ahead as she began to realize she wanted to remain in this Amish community.

Did Joachim have something to do with that?

She nodded imperceptibly. He had everything to do with the way she felt and the sorrow that pulled at her heart.

Chapter 21

Rebecca was right. Sarah wouldn't have been able to navigate the roads. Belle was a well-trained mare, but she still needed a competent person handling the reins.

"Once we get on the main road to Willkommen, we will not have to worry," Rebecca said with assurance. "Belle will continue straight along that road, but first we must make a turn at the next intersection and watch for approaching vehicles. The *Englisch* demand the right-of-way, so we must be careful."

"I'll be on the lookout for cars while you handle Belle."

Rebecca reached back and grabbed her hand. "We must pray for our trip."

"Pray for Joachim, as well. I am worried about his safety."

"*Gott* will provide," Rebecca said with confidence.

"And do not worry about Victor. He will not see you in the back seat nor will he recognize you even if he passes us on the road."

Sarah hoped Rebecca's statement held true.

Both of them bowed their heads and offered a quick prayer. Rebecca squeezed Sarah's hand and then flicked the reins. Belle trotted to the gate and slowed of her own volition while both Rebecca and Sarah checked for on-coming cars. Once they confirmed both directions were clear, Rebecca encouraged the mare onto the roadway. With another flick of Rebecca's wrist, Belle increased her gait to a rapid trot.

Sarah glanced back at the Burkholder farm. Rosie was inside with the doors locked. Hopefully, she and the baby would be safe.

Lord, if You're listening, protect Rosie and that precious baby. Keep Victor far from them and let no other vile men come near the farm.

"We must pass the driveway to the Thomin property," Rebecca said, as if reading Sarah's mind. "Just after that, we will turn right at the intersection. The road heads over the mountain toward Willkommen. Once we enter the town, we must follow the signs for the market. We will find Levi there. You can tell him what happened, and he will take you to the sheriff."

Sarah couldn't control her nervousness when the fence around the Thomin property appeared on their left. As if realizing her upset, Rebecca hurried Belle along. The mare's brisk trot made the buggy creak and groan as it swayed. Sarah's stomach roiled in sync with the back and forth motion. The Thomin driveway came into view.

Her heart stopped and a gasp escaped her lips.

She couldn't look away from the sight of Victor's red pickup idling at the end of the drive. He sat at the wheel, his gaze on the buggy as it approached.

Sarah lowered her head. The black bonnet had a wide bill, but would it hide her from Victor's view?

Please, do not let him see me.

Rebecca acted unfazed and unaffected by the red pickup. If only Victor wouldn't recognize either of them.

Sarah focused her attention on the clip-clop of Belle's hooves and attempted to drive out the fear of seeing Victor, knowing he could swerve onto the roadway, at any second, and brake to a stop in front of the buggy.

Thankfully, the pickup remained stationary. When the buggy was more than fifty yards along, Victor pulled his truck onto the road. Sarah recognized the hum of the souped-up engine. The intersection lay ahead.

"Get going, Belle." Rebecca flicked the reins. The mare increased her pace.

Sarah peered at the oncoming intersection, relieved that no cars approached from either direction. Instinctively, Belle slowed then stepped into the turn, following the slight pressure Rebecca had put on the reins.

The wind tugged at Sarah's bonnet. She raised her right hand to hold it in place. The sound of the truck's engine roared behind them.

Tires squealed and a blur of red passed on the left, then braked to a stop. Her heart hammered in her chest. Rebecca pulled up on the reins. The buggy eased to a stop.

The door of the pickup flew open. Victor jumped to the pavement.

Sarah's heart lodged in her throat. She looked to her

left and right, hoping for some way to escape, but she couldn't escape Victor. He had found her once again.

Twilight descended over the farmland and painted the hillside in shadows as the police car drove along the country road. Joachim sat in the rear, fearing what had happened to Sarah and Rosie and the baby and his sister in his absence. How foolish of him to have considered, at one time, going to the police for help. They had turned a deaf ear to his recounting of all that had happened.

Thankfully, Sergeant Evans had come on duty at the end of the day shift. He had listened to Joachim and was sympathetic to what he had to say.

"I read your statement about your brother's death," Evans said, "and don't see any reason to hold you. The guy who brought you in tries to be a tough dude at times. He hauled you in for questioning, but there isn't any evidence to charge you. If we need to talk to you again, we know where to find you. I'll drive you home. Tomorrow I'll explain what happened to the captain who's been out of town. I have a strong feeling the officer who called you in will be disciplined."

Joachim was grateful for the officer's honesty. At least there was one trustworthy cop in Petersville.

When the police car turned onto the Burkholder property, Joachim should have felt relief and a sense of anticipation to be reunited with Sarah again. He would explain everything to her about his bother and what had happened that night as well as his father's anger, which had forced Joachim to leave.

Would she understand? He would not know until he told her how he really felt.

Hopefully, he would not be too late.

But when the police car pulled to a stop in front of the house, Joachim's stomach soured, seeing his father's face staring down at him from the upstairs window.

He had not expected such a homecoming.

Joachim stepped from the car. The officer turned the patrol cruiser around in the drive and headed back to Petersville.

Mamm opened the kitchen door. Tears streamed down her cheeks at the sight of him. Joachim longed to open his arms and run to embrace her. Then his *datt* eased around her and stepped onto the porch.

His father's eyes were hooded, but the scowl on his face cut into Joachim's heart.

There was no welcome to find in his father's expression.

"Is this the way you come home," his father asked, "in the back of a police car, like a criminal?"

His mother's faint gasp broke Joachim's heart.

"Once again, you are reacting without learning what really happened." The words of reconciliation Joachim had planned to utter refused to issue forth. Instead, he felt the need to vindicate himself.

Joachim fisted his hands, then opened them, consciously trying to overcome the frustration that welled up within him. "You were reacting to your grief when you closed me out of the family and forced me to leave home, but you were wrong, *Datt*. I had done nothing wrong. Rebecca will tell you. Have you talked to her?"

"Rebecca is not here," his father said.

"The only ones here are a young Amish woman who appears scared to death and her infant," his mother added.

Joachim tensed. "What about Sarah?"

Confusion washed over his father's face.

"Who are you talking about, Joachim?" his mother asked. "What happened while we were gone?"

Which was the question Joachim wanted answered, as well.

A sickness filled his gut and he turned in the direction of the Thomin home, fearing Victor had struck again.

Without waiting to explain to his parents, Joachim started running along the drive to the path that cut through the woods. His heart pounded in his ears. The rhythm of his feet hitting the ground kept time with the internal voice that kept screaming Sarah's name.

Victor had captured her. Joachim was to blame because he had left her alone. His gut clenched and pain cut through his heart.

Joachim had saved her once, but would he be able to save her again?

Chapter 22

"Where are you taking me?" Sarah demanded.

Victor yanked her out of the attic closet where he had kept her locked up throughout the past day. She struggled to free herself from his hold, but he slapped her face and shoved her down the stairs.

All around her candles flickered, their light casting eerie shadows over the yellowed wallpaper. The smell of smoke rose from below and burned Sarah's eyes.

Memories of her childhood circled through her mind.

She tried to pull out of Victor's grasp. "What did you do with Rebecca?"

Maniacal laughter was his only response.

"You're insane, Victor."

"That's what my friend George said. He thought he could overpower me, but I proved him wrong."

"George? Was he the man who had Miriam? You killed him, didn't you?"

"Like I killed Naomi. She planned to leave me. I told her to stay, that we would have a good life together. It's fortunate I didn't kill you, Sarah."

She fought against his hold. "I'm not going with you."

"Don't disobey me," Victor screamed, his hand tight on her arm.

"You can't control me," she insisted, struggling to maintain her courage. "I'm not the same person you held captive in your attic. I'm stronger now and I see things more clearly."

"You said you started a fire when you were young. You told me all about it when you were drugged. Your mother left you alone in the house with her boyfriend, and you hid in the closet with the candle. You tried to light it and the fire started. You would have died except Miriam saved you, but she can't save you this time, Sarah. You'll either die in the fire or go with me."

She squared her shoulders and raised her jaw. "I won't go anywhere with you."

He grabbed her by the throat and dragged her down the next flight of stairs. She tripped over her feet and fell. She tried to crawl away from him. He kicked her, then pulled her upright.

The air was thick with smoke. "What about your mother, Victor? She won't survive the fire."

He laughed. "Does that worry you? She doesn't die as easy as you might think. I've tried everything with her, but she's too strong. I stopped her heart medicine, then I gave her sleeping pills. I even tried rat poison, but I must have not given her enough."

"You can't leave her in a burning house."

"Maybe I'll come back for her later. After I take

you someplace safe. A guy in Savannah wanted you, Sarah, but I bought you first. You're mine, and you'll do what I say."

"I don't belong to you." She kicked and pummeled him with her free hand. He caught her wrist and bent her arm up behind her. The pain made her breath catch. She gasped for air.

Her knees went weak and she fell. He kicked her down the steps and ran after her. She landed at the bottom of the stairs. Her gaze turned to the kitchen, where the man with the scar lay bleeding on the floor, his chest rising and lowering ever so slightly. That must be George. From the amount of blood he had lost, she was certain George couldn't live long.

"Where's the other man?" she asked, thinking of the slender guy with shoulder-length hair, the guy she had mistaken for her sister.

"Karl? He's in the basement, dead."

"Why, Victor?"

"Because I had to strike back at someone or something. The electric company said I didn't pay my bills, so they turned off the power." Victor fumed. "Don't they know I'm a Thomin? My family is the wealthiest in this county."

She had to get away from him—but he was stronger and could easily overpower her. Sarah's only chance was to distract him and catch him off guard.

She glanced up the stairs. "Look, Victor. They're coming out of the attic because of the fire. Do you see them?"

He glanced up. "What are you talking about?"

"The rats that live in the attic. They're coming down the stairs."

"No!" He slapped her across the face.

"They're coming after you."

"That's why my mother has to stay here. She never tried to save me."

"Save you from what?"

"From my father. He wanted a son who loved what he loved, woodworking and finance and this house. When I didn't fall in line, he'd lock me in the woodshed. You know what I'd hear?"

"You'd hear the rats."

He nodded, his crazed eyes wide. "At night, they'd crawl over me to get to the food he placed on the floor to attract them. I'd scream, but my mother ignored me. Now, everyone will ignore her."

Victor grabbed Sarah's arm and dragged her to the pickup parked near the front of the house.

She fought against his hold.

He struck her again.

Her knees gave way once more. He shoved her into the truck and climbed in the driver's side. He pulled a weapon from his waist and jammed it into her ribs.

"Do as I say or you'll die."

He gunned the engine and screeched away from the house. She saw movement near the barn.

Her heart lurched.

Sarah jammed her face against the glass and screamed, but he was oblivious to what had happened.

If only Joachim had seen her.

Chapter 23

Joachim saw the red pickup pull out of the driveway, going faster than seemed possible. While he didn't like the idea of the man driving recklessly on the road where others could get hurt, Joachim was still glad he was gone. With Victor out of the way, he could search the house and find Sarah.

"Joachim?" A voice sounded behind him.

He turned to see Levi. "Your father said Rebecca is gone and that you took the path leading to the Thomin home."

Levi pointed to the once-stately home. Joachim turned to see flames licking the roof. They started running.

The front door hung open. They dashed inside and climbed the stairs to the second floor.

"Ms. Hazel." Joachim pointed to her bedroom door. Both men ran to the master suite.

The frail lady lay in bed.

Joachim pulled her free of the coverings and placed her in Levi's arms. "Get her outside. She needs fresh air. I'm going to the attic where Victor kept Sarah."

He climbed the flight of stairs, taking them two at a time.

At the top of the landing, he saw the door and tried the knob. Locked. He pounded on the door. "Sarah?"

Why wouldn't she answer?

Joachim hurled his weight against the door, once, twice, three time before it splintered. He kicked it open and ran to where Sarah crouched, huddled in the corner.

When she looked up, he didn't see Sarah.

Instead, he saw Rebecca.

"Where are you taking me?" Sarah demanded.

Victor was driving like a crazed man. Surely they would wreck before they arrived at their destination.

"We'll go to Savannah and get onboard a ship and head to one of the islands. You belong to me, and you'll do as I say."

"I always obeyed you, Victor," she said, hoping to calm his outrage.

"Until you ran off. Joachim helped you, didn't he?"

Wanting to distract him from thinking about Joachim, she asked, "Why did you keep Rosie and not give her medical care when the baby was born?"

"She never told me she was pregnant. The people I bought her from didn't tell me either. I brought her home to care for my mother. Then after a few months, I realized the truth."

"Are you sure it wasn't your baby, Victor?"

"No!" He shook his head. "I never touched her, but

I let her stay until she got too big. I was sickened that she would bring a child into the world."

"She gave the child life," Sarah tried to reason.

"The child didn't deserve to live. Neither of them did. Besides, I provided food and shelter."

"You call the root cellar shelter? You buried her alive."

"At least she didn't have the rats."

"How do you know? Did your father put you in the root cellar, too?"

Victor nodded. "My mother never questioned my father. Didn't she wonder why I wasn't sleeping in my bed? She had to have known."

"I won't let anyone hurt you again, Victor." Sarah made her voice sickeningly sweet. If she could make him believe she was on his side, maybe he'd let down his guard—giving her an opportunity to get away. "You can trust me."

He shook his head. "I can't trust anyone. The police captured some of the men I've worked with in the past. They're coming after me."

"What about Miriam?" Her heart swelled with hope.

"She's gone. I don't know where they took her. No one knows."

Sarah grabbed his arm. "Someone has to know how to find her."

Victor shoved her away.

Being sympathetic hadn't worked. Sarah needed to try another tactic. She had to get away from him somehow.

"Stop the car," she demanded. "I need to get out. You'll be okay on your own, but let me live."

"I can't, Sarah. You have to come with me."

"The police will find you. You'll go to jail. Let me go now, and you'll be able to get away."

"We need to stay together. I'll dress Amish. We'll live in the country in a small house. They won't find me if I'm with you."

Victor, with his hateful heart, would never fit in with the Amish. "You would stand a better chance on your own. You can save yourself," she encouraged.

"It's too late."

Sarah reached for the door handle. He struck her. Her vision blurred. She grabbed the handle again.

He wove his fingers through her hair and slammed her head against the dashboard.

Pain zigzagged down her spine. Her body went limp and darkness surrounded her.

Chapter 24

Joachim hurried Rebecca through the smoke and down the stairs. "Victor took Sarah," his sister explained. "I saw them drive away in his pickup. He acted like he was crazy, screaming about his father and rats."

"Where did he take her?" Joachim demanded.

"When he was locking me in the attic, he talked about driving to the interstate."

"To get there, Victor will travel along the main road. I will head him off by taking the shortcut. If I can get to the intersection first, I might be able to stop them."

Rebecca grabbed his arm. "No, Joachim. Eli died there. I cannot lose you, as well."

"Then pray I will arrive there before them, Rebecca. Pray Victor will stop his car and will have done no harm to Sarah."

Levi met them at the front door and helped Rebecca flee the house and the fire.

"Oh, Levi," she cried. "I never thought I would see you again."

"I notified the sheriff in Willkommen about what has happened here, but I do not know if he will arrive in time."

Joachim ran for his buggy, the buggy Sarah and Rebecca had taken earlier.

"Hurry, Belle. We have to save Sarah."

The mare seemed to understand the emergency or maybe it was the flames licking the dried wood of the Thomin home that caused Belle to charge out of the drive and onto the roadway. Joachim led her to the bypass, the shortcut locals used that intersected with the main road.

Eli had planned to come home that night so long ago, but he had gotten too carried away with his need to prove himself. If only Joachim had stopped him.

The smell of smoke followed Joachim for some distance; the acrid stench hung on his clothes and filled his nostrils. Ms. Hazel and Rebecca were safe. Now he needed to get to Sarah in time.

He flicked the reins to spur Belle on and glanced into the night sky where stars hung like lanterns, their light helping to guide him.

"*Gott*, I made mistakes and cut you out of my life for too long while I traveled far from home. Forgive me. Forgive my iniquity and my prideful heart. I give You my life to do with as You will, *Gott*, but let no harm come to Sarah."

The wind whipped at his shirt. He tugged his hat

down more tightly on his head and strained to see the road ahead.

The ride never seemed so long.

The intersection loomed in the distance. Joachim's gut tightened, the memory of that night five years ago played over in his mind's eye. Eli's buggy barreling headlong into the intersection. His brother's gleeful laughter as he looked back and taunted Joachim for straggling behind. He had not heard Joachim's cry of warning, nor had Eli seen the headlights approaching the intersection.

Eli had lived life on the edge, always wanting more than the *plain* life offered. He pushed at every chance to break the *Ordnung* and experience life as he chose to live it. Why had their father not seen the truth about his younger son? Joachim had tried to save him that night, but Eli was too reckless and headstrong to listen.

Instead, his buggy had run headlong into the path of the oncoming vehicle.

Seeing it play out again in his thoughts, Joachim cringed, his stomach churned and he wanted to wrench the horrific memory from his mind.

Headlights appeared in the distance. This time, Eli was not in harm's way. Sarah was.

Joachim needed to stop Victor at any cost. He was willing to give up his own life so that Sarah would live.

He guided Belle into the intersection, then pulled her to a stop. He jumped from the buggy, hoping it would provide a barricade, and unhitched the mare, then slapped her on her rump.

"Yah, yah," he screamed, waving his hat and sending the confused horse running into a nearby clearing so she would be out of harm's way.

Joachim turned, seeing the pickup approach. He waved his arms to signal Victor to stop, knowing the crazed man would never do so.

If only Sarah would be safe.

Chapter 25

Sarah groaned and blinked her eyes open. In the glare of the headlights, she saw Joachim. The strong man she had grown to love in such a short time. He flailed his arms, warning Victor of danger. Only Victor was the danger. He continued to push down on the accelerator and steered his truck straight for Joachim.

"No!" she gasped, anticipating the crash and knowing she had to act.

"Rats," she screamed. "At your feet."

Terror flashed from Victor's eyes. He glanced down as if believing a rat was in the car. In that instant with his guard down, she grabbed the steering wheel. The truck veered off the road, jumped a ditch and crashed into a stand of trees. Airbags exploded. Sarah was knocked back, unable to see. All she knew was that Joachim had been saved.

A warm trickle of moisture seeped down her forehead. She touched the wound and pulled her hand back, seeing the dark stain that covered her fingers. Even in her stupor she knew it was blood, her own blood streaming from a gash to her head that she only now began to feel. Gritting her teeth, she ignored the pain. She couldn't waste this opportunity to escape.

She tried to reach for the door handle. The airbag, twisted around her, prevented her escape.

The memory of being in the closet so long ago returned. She smelled smoke from the fire that had started in the main room of the tiny duplex. But thinking back on it now, Sarah realized she hadn't started the fire by her own negligence. He had. The man her mother was seeing. The man who was supposed to watch Sarah when her mother worked. The man who had gotten angry and forced Sarah into the closet. His anger had sent him into a rage so that he knocked over the candles he had lit and later blamed the fire on her, a child only six years old.

All this time, she had thought Miriam had saved her. Now Sarah saw it play out. Sarah had saved herself. Miriam and Hannah were in the adjoining duplex visiting with a friend. Sarah had alerted them to the fire. All the girls, as well as the neighbors, had been saved that night from Sarah's fast action.

Along with the clarity came a sense of relief. She no longer needed to depend on others because she didn't trust herself. She had made good decisions even as a child.

Smoke filled her lungs, along with the pungent smell of gasoline. She untangled her hands from the airbag and grabbed the door handle, but it wouldn't budge.

She looked at the rear of the truck, seeing the flames, knowing she was trapped. This time she wouldn't be able to save herself.

"Sarah?"

Joachim was running toward the pickup. Flames curled from under the hood of the truck. He couldn't save her, and if he tried he would be burned and maybe even killed.

"No!" she screamed. Unwilling to have him sacrifice his life for hers.

Joachim knew he had only a few seconds before the fire would accelerate, sending a fireball of flames into the air.

Please, Gott*!*

Sarah stared at him through the passenger window, her eyes drooping as she became overcome by smoke.

Victor's head lay against the steering wheel, blood seeping from his mouth.

Joachim grabbed the door handle and pulled, but the door refused to budge.

His heart jammed in his throat, a roar filled his ears along with the sound of the fames licking at the truck bed. He needed to act. Now.

He grabbed the handle and tugged with all his might. The door sprang open, sending him flying backward. Regaining his balance, he raced forward and pulled Sarah from the truck. Lifting her into his arms, he ran as fast as he could away from the fire to a clearing, where he placed her on the ground, relieved to see her breathing in spite of her closed eyes and the blood that matted her hair.

He ran back to the truck, this time going to the

driver's side. The door opened on the second try. He dragged Victor out of the truck and away from the fire, just as it accelerated, sending flames into the air. Burning embers fell on Joachim, searing his arms.

Leaving Victor well away from the truck, Joachim ran again to Sarah. Sirens sounded. An ambulance and a sheriff's car from Willkommen were heading toward them. Levi had alerted them. Thankfully, they had jurisdiction in this area near the interstate and had responded to his plea for help.

But would they arrive in time to save Sarah?

He touched her neck, searching for her carotid artery and fearing she was already dead.

Chapter 26

Joachim sat in the waiting room at the hospital, his head in his hands, unable to think about anything except Sarah and the surgeon who was working on her.

The doctor had been guarded in his assessment of her condition, using words like *dislocated shoulder*, *possible head trauma* and *broken femur*. Even more frightening was the threat of internal bleeding.

"We won't know the extent of her injuries until we open her up. What she needs now is prayer."

Except Joachim's mind was numb, and he could not put the words together into some type of a coherent order. The only word that he could utter was her name.

"Sarah" he kept saying over and over again.

Rebecca entered the waiting room along with Levi.

She touched Joachim's arm, offering support, then gasped, seeing the gauze bandages wrapped around portions of his arms. "You have been hurt in the fire?"

He shoved her hand aside. His own injuries were minor compared to what Sarah had experienced, and nothing, not even his sister's concern, could reach Joachim at this moment. All he could think about was Sarah.

"Have you heard anything from the doctor?" Levi asked, sitting in a chair next to Rebecca.

Joachim shook his head, unsure whether he could muster the energy to actually speak.

"I have been praying," Rebecca assured him. Usually, her prayer support would have touched Joachim, but at this moment, her words had no more effect than if she was talking about the weather instead of having asked *Gott* to save his Sarah.

His Sarah. He should have told her how he felt. Why had he kept pushing her aside, never explaining the way she made him feel, like a man who could face any hardship as long as they were together?

"Victor came through his surgery," Levi offered, as if thinking Joachim would get some closure with the information. "I heard two of the sheriff's deputies talking. They will guard him during his recuperation until he can stand trial for his wrongdoings. Not only is he a killer, but they mentioned a trafficking operation that stretched to Savannah and involved shipping women out of the country."

"How could this have taken place here in the North Georgia mountains?" Rebecca asked, sorrow evident in her voice.

Joachim heard footsteps and the swish of a woman's skirt as people entered the waiting room. He ignored the newcomers, intent on his own pain and concern for Sarah.

A hand touched his shoulder. He looked up into his father's face, lined with worry.

He blinked. Surely he was dreaming. Why would his *datt* be here at the hospital—and looking at him that way?

"I was wrong," his father said, his voice deep and sorrowful. He glanced at Levi and then Rebecca. "I have learned the truth about what happened that night."

Joachim did not understand. He rose from the chair, needing to stand eye to eye with his *datt*. Over the last five years, the father who had once seemed strong and self-assured had aged, his shoulders somewhat slumped as if from the heavy weight he carried. In his hand, he held his hat and with the other, he again patted Joachim's arm.

"Some things are too painful to discuss, son, yet I can no longer contain the sorrow I feel about what happened."

Joachim felt that same overpowering sorrow. "I ask your forgiveness for anything I did that night to encourage Eli. He wanted me to race him home, but this was not my desire. I was not racing. Instead, I was following to ensure he got home. But I should have done more—should have tried harder to stop him. He would not listen to my warnings, and I still do not understand why."

His father's eyes were filled with remorse as he spoke. "Only tonight, Levi told me that Eli had boasted about what he had purchased from some of the *Englisch* boys in Petersville. I do not know if he had taken the drugs, and I am grateful the police did not test his blood, but his actions were not what I would have wanted for him."

Joachim's heart went out to his father. Never before

had he heard his *datt* say anything negative about his younger son. Eli had always been the favorite one who could do no wrong.

"You know he was driving Levi's buggy?" his father added.

"Yah," Joachim nodded.

Levi stepped closer. "Eli did not ask to use my buggy. He took it without asking because I had left the singing and was talking with someone behind the building."

"He was talking to me," Rebecca admitted. She lowered her gaze. "I should have told you all of this five years ago, but I was too ashamed. You see, I was at fault for drawing Levi away that night so we could talk about the future. When Eli could not find Levi, he took the buggy without permission. I felt so burdened with guilt that I refused to see Levi for the past few years and I refused to reveal what really happened. It was only with *Mamm* and *Datt* leaving that I needed someone to help me with the farm. Levi volunteered."

"I am the one to blame," his father said. "Eli had not done his chores that day. I had found him in the hayloft with an *Englisch* girl. I told him he would stay at home that night instead of going to the youth singing. But when he asked again that night, I was weak and allowed him to go. I should have kept him home. I was afraid he would leave us for good if I was too hard on him."

"Yet, we lost him forever all the same," Joachim's mother said, stepping around her husband. She opened her arms and wrapped Joachim in her embrace. "I feared I had lost you as well, my son."

He smelled the sweetness of her and knew the fullness of her heart, which had always made room for him. Eli had been his father's favored son, but his mother had loved all her children equally, without censure. Joachim knew that she had never stopped loving him.

"My heart has cried for both of my sons. *Gott* has blessed me by bringing you home again."

"I'm sorry, *Mamm*, for everything."

"*Yah*, we are all sorry about Eli. He lived fast and died fast. As much as it hurt to have him taken from us at such a young age, it was *Gott*'s will."

"Levi has told us of all that has happened while we were away. How is the woman?" his father asked.

Rebecca's eyes were heavy with concern. "The nurse at the front desk said they will know something in the morning. She has been through so much."

His father looked at Joachim. For the first time in perhaps his whole life, he saw pride for his elder son in his father's eyes.

"You saved the woman and both Hazel and Victor Thomin, as well. This is what we were told."

"Victor has come through surgery. I am not sure about Sarah or whether she will survive."

He thought of the truck heading straight for the buggy, then it had turned sharply, leaped over the ditch and plowed into the trees.

"Her shoulder is dislocated and her leg is broken. There are internal injuries, as well."

The nurse came into the room. The sorrowful cast of her eyes made Joachim's heart nearly break.

"You have news?" he asked, hesitant to hear what the nurse would say.

"Ms. Miller is out of surgery and has been moved to intensive care. They're getting her settled. A nurse will notify you if she's able to have visitors."

Moving to ICU could mean her condition had taken

a turn for the worse. Joachim swallow hard, trying to remain optimistic.

His mother reached for him. "This woman is *Englisch*?"

He nodded.

"You have known her long?"

He thought back to the first time he had seen her peering down at him from the window of the Thomin house. Had it been only a few days ago?

"I have not known her long, yet I have been waiting for her my whole life."

His mother drew him close and patted his shoulder. "I will pray for *Gott*'s will."

He wanted to contradict her and insist she pray for what he, Joachim, wanted. He wanted Sarah to live. Most of all, he wanted her to stay with him, but if she could not embrace the Amish faith, then she would leave the area and move on with her life. As difficult as that would be for Joachim, at least he would know she was alive and doing what she wanted.

"When you were a little boy, you had little problems," his mother said, her eyes filled with warmth. "Now that you are a man, you have big problems that weigh upon the heart and soul. I have prayed for you every day of your life and especially over these last five years when you were away from me. I will continue to pray for you and for Sarah. Remember you must use your head as well as your heart, Joachim."

"*Yah*, that is true. But right now all I can think about is Sarah with both my head and my heart."

Chapter 27

Smoke burned Sarah's lungs. She struggled to breathe and tried to fight her way out of the truck. The door wouldn't open. She wanted to scream.

Then she saw Joachim. He was staring at her through the window. His mouth was open. Was he calling her name?

"Joachim," she wanted to shout, but she couldn't move her lips. Nor could she open her eyes or lift her hand. She was trapped in her body, in the truck, surrounded by fire.

"Sarah? Open your eyes." Joachim's voice. He must have opened the truck's door, or was she hallucinating because Victor had given her more drugs? She thought she saw the man from her childhood, her mother's old boyfriend, pointing at her and saying that all of this was her fault.

She thrashed her arm, needing to get away from Victor and the fire and the man who said she had started the fire, when he was the one who had turned over the candles.

"Sarah, it is Joachim. You are in the hospital. You need to lie still. Stay calm and rest."

She wanted to see Joachim, but nothing worked right and her eyes remained closed.

Her head ached. Her left arm felt weighted down.

A hand touched hers. She wiggled her fingers.

"That's right. You can hear me, I know you can, Sarah. I'm here with you at the hospital. I won't leave you."

"My…my sister?"

"What? I saw your lips move, but I couldn't hear what you said. Say it again, Sarah."

But she couldn't. She was too tired, and her mind was starting to drift. Hopefully, she wouldn't go back to the fire. She didn't want to be there.

Please, Lord, I want to stay with Joachim. He always keeps me safe.

She felt his fingers grip hers, then she slipped into darkness and couldn't feel anything.

The waiting room was empty when the nurse ushered Joachim out of Sarah's ICU room. "When can I see her again?" he asked.

"I'll come and get you in an hour. Right now, she needs to rest."

"Can she not rest while I am with her? I will not talk to her. Just being with her is all I ask."

The nurse's eyes filled with compassion. "I understand how you feel, Mr. Burkholder, but nonfamily visits are limited to only fifteen minutes each hour."

"But she has no family. She only has me."

The nurse nodded. "I'm sorry, but I still have to follow the rules."

Rules Joachim did not like and did not understand, even if the nurse felt they were necessary. He walked across the waiting room to the far windows. Staring into the parking lot, he wondered what would happen in the next twelve to twenty-four hours that the nurse said were so important. Sarah had been through so much, yet she was a fighter. If only she would continue to fight for her life.

"Mr. Burkholder?"

Joachim turned as a big man, probably midthirties, entered the room. He was dressed in the uniform of the Willkommen sheriff's department.

"I'm Acting Sheriff Dan Quigley. The nurse said I would find you here. Levi Plank spoke to one of the deputies when he was at the Amish Market in Willkommen. The deputy notified me. I'm sorry we didn't get to the Thomin house before the fire. Everything burned to the ground."

"But no one was harmed?"

"Correct. That's thanks to you and Levi Plank. Mrs. Thomin is being medically evaluated. She's weak and malnourished, but the doctors are cautiously optimistic."

"Victor was giving her sleeping pills."

"He was doing worse than that. The test results haven't come back yet, but the doctors believe that arsenic may have been involved."

The rat poisoning about which Sarah had been concerned.

"Nothing surprises me about Victor," Joachim admitted. "Is he still being held?"

"He's under guard here in the hospital. We won't let him get away. He killed two people today. We think there may be more victims. He'll stand trial in a month or two."

"And Ms. Hazel? Will she testify against him?"

"I can't tell you. It would probably depend upon the judge and how he feels about parent-child privilege. Right now, she's still too weak to communicate very effectively. With Victor out of commission, she would be wise to rent a room in the senior care complex located just outside Willkommen. That is if—"

The sheriff paused a long moment. "Tell me what happened once you arrived at the house."

Joachim recounted trying to find Sarah and instead finding his sister.

"Did you smell gasoline or any type of accelerant?" Quigley asked.

"I smelled only smoke, but the house is so old and made of wood. An accelerant would not be needed."

The acting sheriff made note of what Joachim shared in a small tablet he pulled from his pocket. He pressed for more information and pursed his lips at times as if envisioning what had happened in his mind's eye.

"Rebecca Burkholder is your sister?" he asked.

Joachim nodded. *"Yah."*

"She talked about seeing rats."

"That does not surprise me. Sarah said she heard them in the attic and the basement. I would expect that they ran from the house to escape the fire."

"You had worked on the house. Did you see anything that could have caused the fire?"

"Before my sister left the hospital this evening, she told me Victor had become crazed. Candles were burning. He knocked them over in his rage."

"Then he caused the fire."

"You would have to ask my sister."

"The electric company said Ms. Thomin had failed to pay her bills, and the power had been turned off."

"Perhaps that is why he lit the candles. Ms. Hazel was bedridden, but I thought Victor would take over payment of the bills."

"If there was money."

Joachim looked up. "The Thomins seemed to want for nothing."

"Yet Victor's father died some years ago. A house that size could be expensive to heat and cool. Money can run out."

Joachim knew that too well. He had had to watch his finances over the last five years. "Victor planned to sell the home once his mother passed. He must have tried to hurry her along."

Joachim explained about the scratching sound Sarah had heard and the root cellar. "You know about Rosie Glick and her baby?"

"I plan to talk to her next."

"Talk also to Levi Plank about his sister, Naomi. She worked for Ms. Hazel until Victor came back to the area. She told her family she did not want to work there when Victor was home. Soon after that, she disappeared. The Petersville police thought she had left the Amish way and had run off, perhaps with an *Englisch* man, but the family feared foul play."

"You think Victor had something to do with her disappearance?"

Joachim shrugged. "It is a possibility. A very sad one, but this could be."

"I'll check it out."

"Will you also check out the Petersville police? Some of their actions have been questionable."

Joachim recounted his experience with the officer who had hauled him in for questioning. "The officer's name was Nelson. He mentioned Victor's name a few times as if they were friends. I do not believe this man is above reproach."

"The Petersville chief of police has had problems in the past. I'll talk to him and see what he says about Nelson."

"The Amish do not always trust the police."

"Is that any police or just those in Petersville?" Quigley asked.

"In Petersville. Once trust is broken, it is hard to heal."

Joachim thought of his own father and the trust that had broken between them. Eli had been loved, and in loving indulgence he had been trusted perhaps more than he merited, even after he had broken that trust. Regrettably, his father had given Eli another chance. If only Joachim could have prevented his brother from taking Levi's buggy when he and Rebecca were spending time together. Everyone had a little part to play in his brother's death, but Eli was to blame for his actions that night. He should not have died, but things happened and there was no going back to make them right once tragedy struck.

Joachim would carry the memory of that fateful

night his whole life. At least now, he would be free of the guilt.

Once Acting Sheriff Quigley had asked all his questions, he shook hands with Joachim. "I'll be in touch."

"I have a question," Joachim said before the sheriff left. "What about Sarah's sisters?"

Tired eyes, a drawn face that hung low, a downturned mouth. Sarah blinked at the image.

A dream or...

He moved closer.

"Jo... Joachim?"

"Oh, Sarah, seeing your eyes open has made my heart leap in my chest with relief and joy. I have been so worried about you. Everyone has been worried."

She smiled weakly. "You...saved...me."

He shook his head. "You were the one who saved yourself. You grabbed the wheel and turned the car off the road."

"Victor...would have run...you over."

"I would have jumped to safety, but he needed to be stopped. If he had gotten through the intersection, I would not have been able to catch up to him. Or to you. The police were coming from Willkommen, but Victor would have gotten on the interstate first. He was involved in trafficking, Sarah. He could have known places to hole up. I would not have been able to find you."

He took her hand. "But you are safe now, and that is the only thing that matters. You must get strong and let your shoulder heal and your broken leg mend. You were bleeding internally, but that has stopped. The doctors were so worried, and so was I."

"What of Rosie and her baby?"

"They are both with Rosie's family. I am sure her parents were happy to have their daughter home."

Sarah nodded. "And...a new grandbaby."

"It will be hard for Rosie. She has been through so much. You saved her, Sarah. You heard her in the basement. If you had not insisted that we investigate..." He did not finish his statement.

Instead, he offered her water from the glass on the bedside table. She took a long sip and smiled with gratitude that he knew what she needed, even before she knew it herself.

"Victor's father locked him in the woodshed as a boy when he disobeyed," she said, her voice gathering strength. "He would hear rats. Sometimes they crawled over him. He thought his mother should have protected him, yet he loved her."

"Until she got old and he wanted her money."

Sarah nodded. "Ms. Hazel might not have known what her husband was doing."

"Or perhaps she was like Amish wives who follow their husband's commands within the family."

"You're thinking of your own mother," Sarah said, noting the sorrow in his eyes.

"*Yah*, but *Mamm* never stopped loving me."

"You father loves you, too, Joachim."

"I know that now. Mamie Carver was right. I had to ensure pride did not rule my heart in order to reconcile with my *datt*."

"Does that mean you're staying in Petersville?"

He nodded. "For now. I want to make certain you get stronger so you can decide what you want for your future."

Sarah already knew what she wanted, but she wouldn't tell Joachim. Not now. She needed to rest and, as he had mentioned, regain her strength before she made plans. If only Joachim could be part of those plans. They still had so many obstacles that stood in their way.

She couldn't think of that now; now she wanted to think of the wonderful man who was smiling down at her. He had rescued her from Victor and from the fire and from the guilt she had carried for too long.

Chapter 28

Eight days later, Joachim stepped into Sarah's hospital room, hat in hand. "The taxi will arrive within the hour," he told her. "You are feeling up to the trip?"

She nodded, her eyes bright in spite of the brace on her arm and the cast on her leg. "I'm still amazed that the Amish are allowed to hire taxis. Are you sure the bishop would approve?"

Joachim laughed. "He uses them himself for long journeys. Our trip to my parents' home is not long in miles, but the doctors were concerned about your comfort in the buggy."

"Did you mention that I fell out of the buggy?"

"Some things need to be forgotten," he said with a twinkle in his eyes. "I did not want the doctors to question my ability to lead my mare."

"As I recall, it was my fault for not holding on."

"In truth it was my fault for not holding on to you. That is exactly why we are using Ralph's Taxi Service. Plus, his car has air-conditioning. The day is warm, but we will remain cool as we travel."

"What about your parents, Joachim? Are you sure they don't mind me staying at your house while I recuperate?"

"My mother has been cooking and baking for two days. She always wanted more than one daughter and is happy to have another woman in the house."

"And your father?"

"He gave his nod of approval. Currently, he is busy in the fields. I have been helping him, but thankfully, he has not asked me to join him there today. He knew I needed to be with you at the hospital."

"I promise not to be demanding while my leg and shoulder heal. You need to help your father. I'll stay busy cutting quilt pieces and learning to sew a dress for myself. Rebecca said she would teach me." Sarah looked at the brace on her arm. "At least I'll cut and sew after my shoulder heals."

"You will continue to dress Amish?" he asked.

"Of course."

Her response warmed Joachim's heart.

"Which reminds me," she added. "The nurse said she would help me dress for the trip home. Can you tell her I'm ready?"

Joachim found the nurse and waited in the visitor's alcove until Sarah was dressed. She was sitting in a wheelchair with her leg propped up when the nurse pushed her into the hallway.

"Remember to follow the instructions the doctor gave you," the nurse advised. "He wants to see you in two weeks. Until then, have this handsome guy take care of you."

Sarah smiled. "He'll be getting dirty in the fields working with his father, but his mother and sister will provide plenty of help."

After waving goodbye to the nurse, Joachim pushed Sarah to the elevator and hit the button for the next floor up.

"Aren't we going to the street level?" Sarah asked.

"There is someone I thought you might enjoy seeing before we leave the hospital."

"You're being very secretive for an Amish man," she chided.

"Have you read from scripture that patience is a virtue?"

"Evidently, it's a virtue I need to master."

They rode the elevator to the next floor. Joachim stopped the wheelchair outside one of the rooms. He knocked. A woman's voice bid them enter.

He pushed Sarah into the room and smiled as he saw a very perky and alert woman sitting up in bed.

"Ms. Hazel," Sarah gushed, as Joachim guided the wheelchair next to the older woman's bed.

"I was hoping you would have time to stop by before you left the hospital," Ms. Hazel said with a warm smile. "Joachim has visited me each day and told me about your progress. I am so glad you are doing well."

"The last time I saw you," Sarah said, "I feared you wouldn't survive the night."

Hazel nodded. "The night of the fire." She glanced at Joachim. "I owe my life to Joachim and Levi. They saved me." She patted Sarah's hand. "And you saved me from my son."

"I'm sorry about Victor."

"Victor was a troubled child. My husband thought I was too lenient and insisted our son needed more discipline. I didn't approve of my husband's tactics. He could be an obstinate man and difficult at times, although most people saw only his positive attributes. Today, some might call him bipolar or manic depressive, which only added to Victor's confusion growing up. He never knew how to take his father. And I fear he inherited some of his father's infirmities—most especially the mood swings and the difficulty controlling his temper."

She looked down and sighed. "I didn't know about the rats in the woodshed. Victor never told me, and I'm sure his father thought our son should be man enough to withstand the punishment. Undoubtedly, those nights terrified Victor, and I pray he will forgive me someday for not stepping in." She glanced up with sorrowful eyes. "Hindsight is always easier."

"We all make mistakes," Joachim assured her, thinking of his own mistake. He should have remained in Petersville and dealt with his brother's death and his father's anger instead of running away. But if so, he would not have found Sarah.

She had taught him a lot about facing fear. She had returned to the Thomin home to save Rosie. Her determination meant the Amish woman and her son survived.

"I'm sorry about your house, Ms. Hazel."

"There's nothing to be sorry about, Joachim. The memories of what happened there were difficult. I'm relived it's gone."

"But where will you live?" Sarah asked.

"A new assisted-living home is being built not far from here. I've reserved an apartment and arranged for a woman whose mother worked for my mother to live across the hall. Her eyesight isn't good, but we'll help each other."

"Would that be Mamie Carver?" Sarah asked.

"Why yes. How do you know Mamie?"

"Joachim introduced us."

"You'll have to visit once we move into our apartments. Meals are provided in the main dining room. Come for Sunday supper once you're feeling stronger."

"I'd like that, but if you don't mind me asking, can Ms. Mamie afford such accommodations?"

Ms. Hazel smiled. "Mamie and I have an agreement. She'll help me with my day-to-day needs and I'll cover the cost of her lodging. My husband left me financially secure, which is a blessing. Because of his concern for Victor's poor skills in managing money, he made sure our son never knew the extent of our estate. Plus, I never gave him power of attorney, which is why he couldn't pay the electric bill when I was so infirm. That might have been a mistake on my part, but my husband had everything worked out with a lawyer before he died. I also regret letting the house fall into disrepair. As I struggled with age and my failing health, I left too many things undone."

She turned to Joachim. "There's one more thing I need to mention. Now that the house is gone, I no longer need the land."

The sweet lady smiled at Joachim. "You have always been a good neighbor. I'd like you to have the acreage, Joachim. You're just starting out, and property values are going up. Finding your own farm would be costly. I'll sell you the property for one hundred dollars."

Joachim's eyes widened. "As much as I appreciate your offer, that is far too little," he insisted. "I could not even buy a tenth of an acre for that price."

She shrugged. "My husband always said I wasn't good at math, but that's the price I'm asking if you're interested in buying. You'll have to build a new house, but I don't think that would be a problem."

"Thank you," Joachim said, his voice husky with emotion. "I will buy your land for that amount, but as I mentioned, you are too generous."

"I'm grateful, Joachim. You'll allow me to live the rest of my life knowing some good came out of the land. Perhaps you'll bring me fresh produce from time to time."

He laughed. "You will have your fill of tomatoes, beans and cucumbers. In the fall, we'll gather apples from the trees. Sarah will bake you pies."

Hazel's eyes twinkled. "I like the sound of that. There's one more thing. Mamie Carver has a beagle who needs a home."

Joachim nodded. "He'll enjoy romping with our own dog, Angelo."

The older woman smiled. "Then it seems that we have a deal. I'll have my lawyer stop by your home next week to work out the details."

"I don't know what to say."

"You don't have to say anything, Joachim. Your actions have always spoken louder than words."

The taxi driver was a kindly man who was waiting for them when they arrived at the first floor. Joachim was quiet on the way home, no doubt thinking about Ms. Hazel's generosity. Perhaps he was making plans for his new home.

Sarah mused over his comment about her baking pies for Ms. Thomin. Not that she would question Joachim. There would be time later to talk about his plans. Now she needed to meet his parents. Hopefully, they wouldn't regret their offer for her to recuperate at their home.

Once she was healed, she would need to decide where she would go. She reached out and took Joachim's hand. Perhaps by then they would know what the future would hold.

The taxi turned into the Burkholder driveway and braked to a stop next to the back porch. Two buggies stood near the barn, and horses Sarah had never seen before were in the paddock.

"Your parents have guests," she said, suddenly worried about intruding. "I hate to be a bother."

He squeezed her hand. "A bother you would never be." After paying the driver, he hurried around the car to open her door.

"I will carry you to the porch."

Sarah saw the ramp Joachim had built.

"The wheelchair should have been delivered," he continued. "It will help you get around in the house."

"You've thought of everything, Joachim."

The kitchen door opened and a full-figured woman with big brown eyes and a warm smile stepped onto the porch. No doubt, she was Joachim's mother.

"Welcome." Mrs. Burkholder hurried down the steps and wrapped Sarah in a gentle hug. "We are so glad to finally meet you and to have you in our home."

A man, Joachim's height but with a thinner frame,

pushed a wheelchair onto the porch. "Here is your transportation for the next six to eight weeks."

He looked like Joachim but with less bulk.

"Thank you, Mr. Burkholder," Sarah said. "You all are so generous and thoughtful."

Rebecca hurried outside. "Look at you, Sarah. You have color in your cheeks, which I have not seen before. Joachim, bring her into the house."

"I'm sorry to interrupt your company," Sarah said as Joachim settled her into the chair.

"You must come inside to meet them," his mother insisted.

Joachim pushed Sarah through the kitchen to the main room. She didn't understand his hurry. Meeting the guests was not as important as visiting with Rebecca, who looked like she was ready to burst with anticipation.

Glancing over her shoulder, Sarah saw Levi enter the kitchen, hat in hand. No doubt that was the reason for Rebecca's excitement.

"Here we are." Joachim brought the chair to a stop.

Sarah turned to greet the two couples who had risen from the chairs and were staring at her, their faces filled with expectation.

She blinked.

Her heart stopped. Tears flooded her eyes. Standing before her were Miriam and Hannah, her sisters, whom she'd feared she would never see again.

In one fell swoop, they swarmed around her with hugs and kisses and laugher along with tears of joy.

"How can this be?" Sarah asked once they stepped back to catch their breath.

"Miriam, I thought you were dead or taken by some

crazed man named George." Sarah looked at her eldest sister. "And Hannah, I thought you were in Atlanta."

"I was until I drove to Willkommen to find you and Miriam."

"Only we couldn't find you," Miriam explained as she wiped the tears from her cheeks.

For the first time, Sarah noticed the clothing they wore. "You've dressed Amish?"

"Yah," both sisters answered in unison.

"And we're married." Miriam tugged on the arm of a handsome man in black trousers, white shirt and suspenders. "Meet your brother-in-law Abram Zook."

"And…" Hannah drew an equally good-looking Amish man closer. "Your other brother-in-law, Lucas Grant."

"There's much you need to tell me," Sarah said as her heart nearly burst with joy.

Rebecca invited them into the kitchen for lunch, where they talked about all that had happened since they had last been together.

Sarah had never seen her sisters so happy. Joachim stayed at her side, eager to help when she needed something. She glanced around the table, realizing everyone she loved was in this kitchen. She had thought the past was over and that she would have to make a new life for herself, but God had reunited her with her sisters. At long last, the three girls were together again.

"We have room for you to stay with us," Miriam insisted as the afternoon waned.

"Lucas and I would love for you to stay with us, as well," Hannah added.

Sarah glanced at Mr. and Mrs. Burkholder and then

at Rebecca and finally at Joachim. His face was tight with concern.

"This wonderful Burkholder family has been kind enough to open their home to me. I'll stay here."

"You've made a good decision," Joachim said as he squeezed her hand.

"I'm glad I can stand on my own two feet." Then she looked down. "Well, maybe not stand, but at least know what I want. I like being an independent woman."

"An independent *Englischer*?" he asked.

She shook her head. "I'm no longer *fancy*. I'm an independent Amish woman."

"*Yah*? Are you sure?"

"Cross my heart."

He smiled. "This is a good decision."

Joachim was right. Being Amish was a very good decision.

Chapter 29

Eight weeks later, Joachim lifted Sarah into his buggy. "You are lighter without your cast," he joked playfully.

"The doctor said I can do anything I want. My leg and shoulder have healed, and he doesn't need to see me again."

"This is good."

"Now tell me where you're taking me, Joachim Burkholder. You've been so secretive recently."

He laughed. "Just because I do not chatter on like Rebecca and Levi."

"They have much to talk about with their wedding this fall," Sarah said with a smile.

"*Yah*, they are both excited. This is as it should be."

"The wedding brings joy to the Plank family after the sorrow of the police finding Naomi's remains."

Joachim nodded. "Levi said Victor confessed to kill-ing her because she would not stay with him, which is what he had told you."

"If you hadn't rescued me, Joachim—"

Before she could finish her statement, Angelo ran toward the buggy. Butch followed slowly behind the younger pup. The two adorable dogs brought a smile to Sarah's lips. "Angelo and Butch want to go with us."

"Maybe next time," he said with a twinkle in his eyes. "Today we will go alone."

He flicked the reins and Belle headed for the road.

The day was warm, and Sarah adjusted her bonnet, enjoying the sunshine and the blue of the sky. "Your mother asked me about my plans for the future."

"What did you tell her?"

"I said I needed to make up my mind about what to do and where to go."

"I thought you wanted to stay in Petersville."

"Hannah told me that help is needed at the Amish Inn where she and Lucas met. I am eager to see it for myself when we go there for lunch on Saturday."

"I thought we planned to simply visit with your family. I did not know you would be applying for a job."

"I'll see what the inn looks like and make my decisions then."

He steered Belle along the main road and withdrew into himself. Sarah didn't need conversation. She enjoyed the ride and being with Joachim.

"I want to get your opinion about something," he said, turning Belle into the old Thomin driveway.

"I must start thinking of this as the Burkholder place," Sarah said, taking his hand. "You've working hard planting the fields, but I don't want your woodwork to suffer."

"After harvest there will be time."

"The barn remains standing by the burned-out home site?" she asked.

"*Yah*, but I do not want to build the new house there. I have found a better spot."

He tugged the reins to the right and encouraged Belle up a small incline. At the crest of the hill, he and Sarah looked down onto a lake surrounded to the rear by hardwoods. In the distance, deer grazed and geese flew overhead.

Joachim pointed to a clearing. "I thought a house on the rise would be *gut*. The beauty of the hills and lake would be visible from the porch."

She nodded. "It's so peaceful, Joachim."

"You like the spot I have chosen?"

"Yes, it's perfect."

"And you are meeting with the bishop next week?"

"He is coming for dinner. Your mother said I will be able to talk to him after we eat."

"You are asking for baptism."

She nodded. "Living Amish is what I want. Is that all right with you?"

"It is what you chose, Sarah. You are an independent woman who knows her mind."

She smiled, appreciating his comment. "And the Amish will accept an independent woman into their community?"

"My *datt* has already told the bishop that you are a woman of faith. My *mamm* has assured him of your sincerity of heart." He winked. "Plus, she wants a good wife for her son."

Sarah titled her head, her heart nearly bursting with excitement. "What?"

"She knows her son's heart." He wrapped his arm around hers. "My mother sees the way I look at you and knows how I feel."

Her cheeks warmed and she couldn't stop smiling. "How do you feel?" she asked coyly.

"I feel that life has no meaning without you." He pointed to the hillside and the lake. "All this means nothing to me if I cannot share it with you, Sarah. I love you."

She saw the truth in his gaze and felt overcome with gratitude. "I love you, Joachim."

He pulled her closer. "Will you marry me, Sarah? If you do, I will be a happy man."

"Of course, I'll marry you. I've been waiting for you to ask."

He smiled. "I thought perhaps an independent woman would ask first."

She nestled closer and lifted her lips to his. "First kiss me, then we can talk about how demanding I can be."

"There is something good about a woman raised *Englisch*."

"Oh?" Sarah raised her brow.

"*Yah*, she knows what she wants."

"Joachim, you're all I've ever wanted."

He lowered his lips to hers and they kissed. Sarah's heart nearly burst with happiness and anticipation of their future together.

A new home built on the rise with the water in the distance. Children to bring even more joy and laughter to their home, and a love that would grow stronger with the years.

* * *

The trip to the Amish Inn was pleasant. Sarah talked about wedding plans and what she needed to make for her new home with Joachim, curtains and quilts and the special dress she would sew to wear at their wedding.

Joachim smiled and nodded in agreement, letting her talk and thinking how his life had come full circle. He now had everything he had ever wanted with Sarah at his side.

They arrived at the inn to find both of Sarah's sisters and their husbands stepping from their buggies. Miriam and Hannah greeted them with hugs and then stared expectantly at Sarah.

"What?" she asked.

"I have a feeling there's something you need to tell us," Miriam said with merriment in her eyes.

"You know me too well," Sarah admitted. She grabbed Joachim's hand and pulled him close. "We're getting married."

The women hugged and the men shook hands, and as they walked together into the inn, the conversation turned to wedding dates after the fall harvest and their new home and furnishings.

An older Amish woman greeted them in the dining room. Hannah introduced Sarah and Joachim to Fannie Stoltz, who owned the inn. "I am pleased to meet you," she told them with a warm smile. "The corner table is for your family."

Again the sisters continued to talk, planning the upcoming wedding and catching up on what had transpired since their last visit. The lunch was delicious, and after dessert as they sipped coffee, the talk turned to their mother.

"She is buried on property Hannah and Lucas own," Miriam told Sarah. "We will go there one day."

"I would like that. Mother wanted to find her sister, but none of us ever imagined that we would find a new life and a new faith for ourselves here in the mountains."

"I wish she could have connected with her sister," Hannah said. "I have a feeling some of her struggle and search for happiness was because of the family she had left behind. We've continued the search, but we haven't been able to find any clues."

"No one in the area has heard mention of Annie Miller?" Sarah asked.

Fannie placed the coffeepot on the table and turned to stare at the girls. "What was your mother's name?"

"Leah Miller," Sarah said.

"Miller or Meuller?" Fannie asked.

"Miller is all we ever knew."

"And what was her sister's name, the aunt you have been looking for?" Fannie pressed.

"Annie Miller."

Tears welled in Fannie eyes. "I cannot believe this, but it is true."

The girls waited expectantly.

"My maiden name was Meuller. Fannie Meuller. My baby sister could never pronounce Fannie, so she called me Annie. My sister's name was Leah."

"Mother must have changed her last name when she left Willkommen," Sarah said, putting the pieces together.

"Which means our mother was raised Amish," Miriam said with astonishment.

"And all of us," Hannah added, looking at each of

her sisters, "have found our way back to our Amish roots."

Fannie nodded. "If what you said is true, then I am your mother's sister, your Aunt Fannie or Annie, whichever name you choose to use."

The girls circled the sweet woman and hugged her close. She joined them at the table and told them stories of their mother growing up, of her hopes for the future and her dreams of the family she would someday have. Their aunt also mentioned their mother's struggle with her authoritative father, who never showed his love.

"Mother searched for love and affirmation her whole life but never realized her three daughters loved her more than any man ever could," Miriam said.

Sarah smiled sadly. "And as her dementia started to take hold, she sought to return home to the sister she loved."

Fannie patted Sarah's hand. "I am sure she loved each of you girls deeply. Showing that love was the problem."

Joachim appreciated the importance and healing of the stories and the insights Fannie shared. The three sisters might have questioned their mother's love, but there was no way they could fail to see the compassion and concern that exuded from their aunt.

The family was growing, and Joachim felt sure that in the not-too-distant future, God would bless the couples with children so that the table would grow even fuller in the years ahead.

Going home that evening, Sarah rested her head on his shoulder. "What are you thinking?" he asked.

"I was thinking how God made good come from all the pain of the carjacking. We came to Willkommen to find our aunt, and we also found three wonderful men to love. I'm free of the memory of the fire. Miriam and Hannah both said they never talked about it because of our mother. She knew the man she was seeing had been at fault. Blaming it on me meant that he wouldn't have to face criminal charges, so she forbid them to mention what had taken place."

"Now you do not have to be afraid of fire."

"I don't have to be afraid of anything, Joachim, with you by my side."

"Have I told you how much I love you?" He pulled the buggy to the edge of the road.

"You've told me, but I want to hear it again."

"I love you more than myself, Sarah Meuller. You are my life, my breath, my heart, my soul. You are my everything."

The sun started to set in the west as Joachim pulled her close and kissed her, which was what he had wanted to do every day since he had first seen her peering at him from the Thomin window.

"You rescued me, Joachim," she said. "I'll be forever grateful."

"And I'll be forever grateful for having you as my wife, Sarah. We have much to look forward to."

"Yah," she said, turning her lips to his. *"Gott* brought you into my life at the perfect moment."

He nodded. "And *Gott* brought me home to find you, the woman I will love forever."

They kissed and kissed again. Then Joachim flicked the reins, and Belle continued the journey that would take them to the Burkholder farm. In a few months, they would marry and move into their own home where Joachim would cherish Sarah all the days of her life.

As if reading his mind, she snuggled even closer and sighed. "The pain of the past is over for both of us, Joachim, and tomorrow awaits us." Sarah thought for a moment and then added, "We have a lifetime ahead of us filled with blessings."

"Blessings and love," he added, and then he kissed her again.

* * * * *